sitting practice

Also by Caroline Adderson

A History of Forgetting

caroline adderson

sitting practice

review

First published in Great Britain in 2003
by Review

An imprint of Headline Book Publishing

10 9 8 7 6 5 4 3 2 1

Cataloguing in Publication Data is available from the British Library

ISBN 0 7472 7069 4

Typeset in Baskerville by Palimpsest Book Production Limited,
Polmont, Stirlingshire
Printed and bound in Great Britain by
Clays Ltd, St Ives plc

HEADLINE BOOK PUBLISHING
A division of Hodder Headline
338 Euston Road
London NW1 3BH

www.reviewbooks.co.uk
www.hodderheadline.com

For Patrick Sweeney, who slept through so much of this

Thank you Katia, Lisa, Emily, Kathy and Heather for so generously sharing with me the facts of your lives. *Merci* the wonderful Sherry Caves for making sure I got it right. Louise Young, Zsuzsi Gartner, Morna McLeod and Ingrid MacDonald – I am forever grateful for your invaluable wisdom. Thank you Arnim Rodeck for the recipe and Anna Csepregi for the medical advice. God bless the B.C. Arts Council. Patrick Crean, Charlotte Mendelson, Jackie Kaiser, I salute you. Bruce Sweeney, you are the love of my life.

Passing the berry fields where straw-hatted pickers stooped between the rows, Ross sounded the horn and waved out the window, shouting, 'Come to my wedding! Come to my wedding at two o'clock!' But they were too hard-working, barely pausing to look up at the lunatic driver shouting out in what must have sounded to them like gibberish. Only the imperious hawks on the fence posts abandoned their rigid postures and lifted off in celebration.

The midday sun had burned away the morning's threatening haze. Arriving at the site where two years before they had shot a TV Western, Ross remembered the arrows that had been slung and all the fake blood that had spilled. Now the field vibrated benignly in the unfiltered light, green and silver, depending on which way the grass lay. At one end was a solitary tree and, in the centre, banquet tables arranged in rows. The fire was already burning in a pit next to the caterer's and bartender's scallop-edged tents, with Jaime overseeing it. Standing on top of the stile, his tie in his pocket, Ross called to the servers in their Nehru jackets and to Jaime, 'Who has seen my bride?'

A van pulled up behind him. Four men got out and immediately began unloading instruments and speakers. Ross climbed back down the stile and went over to greet them – a fiddler and a keyboardist he knew, a cellist and a banjo player to whom he was only now introduced. What this miscellaneous quartet was going to come up with, he was curious to hear. 'Play anything you like,' he told them, for he believed this was the way to get the best out of people.

'A couple of other guys are coming.'

'The more the merrier.'

'Mr Alexander?' Approaching was a stranger, tall in a shiny suit, his hand held out to shake. Though Ross could not place him, he was well aware that he had probably invited him. 'I'm the marriage commissioner,' the man said.

'Hello!' Ignoring the hand, Ross pulled him forward for a hug.

The flustered commissioner extracted himself and, clearing his throat, asked, 'Is your fiancée here yet?'

Ross threw back his head, bracketing his mouth with cupped hands. 'STELLA!' he roared. 'Not yet. I guess we should have the ceremony over there.' Pointing to the tree, he struck off, leading the way through the shin-high grass. (When he rented the field it had not occurred to him to ask that it be mowed.) Halfway there, he glanced back and saw the cellist bringing up the rear, walking the flattened aisle Ross and the commissioner had just created, in his arms his own stout, curvaceous bride – his instrument. The sight of the pair alarmed Ross because, in the movie theatre, whenever the strings swelled up in the score, he grew instantly teary in a Pavlovian-style response. He dreaded that this might happen, too, in real life.

They reached the tree and, under its green canopy, the marriage commissioner began his explanation of how the ceremony would proceed. By reflex or habit, if Ross felt someone was trying to teach him something he shut the sound off, as he did watching cooking shows on television. More cars were arriving, parking along both sides of the highway. He wondered what car his parents had rented and would be bringing Iliana in. On and on the commissioner talked. At last Ross glimpsed a promising figure in white, stepping daintily over the stile, holding her long skirt gathered in one hand. He framed her in his gaze: descending into the field, then pausing to look back. She hesitates, *he thought with a pang, until he saw her bend and pluck at the skirt which must have snagged on the blackberry brambles growing in a tangled bank along the fence. Tall and stately, she started towards him, compelling Ross to walk rudely away from the marriage commissioner in mid-sentence. Only as they drew closer to each other did he realize it was not Iliana at all. 'Ross!' sang the brazen impostor, who then took advantage of his already open arms. 'I'm so happy for you!'*

He was furious. 'Mary Ellen? What are you doing here?'

'You invited me. In January when we were shooting that Movie of the Week. Remember? Look how you've changed! Nothing spilled on you at all! Too late for me, alas!' She laid the back of her hand across her brow, pretending to swoon, ever the bad actress.

He had other guests, he noted over Mary Ellen's shoulder as she hugged him again, suddenly some forty or fifty of them, all thirsty from the drive or ready to revel, gathered in clusters around the bartender's tent. Among the men Jaime Rios was recruiting volunteers, explaining in his hyperbolic, heavily accented English how tremendous was the honour of dousing the meat at a man's wedding and helping to heave it into the fire.

'Great to see you, Mary Ellen.' Already he had forgiven her.

At the fire, the six canvas bundles were laid out in the grass. Ross was clapped all over the back and regaled with congratulations, then each of the volunteers armed themselves with a bottle of wine: Jaime, Mike Lambeth, Ross's friend Alan the property master, the Reel Food sous-chef Dmitri, Ross's screenwriter pal Timmy Bonstock who had flown in from LA that morning. Everything seemed symbolic: the rhythmic glugging of the upended bottles, first Ross's, then Jaime's starting exactly as Ross's bottle emptied, then Mike's and so on, as if to signify that the wine would never cease to flow. The fact that they were having lamb. And what was that old proverb about salt? Those without a bottle pushed forward to help Ross lift the first lamb, saturated now with Merlot.

'What's going on?' asked someone just arriving.

'They do it in Colombia apparently.'

Grunting, they swung the lamb, chanting, 'Rosco! Rosco!' It crashed into the fire. Too early for confetti, they had sparks instead, and ash, and by the time the sixth lamb had been delivered to the flames there were sixty or seventy people speckled grey and many with red wine on their hands and sleeves and shirt fronts.

'Only Ross,' said the property master, 'would have a stag party and a wedding combined.'

BEGINNING

1

The day of the accident Ross telephoned Iliana at work. The nurse on duty with her handed the receiver over. 'Your husband's on the phone.'

'Who?' Iliana asked, because he still seemed just Ross. Almost from the moment she met him, he became his own aptest description, as much an adjective as a noun, indefinable except on his own terms. Ross was simply, even very, *Ross* to her.

They had been married less than a month, but because he had been practising it all along in his head, marital nomenclature was easier for Ross. 'Is that my old lady? My blushing bride? My better half? My life's sole reason? I cut out early. How about I pick you up and bring the rackets?'

'I was planning on running home,' she told him.

A single subdued syllable constituted his reply: 'Oh.' It was the ensuing sulky silence that reminded Iliana she had yet to refuse him anything. *He* had, of course, once, that first time he declined to make love to her. But Ross had relented, and so would she because neither of them wanted marriage to mark the cessation of their mutual indulgence.

'I've got my shorts and shoes with me,' she said. 'I'll see you at seven.'

On the court now he hung forward, arms long as he gripped the racket handle, swaying from foot to foot. Iliana, bouncing the ball, looked up and frowned.

'What?' he called to her.

'Tie your shoe!'

He squatted, letting his Yonex clatter on the asphalt, and while he was down and vulnerable, she fired a ball that nearly clipped him. He ducked, lost his balance and toppled ignominiously on to his seat.

'That's a warning shot! That's for not even trying!'

'I'm trying!' he complained. 'I'm trying to tie my shoe!'

He brushed himself off and, like a urinating dog, shook one leg out before resuming his troglodytic ready position. (He played like *Ross*; there was no other simile.) Because she loved him, Iliana let the serve drop within easy reach, but rather than darting forward he straightened idly and took two loping flat-footed steps. (She pictured him pausing to scratch and yawn as well.) Somehow he reached the ball in time. Iliana didn't even bother turning to watch it soar over the perimeter fence. She saw how hard he hit it.

'Sorry. I'll go get it.'

She was not prepared to wait that long. 'Never mind. We can play with two. What's the score?'

'Love.'

'And what else?'

'What else is there?'

On the next point they managed a rally, Iliana placing the ball farther and farther from him with each shot. 'Run!' she screamed. 'You are so lazy! Run! Run!' Ross, flushing from exertion and the pleasure he took in her abuse, paused for a water break.

Halfway into the set (three–love Iliana), they thought they

lost a second ball. Ross, warmed up now, played marginally better, while Iliana, grown reciprocally less forgiving, returned his shots in an impatient bombardment. One plopped straight down from the lob. 'Smash it!' she cried, seeing him approach it as a forehand. For once he took instruction, leaped and brought his racket triumphantly down. Iliana, backing up for the return, looked expectantly at the sky empty of everything but clouds, then at Ross just as puzzled by the ball's apparent mid-air vanish.

Shrugging, they turned their backs on each other and went searching. In the long grass around the fence they found balls stained by weather, mould-coloured, fruit-soft, gnawed by dogs. Balls that belonged to other people. Theirs was nowhere to be found. Still shaking their heads at the mystery, they took their positions once more. Ross tossed the remaining ball and, raising his racket, saw double: the missing one wedged tightly in the V in the handle. Serving was difficult enough for him without trying to do it through disabling spasms of laughter. He misaimed, sent the ball ricocheting off the net post, then the fence top, then across the road.

Final score: six–love Iliana.

It was only ten to eight; there would be time enough once they got home for her to go for her run after all and work up a decent sweat. She skipped over to the net, hand held out for Ross to shake. Ross grabbed it and, pulling her over, pressed a sloppy kiss to her face.

Their rackets and the ball they tossed in the back seat of Miss Stockholm. 'Was that fun, or was that fun?'

'It was fun,' Iliana conceded as they drove off into Friday night's impatient traffic. 'It was especially fun to see you execute a backhand while pulling up your shorts.'

'I do everything that way. On set today I flipped a hundred

7

salmon burgers pulling up my shorts. What do you feel like for supper, by the way?'

'I've been thinking about the wedding.'

Ross lowered the sun visor. 'Tell me again. Wasn't that the best meal ever?'

'Remember Phyllis and Ham and Mike and Ed dancing?'

'Mike danced with Ed?'

'Can we take dance lessons, Ross?'

He got into the turn lane at the intersection. 'I already know how to dance.'

'Gosh,' said Iliana. 'You already know how to play tennis, but you let me make suggestions.'

The indicating arrow, amber while they waited, changed just as Ross was about to turn. He went anyway, veering sharply, accelerating. Iliana clutched the dashboard. At the wedding, Ross had taken her in his arms and, squashing her against his softness, swayed enthusiastically from side to side. It was his idea of a waltz. In the grip of it she knew she had found an activity they could pursue as equals. 'I'd like to learn. Dancing was out of the question growing up. He claimed it was just fornicating standing up.'

'We definitely do not need lessons in fornicating standing up. I'd say we've pretty well mastered that.'

As if to make up for his earlier recklessness, at the next red Ross braked well in advance of the line of cars. The pedal depressed only part way. Alarmed by the rubbery resistance underfoot, he looked down and saw the ball jammed behind the brake. When he lifted his foot, it unsqueezed and rolled free again.

Though Iliana didn't know what had happened, she heard the hop-to-it tone in his voice.

'Get the ball.'

She looked over her shoulder to the back seat. 'Where is it?'

'On the floor somewhere.'

8

Undoing her belt, she leaned sideways between the seats trying to feel under Ross's.

The light turned green. 'Did you get it?' Ross asked.

Her hand crabbed around on the floor mat. 'Just a sec.'

He drove grindingly on in second gear, letting the space between them and the car in front widen until someone behind honked and he had to accelerate. Shifting to third, he glanced behind in time to see Iliana's hand close around the ball. It was her left hand, he would always remember, because he also saw her wedding ring.

It rolled right to her. 'Got it!' she cheered the second before everything went black.

In his eleven years in the film catering business, Ross had witnessed a shocking number of motor vehicle accidents. He'd seen a score of car chases, several Icarus plunges off bridges, and cars that, in swerving to avoid head-on collisions, violently compacted themselves against trees. Before his very eyes cars had exploded or rolled over like obedient dogs, and in the aftermath of this carnage Ross could usually be found trotting towards the charred or twisted body of the wasted automobile bearing a suitably fortifying beverage for the stuntman. Not one of these accidents, so terrible later on the screen, seemed particularly tragic at the time. On the contrary: when the camera stopped rolling, the crew would usually clap and cheer.

In one moment Ross saw his wife of three and a half weeks reaching to capture a wayward tennis ball. In that same second a moving truck, taking advantage of the break in traffic (the interval between Ross's Volvo and the car ahead of it) without realizing the gap was quickly closing, entered the intersection. Ross heard, in a succession so rapid that the sounds almost overlapped, the shriek of brakes, the punch of metal, the gritty tinkle of shattering glass, the ominous thud of Iliana's unrestrained body meeting the dashboard. He did not actually witness the collision because he had instinctively shut his eyes. Had he the presence of mind to compare it to all those other crashes, he would have judged it remarkable only in how devoid it was of drama.

So pervasive was the influence of the motion picture in Ross's life that, like many people's, his dreams and memories came to him in its basic three-act structure. Even the way he thought was subtly affected; he made his living, after all, in Hollywood's northernmost sweatshop. What happened next Ross perceived as if it were happening to someone else, a stand-in for himself, and he, Ross, had been invited (as he sometimes was) to view from a theatre seat the rushes of this tragedy. It did not occur to him that this was the detachment of shock.

All the shots were, in the parlance, from Ross's POV: two huge cartoon hearts on the logo of the moving truck broken into myriad tiny Cubist tiles through the shattered windshield. On the soundtrack: sobbing, a distant siren.

Iliana's bloodied head half buried in Ross's lap.

Gradually, blurred faces filled the screen. They were peering in at Ross and Iliana from both sides of the car, but the focus – soft, almost liquid – rendered them featureless. At his window, a man was telling Ross not to move and not to touch Iliana until the ambulance arrived. 'Here it comes,' he said.

'My wife, my wife, my wife, my wife, my wife . . .' Ross sobbed with the approaching siren.

Next he was strapped to a board and transferred to a trolley where, buttressed with sandbags, he lay utterly immobilized, unable even to turn his head to take one last look at Iliana. Involuntary tears streamed out of him and pooled in the auricles of his ears. He felt himself being raised up, up into the ambulance. He and Iliana had been playing tennis on the courts across from Vancouver Hospital and had afterwards driven just over twenty blocks up Oak Street. Now this pair of his-and-hers ambulances was bringing them back, retracing their very route, keening, lights flashing. Iliana *worked* there. It was where they had first met, though Ross had not been back inside it since. The mere smell of the place left him queasy and perspiring. He always waited for her outside.

The sum total of his hospital experiences: his own birth, or rather (he was a twin) his *co*-birth. His nephew Bryce's. The time he poked three cultured pearls from the broken string in his mother's jewellery box up his nose as far as they would go. The time he broke his nose playing sloppy junior hockey, leading in a karmic-like progression to day surgery two decades later.

After the break, the right nostril on its own could not deliver oxygen adequate for an endomorph. All those years Ross had relied on his mouth to supplement his breathing. Having come into manhood in this condition, he was used to his own heavy, uvular respiration. Other people had not been as indifferent. His sister Bonnie said it was gross and he knew she was right. While it never affected his sex life (women were always happy to come home with Ross), once the fun was over and he and she were curled cosily up in drowsy post-coitus, his snoring did tend to close the evening down. His couch offered refuge from the din, but more often than not a cab was called. Of his long-term relationships, and there were several (Ross was lucky in love), none had led to cohabitation.

Only after his sister had a baby did Ross decide to take action. With the birth of his nephew, he discovered that he liked babies very much. As children, he and Bonnie used to play house, Bonnie the mother, Ross the father, a battered collection of dissimilar dolls their copious offspring. Back then Bonnie had been in charge of the children; she still was, always asking Ross to give Bryce back too soon. The second Ross relinquished his nephew, he felt the palpable ache of loss. It made him want to settle down, though that did not seem very likely. After all, he couldn't honestly expect a woman to spend her life with him when so many couldn't stick it out an entire night.

Surgery had been the only means of unblocking the culpable left nostril. He had tried every alternative short of a sharp stick. While not admitting to a phobia, Ross was frank about his fears. 'I might die,' he told Bonnie, who went with him to the outpatient clinic.

'That would be really embarrassing.'

She was right; it was not a cause of death he'd want cited in his obituary. He fell into an anxious, uncharacteristic silence, but not for long. Hunger goaded out of him another far-fetched statement. 'I might starve to death.'

Bonnie snorted.

'I haven't eaten since last night. By the time this is over, I'll look like a famine victim.'

'Maybe a group of famine victims,' Bonnie quipped.

Thank God for general anaesthesia. He got through the ordeal and Bonnie was there again, waiting with Bryce, the baby, when he woke up. 'How do you feel?'

There was an impossible length of petroleum-jelly-coated gauze packed into his nostril. 'Congested,' he replied, holding his arms out for his nephew.

He was supposed to take a week off work, but that very night, when he was sure the anaesthetic had worn off, he self-administered Ross's Cure-All, his Morning-After Miracle (a 222, an extra-strength Tylenol, and an ibuprofen washed down with Gatorade) and drove out to the set to make sure they did not overcook the ribs. His breathing sounded especially laboured and no one would take him seriously with his new cartoon voice. He was the boss, but when he said, 'Obey me,' everyone tittered.

Over the next twenty-four hours the thickheaded sensation symptomatic of a hangover worsened, as did the acute ache behind his eyes. The thought of gauze and its filmy, lepidopteristic connotations made him want to laugh. Back at the hospital the next day, sitting on the edge of the table in his paper dress waiting for the gauze to be taken out, he found himself recalling an observation he'd once made while catering a kung-fu movie – how a North American pointing to himself points to his chest, to his heart, but an Asian points to the nose on his face. He wondered what the hell it meant.

A light knock on the door, then the nurse entered on springing steps. She was younger than Ross, but almost as tall, athletic he saw by her gait and her well-defined calves. (*Definitive* calves, he would even have called them.) A simple elastic held back her blonde hair. Her face was triangular with slightly pronounced Slavic cheekbones and a smallish chin. All this he noted automatically, as well as that she wore no make-up and no rings. 'I'm going to take your dressing out, Mr Alexander.'

'Ross. What's your name?'

'Iliana.'

'Iliana! What's a girl with a nice name like that doing in a place like this?'

Smiling, she went over to the cupboard and took out a box from which rubber gloves were dispensed like tissues. 'I like it here.'

'Is this going to hurt?'

'Maybe a little.'

Cold in the paper dress, he suddenly realized why they had asked him to strip to the waist and put it on. 'Blood?'

'Maybe,' she said cheerily.

'No,' said Ross. 'I must not bleed.'

She laughed. Like everyone else, she seemed to think he was kidding. Carrying a stainless steel tray and a tweezer-like instrument, she brisked over, stopping in front of him and asking in that joky nursy way if he could just tilt his head back a little. He realized then that this was going to be worse than the actual operation for which, after all, he had been unconscious. The gauze would be bonded into a solid mass by now, like a brick stuck in his face, and he imagined it would be removed about as easily as a brick could be drawn down through his nostril. Panicking, he reached out and clutched the bare wrist of the hand holding the tweezers, above the latex protection of the glove. 'No blood,' he commanded nasally.

All he wanted was to be taken seriously. He never meant to behave, or to seem to be behaving, aggressively. That would not have been in character. She didn't know Ross's character then, of course, how woozily affectionate he was, particularly towards society's most vulnerable: has-been American actresses, the elderly, babies (especially babies). He was a softie; a finger poked in anywhere on him would sink to the second knuckle.

She stared down at her own wrist in his desperate clutch. Ross let her go. 'Why don't you lie down?' she suggested, flexing the wrist.

'Can I?'

'Of course. Let me help you.'

He turned sideways, lifting his legs up on the table. Iliana eased him back. Everything rustled as he moved, the paper liner on the table, the paper gown, so once he had settled and closed his eyes the room seemed quiet for a moment before it filled up with his breath. Twice as loud as before the operation, it seemed vaguely obscene, as if they were hearing it over the telephone long past midnight in the good old days before Caller Display. Her cheerful chatter, intended to distract him as she slid the tweezers up inside him, was ineffective; he was very much aware of his hairs parting for the steel, the tip of the tweezers separating and touching the sensitive inside walls of his nasal passage, then closing.

It was the strangest sensation, like a long loose bowel movement, but coming from his head. He felt mentally evacuated, his mind astonishingly empty. Rushing to fill him up (for the first time in twenty-two years through the left nostril) was air, sweet and cold, so much of it at once, double his usual dose, that he was instantly hyper-oxygenated. Giddy, high, he opened his eyes. There was Iliana, his future, smiling down on him.

He felt like laughing and crying at the same time.

'Excuse me! Hel-*lo*! I want to speak to someone!' he called from behind the cubicle curtains in A and E. Though they had told him not to move his arms, he was waving them insistently, his shouting only adding another track to what was already a sound-congested background. He wasn't the only one raising his voice. A woman in another cubicle kept intoning in a flat coarse bellow that she was in the methadone programme.

Finally, a nurse with a clipboard appeared. 'Where's my wife?' Ross demanded.

'I'm from Admitting. I need your next of kin.'

'We're each other's next of kin!'

'I know that, sir, but you're both patients at the moment.'

He gave Bonnie's name and number, and Iliana's parents' names, though she was no longer in contact with them. 'I want to see my wife,' he insisted.

'Oh, bring him his wife!' hollered the woman in the methadone programme.

'You have to have an X-ray,' the nurse told him.

It dawned on him then that she was being evasive. He fell silent, but the methadone woman kept it up for him. 'Where's his wife? Give him his wife! He wants his wife! Hell, *I* want a wife!' Laughing loosened her phlegm; it sounded like stones rattling in a box.

His closed eyes made a dark screen, but now there was no movie and no soundtrack. What was happening could not be acted out because it was an internal drama. Breathing arrhythmically, arms folded on his chest, he probably seemed to be asleep. He was caught – rigid in the plastic collar, restrained by nylon straps, bound in an oxymoronic predicament – a man with nothing to occupy him but his thoughts, trying not to think his wife was dead.

Eventually they came to get him for the X-ray. Afterwards the nurse told him where Iliana was. A different nurse from the one from Admitting, she unstrapped him and helped him to sit up. Her kindness reminded him of Iliana's that first time. Back then it had not occurred to him that Iliana had simply been practising her profession. He had thought she liked him. He assumed this of most people.

'I have some news about your wife. She's in ICU. She's from here, right? I mean, she's a nurse.'

Immediately, he began to weep from relief. 'Where is she?'

'Wait. The doctor has to see you.'

Ross stood to go just as a harried-looking doctor came through the curtains with Ross's X-rays. 'Good news. There doesn't appear to be any skeletal damage.' She asked Ross to tilt his head forward and back, and to turn it side to side. As Ross looked right, something jammed in his neck, preventing him from lining his ear up with his shoulder on that side. A shaft of pain shot down his back.

'Whiplash,' the doctor told him.

That, apparently, was the only thing the matter with him.

Stumbling out of the elevator, he faced a set of oversized blue metal doors. There was a button on the wall, palm-sized and square with a blue pictograph of a person in a wheelchair. When he pressed it, the doors swung suspensefully outwards on a brightly lit nursing station. He asked directions and was pointed to ICU. On the way he passed a lounge where a man sat alone dressed up in the costume of a mime. Perhaps by association Ross read an exaggerated despair in his posture and expression. He did not look twice. More surprising was the realization, thanks to the darkened view from the window, that it was night.

At the end of the corridor he came to yet another set of forbidding doors. A sign informed him he had to use the intercom in the lounge to gain access. He retraced his steps. The mime glanced up as Ross pressed the intercom button but, naturally, said nothing.

The habit of sending hospitalized friends and acquaintances exorbitant bouquets gaudy with bird-of-paradise so he wouldn't have to visit had left Ross especially unprepared for an intensive care unit. When the doors opened to admit him, what struck him first, after the eye-watering blast of antiseptic, was the hissing. He had stepped into the sound of a hundred inflatable objects leaking – a steady, numbing, unmodulated sibilance. A big black-rimmed clock, positioned to meet the eye, read twenty to one. To the left was the nursing station, to the right a wall of pale yellow curtains. No one was in sight, but he could hear conferring voices and the nauseating foley of a medical procedure being carried out behind one of the curtains. A moment later it jerked open and a very pregnant nurse in a bright pink T-shirt stepped out, beckoning. 'I've paged the resident,' she said. As she led him along, Ross thought of Bonnie, who had also walked in this comical fashion during the last stage of her pregnancy, he following behind with his thumbs hooked in his armpits, flapping his elbows. It had seemed funny at the time.

'I'll leave you. The doctor will be right up.'

She pulled the curtain back revealing Iliana in a large elevated bed between curved chrome safety bars. On her side like this, with her knees drawn up (not how she slept at home), she appeared much smaller than she was and, with the tubes and

17

wires attached to both limp hands and coming from her nose, as inanimate as a collapsed marionette. Her hair was loose, tangled on the pillow, straw-coloured. Seeping though the bandage on her forehead, red.

He took a step back. 'I'm going to faint.' The nurse had let the curtain drop behind him. She freed him from the tangle of fabric he was trying to escape and, taking his arm, duck-walked him briskly out of the unit. The mime was still in the lounge, so she steered him across the hall to some kind of activity room where she helped him to lie down on a raised platform. He was shaking all over, teeth chattering.

'Will you be all right here for a minute? I'll send the doctor in right away.'

Eventually he was able to open his eyes. The nurse had turned off the light. He stared round at the shadowy contents of the room, the weights hanging from pulleys on the ceiling, the set of parallel bars that ran half the long length of one wall. There were different kinds of wheelchairs, electric and standard, the electric one blocky with a moulded headrest, uncannily reminiscent of the death row model. All at once the light came back on, mercifully blinding him to the implications of these objects.

A young, tired-looking man with messy brown hair tiptoed over. 'How're you doing, Mr Alexander?'

Ross stared up at his white coat.

'I understand you're feeling light-headed.'

'I'm fine now.'

'I'm Dr McCracken, the resident on duty tonight. I'd like to explain to you your wife's condition. Are you sure you're okay?'

'Yes.'

'Can you sit up?' He offered his arm. Ross took it and allowed himself to be passively hoisted.

'The injury,' Dr McCracken began when Ross indicated he was

ready, 'is at the level of the tenth thoracic vertebra. The one right about here.' He turned away from Ross, pressing his thumb to the white fabric in the small of his back, and in doing so faced the shelf of books and equipment that lined one wall. Something caught his eye. He walked over and took from a cubbyhole a life-sized model of a spinal cord and pelvis. Bringing it back to Ross, he showed him the tenth thoracic vertebra again on the model, the snaggled line of them strung together on a thick rubber stem. Made of plastic or fibreglass, the model was the very colour of bone and Ross felt himself recoiling from it as if it were an actual part of a cleanly picked human carcass.

'During the accident your wife's spine was subjected to a sudden hyperflexion and rotation, like this.' He pulled and twisted the model so the hollow butterfly of the pelvis knocked against his thigh. 'The X-ray shows that the tips of the vertebra broke off here. We'll have to do surgery to remove them and stabilize the spine, probably early next week.'

'Is she going to be all right?'

'Unfortunately, we won't know the full impact of her injuries until she regains consciousness.'

'She's unconscious?'

'Yes. In terms of a prognosis, I have to tell you that a person with this level of injury—'

'She's not going to die?'

'Oh, no. Her surgeon, Dr Chapman, will be doing rounds in the morning. Maybe you should have this conversation with him. You're obviously distraught. Are you staying?'

'Can I?'

'Certainly. Have them page me if you need me. She's a nurse here. Is that right?'

'Yes.'

'Well, rest assured she'll get the best possible treatment.' He stood there for a moment looking at Ross as if he expected him to say something.

'We just got married.'

It came out sounding like a plea for exemption, as if newly-weds should not be expected to go through something like this. Technically, they qualified as newly-weds for a full year, the same length of time etiquette allowed for those invited to the wedding to fork over a gift. For a whole year they should have been bubbled in safety and bliss. But all Ross was really doing was stating a fact: his marital status had recently changed. Implied in his eagerness to impart this information to everyone he met was his own ludicrous happiness.

'When?' asked the doctor.

'August the second.'

'Big wedding?'

'Yes.'

'That's just marvellous.' Dr McCracken ran a hand through his hopeless hair. 'Congratulations.'

After the doctor left, Ross sat for a while pressing the heels of his hands against his eyes. He moved slowly off the platform and began to make his way across the room as though drugged. At the door, he glanced at the parallel bars that ran along the wall level with his hands. Meeting his own reflection in the full-length mirror at the end, he started. Blood stained the front of his shorts and streaked his bare legs. He looked castrated.

He wandered down the corridor in search of a washroom. The mime was there, standing at the sink squirting bright pink soap on to a pad that he had made out of folded paper towels. From the urinal, Ross saw him lean close to the mirror, scrubbing harshly at one cheek, the patch of skin under the whiteface as pink as the soap. Wetting a paper towel himself, Ross began to clean the blood off his legs. It was Iliana's blood. If he'd been alone he would not have been able to do this, not without weeping. When their eyes met in the mirror, the mime gave Ross a silent, solemn nod.

Half past one by the time he returned to ICU, he took the chair next to the bed, leaning a little forward, watching Iliana as attentively as a dog commanded to sit. It was far from the first time Ross had set himself the task of waiting for her to wake. When she worked the night shift, he'd often arrive home from a long day on set and, impatient, go right into the bedroom to admire her sleeping with her long arms and legs tossed to the four corners of the bed. (She wore earplugs and an eye mask; he didn't worry about disturbing her.) Now she lay closed up, forehead bandaged, hair crusty and powdered with dried blood, a tube in each nostril. He stayed well back, closer to the foot of the bed than the head, and did not touch her. Technology was taking care of her. On the other side was a pillar on which a confusion of equipment was mounted, most prominently a monitor showing in bright green lines and boxes her vital signs. This pillar was her life support; Ross had not imagined it would literally be holding the ceiling up.

He spent the night in the chair with a blue hospital blanket over his legs. Every few hours two of the nurses would come in and, using the bottom sheet, very carefully roll Iliana and check her vital signs. Without realizing he had been sleeping, Ross would start awake into the nightmare. Normally a sound sleeper, the only other time he'd experienced such a regimen of forced wakings was the two weeks he'd gone to stay with Bonnie after Bryce was born. Then each rousing had exhilarated him; it was an alarm sounding a new life. At the end of the two weeks, nearly psychotic from sleep-deprivation, he'd felt the happiest he'd ever been.

Because of the nature of their work, he and Iliana did not always sleep together, but from their first night they had shared a bed.

Even if she was not in it, the smell of her was, and the memory of their hasty lovemaking before they had to part. He had come to assume that trying to sleep somewhere else now would be like trying to sleep standing up. Here he was, sleeping *sitting*. It was his body's act of mercy towards him because, asleep, he did not think or dream. Awake, he watched Iliana, her face appallingly serene, or the line of her damaged spine, depending on which way they had turned her, agonizing over the exact moment he became culpable for all this. Was it when he had ordered her to capture the ball rolling loose on the floor of the car, or back on the tennis court, swinging his racket and almost intentionally sending the second ball into the blue? Or even earlier? On set that afternoon he had thought of her on the court rushing at him with the same fervent energy with which she responded to even his slightest sexual hint (Iliana was always, always ready). Suffused with nostalgia, he had decided to cut out early and get her to play with him.

But if it was possible for blame to be retroactive, he might have to go back further than that, though to what point exactly he couldn't say. Their wedding day, or even that first, nearly disastrous date? The first time they slept together? (These last two were the same.)

2

The week after they met at the outpatient clinic as nurse and patient, Ross (virtually healed but for minor spotting) pressed the button on the intercom outside Iliana's building. Buzzed in, he went over to the lobby sofa and, while he waited for her to come down, could not help but wonder how much of who a person was was reflected in where he lived. It was certainly true of Ross that his Kerrisdale apartment and even his pensioner neighbours were part of how he defined himself. Iliana's was one of many similar low-rises clumped around the hospital, not new, but at least a decade short of being interestingly old. With its imitation Spanish décor and obvious lack of maintenance, it seemed the kind of place someone might stay only temporarily, and even then would not invite guests to without offering that excuse for bad architecture everywhere: location, location, location. Presently, Iliana appeared at the top of the stairs and he left off these musings. First her legs came into view, then, almost anti-climactically, the rest of her.

'Sorry,' she said. 'I had to change.'

Out of uniform, she looked different. Partly, it was the shorts, or rather the legs they revealed, not only in full elongated display, but seen like this, from below. Also, when Ross had first met her she'd had her hair sensibly pulled back; now she was wearing it in braids which, to him, looked ridiculous on a grown woman. She had seemed so unlike the film types he usually dated (a veritable breath of fresh air), yet here she was, as guilty as the next woman of wearing obviously uncomfortable clothing and doing irrational things to her hair. Holding the door for her, he had to resist the urge to tug a braid and say, 'Toot toot.'

'How's the nose?' she asked.

'Okay, so long as I don't blow it.'

He rejected her suggestion that they walk the few blocks to the courts, ushering her over instead to Miss Stockholm, parked in front of the building. She glanced in the back seat as she got in, at his repository of paper coffee cups and old *Province*s, at the borrowed wooden racket with the broken string. 'Do you play much tennis?'

'I used to quite a bit.' He meant those late summer days when school was starting to look good again, hitting against the garage door the ball he'd stolen back from the dog. About grade six. The day before, he'd borrowed the woody from a seventy-year-old neighbour.

'We don't have to play.'

'I want to,' Ross said.

Call it innocence or call it egotism, but only when they were out on the asphalt and Ross saw her stretching and heard the ungodly grunts made by the players on the next court every time they returned the ball did he realize he was going to embarrass himself. (*He* was the one who'd suggested they play. His opener: 'You seem the sporty type.') While Ross cleaned his sunglasses on his shirt, trying to forestall the shame, Iliana grasped an ankle and pulled it behind her so the heel of her running shoe touched her buttock, barely covered by the little shorts. 'I don't warm up,' he explained. 'It's kind of a policy of mine.'

'You might hurt yourself,' she chided.

'That's right. I might hurt myself if I warm up. I might overheat.'

She began hopping up and down on alternating feet and, like that, the braids bouncing, seemed about twelve (a very tall, possibly debauched twelve). 'That's not blood, is it?'

Looking down, he saw she meant the dark trickle on his T-shirt and the splotch on one leg of his shorts. 'It's Ring of Fire Sauce. I didn't have time to change.'

'Are you a cook?'

'A caterer.'

She crossed her bent arms at the elbows and twined them around each other. 'I can cook three things. Tuna fish casserole with potato chips crumbled on top, scalloped potatoes with potato chips crumbled on top, and toast.'

'With potato chips crumbled on top?'

She laughed.

'Don't think I'm a gourmet. The real secret of my modest success is quantity.'

'I might have guessed that,' she said with a glance to his mid-region. 'Heads or tails?'

'Tails.'

She spun her racket and let it fall, then showed him how the logo on the end of the handle was upside down, meaning he got to serve or choose a side. 'I choose this side,' he said. 'Then I won't have to walk all the way over there.'

She jogged there, took her place behind the service line and, after a few preliminary bounces, tossed the ball. For a second it hung in the air above her – a furry yellow orb against the blue sky, a second sun, seemingly benign – before her racket strings hit it. Ross was taken completely off guard by the force of the shot whizzing past, and by the sight of this demented Heidi now rushing towards him (thank God for the net). He thought she was going to leap right over it, so earnestly did she charge, yet nothing on her body bounced, she was that strapped in or toned.

For twenty minutes they played without keeping score, Ross loping back and forth attempting to return her tempered shots (*baby* shots), flowers of perspiration blooming on his chest and back and in the Eden of his armpits. A crow flew over the court and Ross swiped at its shadow by mistake. Mid-swing, he let go of his racket. Her final lob rising in a high parabola above his head, he leaped to smash it, shirt hiking up. He drove the ball straight into the net, groaning because he'd accidentally shown her his fat.

'Had enough?'

Panting, he staggered off to the side. 'Where did you learn to play?'

'Camp. I was girls' champion five summers running.'

'Now you tell me.' He closed the wire fence behind them. 'There's nothing like humiliation to stoke the appetite. How about you? Are you hungry? You still have your pride, but can I make you dinner?'

He fully expected her to beg off, but instead she brightened. 'At your place?'

'It doesn't have to be. We can do the restaurant thing if you want.'

'I'd rather go to your place.'

'All right,' said Ross, as pleased as he was surprised.

The day before, preparing for the possibility that he might be cooking for her, Ross had decided on pasta because it was something that only the pathologically picky disliked, but since she had mentioned tuna he changed his mind. 'I know a great place for tuna,' he told her as they got in the car. Detouring down to Fourth Avenue, he left Iliana in the Volvo while he dashed into the store.

Kerrisdale was a leafier, more gentrified part of Vancouver. He'd been in the same apartment there for years. The building, the Victoria Arms (four stuccoed storeys with a penthouse), was co-operatively owned. 'I'm the youngest person in the building,' Ross told her as they entered. 'I'm the surrogate grandson-in-residence, yet any one of my neighbours could probably beat me at tennis.' In the elevator, he said, 'I guess you'll want a long, cold drink after that tremendous workout.'

'A glass of water would be great.'

As soon as he let her into the apartment, she asked to use the bathroom. Pointing her down the hall, he headed for the kitchen to put the tuna steaks into the fridge. From the freezer he took two glasses, filling one with beer for himself, the other with water. Hearing her come out of the bathroom, he waited with the glasses in hand, the frosted effect becoming less dramatic by the moment.

He went to find her. She was in the bedroom, sitting on the bed, looking curiously around. 'This is the bedroom,' he said from the doorway.

'I know.'

He began to wonder about her then. The fact that she had seemed so wholesome was one of the things that had attracted him in the first place. To a man like Ross, because of the business he was in, wholesome was refreshing. Wholesome was strange and new. But on the court she had seemed exasperated, even ruthless, and here she sat in another guise: cross-legged on his bed, leaning back on the heels of her hands, smiling in a manner he would have to call unnatural or forced. Maybe she was grimacing. The shorts were obviously cutting her in half. 'Come on,' he told her, holding out her drink. 'I'll show you my faux food.'

One wall in the living room was scaffolded with the wall unit that housed his collection, his smorgasbord of culinary realia. Opening a drawer and stirring inside, he closed his hand around two chunks and held them out: the splayed shrimp butterfly of the *Ebi* and the yellow *Maguro* strapped on to the rice by thin seaweed ribbons.

'What is it?' Iliana asked.

'Sushi.'

'Are they shellacked?'

'It's plastic.' He tossed the pieces back and lifted a plate from a shelf. The plate was real. 'Spaghetti and meat balls.' The shiny mass of strings and balls came off in one clump that he held against his heart. 'There is just so much to say about plastic food. I mean, it's beautiful. Beautiful and at the same time, I don't know, sick. Whole philosophical tomes could be written on the subject.' The phone began to ring. 'Look at it. Go ahead and look at it while I get that.'

It was his sister on the phone. When he returned with the bad news Iliana, tugging at the crotch of her shorts, was reading one of his movie posters. 'Seen it?' he asked.

'No.'

'You might have on an aeroplane. Awful, but the people who worked on it were nice. Look, something's come up. Can we take a rain check?'

'What?' she cried with what seemed like genuine, even excessive, disappointment.

'My sister needs a babysitter.'

'Do you have to?'

'I want to.' As soon as he said it, he realized how insulting it sounded, though Iliana did not appear to be insulted.

'How many kids does she have?'

'Just one.'

'I'll come, too. Will she mind?'

Ross didn't see why Bonnie would since she wasn't even going to be there. 'This is great,' he told her, packing up the steaks and a bottle of wine. 'You'll get to meet my nephew.'

Driving over to the West End, Ross told Iliana about Bryce. 'He was one of those happy accidents. Bonnie didn't really want a baby, but I managed to convince her. I was even in the delivery room part of the time.'

'Where was the father?'

'Oh, he passed. I'm very involved. I'm like the father. On call twenty-four hours a day.'

He always had been, even before Bryce, at his sister's beck and call.

Bonnie lived on the twenty-first floor of her building and didn't have a barbecue. He'd have to pan-fry the tuna and abandon the grilled vegetables he'd planned. Forced to rethink the entire menu on the spot for the third time, he stopped at a little produce store on Davie.

Bonnie was all ready to go when she answered the door. She

didn't even have time for introductions, just looked Iliana up and down and said, 'Who's she standing in for?' Once, just once, Ross had gone out with the stand-in for a certain Hollywood actress, then made the mistake of mentioning it to Bonnie, and of admitting that he had slept with the woman. 'Nobody,' he said now. 'She's a nurse.'

Behind them Bryce sat in his high chair, circled by wreckage, his face boiled-looking and wet, quivering tongue bent back in his mouth, arms held straight out and stiff as if he was signalling in semaphore. Bonnie slipped past and out of the door, fleeing her child's cries, heading for the elevator without so much as a goodbye.

'*Bonjour! Bonjour!*' Ross called out to the baby.

'Is she angry?' asked Iliana.

'It's a boy. Bryce. Didn't I say that?'

'Your sister.'

He set the groceries on the kitchen counter. 'Why would she be angry?'

'Maybe I shouldn't have come.'

'Forget it,' said Ross.

'She doesn't look like your sister.'

'Everyone says that. Actually, we're twins.' Like everyone, Iliana expressed her surprise. When she asked him what a stand-in was, he sighed.

'Look who's here!' Ross crowed, going over to Bryce. '*Bonjour! Bonjour!*' To Iliana he said, 'See how he lights up when he sees me? He thinks I'm his dad. If you're happy and you know it clap your hands! If you're happy and you know it clap your hands!' Ross clapped. Bryce kept on shrieking. 'Clap with me,' he told Iliana.

Iliana undid the buckle on the high chair, liberating Bryce from his fire-tower perch. Lurching backwards, arching his whole body, he might have tumbled out of Iliana's arms had he not grabbed the lifeline of her braid just in time. Ross recognized at once the practicality of the hairdo. 'Easy there,' said Iliana.

'He only understands French. This has been the problem all along. We talk to him and he doesn't understand us, so he cries.' Ross had made this surprising discovery during Bryce's colicky months when, desperate for any way to soothe him, he had picked up and read aloud from the instruction manual for the VCR. 'Halfway along, I turned the book upside down and started on the French, botching the pronunciation, but no matter. Bryce definitely turned the volume down. Now I reach for the cereal box, or whatever French is handy. I'm going to get a pocket copy of *A la recherche du temps perdu* and keep it on my person at all times. Hey, it's me, Monsieur Champignon, the chef,' he told Bryce. '*Roux, roux, roux.*'

'You cook. I'll give him a bath.' She toted Bryce off.

Ross set the red skins on to boil, hearing the bath running in the pauses between Bryce's screams. He trimmed the green beans to the music of his nephew's furious vocalizations and was just opening the wine to let it breathe when he felt the sudden switch to silence. Not that he minded Bryce's crying, but now that it had stopped so abruptly he understood why his sister was on edge so much of the time. What did it mean, though, this cessation of wails, so out of character? He hurried with the half-opened bottle to the bathroom where Iliana was kneeling on the bathmat steadying Bryce in the water as he sucked a washcloth. Lifting his eyes to Ross, Bryce smiled with his whole body.

'You're good with babies,' Ross told her.

'I have nieces, though I haven't seen them for a while.'

He took the glass off the vanity and joined her on the mat, uncorking the wine and filling the glass for her. He offered Bryce the corkscrew, its sharp part disabled by the cork. Bryce dropped the washcloth to accept it, turning it deftly over in his raccoon hands.

Ross loved his nephew. He loved counting the rolls of fat on his stomach (six – two more than Ross), the creases and indentations, the white perfection of his skin, the crooked seam running from the baggy tip of his tiny penis, down the little shaft, over and under his testicles and into his anus, like a string tucked in. Changing Bryce's diaper, Ross would munch his bare, drum-tight tummy, suck his toes, suck his whole foot. Bryce's shrieks at changing time were shrieks of laughter. 'When you see a naked baby,' he asked Iliana, 'do you immediately think of different ways to cook it?'

'Gosh.' She gave a little shudder. 'I couldn't. I'd have to eat it raw.'

He laughed, but her comment gave him fourth thoughts about the tuna. Maybe he should have served it as sashimi. 'Could you really eat a person?'

She sipped the wine. 'It depends. They'd have to be dead already.'

Ross, getting up to check on the potatoes, agreed. 'We wouldn't want anyone to get hurt.'

The tuna steaks were wrapped in brown paper. He opened the package and lifted one out, an inch and a half thick, almost as red as the Merlot they were drinking. Another idea came to him then, his fifth that night, making the evening already memorable for this fireworks display of inspiration. His original impression of Iliana restored now, he had even noted additional favourable traits: a sense of humour, maternal expertise. (He knew by observing his sister's struggles just how important the latter was.) The cheesy short shorts and bizarre pose on the bed he chose now to disregard.

She emerged carrying a fresh-faced Bryce, sleeper-clad, snake-charming her braid. 'What are you making?'

'Salade niçoise.'

In her arms, Bryce lunged forward, reaching out for Ross. 'See?' he said. 'Salade niçoise! Salade niçoise! Châteauneuf du Pape!'

'Does he have a bottle?'

It took her almost half an hour to get Bryce off to sleep. Ross waited for her before searing the tuna pockets. Transferring them to heated plates, he removed the toothpick sutures that held in the stuffing and carried them over to the table anticipating her delighted 'Ah!' She just looked perplexed. While Ross didn't mind disappointing her on the tennis court, his pride was at issue now. He took his seat and cut into his own steak in order to demonstrate the brilliance of his idea, not only how the inside was stratified from the cooking (the seared part white, the raw inside red), but that he had carefully carved a pocket in each steak and filled it with minced salade niçoise. The salad was on the inside!

'What do you think?'

She took a bite and nodded. 'Good.'

'The salade niçoise is on the inside.'

'What are the black bits?'

'Olives! Are you telling me you don't know what salade niçoise is?'

If she had not already betrayed herself, he would have guessed by the way she handled her utensils that she was a practical and uninspired eater. At least she wasn't a food rearranger like Bonnie. Bonnie poked her food around the plate, seeking configurations that might disguise how little she actually ate. Suspicious of other people's cooking (Ross's especially), she sniffed everything, quizzing him on the Best Before dates. Bryce, by contrast, took a happy tactile approach to food, a projectile approach. (He was not above smear tactics either.) Iliana cut and chewed and chewed and cut, worker-like. Except hers were not a worker's hands, but clean and smooth with long slender fingers. His eyes wandered to her wrists, the left adorned by a small gold watch with an expandable strap, then to her bare, hairless forearms held close to her body, bent at the elbows as she worked the knife and fork, her tight biceps at right angles, framing small breasts.

'I guess you went to cooking school,' she said.

'Actually, I'm self-taught. I'm really just an entrepreneur who loves to eat.'

'That's funny. I'm just a nurse who hates to cook.'

'We were talking about eating people. I have a theory. It came to me once during a dinner party and now I can never go to or throw a dinner party without testing my theory.' He used a nub of olive impaled on his fork as a pointer, waving it as he talked. Like all autodidacts, he had a pedagogic streak. 'When you sit down to eat with a group of people, imagine that you are on a plane with them and the plane crashes and you are the only survivor. Then ask yourself who you would eat. Pick the people you would eat then ask yourself, out of all the people sitting at the table, who you like best.' He bit into the olive, a salty detonation. 'What I found was the people I really liked and the people I'd eat were the same.'

Iliana set her utensils down. 'Would you eat me?'

He openly appraised her as he already had in secret. 'Most definitely.'

'When is your sister coming home?'

'I'm not sure.'

'Do we have time to sleep together?'

'Probably,' said Ross, pleased that she had liked the meal after all. 'Can we finish eating first?'

'I'll go freshen up.'

'Aren't you going to finish?'

'I can't.'

As soon as she had left the table, Ross sniffed briefly at his armpits because, rightly, he was the one who should have freshened up.

'I forgot about the baby,' she said when she came back. 'Will he wake up?'

Ross was swabbing his plate with a chunk of bread. 'Good question.'

'Maybe we should do it on the couch.'

'The couch definitely. Bonnie would kill me if we used her bed.' He reached across the table with his fork, aiming to spear a piece of potato off her plate. With a cry of exasperation, Iliana grabbed his wrist. Both of them recognized the gesture. When the kiss happened, Ross tasted dinner on her.

'Remember the camp I told you about?' she pulled away to say.

'What?'

'Camp Pentecost.'

'Is that where you learned to kiss? At camp?'

She sat down in his lap. 'Ooof,' said Ross.

'You're so soft!' Iliana exclaimed.

'Plee-ease!'

'Do you have a condom?'

'I don't,' said Ross. 'I thought we were playing tennis.'

She went and got her handbag, digging through it, pulling out a long cellophane strip. Ross said, 'We definitely don't have that much time.' She tore an envelope off and, hauling him from his chair, led him to the couch where Ross took the initiative, circling her in his big soft arms and covering her mouth with his, tongue sweeping between her teeth and the slippery inside of her lips. He sucked her tongue and, while they were still fixed face to face, she began tugging on his shirt. Ross was the one who drew back then. He always felt he had to warn a woman. 'I've got titties.'

'So do I.'

'Mine are bigger.'

Falling back and drawing her on top of him so he would not

34

be wobbling above her, he placed a hand over each of her breasts. They were shockingly firm. Did she have muscles in her tits? Lifting her T-shirt to inspect them, he discovered that she was wearing one of those sports bras with no obvious entrance. Obligingly, she peeled off both the shirt and the bra, revealing two solid cones of creamy flesh with brownish tips, like a pair of individually packaged gelato desserts, cappuccino-flavoured. Her legs hooked around his hips, his erection joined them, though Ross wasn't nearly finished kissing yet. He almost liked the kissing best. It was the thing he regretted most in how his relationships progressed, that he so often slept with a woman on their first date and therefore forfeited the kissing stage and its playful unirrevocability. In matters of sex, there seemed to be no retracing steps. He could not very well tell a woman he had had intercourse with that tonight he only wanted to kiss her. It would offend her honour and cast suspicion on him. And now that he had allowed in regret, it was only natural that he should succumb to his inevitable melancholia. This time it was more than the usual spasm of precoital loneliness: he was sorry they were at his sister's because, now that he had got his nose fixed, she might actually have stayed the night.

Iliana said, 'We should put a towel down.'

He pulled the hair elastic off a braid. 'We've got condoms.'

'We're going to need a towel. Do you know if she has any old ones?'

He told her where the linen cupboard was. Up she sprang. Cringing, he watched her go. Was she menstruating? She didn't seem the ghoulish type. She came back hugging a bath mat to her chest, hair hanging to her shoulder on one side. 'That camp,' he said, testing his awful hunch. 'What was it called again?'

'Camp Pentecost. It was Bible camp.'

Ross himself had been raised a Catholic and, though he no longer believed, there were certain things he would always be superstitious about: hanging a crucifix upside down, being rude to nuns, deflowering virgins. He sat up, hand to his forehead. 'My God, you *are* wholesome.'

Iliana said, 'I'd like to change that.'

'It's hard to believe. I mean, didn't some nice Christian boy ever—'

'They wouldn't dare. I was the minister's daughter.'

'You don't want to start with me.'

'I do,' said Iliana.

In a flash he recalled her opening serve almost taking off his ear, powered (he realized now) by repressed sexual energy. He pictured her reclining on his bed. 'You planned this.'

She coloured and was all the more tempting in red.

He should have felt offended – used, in fact – but he was flattered. 'Did you decide when you met me?'

'No. When you buzzed this afternoon.'

He slumped. 'So you didn't like dinner?'

'No, I did. I did. I just can't eat when I'm nervous.'

She started towards him. Alarmed, Ross waved her back. 'No. Don't make me. I'd feel awful later.'

'Why?'

'I just would.'

She stood pushing the loose hair back, perhaps expecting him to relent.

'Don't be mad,' he begged.

'I'm not.' Turning, she calmly reversed the burlesque. He found her modesty sexy, too, more than if she had thrown herself at him. There: the incipient wings of her shoulder blades, the bumpy line of her spine as she bent to retrieve her T-shirt. Smartly, she rebraided her hair, then, facing him again, held out her hand for her hair band. All the while Ross sat shrinking on the couch. Many of the women he dated were actresses for whom waitressing between auditions did not provide sufficient outlet for their pent-up dramatic tendencies. They thrived on scenes and were ever vigilant for cues that one might be provoked. Though the pretext might be slight, the scene was usually worthy of the grossest Hollywood disaster epic. Ross had dubbed these exchanges 'hurricanes': Hurricane Paula, Hurricane Mary Ellen. His sister, though a restaurant hostess, not an actress, before she had Bryce, possessed the same meteorological temperament.

Iliana pulled her ankle up behind her so her heel touched her buttock. 'What are you doing?' Ross asked.

'I'm going home.'

'Don't,' he cried. 'Wait for Bonnie. I'll drive you.'

'I need a run.'

'You're going to *run*? Are you crazy? It'll take you a month!'

'It would take you a month.'

'I'd take a cab.' He followed her to the door. 'Are you sure you're not mad at me?'

'If anything,' she told him, 'I'm mad at myself.'

'Can I call you again? Maybe if we saw each other a few more times I'd feel better about it. In the meantime, why don't you sleep with someone else?' He stepped into the hallway, naked from the waist up, fly unbuttoned (hardly a shocking sight from what he knew of Bonnie's building, a high-rise Sodom and Gomorrah), and watched her jog over to the elevator. Hands on the wall, she bent one knee, forming a delectable angle with the straightened leg behind her. 'Don't be mad,' were his last words as the elevator opened. Immediately he regretted what he'd done. Over a matter of scruples he had let a consenting woman walk out of the door. How often did that happen in the post-modern era?

Glumly, he went back in to clean up. Confronted by the uneaten half of Iliana's meal, he sat down to it shirtless rather than throw it out. Bonnie would certainly not eat it. Afterwards he felt worse. He hated eating alone.

In the next room his nephew slumbered. Nursing in his dreams, making barely audible sucking sounds, Bryce was still in his deepest phase of sleep and could be safely lifted out of the crib and carried to the bed. Ross climbed in, careful not to jar the baby as he settled down beside him. Sensing another body's warmth, Bryce turned his sleeping face to Ross. Ross wriggled closer. Oh, joy! Bryce latched on to a roll of fat.

How many different kinds of love had he known? He had married his own sister countless times in childhood ceremonies, she with an antimacassar on her head, he cummerbunded with an old tie. Scores of girlfriends had come and gone. He used to feel that he abandoned his sister every time he loved another woman. He sensed her resentment even as she pursued her own bizarre affairs. Now she had this child and, though he was only pretending it was his, it had given him the taste of a true love other than a twin's.

By the time Bonnie came home, he had finished cleaning up. 'Where is she?' she asked, eyes jealously slitted.

Ross seized both sides of her face, kissing. 'Gotta run.'

'Please, Ross. I'm so depressed.' She backed against the door, clutching the frame, barring his way, forcing him to choose.

He got to Iliana's place ten minutes before she did, which allowed him the additional pleasure of watching her through the lobby window as she performed her complicated stretching ritual. When she unlocked the door and stepped into the lobby, Ross, on the sofa, stood to greet her. Flush-faced, she stared, as if he had appeared by magic.

'Bonnie came back,' he explained. 'Your neighbour let me in. Let's go make a baby.'

'Oh, sure.'

He put his arm round her shoulders and, together, they climbed the stairs. She was damp to his touch, hot. He could feel how erectly she carried herself, the whole of her skeleton beneath his eager hand. *Who's she standing in for?* Bonnie had asked. The truth was (he knew it now) that all of the others had been standing in for Iliana. A song burst from him. *'If you're happy and you know it—'*

'Clap with me,' he urged.

3

When the nurses came in at 4 a.m., Ross took a bathroom break. Passing the lounge, he saw someone curled up across the blue vinyl seats, not the mime, but a ballerina, the pink spangled netting of her tutu crushed under her sleeping form, so small she seemed not much older than a child. He wondered if he was dreaming after all, or hallucinating, and in the washroom splashed cold water on his face.

At 7 a.m. the nurses changed shifts, opening the curtains so they served only as partitions between the beds. Dr Chapman appeared then on his rounds with a trio of students and Dr McCracken, who apparently did not sleep. Chapman was English and bald with frizzy reddish curls around his ears. A foolishly patterned tie (hedgehogs?) complemented his clown-wig hairstyle, further reducing his credibility in Ross's eyes. As he explained what Iliana's operation would entail, Ross found it hard even to listen. 'It will not negatively impact upon her recovery. I believe Dr McCracken explained all this to you last night.'

Ross raised his throbbing head. 'What?'

'Her prognosis.'

He stared, not quite at the surgeon, at the empty space above his shoulder, next to his ear.

'It's unlikely she'll walk again.'

Ross leaped to his feet. 'That's *bullshit*!'

The incoming nurses stopped what they were doing and turned to look at Ross. 'You mustn't raise your voice in here,' said Dr Chapman, not unkindly. 'Let's step outside, shall we?'

Ross did more than that; he stormed out, pounding his fist on the button that opened the big blue doors. They couldn't open fast enough for him. He punched the door as well.

One of the nurses came after him. 'Mr Alexander? I understand you didn't get much sleep last night. Why don't you go home?'

'I'm waiting for her to wake up!'

'If she does, we'll call you right away.'

'I want to be here!'

'But she may not wake for days.'

Ross, receiving this news like a slap, teetered slightly.

'Would you like someone to come up and talk to you? The social worker? We have chaplains, too, of all denominations.'

'No,' said Ross.

'You have to look after yourself. Is there a family member you'd like me to call?'

'No.'

'Then why don't you go down and get some breakfast?'

He did, solely in order to get away from Chapman. In the cafeteria, he bought a coffee, and walked out with the steaming cup in hand, moving in the half-trance of a dislocated animal recovering its bearings, right back up to ICU. The mime and the ballerina were walking ahead of him, the ballerina drawing the bemused attention of people coming down the corridor in the opposite direction. By the time Ross reached the elevator, he'd caught up with them.

They looked wrecked, in their costumes like Hallowe'en revellers who had refused to stop partying all the way into All Saint's Day. The girl, hair harshly peroxided, complexion pitted, was peeling the wrapper off a Mr Big like it was a banana. The mime was short and conspicuously muscled, with a broad forehead made more prominent by hair ebbing at the corners. He was carrying a sandwich packaged as an isosceles triangle. They all got in the elevator, where the mime immediately turned on Ross a pair of arrestingly pale, deep-set eyes. He spoke loudly, with a ponderous Slavic accent. 'What bring you to this fucking place?'

'My wife,' said Ross and he took a sip of the scalding coffee so he wouldn't start to weep. 'What about you?'

'My brother. We are aerialist.' He pointed to himself and to the girl who was standing next to Ross but not looking at him. 'She is fiancée. We are with Moscow Circus. Last night my brother fall.'

The elevator opened on the ninth floor and the three of them got out. 'How is he?' Ross asked.

The man lifted his empty hand and squeezed it into a fist. 'He don't know who the fuck is he. Who am I. Who is Anna. My twin brother!'

Rattled, Ross muttered that he was himself a twin and, without warning, the man embraced him. Ross had to hold his arm out straight to avoid spilling coffee on him. Smelling powerfully and acridly of sweat, the hug was tight and brief and oddly reassuring. It was a twin's hug, implying an understanding of that strange bond – uterine, genetic, curse, gift. The girl asked something in Russian and the man released Ross in order to berate her and wave the sandwich. When he turned back, Ross saw his eyes were filled with tears.

'You know what I feel, man.'

They parted at the lounge. A few more visitors had arrived and were sitting in pairs or standing alone staring out of the window. Ross asked to be readmitted to ICU and, leaving his coffee behind, entered and asked the nurse to phone Bonnie. He had not wanted to call her earlier, but felt more than a little comfort now in the prospect of her coming.

The nurse nodded in the direction of Iliana's bed. 'She has another visitor.'

A woman was sitting in Ross's place. She wore a long-sleeved grey dress with a white collar and a dark kerchief over her hair, clothes that were so similar to the habit of a certain order of nun from his childhood that Ross turned to glare back at the nurse for having ordered her up against his wishes. Physically unable to look over his right shoulder, he had to swivel stiffly from the waist, but by then she was busy at the computer, oblivious of his reproach. Most annoying of all was that the nun had taken his chair. He went to find another. Returning and setting it on the opposite side of the bed, he resumed his vigil.

They had turned Iliana, and if the nun had not taken his place he would have had her face to look at now rather than the back of her head. This was the side of the bed the catheter bag hung on. He resented that, too. Her legs stirred, but he knew now it was not her legs but the continuously inflating and deflating plastic sleeves around them that stimulated her circulation. Dr Chapman's words came back. He felt nauseous and unthought them.

The nun, her face lowered in prayer, did not disturb him. He had almost forgotten she was there by the time she spoke. 'What is that thing on her finger?' He looked up with a start. She meant the white plastic sheath with the glowing red light on the end attached by a wire to the pillar of life. Ross had asked this question himself sometime in the middle of the night, it being the most obvious one after the one he had deliberately not asked.

'It measures the oxygen in her blood.'

'What for?'

'I don't know.'

The nun tsked. 'I'm astonished at these machines.'

42

For someone who ministered in a hospital, this seemed to Ross a loopy comment. In his opinion it was well nigh time she moved on to another bed and, again, he tried to look back at the desk in order to enlist the nurse's help. Turning halfway round in the chair, he caught her eye. Her sympathetic smile, a single maddening second long before she returned to the computer screen, confirmed for him that the nun had indeed been summoned.

Hoping a quick chat might satisfy her, Ross asked, 'Were you praying when I came in?'

'Yes. Will you join me?'

'You go ahead.'

'Do you know how to pray?'

He laughed jadedly. 'Hail Mary full of grace.'

'That's not praying.'

He did not know how to evict her, nor did he possess the energy to, so in self-defence he closed his eyes. If he kept his eyes closed, he reasoned, she might take the hint and leave. It seemed to work; for a time she said nothing and eventually he heard her rise to her feet. She had stood in order to reach across the bed. 'Give me your hands,' she said and, as though hypnotized, he did. Across Iliana's body, their four arms formed a bridge. The continuous wearying hiss of oxygen and suction, which had faded to ambience hours ago, gradually reinsinuated itself into his consciousness.

'Will you pray with me?'

'Yes,' Ross said, eyes still closed.

'Oh Lord—'

She paused and he understood that he was to repeat what she said. 'O Lord.'

'Look upon this child who lies here broken—'

'Look upon this child who lies here . . . broken.'

'—requiring of You Your infinite love—'

'Requiring of You . . .' He began to sob. 'Your infinite love.'

Opening his eyes, he saw the nun's face tilted up and glowing as if there were a light source above the bed, tears coursing down her cheeks.

'And Lord, forgive the ones into whose care You placed her. Forgive their faults and their mistakes.'

He thought she meant him and yanked his hands away. Startled, she muttered a hasty 'Amen' and nervously touched the edge of the kerchief that concealed her hair. She was no nun, Ross already knew by her prayer, but only looking up at her formidable height and seeing when she turned her face away the blonde-grey bun beneath the kerchief, did he recognize Iliana's mother. He remembered sitting across the kitchen table from her and thinking exactly this: that if he happened to meet her again by chance, he probably wouldn't know her.

'Why are you here?'

She couldn't meet his eye. She wouldn't dare. 'They phoned me.'

'You wouldn't even come to the wedding! How could you not come?'

'Tell her . . .' Her voice began to come apart. 'Tell her that we love her.'

'You tell her,' said Ross. 'She's right here.'

As soon as Ross and Iliana had become engaged, the matter of her family began to trouble Ross. Her parents lived little more than an hour away, as did her two older married sisters and their families. Not only had Ross not been introduced, Iliana was not going to invite any of them to the wedding. Ross's parents, Pal and Teddy, had retired to Arizona two years before at the close of Teddy's twenty-five-year career as a Danish cheese representative (the Cheese Ambassador, they still called him, the Hamlet of Havarti). Ross loved and admired his father. It was partly due to his influence that Ross had ended up catering for film and television; as a boy he used to be allowed to stay home from school to watch his father whenever he appeared on cooking segments of local talk shows. Though she was harder to get along with, he loved his mother just as much. He couldn't imagine bearing a grudge against his parents, or Bonnie, or anyone. He decided to speak frankly to Iliana. 'I think you should invite your parents.'

'Why?' she said. 'They won't come.'

'Then it will be on their conscience that they refused to attend their own daughter's wedding.'

'That won't bother their conscience in the least. They'll think they're in the right.'

That was January, shortly after they had become engaged. The wedding was going to be in August. Sometime in the spring he announced that he could not abide by her decision and was going to invite her parents himself.

'You don't have to feel guilty about inviting more people,' she assured him, guessing correctly that he would soon inform her of new additions to his list. While Iliana had invited two or three nursing friends, Ross's list topped thirty now that he'd spilled the beans to his staff and some of his suppliers. Thirty people meant at least fifty for the number who would bring dates, pushing the celebration out of the 'intimate' category, which was what they planned for after Ross went ahead and invited several of their neighbours to elope with them.

'What's the phone number?' he asked.

If she had forbidden him to call, he wouldn't have. Instead she stood by while he dialled, turning and fleeing only at the last second. Iliana's father was a minister. She had told Ross that as a child she had confused her father with God. Now that she was an adult she understood that he was just as confused as she had been, doling out threats in the name of God, as if by proxy.

Evidently, though, he still inspired enough trepidation to drive her from the room while Ross talked to him.

After he had hung up, he found her in the bathroom, in the tub, steeping in her dread. 'What did he say?'

'We're invited for supper on Saturday.'

'*What?*'

'I told him that I'd heard so much about him, I'd like to meet him.'

'Ha!' said Iliana, rising out of the bubbles. 'See how vain he is?'

There are more churches per capita in the Fraser Valley, more Bible-pounders and Bible-rifflers, more people who would use the Bible as both a rhetorical weapon and one to slam down hard across a child's knuckles, than anywhere else in the country. What else would Ross have thought about driving out? A detour around the first border crossing put them on to Zero Avenue. Though hazy on the doctrine of his youth, he knew enough to comment that Zero Avenue sounded like the road to Purgatory. Mount Baker reared up on the horizon, a pure white cone. No wonder it was the Bible belt: visible from the highway, or any of these back roads, was the throne of God.

'Are you an agnostic or an atheist?' he asked Iliana.

'Atheist. Aren't you?'

'I'm not sure. I want to say atheist, but what if I'm wrong? What if there is a God? If you're agnostic at least your ass is covered.' They were driving past fields of raspberry canes, clapboard farmhouses, pink Punjabi mansions. 'What should I talk about?'

'It doesn't matter. Nothing you say will change his mind about me or you.'

'I just don't want to say the wrong thing.'

'Then don't call me your Mennonite Mama. He hates the Mennonites.'

'How about my Baptist Beauty?'

Iliana laughed.

'My Pentecostal Pussy?'

Eventually Zero Avenue split into two narrow roads separated by a shallow ditch. Iliana pointed to the field on Ross's side. 'These raspberries are Canadian.' She tapped the passenger window. 'Those are American.'

'You mean that ditch is the border?'

'Yes,' said Iliana.

'That ditch is *it*?' Ross was incredulous. 'Are you telling me that all that protects us from the Yankee Menace is a ditch?'

At the next pink mansion, he pulled into the driveway and left Iliana sitting in the car while he marched across the road. Opening his fly, he attempted to urinate across the ditch, not out of any nationalistic sentiment, but just to say he had straddled two nations with his piss. He actually had no political convictions. As for the Yankee Menace, he was overjoyed when their mobile dressing rooms rumbled over this very border and their detoxified stars jetted in.

Back in the car, he drove on past greenhouse complexes etched with reflected clouds. Somebody's Rottweiler chased the car. The expanse of tarmac at the T-junction was the airport. 'Turn here,' said Iliana. 'It's on the corner.'

They came to a little wooden house and shambled outbuildings in a yard dotted with muddy pools. Moss grew thick on all the roofs and the tops of the fence posts, as if a layer of bright green snow had fallen. There it was – the sign – weathered and not quite as looming as he had imagined when Iliana had told him about it, facing the four-way stop: *The wages of sin is death*.

Ross shook his head.

'I told you,' she said.

Just then a dog came loping out of nowhere, baying sonorously. As it drew near the car, Ross saw its one normal sad brown Labrador eye and the other bulging grotesquely. 'Don't get out!'

'It's only Dora,' she said, stepping right down in the muddy track they'd parked in, crouching so the dog could lick her face. He heard her conspiring murmur. The dog, she was telling it, was the only one she missed.

The side door to the house opened (the front, Ross observed, had a sheet of plastic stapled over the frame) and a man in green work pants and plaid shirt stepped out. 'There he is,' Iliana said.

That the man on the step could have engendered a long-limbed wonder like Iliana was nothing short of a miracle, Ross thought, but now the sign made sense. Only a very short man would feel compelled to post such a message to the world. Hesitantly, Ross got out of the car. (It was not the dog he was afraid of, but its terrible eye.) Iliana's father whistled, one quick commanding blast produced without the aid of fingers, just the pent-up energy in his mouth. Instantly, the dog ran off, disappearing behind the barn.

Not one for public displays of affection, Iliana surprised Ross by taking his hand and leading him to the house. 'Dad? This is Ross Alexander.' At the bottom of the steps looking up at him, Ross felt as though they were standing before the pulpit. He nodded to Ross but did not acknowledge Iliana in any way, simply stood aside to let them in the house.

Like the outside, the inside of the house suggested poverty, though Iliana had warned Ross not to believe it. For years real estate agents had been driving their Cadillacs into the yard and offering her father greater and greater enticements if he would only move over for the encroaching subdivision, yet her father still sent Dora to bear witness with her evil eye against the emissaries of mammon. The Popsicle-green cupboards had never been repainted and the lino had worn through to the underflooring in a path from the stove to the table. Plastic sheeting stapled over the window above the chipped enamel sink sealed in the smell of cooking. There was a tall, nervous-looking woman with a grey-blonde bun standing at the sink. She was not introduced, but as she turned to look at them Ross saw that, in appearance, Iliana was her mother's child.

Right away, he realized no one was going to put on the Ritz for them. He was not shown the rest of the house, not even the living room. Instead, Iliana's father gestured for them to take a seat at the table already set with unmatched plates and cutlery and a bottle of ginger ale, which he offered to Ross to pour out for himself. Iliana got herself a glass of water. Without uttering a word, her mother stepped sideways at the sink so Iliana could get at the taps. Someone had to speak first and, as this was a responsibility that usually fell to the loquacious Ross, one he usually welcomed, he cast around for something to say. The first thing that came to him was to point out how valuable some of the stuff in their kitchen would be, the curved, chrome-handled 1950s era appliances and the Formica table in particular, to set decorators who were constantly scrambling for authenticity when doing period movies, but he feared he might be labelled an emissary of mammon himself. Outside, the whine of a small plane engine started up, then stopped. 'Does it bother you living so close to the airport?' he asked.

'Can't say I notice,' said Iliana's father, closing down that subject. He looked fixedly at Ross out of grey-green eyes, close-set and mirthless under thick patriarchal brows. His head was large for his body and he used some kind of unguent to keep his hair in place. Ross wondered if that was what made him look severe, or if because of all Iliana had told him he read condemnation in

49

the man's gaze. Maybe it was the sign. Ross shifted and, under his weight, the vinyl seat hissed like the audience at a melodrama.

'Any of those agents come by recently?'

Although Iliana had asked the question, her father looked at Ross with the answer. 'A few weeks back.'

'What did he offer?' Iliana asked.

'Eight hundred thousand.'

Ross, to whom this reply was likewise addressed, sputtered a cough as the ginger ale backed up his nose.

'Oh, Dad,' Iliana chided. 'With that kind of money you could really fix up the church.'

'A church is not a building,' he told Ross, who, dabbing with his shirt cuff at the pop running out of his nose, was beginning to feel like a ventriloquist's dummy. The man would apparently not even look at his own daughter. 'It's a gathering of believers.'

'Even believers might appreciate rainwater not leaking all over their heads.'

He reached out and tapped his forefinger twice on the table to punctuate his point. 'True believers wouldn't notice.'

Then Iliana's mother brought to the table a ham in an aluminium roasting pan baked black, followed by a bowl of mushy-looking Brussels sprouts and a casserole dish whose steaming contents were, Ross grinned to see, hidden under the famous crumbled potato chip topping. 'It looks great,' Ross told her, but she did not acknowledge the compliment. Ignoring both Ross and Iliana, she never once lifted her face.

While her father carved the ham and shook a piece off the long fork on to Ross's plate, Iliana spooned out the scalloped potatoes. Ross took up his fork and prodded at the meat with the tines, then cut into it and looked inside.

'We haven't thanked the Lord yet,' said her father.

Mortified, Ross let go his utensils and clasped his hands.

The prayer was long. It seemed interminable. The Lord was invoked, then Jesus Christ, then the Lamb of God and the Son of Man. Only partway in did Ross realize that these were aliases, which made him hope the conversation would not turn theological over dinner. Yet it seemed inevitable that it would. What should he say, atheist or agnostic? An agnostic was less of a lost cause. On the other hand, Iliana's father struck him as the type who might actually respect an atheist for at least having convictions.

Outside the little plane started up again with more determination, the whining thrum intensifying until it climaxed over the house. As the words 'unworthiness' and 'corruption' were intoned, Ross thought of flying away on the plane with Iliana beside him and her parents in the row in front. As always, the engines of his imagined plane cut out just above the inevitable uncharted wilderness; the plane, descending in a spiral, crashed, leaving Ross the lone survivor. His eyes strayed to Iliana, who just then glanced sidelong at him, apparently to see if he was taking any of this personally. He leaned a little towards her and she to him. But then the prayer ended, Iliana's father's 'Amen' seconded by her mother, who was not mute after all.

Now that he was free to eat, Ross had to admit that the mouthfuls of scalloped potatoes with the salty crunch of topping were delicious and that the meat was excellent. 'You have a good butcher.'

Iliana's father said, 'I do the butchering myself.'

'Really?' said Ross, freshly appalled. 'Do you have many animals?'

'Enough so we're self-sufficient and don't have to mix with that bunch in town.'

'Who?' asked Ross.

'Everybody.'

Another uneasy silence fell over the table, except for the sounds of scraping cutlery and chewing. Ross could no longer think of anything to say, not even that he and Iliana were getting married (the first thing he was apt to say to anyone, even perfect strangers whom he had lately taken to seeking out for the very purpose of giddily confiding this information). The silence, heavy with judgement, disturbed him and he wished another plane would take off so he could imagine just himself and Iliana on it; this time he would not let it crash. Even a theological discussion would be welcome now if it could release this terrible tension. When next he looked up, he saw to his surprise that all of them had already cleared their plates of food, which was apparently what happened when the conversation was taken out of dinner.

'Is there pie, Mother?' Iliana's father asked.

'It's warming.'

'Then I'll show him the pig.' He scraped his chair as he stood. At the door, lifting a worn brown corduroy jacket off a hook, he turned back to look at Ross.

'He wants to show you the pig he's going to kill next year,' Iliana whispered.

Ross's 'What?' sounded strangled even to him. He rose from the table, entreating Iliana with his eyes.

In the yard, he fastidiously sidestepped the puddles in his dress shoes. Iliana's father, wearing lace-up work boots, marched on ahead, heedlessly splashing. The man possessed a Popeye strength, Ross could tell by the way, when he threw open the barn door, the rusty rollers squawked. From inside came the sound of bolting and frightened bleats. When he caught up Ross saw half a dozen black-faced sheep huddled fearfully in the corner of a pen. Iliana's father strode on to the back of the barn, but Ross, nervous of meeting the dog again, proceeded cautiously until his eyes adjusted.

At first he thought the drone was another plane ready on the runway. Then he noticed that the light coming through the window was moving; it was moving because a living torn curtain of flies covered it. The barn was full of them and, as Ross made his way to the back, he felt he should excuse himself every time he collided with one, they were that formidable. He found Iliana's father standing before a stall in which a small pig was sleeping. Whitish-grey, it was packed so tightly inside its own hide it looked inflated, reminding Ross of his taut-bellied nephew. The pig opened one eye. 'Peek-a-boo!' Ross sang out, to Iliana's father's evident scorn. Encouraged, the animal sat up smartly and began a coy rooting through the niggardly bit of straw, tossing it, then stopping to watch its own ear jiggling from the corner of its eye. It was the single living thing Ross had seen here that had a spark of joy.

'Iliana and I are getting married,' he announced. He said it to the pig.

Her father said, 'I guessed as much.'

'Will you come?'

Surprisingly, he didn't say no. He thought a moment, then asked the dreaded question. 'Do you have a religion?'

Where all his theological pondering had only left Ross undecided, now the answer came to him unforced. He believed in the twin sacraments of garlic and red wine, but he was not about to confess to that. Instead, he found himself avowing something just as true. 'I do. I love your daughter.'

'That's blasphemy.'

'How could it be?'

'I see you don't know the Bible.'

Ross said, 'I know my heart.'

Apparently this counted for naught. 'She's proud,' Iliana's father warned. 'She's headstrong. I've even known her to be wicked.'

Ross licked his lips.

'She's the youngest of my three girls and I favoured her because of that. I let her do things I would not have allowed her sisters and now I can see how wrong I was. I let her go to Vancouver and live in that dormitory. That was when she changed. Now she's come home with a winebibber. Am I right?'

Unmasked, Ross chuckled nervously. 'We'll send you an invitation in case you change your mind.'

'And we'll keep on praying for you both, in case you do.'

The pig pushed its way backwards through the straw then looked up as if expecting applause. 'I imagine you must get attached to your animals,' said Ross, for lack of anything else to say. 'It must be hard when the time comes.' He nodded at the pig.

Iliana's father sniffed. 'I hit it over the head with a shovel. Then I use a knife.'

When they got back from the barn, Iliana met them at the door in her coat. 'Mom has a headache. She's lying down. We'll be on our way now, Dad.'

For the first part of the ride back the silence of the mother seemed to have infected the daughter. Now and then Ross glanced at Iliana and shook his head as if she had come back from the dead. 'Is it always like that?' he finally got up the courage to ask.

'They were shunning me, thank God, otherwise he would never have shut up.'

'He didn't ever hit you, did he? Tell me that he didn't.'

'He threatened to. You know, spare the rod, blah, blah. He's all talk. He used to stand there shouting at us as he undid his belt. We'd all start screaming. He loved that. He thought we were afraid of him, when in fact we were afraid of his pants falling down.' She put her head on his shoulder and giggled.

Ross was appalled. 'That's funny?'

'It must have been awful for them.'

'For *them*?'

She placed a hand on his thigh. He felt her warmth through

the fabric of his pants, sliding up to join his heat. 'To see us so happy.'

4

For Bonnie, the blitz of motherhood, the air raid siren wails that tore her out of sleep two or three times every night, had taken her completely off guard. Boot camp, she thought at the time, would be a holiday compared to boob camp. It was nearly a year before she was able to get six consecutive hours of sleep and be civil again. Civil was all she could have claimed before she'd had a baby. Then, just after New Year, when Bryce was eleven months old, she actually experienced a flush of friendliness (probably hormonal) and invited Iliana to take a power walk along the seawall in Stanley Park.

Bryce slept in the jogging stroller, chin tucked in his chest, dressed in the present Iliana had got him for Christmas at the hospital bazaar, a white hand-knitted bunny suit with a hood and floppy ears. A *dangerous* suit, Ross had said when he saw it. He had entreated Bonnie not to take Bryce out in it lest someone steal him. Though Bonnie was supposedly setting the pace, Iliana, longer of leg and in much better shape, kept unintentionally accelerating. As she struggled to keep up, Bonnie told her about losing not one but two boyfriends to men living in her own apartment building. Neither, she explained to Iliana, had been gay to start with. 'I'm absolutely sure of it. I even remember one time getting into the elevator with Randall. My nice neighbour from upstairs, Barry, was already in the elevator and he looked Randall shamelessly up and down. I mentioned it to Randall as we were leaving the building, to tease him. He flipped right out. He absolutely freaked. Now he lives with Barry on the twenty-sixth floor.'

'In your building?' Iliana sounded scandalized. 'What if you run into him?'

'Oh, I do, all the time. It's all right. They babysit.'

'Is he Bryce's father?'

'No, that was the other not-gay guy who had the decency to move to San Francisco.'

Iliana said that she wouldn't be able to tell either if a man was gay or not. She said she hadn't even known what gay meant until a few years ago.

'You're missing my point,' Bonnie told her. 'I *can* tell. I can tell a mile away. I'll show you. Every time we pass one I'll say—' She fished around for a word. 'Rabbit.'

Someone was approaching from the other direction: jeans and a denim jacket, a plaid wool scarf poking out from under the collar. 'Rabbit,' Bonnie said as soon as he had passed.

'But how did you know?'

Bonnie was puffing (she could see her breath) and, when she sighed, she could see that, too, a great gust of incredulity. 'You've never seen an earring on a man?'

'That's it?'

'Sometimes.'

'Ross used to have an earring. He still has a scar on his earlobe. Should I be worried that Ross is gay?'

'Ross?' Bonnie snorted. 'Ross is a big fat pig. Rabbit, rabbit.'

They had overtaken Iliana and Bonnie from behind, one with a shaved head, the other sporting a goatee, both wearing leather jackets. 'The one on the left didn't have an earring,' Iliana pointed out.

Bonnie tugged her sleeve to slow her down. 'It was the goatee. Didn't you notice?' The concession stand came into view. 'Rabbit, rabbit, rabbit, rabbit, rabbit, rabbit, rabbit, rabbit, rabbit.'

'What? All of them?'

'Send out a posse. You won't find a decent straight man in Vancouver.'

'There's Ross,' said Iliana, as if that would give Bonnie hope.

Bonnie said, 'I rest my case.'

Ahead of them, beyond the turquoise swimming pool drained of all but rainwater and dead leaves, the Canada geese were busy denuding the bank of grass. Bryce woke shrilling his one word, the one that to everyone's embarrassment, but no one's surprise, sounded a lot like 'fuck' (but that Ross heard as *phoque*), pointing and demanding with impatient grunts to be unbuckled and set free. Bonnie, glad to stop before Iliana had them breaking into a canter, released him. Setting him on his feet, she looked at him in his white suit – yet another rabbit. He would surely turn out to be one, and not only because of his paternity. Bonnie was a warped Queen Midas: every man she touched turned queer.

They each took a hand, but Bryce pulled away and set off unsteadily towards the geese, a long-eared imp, his determined face framed by the hood. 'Uck! Uck!'

Iliana chased him down. 'Tell me how Ross is flawed,' she asked when she had shepherded Bryce back.

'He's fat.'

Iliana rolled her eyes. 'What else?'

'He breathes through his mouth.'

'He doesn't, though. He had his nose fixed, remember? That's how we met.'

'I still hear it. I look at him and hear it.'

'I have a reason for asking. What else is wrong with him?'

'His cooking, but you know about that.'

'I like his cooking.'

'He underdoes everything.'

Bryce bolted again, this time for the seawall's edge, and Bonnie went after him. What did Iliana expect her to say? Ross was her brother and she loved him, loved him too much. Twins are inherently afraid of being alone and, while Ross countered this fear by surrounding himself with people, Bonnie only wanted to be with her brother. A therapist she used to see had explained this and Bonnie subscribed to the theory wholeheartedly. Not that there was anything incestuous in her feelings, far from it (the therapist, fortunately, had not been Freudian). But none of this negated the fact that Ross was what he was, or Bonnie's right as sibling and twin to *say* just what he was: a fat former mouth-breather spreading salmonella all over Hollywood North.

Iliana caught up. 'We're getting married.'

Bonnie heard a crash. It was a wave slamming against the rocks below, but it might easily have been the sound of her status quo collapsing. She pulled Bryce back from the brink, as Ross had done for her so many times, sure she was going to cry, and not from happiness.

Ever since Iliana's announcement that day, Bonnie had been expecting bad news. She always expected the worst (she lived for it) and when things turned out to be merely disappointing instead of catastrophic, she felt the double sting of someone not only dumped on by fate, but also proved wrong. First she had expected Ross to break his engagement to Iliana because of what she considered his Casanova proclivities, then that Iliana would have sensible second thoughts and back out herself. The worst came true and they actually did get married and Bonnie, who had not felt so abandoned since birth, had to come to terms with their obvious happiness. She behaved like a fool at the wedding. Never had she expected to be rushing to the hospital, except in the event of her own suicide.

She announced herself through the intercom in the waiting room. A young doctor with a Scottish name she did not catch came out to meet her, taking her into a small room reserved for devastating chats and explaining just how much worse things actually were even than Bonnie had imagined.

'Your brother seems unable to hear this,' he said. 'Maybe you can be of help here.'

Bonnie recoiled. 'Me?'

Afterwards, a nurse led her through a set of big blue double doors. She was still reeling from what the doctor had told her and, at the sight of Ross in the chair at the foot of Iliana's bed, barely recognizable as her brother, she burst into tears.

He did not stir or even look at her. Hunched, elbows on knees, hands over his mouth, stifling himself, he stared on at Iliana. 'Ross,' Bonnie whimpered. He turned slowly, with his whole body, and she rushed to him instead of the other way round. As she held his big shaking body, it was with the sinking understanding that he would not be rescuing her this time.

'Oh, God, Ross. Oh, God.' She pushed him to arm's length, searching his face. Bronze stubble roughened his jaw. His eyes were so bloodshot his tears looked pink. 'Are *you* all right?'

'I love her so much, Bonnie.'

'Are you hurt?'

'No.'

'Thank God.'

From the other side of the curtain someone was barking in what sounded like Polish.

'Did they tell you what I did?' Ross asked.

She rushed to his defence. 'It was an accident!'

'I know,' he told her angrily. 'I was the one driving!'

Bonnie went over to the other side of the bed, still not daring to face her sister-in-law, and dragged back the chair that was there. Sitting down beside Ross, she offered him the small comfort of her hand. He took it, squeezing too hard. 'We were playing tennis,' he said. 'There was a ball rolling around on the floor. It got stuck under the brake.'

'Shhh.'

'I asked her to get the ball. I looked back to see if she had it yet. A truck was trying to cross. I didn't slow down. I didn't see it. I was looking back.'

'It wasn't your fault.'

'I should have pulled over. Why didn't I just pull over?' He let go of her to bury his face in his hands. Hugging him again, Bonnie peeked at Iliana, pale and bandaged, seeming tethered to the bed by clear plastic tubing, tubes even in her nose.

'How will she ever forgive me?' Ross said.

It was Bonnie's very question to herself. In the months leading up to the wedding she had not offered assistance in any way, not until Iliana asked her outright to come and help her choose between the two dresses she had picked out. At the wedding, instead of giving them her blessing, Bonnie had cried her eyes out. It had nothing really to do with Iliana; Bonnie would have felt jilted no matter whom Ross married. But now Iliana was lying here in a coma. Religion, or Hollywood, had given Bonnie the notion that the comatose, like the dead, were all-seeing and all-knowing. She even ascribed these powers to the unborn. Bryce, as a foetus, had helped make all her decisions by kicking once for 'yes' and twice for 'no', although she was less interested in his opinion now that he was actually born. Did Iliana know Bonnie was here at her bedside? Did she know what Bonnie had said and thought about her?

'Those things I said about her, Ross,' she told him just in case, 'I didn't mean them.'

'What things?'

'That she was too young to get married. That she says "golly". That she has awful taste in clothes.'

The first time she told Ross this, he had gaped in astonishment.

Apparently, he had looked Iliana over countless times, as a jeweller wearing a magnifying eyepiece scrutinizes a gem, and concluded that she was perfect. Discounting Bonnie's criticisms, he had flared angrily, saying that they came from a woman who dressed like a cat burglar whatever the occasion. His reaction now was much worse: he said nothing.

The nurse was back on the other side of the curtain trying again to silence the guttural one. 'Please! You're disturbing the patients!'

'I took the nicer dress for myself,' Bonnie confessed.

Ross lifted his face out of his hands. 'What are you talking about?'

'Her wedding dress. I told her to take the blue one. I was upset. She's a wonderful person.'

Ross gripped her arm. 'Bonnie. Did they tell you she won't be able to walk?'

She couldn't do it. She couldn't be the one to hurt him. Looking to that most convenient prop, her watch, she drew upon every mother's excuse, her child. 'I should go phone Randall and Barry. They're watching Bryce. I'll be right back.'

Stepping out from behind the curtains, she almost collided with a man. Stocky and tightly packed into his T-shirt, he gave her a puncturing look in reply to her 'Excuse me'. She took no offence because she took it for granted that he could not understand her. He was the angry voice from the other side of the curtain.

'Was it your sister?' Vladimir asked.

Ross turned sideways in the chair to look at Vlad filling the opening in the curtains. He flinched with the nod.

'She don't look like you.'

'How's Steve today?'

'They are move him out of ICU. This morning I told to him,

61

"You better move your fucking legs." He looks scared and, man, he move them.'

'He did?'

'Yes. These people here are fuckers. They suck big one. Do not listen what they say.'

Behind Vladimir, the blue doors opened on Anna, who disappeared quickly behind Stepan's curtain. Ross had still not figured out which brother she was engaged to. Vladimir did all the talking; once the mime's whiteface had come off there was no shutting him up. English he had apparently learned from rap and Quentin Tarantino movies. Profanity in other languages, Ross knew from throwing every word of French he could come up with at his squalling nephew, rarely had the same punch as in a mother tongue. Probably Vlad didn't know how he sounded. Or he sounded like that in Russian, too.

The Moscow Circus was performing now in Calgary, Vlad told Ross. 'We are meet them in Montreal in October third. All of us. Me, Steve, Anna. You better believe me. Fuck.'

Ross's first inclination was not to. He had looked in on Stepan last night and seen him lying in a halo brace with his face, Vladimir's face exactly, contorted in a soundless sob as Vladimir barked at him the facts of their lives. Everyone overhearing those harsh, incomprehensible syllables understood about as much as Stepan. At the same time, Ross wanted to believe, to hope.

In the lounge, Bonnie phoned their parents first. 'Daddy, it's me. I've got some awful news.' Because this was not so unusual a way for Bonnie to start a telephone conversation, her father chuckled. She explained. A long pause followed. 'Is Ma there?'

'She's shopping.'

'Good. You can tell her.'

'We'll come.'

'For God's sake, don't bring Ma here!' she shouted before dissolving in girlish sobs. 'What am I going to do, Daddy? She's going to be crippled. He'll have to look after her.'

She phoned Randall and Barry and said she'd try to be back by dinner.

On her way back to ICU a nurse stopped her in the hall. 'Do you think you can get your brother to go home and sleep?'

'No,' Ross told her when Bonnie put it to him. He seemed to have pulled himself up in the quarter of an hour that she was gone. 'I'm staying right here. I'm not leaving her. She's going to be all right, Bon.'

Even as children Ross had looked on the bright side while Bonnie had glared into the dark. It used to make her angry. Now it broke her heart.

On the phone Teddy had said that he loved her, that he loved Ross and Iliana. He said, 'Tell Ross we're praying for her.' This was something Bonnie was not above doing herself whenever she realized that she wasn't going to get her way. Sitting back down beside Ross, she immediately set to murmuring the old formulas. They meant nothing to her, but there was something soothing about the repetitive cascade of empty syllables and how they filled her mind.

5

Long after Iliana had rejected her religion, she still found herself preoccupied by it. Mostly she would remember what she had once believed and be baffled as to how she could have. You were damned if you did not accept Jesus Christ as your saviour, yet faith was a gift from God, not something you could go out and acquire on your own. Who in their right mind, she wondered now, could endorse so frustrating and cruel a paradox?

Even as a child earnest in her faith, she had envisioned a different life for herself. Her sisters had not gone to Bible camp; they had preferred learning to make piecrust with their mother. Iliana came back from Camp Pentecost her first summer converted to tennis, yet so charged with the Spirit as well that her parents encouraged her to go every year after that. (They also let her go into town at weekends to use the tennis courts.) Many of the counsellors had been missionaries and so Iliana, at the impressionable age of ten, decided to become a missionary, too. To be a missionary, she would need a practical skill.

Her father was right to have fought her, for nursing school did in fact disabuse her. No one incident caused this to happen, rather a slow accumulation of observations drawing her towards an inexorable atheism. When she first moved into the residency, she continued to pray as she had at home. It didn't win her friends among the girls who every night unplugged the hairdryer and plugged in the blender for strawberry daiquiris. They played pranks on each other, usually involving panties. (Iliana kept hers locked in her suitcase under her bed.) Eventually she cut out the prayers. Not only was she afraid of being completely ostracized, she saw these girls having a great time and admired them for it. In the hospital, she saw people cured without regard to their beliefs, healed by science, not faith, and began to feel that she had been made to grovel for every little thing, quite unnecessarily, all her life. It was one thing to feel thankful for what you had, another to live with God's foot on the back of your neck, holding you prostrate. So she stopped. She just stopped and waited to see if she would be smitten and, of course, quite the contrary happened.

After graduation, when she refused to return home, her mother began to send the cards. They came infrequently enough to catch

Iliana off guard every time. In the eighteen months between graduating and meeting Ross, she received three. Stopping in the lobby to empty her mailbox of the accumulated bills and fliers, she would find among them a plain envelope with no return address and, unthinking, unsuspecting, slip a finger under the flap and rip. Inside would be a Bible passage typed out on an index card with a ribbon so desiccated the pale print seemed on the point of dissolving into spirit matter. At first she would simply stare at the message, then, jaw setting, tear it up.

She was slamming drawers over one of these cards when Ross called on the intercom to tell her he was there. She pressed the buzzer twice in curt, angry stabs, letting him into the building. Her mood threatened to spoil their date, which was, of course, the real purpose of the cards. They were meant to make her lose her confidence in the wider, secular world. Back in the valley they were all raw-kneed from praying that the prodigal daughter would come home bawling, but if they knew what she was going to do instead they would gnash their teeth and tear their hair. The contents of a drawer strewn about the bed, she deliberately picked out a pair of shorts she would never normally have worn, too short for comfort, constricting; she felt cleaved by them, but, more important, she looked it.

Yet only on the tennis court did she know she had the nerve to do it. She looked across the net at Ross, shirt riding up, hairy stomach jiggling as he reached for the ball. On its own, isolated from the rest of his body, his stomach reminded her of a squishy invertebrate animal with an air hole. He seemed so utterly harmless, an unlikely candidate for relieving anyone of her virginity. She guessed he would not mind.

That day the offending card had read: *Ye must be born again.* Many a childhood Sunday she had watched the repentant line up for submersion in her father's makeshift baptismal font. She had

65

observed this ritual, even taken part in it, but she no longer believed in it. There had been no difference in these people afterwards, other than that they were sopping wet. During nursing training she had had the opportunity to assist during labour, which was where she saw for herself how ludicrous the notion of rebirth was. That pause when the head is born, face upside down, looking beyond its mother's backside, that happens only once in a life.

When she opened her eyes she was lying on her side. She must have been sleeping through her break on the nightshift and, though she could not remember the dream she had been having, she was still swimming, dopy and amazed, in its after-effects. Yet the noises and voices sounded so clear! The light stung. Odours, not yet classified or evaluated, burned her nose and throat. These were strangely pure sensations, intense and utterly without reference to her life. The entire moment was out of context and, for that second, as free of fear and consequence as when, twenty-five years earlier, she had taken her inaugural breath.

Ye must be born again was what she thought.

Two nurses were standing over her. 'Hello!' one chirped in surprise. The other said, 'I'll get Dr McCracken.'

Confused, Iliana attempted to sit up but could not seem to lift herself at all. The nurse who had stayed kept on smiling down on her in a manner Iliana could only think of as demented. 'We were rooting for you.'

All at once a white coat burst through the wall of curtain. 'Hello!' cried the doctor wearing it. 'Welcome back. Do you know what day it is?'

'Friday.' She felt herself gagging on her voice.

'It's actually Tuesday already, so you see, you've been away. I'm Dr McCracken, the resident. Do you know where you are?'

'Vancouver Hospital.' She coughed, but could not clear the obstruction in her throat.

'Good. Why?'

'I work here.' Even as she said it, Iliana knew it was not the answer he wanted. She was aware of her own confusion, though not its cause, and of the ponderous weight that was her lower body.

'Actually, you've had a car accident. Yesterday you had an operation.'

The burning in her nose, the block in her throat, was a gastro nasal tube. She turned her head and saw two IV bags hanging on the stand above her, fruit on the medical tree of life. 'What's in the other bag?' she asked the demented nurse.

'Solumedrol.'

'What for?'

'What's your name?' the doctor asked.

'Iliana – am I on morphine?'

'Indeed you are. How old are you?'

'Twenty-five.'

They were testing to see if she had a head injury, Iliana knew, because next they asked for her address and telephone number and that she start counting backwards from a hundred.

'Your husband's very anxious to see you,' said the doctor, interrupting her at eighty-three.

'Who?'

Worry sprang on to their faces. Each looked at the other two.

'Oh, *Ross*! You mean *Ross*!'

Seemingly cued by her rasping exclamation, a man who had been waiting behind the curtain stepped tentatively inside. Iliana looked right at him, then beyond him, still waiting for Ross. Only when she sensed the renewed flurry of alarm from the medical staff did she realize it *was* Ross. Dr McCracken said, 'Your surgeon's on the ward. I'll leave you two alone for a minute while I fetch him.' He ducked out of the curtains with the nurses.

Iliana held out a hand, the one that was attached to the oxygen saturation monitor, the glowing red bead pointing at Ross. He approached the bed and stood over her, taking her hand without applying any pressure to it, as if he were weighing it. His eyes were looking all round her, outlining her. It was the first time he'd come within four feet of her and not tried to lavish her with kisses.

'He said I had a car accident.' She seemed only able to mouth the words. Ross, leaning in to hear, nodded.

'Where were you?'

'I was there, too,' he said.

She was still trying to figure out what was different, why she hadn't recognized him at once. He was growing a beard. He needed a bath. 'You're moving funny. Are you hurt?'

'My neck's stiff, that's all.'

The nervous flit of his gaze finally settled on her face. His eyes were floating in a brine of tears. His expression, she understood then, was her own fate, known to him already, reflected back down on her. This was his disguise.

'Ross,' she told him, 'you look so sad.'

Because they made love, Iliana barely had time to go for her run and shower before her appointment with the hairdresser – a man she knew beyond a wisp of doubt was a homosexual. Afterwards, she dressed at Bonnie's so Ross wouldn't see her in the dress before the wedding and so Bonnie could effect upon Iliana's face the improvements she deemed necessary.

Equipped to professional standards, Bonnie worked out of an actual toolbox. Paints, pastes, laminates, tubes, powder cakes, puffs, pencils, swabs, sponges, sable brushes of graduating thicknesses: as soon as Iliana saw it all, she understood why it was impossible for Bonnie to get a job. Who could juggle looking after a child, work and putting on make-up? There are only so many halves in a day. Draped in a protecting towel, hair in a French twist with two discreet side curls to distract from her ears, she perched on the lid of the toilet, wincing as Bonnie incised with a sharpened pencil a border around her mouth. Bryce, in the bottom of the tub, played with the brushes, chattering away in an incomprehensible tongue.

'There aren't going to be speeches, are there?'

Iliana had to wait for Bonnie to close the stinging outline before she answered. 'I don't know. Ross is in charge.' She dabbed at her lip, certain there would be blood.

Bonnie batted her hand away. 'Don't.' She threw the pencil back in the box and began uncapping lipsticks. 'Has Ross explained about our mother being a hopeless drunk at weddings and funerals? At any party actually.'

'No.'

'Under no circumstances must she be allowed to speak. She says appalling things. She drank too much sherry after our confirmation and bragged to everybody at the luncheon that Ross had already lost his virginity.'

Iliana saw in the bathroom mirror her own shocked face with its traced, open mouth. 'How old was he?'

'I think you're supposed to be ten, but one year we had the mumps and the next they were in a golfing tournament or something.' She chucked Iliana under the chin and in three expert flicks applied the lipstick, demonstrating with her own painted mouth how Iliana should burnish her top lip with her lower. 'Didn't Ross tell you about losing his virginity?'

'He didn't tell me he was twelve.'

'He might have been thirteen. I wonder what else he hasn't told you.' She was digging in earnest through the toolbox. 'How old were you?'

'Twenty-four.'

'You're kidding, right? Anyway, it's not too late.'

'Too late for what?'

'To back out.'

'Of the wedding?' asked an astonished Iliana. 'It's in an hour.'

'So? You just don't show. It happens all the time.'

'I want to get married.'

Bonnie, still rooting, sighed. 'Have you ever had electrolysis?'

'Should I have?'

'I was just going to warn you off it. When they say "painless" they actually mean "very, very painful".' She turned back with a strange instrument in her hand.

'What's that?'

'An eyelash curler. I'm going to put mascara on you, too, but please don't forget to take it off before you go to bed. The last thing you want is for your eyelashes to break off on your wedding night.'

'Bonnie, this is awful!'

Bonnie seemed surprised. 'Aren't you having fun?' The doorbell rang. 'God! They're here already!'

Opening the door on her desert-dwelling parents, Bonnie was greeted by Teddy, both greyer and browner than when she had last seen him, smiling with familiar delight at the sight of his little girl again, and behind him her mother, chemically blonde, her parched seventy-year-old face atop her lithe fifty-year-old body. (They kept in shape under the sun, but it was murder on the skin; Pal's actual age was the median sixty.) She wore a tasteful mint dress with matching pumps and a look of such scathing maternal disapproval that Bonnie's voice quavered as she asked, 'What's the matter?'

'You should be ashamed of yourself.'

Brought instantly to the point of tears by the slicing comment, as a daughter can only be by a mother, and vice versa, Bonnie rushed to her own defence. 'It cost six hundred dollars.' She knew she had to have it the moment she saw it on Iliana. In it she felt sweet and airy, despite white's being the colour that adds the illusion of weight. The diaphanous layers of the bias-cut skirt and sleeves, moth-light, lifted her, as did the buoyant swell of her own milk-plump breasts half revealed. This was her last chance to show off her breasts because next month she was going to wean Bryce.

Pushing her way into the apartment, heading for the bedroom – followed by Bonnie, sobbing now, and Teddy in automatic placating mode – Pal went straight to Bonnie's closet, hangers screeching on the rod as she rifled determinedly through Bonnie's wardrobe. Iliana, still in the bathroom with Bryce, blotted her peony mouth on a square of toilet paper in an attempt to subdue the colour. The impression on the square was of a smile; it pleased her to be marrying into a family that actually expressed itself.

'What's the matter with the dress, Pal?'

'It's white, Teddy. White is for the bride.'

He tried to console Bonnie by stroking her hair, but Bonnie stopped him. He was messing it and, besides, she'd won this fight. Everything her mother pulled out of the closet was black, the very worst colour for a wedding.

MIDDLE

1

From halfway down the block Ross caught sight of Iliana, her give-away blondeness, her posture in the chair exaggeratedly, almost balletically, erect. Ross saw her, but didn't realize it was her, not until he was right beside her putting the car in park. For a moment he sat behind the wheel, shocked that he had not recognized his own wife, his better half, the love of his life. It was the chair that had thrown him off. He still expected her to be standing at her full, impressive height.

Then exactly the same thing happened the other way round. He got out, hurried round to open the passenger door, strode right over grinning idiotically to compensate for his unforgivable slight – and she didn't recognize *him*. 'Babe,' he had to say.

She looked up in surprise. Ross had always claimed that the Volvo was the most beautiful of automobiles because of how the diagonal bar across the grille resembled a beauty pageant contestant's sash. Iliana didn't know him getting out of something else. 'Where's Miss Stockholm?' she asked.

He cringed. Of course he expected to be called to account for the accident. In a way it was what he had been waiting for all those days Iliana had been unconscious in ICU – for her to wake and turn her pretty jutting ear to him. Some atavistic Catholic impulse compelled him to press his face right up against the confessional screen, hard, until it marked his forehead like the ritual scarring in a tribal initiation. What he had not expected was to be put through the ordeal again and again. In the hospital she'd asked him every morning to explain. The square peg of the incident apparently could not be pounded into the round hole of her memory. Now that she'd moved to rehab, he'd hoped these torments would cease.

Perceiving his distress, Iliana smiled and lifted up her arms. He bent in submission and hugged her hard and long. It was a second, competing embrace. He could feel that, beneath her sweater, she was already in the metal arms of the Jewett brace she wore to stabilize her spine.

'You look good,' he said, straightening.

'You, too.'

Running both hands down his chest, he puffed himself. 'I changed my shirt.'

'Well!'

They laughed with the staccato awkwardness of strangers or the long separated, though in real time he was last here yesterday. As he stepped behind the chair to push her, she said, 'Don't. Let me.' Bag in her lap, she began to wheel herself towards the kerb where the car waited – curvy, green, new, the interior perfumed with vinyl, its seats unlittered. 'This is not a Ross car,' she told him.

'It's only leased.'

So was the wheelchair, a loaner she was borrowing until the one made to her specifications arrived. She heaved herself out of it and on to the car seat with some effort and less grace, in part because of the restricting brace. Lifting her legs in after her was now a conscious action. She had to remember to bring along her lower half.

Ross, hands on his hips, said, 'Now tell me how to take this thing apart.'

'It's an intelligence test,' she teased.

The name of the rehab hospital was, hilariously, G. F. Strong. It was stencilled on the back of the chair, *Property of* . . . (R. P. Tired, Q. Z. Weak, A. B. Flaccid, Iliana had joked). As they drove away from the blocky brick and concrete structure Iliana, looking out of the window, made a chagrined observation: the leaves on the trees had already burst into the colours of flame, one season giving way to another, without waiting for her. It was not only that her personal disaster meant nothing in the wider, leaf-strewn world, but that autumn always presaged for her an inevitable melancholia.

'I feel sad.'

'Don't,' Ross pleaded. 'Please don't.' They reached the end of the street. 'It's going to be great finally having you home. I wish it was for longer than the weekend. I wish it was for good.' He touched her leg, then remembered and fumbled for her arm instead.

He had misunderstood. 'Because it's fall, I mean.' She offered her hand and he placed the back of it on his thigh, weaving his fingers between hers, squeezing, his grip sweaty. When he released her to make the turn, her palm, left lying open on his leg, felt cool and empty.

At the intersection an impromptu procession of children from the school on the corner crossed in bunches, skipping, walking backwards, swooping to retrieve a construction paper masterpiece. The windshield was so clean it almost seemed to magnify them. The lights changed and Ross turned on to Oak Street, driving along in what was to him a suspenseful silence. When they reached the exact spot where the accident had happened, he looked at Iliana. Because he could not turn his head to the right without bringing along his left shoulder, she saw from the corner of her eye his unsubtle glance. The one she returned asked a question: *What?*

Ross looked away again, satisfied that she really did not remember.

It occurred to Iliana then that this strange feeling that Ross was withholding something might only be him favouring his own injury. 'Have you been going to physio?'

'What for?'

'Your neck.'

'It's nothing.'

'It makes you seem nervous.'

'I am nervous. I'm sweating like a pig. I was less nervous on our wedding day.' He lowered the automatic window and shouted out across three lanes of traffic, 'I just want everything to be okay!'

Entering the apartment lobby, they saw the banner strung across one wall: WELCOME HOME ILIANA! Ross, touched by the gesture, remembered their neighbours' reaction last winter when they learned that he and Iliana were getting married. He'd invited a few potential investors over to hear his latest pitch: ground chicken moulded into the shape of various exotic meats. (His slogan: *If it tastes like chicken anyway* . . .) He had in mind escargot and rattlesnake, but for his prototype had used a mould borrowed from his friend Alan, the property master, who'd designed it to make severed fingers out of wax for a horror film.

As in previous years, after Ross's presentation, things deteriorated pretty quickly with Mike Lambeth topping up everybody's whisky and shaking his full head of white hair. 'Ross,' he began, and Ross knew everybody was going to take his word as the Almighty Truth. Mike was his mentor, the person he was really making the pitch to. The retired Canadian president of a multinational oil company, he still sat on the board of a couple of smaller companies in addition to managing his own portfolio on-line. Ross had lost count of the times he had come home at three or four o'clock in the morning after a night shoot to find the penthouse lit up like the building's one good idea, Mike Lambeth trading stocks, making obscene amounts of money in his pyjamas. 'Supply and demand, Ross. Supply and demand. I've said it once, I'll say it twice. Supply and demand.'

'Actually, that's three times, Mike,' said Ross, falling back sulkily in his chair. The others clinked their tumblers together and Ed Snow from next door (who had not been invited) reminded them of the previous year's meeting (which he'd also gatecrashed), when Ross had tried to interest them in a latex brassiere that would allow men to breast-feed. The oldsters renewed their hoots and chortles. They couldn't understand his fascination. Who but a man who catered from a mobile kitchen could appreciate such perfect portability, a man whose ultimate aspiration was to achieve a sense of closeness to the people he fed? If he could only get through those idle Januaries and Februaries, they all agreed. 'He should try his hand at writing,' was Ed's opinion. 'I'd even let him have a crack at adapting my memoirs for the screen.'

Ham Hamovitch spoke for his wife. 'Phyllis says he should do a cookbook.'

'I hear he's got a wedding to plan,' Mike said offhandedly. 'You'd think that would keep him busy.'

A spontaneous roar of surprise, a 'son of a gun!', an 'I'll be damned!' but no one was more surprised than Ross, who was supposed to be eloping. As the bottle made a congratulatory round, the men assured Ross that they were all of one opinion, reaffirmed now as if this were a residents' association meeting, that Ross had stumbled upon a godsend when he met Iliana. Even so, they were thankful to all his old loopy girlfriends for the chuckles they had provided in these, their twilight years. Their building was named the Victoria Arms and now Ross learned that every time they met a woman under fifty in the lobby they nudged one another, signalling an unspoken wager that Ross had lain the night before in Vicky's arms.

'But that Iliana,' Ed Snow had said, garrulous by then with drink, 'there's a girl you'd want to settle down with.' Naturally he felt this way. Every time he ran into her in the elevator, he'd describe to her that morning's bowel movement. And it wasn't only Ed Iliana reassured. They would phone over or stop her in the hall. To them she was a Florence Nightingale in Reeboks serving in the Crimea of their constipation. Ross himself admired her in these moments, for how she stomached it. In case of emergency, she was there in their midst, a qualified professional. Her diploma made them feel safe; her smile, immortal.

The night of his pitch Ross's Morning-After Miracle failed him. He hadn't felt that much pain since he'd had his nose fixed. Part of the agony was the hangover, part his wounded entrepreneurial pride, but the worst was the smarting memory of having invited Ed Snow to his wedding.

Iliana frowned at the banner. 'You're not having a party, are you?' Though Ross denied it, she hesitated before pushing the elevator button, half expecting the doors to open on all their neighbours chorusing, 'Surprise!' At their apartment door, she paused again. 'You're sure there's no party?'

'Bonnie and Bryce are coming tomorrow for Thanksgiving. I told you that.'

He'd asked everyone to stay away until the next day so that he and Iliana could be alone. The plan was that, as soon as he closed the door behind them, he was going to scoop her up and carry her across the threshold to the bedroom where he would lay her out on the bed, undress her and bend over her with an open, eager mouth. This was the homecoming moment he had rehearsed in his mind every one of the deprived nights he had shivered in the queen-sized bed, alone but for the cheerless company of his right hand. But now he found himself dithering. She was so touchy about what she wanted him to do for her and what she wanted to do for herself. There were rules; Ross had spent many hours at G. F. Strong with Iliana and her team learning these rules, but he still felt inept. He had not accounted for the presence of his rival Jewett of the Jewett brace in his plan, either, and didn't know how he could extract Iliana from the hold he had on her. So he hesitated, even with her looking inscrutably up at him, perhaps expecting something, perhaps not. She lifted the bag from her lap and dropped it on the floor. *Thump.*

Moment gone.

Off she went in search, he thought, of neighbours waiting to ambush her with their jubilation. It was a terrible thing for an old person to have to endure the suffering of someone young. She had no idea how happy they were that she was even alive.

Stopping in the kitchen, she reached over the counter so her fingers just grazed the espresso machine. 'I guess you're going to have to make the coffee from now on.'

Ross stared at her.

'Kidding.' She moved on.

She couldn't get the wheelchair past the dining-room table. Ross hurried over and pulled the barricade of chairs out of her way. 'Thanks,' she said, passing.

Obviously the coffee table would have to go. Like most of his furniture, he had got it cheap after a shoot when the art department sold off what it could not return to unsuspecting stores. The wedding album, which Iliana had not yet seen, was lying there. He tossed it on the couch, then lifted the thick rectangle of frosted glass off the trestles and carried it sideways out on to the balcony. He went back for the legs, clearing the way in time for

Iliana to wheel on through the living room and round the corner to the hall.

Finding her in the bedroom doorway looking in, he came and stood behind her. For a full minute they remained like that, gazing on as if wordless before a highway viewpoint or a plaque explaining the significance of a historical landmark. Finally Iliana spoke in a voice softened with what he could only think was awe. 'Oh, that bed.'

Emboldened, he lifted his hands and placed them carefully on her shoulders. (Jewett Brace: *fuck!*) 'Want to get in it?'

She smiled up at him with that familiar complicity. 'I'd better freshen up.'

He dogged along behind her to the bathroom, in case she needed help. For once, it was the right thing to do. There wasn't enough room for the three of them: Ross, Iliana, the chair. 'I'll lift you,' he offered.

'We're going to have to renovate if we're staying.'

'What do you mean "if we're staying"? You don't want to move, do you?'

She was washing her hands at the basin. 'Well, we have to renovate then.'

'I've lived here eight years.'

'Can you bring my purse? It's at the door.'

When he came back he asked, 'Why are you talking about renovating so soon?'

'Because it isn't done overnight. When I'm discharged I'd like to come home to a liveable place.'

'But things will be different when you come home. You're only halfway through rehab. You've been using the walker, right? We may not need to lower the counters.'

'The walker is for exercising, Ross. I won't be walking round the apartment.'

'You're doing so well, babe. I've never seen anyone so single-minded about anything. Your attitude's fantastic. Everybody says so. In four or five months—'

She looked at him, then at the ceiling.

'I wouldn't be surprised, babe. Remember the Russians.'

'He had a head injury, Ross. If it was a spinal cord injury, it was incomplete. Lift me?'

Ross pulled her back out into the hall and lifted her there, staggering forward and dropping her on to the toilet seat.

'Don't go. Can you help me with my pants?' She leaned into him as if for an embrace, raising herself off the seat with her arms. Ross wriggled pants and panties down as one, abandoning them at her knees. She eased herself back, gripping the edge of the basin for balance.

'Call me when you're finished.'

'I'm going to need your help, Ross. My purse.'

He picked it off the floor and handed it to her.

With one hand on the basin, she took the catheter in its package from the bag and held it in her teeth while she sifted again for the antiseptic towelette. She didn't see the ashen look that Ross saw in the mirror. He'd watched the procedure before at G. F. Strong, in the company of a nurse and an occupational therapist who had been training him to be her support when she came home. Iliana was a nurse herself and unembarrassed by such things. 'What do you want me to do?' he asked.

'Just hold me steady. I need both hands.'

He squatted, gripping her shoulders, head turned. The smell of the alcohol off the towelette made him slightly queasy, as did the rustling of paper and plastic as she opened the packaging. Under his hands, her arms moved, performing the task he could not bring himself to watch. He heard the music of the draining urine.

81

'Okay.'

'Did you take it out?' he asked.

Obliging, she stirred around between her legs. When he looked up, he saw to his horror that she had dropped the thing in the basin. Quickly, he looked away. She straightened her arms, lifting herself off the seat. 'Pull my pants up?'

He did, keeping his eyes averted. Her right leg began to spasm. 'Oh, God,' she moaned, trying to still the trembling with her hands. The first time this happened, Ross had thought Iliana's movement had come back, but now it was just a cruel taunt.

He didn't know if he could lift her now. 'Hold on. Let me stand up.' When he straightened, the blood rushed to his head and he almost lost his balance. He had to pause for a long moment, breathing deeply, one hand braced against the wall.

'Oh, great,' said Iliana. 'Just what we need. Both of us keeling over.'

Her arms round his neck, he slid his hands under her knees and managed to hoist her. 'Where are you going?' she asked, once he had dumped her in the chair.

He stumbled to the living room, to the couch. 'I'm sorry,' he told her when she caught up. 'I'm not feeling so hot.'

'Because of me?'

'I think I'm coming down with something.'

She laid a hand across his forehead. 'You do feel a little clammy.'

'Could you get me a cold cloth?'

He felt worse for sending her on this specious errand. The tap ran; he could hear the chair collide with the wall. When the phone began to ring, she called, 'Should I get it?'

'No!'

At long last she made it back and placed a cool folded cloth over his brow.

Unable to look at her, he closed his eyes. 'Thank you.' Blind, he felt around for her hand and, seizing it, asked her to forgive him for the thousandth time.

The evening was far from over, Iliana reasoned brightly. She wasn't going to get depressed. She hoped, in fact, to skip the whole depression stage of recovery by simply acknowledging her losses and moving on. Yet she could not really do this until she returned to normal life. She was like the person who arrives home and, at a glance, realizes she has been robbed, but beyond the obvious knows not of what.

What she would not allow to be taken was her independence, so while Ross slept she took a pad of paper and wrote down all the things they were going to have to change in the apartment. Afterwards, she almost made herself a cup of tea. She grabbed the kettle's lead, pulled it to the edge of the counter, filled it sitting sideways to the sink, plugged it in in the hall, everything made twice as awkward because of the brace. She felt like a punching bag, teetering from the waist. Because of a tea bag she ultimately failed the test of normality: the canister was in the cupboard above the sink.

Ross didn't look that much better when he woke. 'I'll cook supper.'

Iliana, who had never heard him utter those three words with so little enthusiasm, suggested a take-away. When it came, Ross watched fondly as she ate out of the styrofoam containers.

'You're a rarity.'

'How's that?'

'A Vancouverite who eats Chinese with a fork.'

She laughed. 'Sure you're not hungry?'

'No.'

'Gosh. You must be dying.'

'Ha ha.'

She sucked the last wriggling noodle up. 'Maybe there's a movie on TV.'

Though Ross was as addicted as the next man to the hockey opiate, he normally taped the games. Television was not something he and Iliana did together. They didn't even do movies. When he first met her, part of her allure lay in the fact that she was the only woman he had dated since starting Reel Food who was not writing a screenplay. (Possibly she was the only person in Vancouver not writing a screenplay. Certainly every actor and extra, every gaffer, focus puller and grip who had fed at the Reel Food trough, every person he met who learned he was connected to the film industry, albeit in a parallel fashion, turned out to be writing a screenplay and wanted to tell him about it, usually scene by scene. Ross himself had even started one. It was somewhere in a drawer.) Once while they were still dating they went to see a film Ross had catered. Iliana, squirming at his side, heaved the same kind of agonized sighs Bonnie had during labour. She left her seat three times. Movies, she told him afterwards, were one of the great disappointments of her life. Growing up, she had been forbidden them, so when she had finally come to Vancouver to study nursing she had gone immediately to the nearest cinema and been disabused of their allure in ninety minutes.

'Does it have to be so loud?'

'That's surround sound,' he explained.

'And the point of it? The story, I mean.'

'Escape.'

Iliana said, 'I felt trapped.'

Now she asked him, 'What else can we do?'

TV, Iliana discovered, was actually interesting to watch in Ross's company. He pointed out things a person would only notice if he had been behind the scenes and privy to how the strings were pulled and the gears turned. The spark in a lover's eye came not from within, but a light on a stand behind the camera. How the women seemed to melt in the hero's presence was a simple trick of a filter. Nothing anyone said, not even a dog's bark or a bird's trill, no cough or footstep or car engine turning over, was actually original. Every line of dialogue was re-recorded in a studio months after the fact, all sounds replaced with clearer, digital ones. He pointed out a shadow bobbing briefly above someone's head – the sound boom almost coming into frame. In the upper right-hand corner of the screen a momentary sunspot appeared. 'Reel change!' Ross crowed. It seemed to Iliana that he possessed the omniscience of a deity.

Explaining all this seemed to reanimate him. He was sitting up by the time the movie ended, but Iliana, on rehab's boot camp schedule, was fading and suggested bed.

The catheterizing was easier the second time. Ross knew better what to do. In the bedroom he stood by while she removed the brace and transferred on to the bed. 'What are you thinking about?'

He was ruing the end of an evening so freighted with expectation. It had been their first chance at intimacy in months, yet they hadn't even been alone. The chair had been with them from the beginning, and that bastard Jewett. (Ross had seen how Jewett was hurting Iliana, leaving red inverted welts on her torso like the marks of incised ribs.) Then the TV, too: a veritable *fivesome*! He might as well have invited all the neighbours.

'What do you want to do tomorrow?' he asked, trying not to sound as dejected as he felt. 'We should have some time in the morning before I have to cook.'

'How about the beach?'

The phone started to ring.

He rubbed the stiff side of his neck. 'All right.'

'Aren't you going to get that?'

'It's only Bonnie. I specifically asked her not to call.'

'Are you coming to bed?'

'Mmm,' said Ross, not moving. Eventually the phone tired itself out. Ross heard the pause, then the short, appended ring that signified a message being taken. He was thinking about the catheter curled up in the basin, clear with a shockingly blue tip.

'We should put down a towel, just in case.'

He went to get her one. 'Not a good one,' she told him when he returned with one that had been a wedding present. 'Get an old one.'

He helped lay it out under her. 'I'm sorry,' she said.

'What for?'

'The lack of spontaneity.'

'I'm sorry for ruining everything!'

'You didn't.'

He kissed her forehead.

From where Iliana lay waiting, she heard Ross in the bathroom, peeing and flushing, the tap blasting. She imagined these noises erased and Ross going through the motions of getting ready for bed in the profound silence of a vacuum. For a minute everything was quiet, then, in the kitchen, the fridge door popped its seal, exhaling audibly. She did too, sighing with exhaustion, but how long could she reasonably expect him to go without eating? The jars clinked as he removed them from the door rack. She heard rustling, bread sawed, then dropped on to the toaster's springs. The second before the toast popped, she smelled it. He put everything back and turned on the tap (she knew him so well) to wet the dishcloth to wipe the counter. Smiling, she listened for his approaching steps.

Instead, from the living room, came the plasticky rattle of a VHS tape being swallowed by the machine. The volume was still set at the level it had been at when they watched the movie. From hearsay, not experience, from the idle complaints of the women she worked with (they dubbed themselves *widows*) she recognized the sound. Though Ross muted the set immediately, in the second before the silence she heard a full arena's aborted cheer.

Accustomed now to a hospital's nocturnal comings and goings, she slept through the night's unnatural peace in fits furious with REM, waking unrefreshed to find the space beside her undisturbed. She had fallen asleep waiting. Now she stared at the empty side of the bed, wondering what it meant. Throwing back the covers, she got up to find out. Her intention was genuine. Every morning the first of the day's tasks was to readjust her perception of herself. The wheelchair was there where Ross had left it the night before, out of reach. 'Ross!' she called and when he did not reply, a sickening feeling came over her. '*Ross! Ross!*'

He stumbled into the doorframe, hair pressed in a weird whorl on one side of his head, eyes wild with apology. 'I fell asleep!'

She gestured to the chair, but he swooped down on her instead, actually sank to his knees, demonstrating how little he understood. 'I'm sorry. I don't know what happened.'

'Just bring it over!'

He got up and manoeuvred the chair to the bedside.

'The other way!'

'Let me—'

'No!'

He stood there helpless before her struggle. He'd had no idea of the heroics involved in simply getting out of bed. It took two tries for her to throw the covers clear of her feet. Balancing on one hand, she used the other to tip each leg off the bed. With feet dangling, her upper body twisting into the bed, she clutched the covers and awkwardly lowered herself into the chair.

She meant to move forward in a cocky lurch, like a car that on the green light tries to beat the pack into the intersection. Ross stood in her way.

'All I wanted to do was hold you. I can't tell you how badly I wanted that.'

'I thought you'd already got up and gone out! I thought I was stranded! I'm completely at your mercy! Don't you understand that?'

He knelt before her again. 'No, babe. No. I'm at yours.'

After breakfast they drove to Jericho Park to walk the path that linked the three beaches. Iliana was nervous about going out. She asked him to get her a menstrual pad from the cupboard. 'Just in case.'

'In case of what?'

'In case my bladder lets go.'

Ross said, 'Oh, Christ.'

Only after they had arrived did Iliana realize this favourite former walk was no longer the best choice. A lot of the path was unpaved and therefore difficult to negotiate. But they were already out of the car and Iliana in the chair so they set off anyway. Ross did not offer to push.

A thousand other people had had the same idea. What she noticed about those coming toward them was that they either looked at her a little too intently, as if they were wondering about her, or self-consciously averted their eyes. It was her first time out in the real world since the accident, so she could not be sure if she was imagining this or not. Once she had walked in a different park with Bonnie, sizing up all the people that they passed. Back then she had wondered if she could more easily spot the Christians walking on the seawall than Bonnie's rabbits and decided to mentally label 'sheep' any that she saw. In the next five minutes they passed no obvious sheep but according to Bonnie at least a dozen rabbits, so Iliana came to the conclusion, which she had always believed anyway, that you couldn't really tell that much about people just by looking at them.

When people looked at her now, they saw the chair. What she feared was that she would be defined by the chair, that her every mood would be interpreted *vis-à-vis* the chair. If she was depressed, it would be because of the chair. If she was happy, it would be in spite of it. She would never again be a normal woman with a normal range of emotions responding to the normal ups and downs of life. After an hour, she wanted to go back home: not because of the chair. Because she was tired.

'Okay,' she told him. 'Your turn. You push.'

Leaving that morning with still no sign of their normally early-rising, out-and-about neighbours, Iliana had begun to wonder if the building had been evacuated. When they got back, Phyllis and Ham Hamovitch were just stepping out of the elevator in their matching robin's egg blue windbreakers. Screaming, Phyllis rushed at Iliana with open arms, joyfully baring teeth, the way she would ambush a grandchild. Pulled into her squashy, perfumed bosom, Iliana felt the momentary panic of suffocation. Ham stepped in to shake her hand, but could not contain himself and hugged her, too.

'Look at her, Ham! It's our Iliana!'

'Hi, Phyllis,' said Iliana. 'Ham, how are you?'

'She's back!' said Ham.

'Ross, it's noon. Don't be angry.' Phyllis showed Ross the innocent face of her watch. 'He wouldn't let us out!' Iliana leaned away from the still-raised voice directed at her. 'We had a curfew, just like on your wedding night! Doesn't she look well, Ham? You look your beautiful self! How do you feel?'

'I'm all right, Phyllis. What about you? You've done something with your hair, haven't you?'

'We were praying for you, weren't we, Ham?'

Ham, who was definitely staring (he hadn't taken his eyes off the chair), said, 'Yes.'

'I don't know that it did any good, but thanks anyway.'

At that, Phyllis made a sudden half-turn away, urgently patting pockets for a tissue. Ham whispered something to her while Iliana and Ross waited in embarrassed silence. At last she lifted her nose out of the tissue and forced a smile. 'I'm sorry! We'll let you get on with the honeymoon. We'll talk tonight!'

Ross punched the elevator button. The doors, waiting for them, opened right away. 'What's tonight?' asked Iliana.

'Thanksgiving dinner.'

The doors closed and they began to ascend. Ross said, cringing, 'I invited Mike Lambeth, too. I was going to tell you, babe.'

If, on his wedding day, a fortune-teller had warned Ross that very soon something would happen that would change everything for him and for his bride (their lives, their livelihood, their marriage), he wouldn't have believed it. With equal incredulity would he have heard the prophecy of an impending quarrel. Iliana had yelled at Ross before, of course. He was one of those likeably infuriating people everyone yelled at, who, prone to outbursts himself, was not offended by being addressed at heightened volumes. Anger, however, had never seemed the combustible in any of Iliana's flare-ups, only the dry tinder of impatience, or, like this morning, the oil-soaked rag of frustration.

Iliana slept most of the afternoon. When she woke, she asked if he needed any help with dinner. It was a question she asked every time they had guests. Ross, who normally did all the housework, always answered in the negative, freeing her to do whatever it was she really wanted. 'No, thanks,' he told her, peeling a potato into the sink in a continuous paper-thin spiral. The rough brown Slinky of paring dropped, naked potato leaping from his hand like a squeezed bar of soap into the cold water.

'I don't want just to sit here,' said Iliana, still in the doorway. 'I want to do something.'

The mistake Ross made was to laugh. He thought she meant she wanted to cook. Iliana did not indulge in anything culinary. Once he'd made the mistake of letting her run the dishwasher but after that had discouraged her from even cleaning up. (Ross had a system for loading the dishwasher, a System, combining Art's improvisation and Science's precision; he shouldn't have expected Iliana to understand this, or even to put the glasses in the top rack where Art, Science and the System had intended them to go.) Ross laughed, prompting her to shout, 'Give me that!'

Startled, he handed over the knife. Taking it, she held out her other hand. It was like that familiar scene in all the cop movies where the punk is disarmed, this time of his potato, too. Ross got her a cutting board, snappily, and brought everything over to the table, the bowl of cold water, the unpeeled russets. Hovering over her, he tried not to disapprove as she chipped away. He was tempted to ask what she was whittling, but bit his tongue. She jumped on him anyway. 'What?'

'Nothing.'

Retreating, he took the mushrooms and pine nuts from the fridge and, from the cupboard, a net bag of onions. Before starting on the stuffing, he sneaked another look and, seeing her slicing the potato into thin medallions, cried, 'No!'

'I'm making scalloped potatoes!'

He tried reasoning with her. 'Babe, I have a menu.'

She tilted the board, sweeping the slices into the bowl of water before going fishing for the potato that had been soaking. It, too, she attacked with sharp, defiant clips against the board.

How, Ross wondered, do you have an argument with a person

in a wheelchair? He would have found it difficult not to capitulate to Iliana in any circumstance, but those big wheels, the back with its stencilled letters, as if it were in a child's possession and likely to be lost on the way home from school, made it impossible for him. Life, that double column of gains and losses, which at the end must cancel each other out, owed Iliana anything she wanted. 'I'm sorry,' Ross told her. 'Scalloped potatoes will be great.'

It was too late. She would not deign to meet his eye. He repeated his apology, and again, until it sounded as condescending to him as it probably had to her the first time. By then his armpits were sopping. He switched on the stove to toast the pine nuts. How many recipes did he have in his head (thousands?) yet he didn't know how to fight or make up with his wife. When she finally finished and started towards him, he swung round with a fawning grin, eager for reconciliation. Out of a drawer she took a plastic bag and, snapping it, lifted in the dripping peel, knotted it smartly and set it in her lap. 'Excuse me,' she said, trying to get past.

'Where are you going?'

Almost the moment she closed the door behind her, Ed Snow's opened (he always knew when one of them was leaving; it was uncanny). He stepped out in his socks, wisps of dyed brown hair floating around his tonsure, barely five feet tall, chains flashing. 'Iliana!'

'How are you, Ed?'

He continued to speak at the volume he had used to call out to her. 'Not bad, not bad! Just a little off. Nothing too serious.'

'I'm glad.'

'You?' he asked.

'I'm alive. I'm glad for that.'

'Hear, hear! Are you out now, then?'

'Just for the weekend.'

'Having a big dinner?'

'You know Ross.'

'His usual and all the fixin's?'

'He's in charge.'

'Having a great big bird, I bet!'

'I'm just taking the garbage down, Ed. I'll see you later.'

He raised one hand and waved as if she were driving away. Iliana sensed him still standing there tocking his arm like a metronome, watching the chair move down the hall towards the elevator.

Mrs Fredricks's door opened before Iliana reached it, Mrs Fredricks calling out as she fumbled with the chain. 'Iliana!' It dawned on Iliana then that they had been watching the chair all along through apartment peepholes without her realizing it.

'Hi, Mrs Fredricks,' she said, passing, but Mrs Fredricks, who walked with a cane, was able to use her physical advantage to catch up with Iliana and overpower her. She was still in her housecoat.

'Oh, my darling. Oh, my darling.'

Embraced and briefly wept on, Iliana finally fended off Mrs Fredricks, made the elevator, and descended to the concrete sanctuary of the basement where, bellowing her frustration, she flung the bag of peel into the dumpster. Staying there for the rest of the weekend seemed not too bad an idea. She rode back up alone despite her foreboding, reaching the apartment door without any further dampening encounters.

Ed Snow popped out again just as she was about to go in. 'I should have offered to take the garbage down for you, Iliana!'

Her hand on the doorknob, she paused without looking at him. Ed was one of the few people Ross could not stand and now Iliana was reminded of why: because he was nosy and boring. Because he was lonely. The curfews Ross jokingly placed upon the whole building were really only meant for Ed. 'Actually, Ed, I appreciate that you didn't.'

'I'm not doing anything!'

'I want to do as much as I can for myself.'

'I'm just sitting around! I'm glad to help out!'

Ross, hearing her talking to Ed, rushed to the peephole to see what it was he wanted, then back to the kitchen before Iliana caught him spying. When she came in, he took her smile as an unexpected windfall and grinned back in relief.

She was beaming with revenge. 'I invited Ed.'

Phyllis and Ham were first to arrive. The moment Phyllis came in the door, she adopted the same exclamatory tone as that morning, which Iliana found especially baffling now that they were sitting side by side looking at the wedding album. Weary of her own bad mood, she decided to be charitable and assume that Phyllis was talking this loudly because she was trying to include the men in the conversation even though they were in the kitchen.

'It was like a movie!' Phyllis was saying, not surprisingly, because the photos were black and white eight-by-ten glossies, taken by a friend of Ross's, a still photographer. 'I felt I was in a movie just being there!'

Turning the page, they came to a picture of Ross caught unawares, seen through the open flap at the back of the catering tent, stripped to the waist, wine glass in hand, as droopily teated as the Buddha. 'Hasn't he lost weight!' cried Phyllis just as Ross came in with a tray of appetizers and Ham in tow. He was wearing his shirt tucked in and, seeing the waistband of his khakis bunched up under his belt, Iliana was reminded of a painful fact: the weekend was half over and she had yet to see him naked.

The next photograph was of Iliana under the tree in the middle of the field with the cellist behind her. She was looking out, watching for something, brow pleated with concern.

'She was worried you weren't going to show, Ross,' Ham joked, coming over to stand beside Phyllis.

'No, I wasn't.' Iliana remembered the moment perfectly, the smell of smoke and the zing of insects as she stood in the shin-high grass, the cool hands of the tree's shade touching her bare shoulders. 'I'd just realized that I'd left my bouquet in the car.'

'It was a wonderful wedding! So original! How I cried! Didn't I, Ham?'

Ham said Phyllis's name, warning. She ignored him. 'I didn't cry nearly as much at our own son's wedding! Well, why would I? Those two didn't last a year!'

'Phyllis.'

'What?' She grew flustered then and, lifting the album out of her own lap, made to set it in Iliana's. Stopping herself with a horrified gasp, she flung it on to the couch instead and, after two abortive attempts, got to her feet and fled the room. No one seemed to know what to say after that. Ham and Ross just stood there and Iliana, embarrassed by their embarrassment, looked away. There was a timely knock at the door: Ed. (There *was* a reason for Ed Snow.) Ross had to admit him despite the quality of the wine he'd brought. 'For External Use Only,' he pretended to read off the label.

Mike Lambeth arrived on Ed's heels with flowers for Iliana. He had been somewhere to rejuvenate his tan, Iliana noticed, and his hair looked whiter for it. Phyllis came back then, the sides of her nose tinged red from blowing. She brightened with a purpose when she saw Mike's flowers. 'I'll take those for you, dear!' and, like an over-zealous maternity nurse, she whisked them off to the kitchen before Iliana got a chance to hold them.

Ross passed round the appetizers. 'What's on the menu, Ross?' asked Ed.

'It's a surprise.'

'I could smell that bird at eight o'clock this morning.'

'That's funny.'

At gatherings of this kind Iliana usually found herself in great demand, both for the health advice she could provide and as a fresh ear for tales of Ross's escapades before she'd met him. Now she sat alone. Probably they didn't know what to say. What were arthritis, poor circulation, a uterus succumbing to gravity, compared to what had happened to her? Who were those underweight actresses tantrumming in the lobby to any of them now? Theirs was a generation that abided by the rules of etiquette as if they were commandments. If they couldn't be sure of saying the right thing, they wouldn't say anything. Ross came over, but instead of words he offered an appetizer and a napkin. At last she was approached by Phyllis again who, bending over her, apologized too loudly for having cried. 'Don't be sad, Phyllis,' Iliana pleaded. 'It only makes me feel worse.' Everyone heard this; it had the effect of immediately suspending all conversation. A default subject was quickly taken up.

'What's different in this room? Did you get new furniture, Ross?'

'I got rid of some.'

'It feels so spacious,' said Phyllis who was actually standing there with her hand on top of Iliana's head.

Why was she so fond of these people? If it was because they were her neighbours, who said she had to love a person just for that? She wished they would all just sit down. Her neck was tired. When she lowered her gaze, it was level with everyone's crotch.

The door flew open and Bryce darted in. Seeing all the people gathered, he froze, threw back his head and, from under his cap brim, scanned the room for Ross. Spotting him, he squawked. Ross immediately gave chase, nabbing Bryce within three paces, raising him horizontally. 'Helicopter!' Ross whirled. Tummy-down on the top of Ross's head, Bryce squealed. Centrifugal force flung off his cap.

'Careful!' Phyllis entreated. 'Oh, be careful!'

Ross dropped on to the couch and, using his extended legs as a ramp, log-rolled Bryce down them. Everyone was made dizzy watching these acrobatics, except Bryce who landed in an ecstatic sprawl, leaped up and ran in a straight line to the wall unit where he opened a drawer and turned expectantly to Ross.

'Watch this,' said Ross, one hand to the side of his neck. 'Is this kid smart or what? *Tamago!* '

Bryce began a two-handed dog-dig through the drawer until he found a rectangle of yellow plastic tied on the plastic rice with a seaweed ribbon. He held it out.

'That's the stuff ! *Tekka maki!* '

Bryce dug again.

'That's Kappa maki. Find me Tekka maki. That's right. Good boy! Now *California Roll.*'

'He loves that child so much!' Phyllis exclaimed. 'Oh, it breaks my heart to see how much he loves him!'

Bonnie, who had arrived in the middle of the show, acknowledged everyone with an outraged look. 'Come here, baby. Let me take off your jacket.' Bryce trotted over to where she squatted beside Iliana's chair. Squirming out of a sleeve, he pointed at the wheelchair. 'Troller.'

'No, it's not a stroller, sweetie.'

Only Iliana laughed.

Once Bryce had been extracted from his jacket, Bonnie made a motion to shoo him back to Ross. 'I'm in love,' she whispered to Iliana.

Escape. Iliana clutched Bonnie's arm. 'Let's go into the bedroom where we can talk.'

Ross filled his mouth with sushi pieces then blew them against the wall – one, two, three – with the potent force of an air gun.

In the hall, Iliana asked, 'Why didn't you bring him?'

'Ross said it was just the four of us. Now I want to kill him.' She let Iliana go in first, then shut the door and threw herself across the bed, rolling back and forth, moaning in echo of the night before, and from the agony of separation. Iliana, who had never seen her sister-in-law evince enthusiasm of any kind, looked on in amazement. Love seemed to have affected her like gall stones. At last Bonnie came to rest on her back with her arms and head hanging over the edge of the bed.

'Tell me about him.'

Her inverted face filled up with blood. 'He's Japanese!'

Iliana waited for more information. Bonnie moaned again.

'What does he do?'

'He's Japanese!'

'Gosh. Does it pay well?'

Giggling, Bonnie reached for a pillow (she always had to be hugging something). She sat up but her face stayed flushed. 'He's a dancer. Oh, my God, you should see his body. You'd think he was made of stone. Yet he's so sweet. His English isn't great, so he says the cutest things.'

'Like?'

'He called a carrot a radish! Imagine being so innocent that you don't even know your fruits and vegetables? He asks me the names for things, just like Brycie does. He went round the whole weekend saying, "Va-geen-a, va-geen-a." He said it was a beautiful word. He said if he ever had a daughter, he was going to name her that.'

'She's going to get teased in school.'

'My lips are like futons. He says that kissing me is like eating tuna. When he leaves he tells me he has eated cherries on the mountain.'

'Where did you meet him?'

'In the elevator.'

'He lives in your building?'

'No, no, no, no, no, no, no! He was *visiting* someone! I've got to tell you what happened last night—' A knock. 'What?' Bonnie called.

Phyllis popped her head in. 'We're sitting down, ladies.'

'What happened last night?' asked Iliana.

'Oh, God!' Bonnie clapped both hands over her mouth. 'Last time I saw you you were in a coma!'

'Please!' Iliana waved the subject off.

'I haven't even asked how you're doing!' said Bonnie, following her out of the room.

'Thank you. Thank you for not asking.'

'Your posture's wonderful.'

'It's a brace.'

'How long do you have to wear it?'

'A few more months.'

'Then can I borrow it?'

Entering the living room ahead of Bonnie, Iliana saw the hole in the seating arrangement she was expected to fill between Mike and an empty chair. Ross held between bear-paw-sized oven mitts her scalloped potatoes which he placed with a flourish in the centre of the table, clapping the mitts soundlessly in her direction to give her credit. He returned from the kitchen again with a platter of stuffed portabella mushrooms, eliciting another round of 'oo's. On his third trip, he carried in a crock-pot of stewed peppers. Ed said, 'This is what I call fixin's!' Rolls and a green salad. 'It just keeps coming!' Butter, a vinaigrette, pickles, then Ross took a shorter trip to the sideboard where four bottles of red wine were lined up alongside the flowers Mike had brought and Phyllis arranged.

'I've left these breathing. It looks like Ed's might require artificial respiration, so let's start with the Cab Savs.' He passed one of the bottles down to the far end of the table and took his seat.

They were all looking at him. The last thing Ross had cooked for them was his own wedding feast. After a triumph of that magnitude, it was natural that they had expectations. They probably expected turkey. 'It's Thanksgiving. Thanks for coming,' he said. 'Dig in.' They laughed and Bryce slapped both his palms against the high chair tray. Only when he took the initiative to begin the dishing up did Ross realize he'd forgotten the serving utensils on the counter. 'Sorry.' He slipped back to the kitchen.

'White meat for me!' Ed called after him.

When he came back with the utensils, the laughter fell away, replaced by a long, disbelieving pause. All around, throats were cleared, and finally Mike quipped, 'I guess I'll carve.' He stood and, with a flipper, cut the maiden square out of the scalloped potatoes and deposited it on Iliana's plate.

The rest of them helped portion out the meal. With many perplexed glances in their host's direction, they passed the plates from hand to hand. 'Not so much,' Bonnie said. 'No, none of that.' When every plate but Bonnie's was full, Mike stood again with his wine glass raised for a toast.

'We have so much to be thankful for, not least of which is the fact that there's a KFC in the neighbourhood.' He turned to Iliana. 'And thank you, Iliana, for being here.' Ham started to clap, and then Bryce. 'We had an inkling you were one pretty tough lady. Now we know. To our Iliana.'

Everyone drank and Bonnie, putting an arm around Iliana's shoulder, kissed her cheek.

'Please, everybody,' said Iliana, colouring, 'just eat your dinner.'

The night before, Shiguru had come over to Bonnie's apartment on the flimsy pretext of breaking up with her again. Too much sex, his excuse. Their sex was sapping his creativity. Crying, she'd treated him to a performance of her own, sobbing and throwing things round the room. Somehow they'd ended up on the floor, fully clothed, he cross-legged, she in his lap, her ankles hooked behind his back. They held each other like that for a long time before they began to kiss, their open mouths pressed exhaustedly together, barely moving. Eventually these vegetable kisses petered out, but their mouths stayed attached, he swallowing her exhalation, she his. Slowly, not even touching or rubbing each other, just with their breath, playing with the tempo and the force of it, they'd brought each other to orgasm. All through dinner Bonnie smiled indiscreetly to herself. As soon as it was possible to leave the table without seeming too flagrantly rude, she excused herself and went to call him to find out what he was doing later.

The rest of them, unable yet to face Phyllis's pumpkin pie, retired to the living room for coffee. 'I didn't miss the turkey,' Ed announced there. 'The fixings are the best part anyway. Is this decaf?'

'We saw your name in the credits of a movie last week,' Phyllis told Ross as he handed the cup to Ed.

'Not my name.' He glanced at Iliana in the corner, examining the ends of her hair, then went back to the kitchen to make the next round of cappuccinos.

'Well, Reel Food's then.'

'Along with Mrs Fredricks's,' Ham added.

'Is she with Extra, Extra?'

'Aren't we all?'

'Jim Marchand is with Extra Casting Inc.'

'Do you know them, Ross?' Phyllis called.

He stuck his head out of the kitchen. 'What?'

'Do you know the people at Extra Casting Inc?'

'To say hi.' He resumed foaming the milk.

'How did *that* happen, then?'

'I think he wasn't wearing the right glasses when he called.'

'And Mary Lum's with Asian Extras, of course.'

'I never get called,' griped Ed.

Bryce had the sushi drawer on the floor beside him and was very carefully lining up each piece against the wall. When he reached the couch, he placed the California Roll at right angles to the Tobiko with Quail's Egg. In the hallway, Bonnie was pleading in a whisper on the phone.

Ed turned to Iliana. 'Has Ross got you started?'

'What?' she said, letting go of her hair.

'In the extra business.'

'Oh, sure. Me and Christopher Reeve.'

Ross came in carrying Phyllis and Ham's coffee. 'Who is Christopher Reeve?' Ham asked and Phyllis elbowed him. Coffee and foam sloshed out of his cup and down the front of his cardigan. 'What did you do that for?' he snapped.

Ross, wondering how the hell they'd got on this subject in the five minutes he'd been out of the room, handed Ham a napkin.

'He was that actor who played Superman, wasn't he?'

'He's doing marvellous things now.'

'Well, he's not quite leaping tall buildings in a single bound,' said Iliana.

'And there's that fellow living right here. What's his name? He went around the world in his wheelchair.'

Ed said, 'Terry Fox.'

'For Christ's sake,' Ross muttered. Bryce's drawer was almost empty. Ross went over and pulled another out for him.

'I know who you mean,' said Mike. 'It's on the tip of my tongue.'

'I saw a documentary about him on television. It showed him wheeling his chair along the Great Wall of China.'

'They can do anything now,' Ham encouraged. 'A patient of mine has a son in a wheelchair. He's some kind of basketball star.'

'A very nice-looking man. Steve, I think. Steve somebody. Ah!' Phyllis shrieked and drew her feet up. 'Oh, my goodness! It's just the child.'

Bryce, crouching under her, waited for her to put her feet down so he could outline them in sushi.

'What was I saying?'

'It's definitely not Steve.'

'I can get his number,' offered Ham. 'They play over at the high school.'

'So handsome. Afterwards he married his physiotherapist and they even had children. I don't know how, but they did.'

'Hansen,' said Mike. 'Rick Hansen.'

'That's it!'

Bonnie appeared in the doorway, smiling triumphantly.

'Do you know him?' Phyllis asked Iliana.

'Oh, sure. He came to visit me in the hospital. He brought me a lollipop.' Her watch beeped, reminding her to shift position in the chair.

'What time is it, anyway?' Ross asked, hoping they'd take the hint. Fuck the pie.

'Time to go, sweetie,' Bonnie sang to Bryce.

After he had finished cleaning up, Ross came and stood in the bedroom doorway, listening for Iliana's breathing to tell him if she was awake or not. From where she lay, she saw his slouching silhouette and felt sorry for it.

'Dinner was delicious, Ross.'

'Look, babe. I apologize. It was a terrible idea having them over. I'm sorry I put you through it.'

'It's all right.'

He ran a despairing hand through his hair. 'All night that expression kept running through my mind, "There's no fool like an old fool".'

'They're not fools. They just don't know what to say. Anyway, it was great seeing Bonnie. I like Bonnie.'

'Nobody likes Bonnie, babe.'

'Well, I do. I appreciated talking about her instead of poor old me. Are you coming to bed?'

He shuffled in and began to undress in the dark, hanging his shirt in the closet, undoing his belt, stretching out his arm to free it from the loops. Iliana watched him step out of his khakis. Bending, he shucked his socks. When he climbed into the bed, he still had his briefs on.

'She has a boyfriend.'

'Oh, Christ.' He chopped disgustedly at the pillow before throwing his head down on it and wincing in pain. 'Who is he?'

'A Japanese dancer.'

'Christ.'

For a long moment they lay there, Ross on his back, Iliana on her side facing him. 'What happened to the turkey anyway?'

'I didn't buy one. I didn't feel like it.'

'That doesn't sound like you.'

'I was at IGA about to choose one when I had this horrible realization: an uncooked turkey looks just like a decapitated baby.'

'And you couldn't think how to cook it? I don't believe it.' Teasingly, she put one finger on his arm. It made him jump. 'We can still have a baby, you know.'

Ross grimaced. 'It's hardly the time.'

'Do you want to make love?'

It was the only way to put the weekend right. Salvage rested on his answer.

For Ross the worst moment of the evening had been during the meal, when everyone was eating and no one was actually saying anything awkward or offensive. He happened to glance round at them, as was his habit, and right away rejected Ham and Ed. Age, Ross had long observed, magnified the features of men. Their ears seemed huge, their noses drooped, their eyebrows (Christ, those eyebrows!), they stuck out to *here*! He looked at Phyllis and looked away. Of course he admired and respected Mike, he was like a second father to him, but he did not think he could ever eat him. His sister, his own flesh and blood, his womb-mate, she would be lean, not fatty. Even so. Bryce, at twenty-one months, was as tender as they came; Ross had shuddered. When he came to Iliana, he found that she was smiling at him, her first real smile since they had quarrelled that afternoon. His co-conspirator, she knew what he was thinking, yet not even she, once his preferred delicacy, had tempted him.

Lying beside her, he froze. All of him stiffened except the part that should have. 'It won't be very much fun for you, will it?'

'I don't know yet. Anyway, I can always do something nice for you.'

Under the covers, he squeezed himself through the briefs. It actually *retracted*. 'Why don't we wait?'

'Wait for what?' she asked.

2

Ross was not at all taken with the Camry. He associated it with the accident and, for this reason alone, could not commit to it beyond a lease. It was also an automatic, which was not an interesting drive.

Miss Stockholm had been fun. She'd had a manual transmission and a personality – her own special shriek for when he ground the gears, a quirk in her wiring that caused the horn to sound a rebuke whenever the steering wheel was cranked too sharply, an enigmatic paint job, something between blue and black (Ross had called it Midnight). The Camry was a light, almost iridescent green with the new non-bumper wrapped right around and tucked in under, just begging to be rear-ended.

Even if Miss Stockholm had survived, the thrill was gone for Ross. Though he was barely able to shoulder-check and, before the accident, had never done so anyway, now he felt it morally incumbent upon him to twist painfully round in the seat and thoroughly scan the road before pulling out of park. He signalled a full block in advance of every turn. Never again Ross's Roll-On, his infamous pseudo-stop. Never again the *Province* spread open on the steering wheel, Ross checking the hockey scores *en roulant*. The windshield wipers set on low set the pace at *andante*. Doing forty-five down the Arbutus hill, hands at ten and two o'clock, he could easily have been taken for just another senior driving Sunday-style out of Kerrisdale.

He parked on the street. Under the store's chlorophyll-green awning, stacked straw bales formed a shelf to hold rustic bushel baskets of heritage apples. There was a flower stand, a cart of freshly squeezed organic juices, a dappled mechanical horse. Stepping inside and throwing off his hood, he saw it was smaller than the supermarket where he usually shopped, but brighter, and even at first glance he could tell that it was stocked with vastly different goods. Displayed in a stand next to where he grabbed a basket were sticks of incense in sleeves of coloured paper, rainbow-patterned beeswax tapers, handmade soaps. He made his way to the back, passing a juice bar, a long deli counter, a cheese island. He didn't bake, so it was solely out of curiosity that he stopped to look at the multitude of plastic sacks lining the pine shelves. Different kinds of flour: soy, spelt, tapioca, triticale, organic stone ground, organic pastry, seven-grain, millet, kamut, whole barley, brown rice, white rice, sweet rice, potato, oat, amaranth, buckwheat, quinoa, white corn, blue corn, yellow corn, rye.

What the hell, Ross wondered, was *kamut*?

February was the slackest month for shooting. With the sound studios and editing suites forcing the Reel Food fleet of two into seasonal redundancy, every morning after breakfast Ross stationed himself at the higher of the kitchen counters at home and set to work concocting his potent marinades and incendiary coatings. A virgin grey-white slab waited on the board. This year he was experimenting with tofu to see if there was any method by which it could be made to hold some flavour. He pushed garlic slivers and crimson chilis into the unresisting vegetable flesh. He deep-fried, seared, blackened. 'I wonder if tofu has been fully exploited,' he told Iliana that morning. 'As a non-food substance, I mean. Have they tried hollowing it out, for example, and transporting nuclear waste in it?'

Still at the breakfast table, coffee bowl empty, apparently engrossed in the eradication of her cuticles, she looked up. 'What?'

'I'm wondering if something this non-reactive is safe to eat.'

She nuzzled the skin at the base of her middle nail. 'What is?'

'Tofu.'

He had been sourcing it at his local Oriental market until he got the belated notion of investigating the competition. *Soy Products*, read the sign high on the back wall of the store, demonstrating just how serious the competition was. It came in a spectrum of consistencies: X-tra firm, firm, soft medium, lite firm, lite X-tra firm and silken style. He could indeed have it flavoured (savory herb, vanilla, mocha or amaretto), or moulded into patties, breakfast links, hot dogs, bologna-style slices, faux-pepperoni sticks, pâté-substitute or imitation bacon strips. There was a line of baked tofu in Italian, Szechuan and Teriyaki sauces, and something called a 'soy based chunk product'. *American Flavour!* read one label and Ross could not help but think of some former president offering the endorsement: 'It tastes like me!'

'Ross?'

He turned. Standing behind him at the Reverse Osmosis Purified Water Centre was Paula Falcone, silken style, amaretto flavoured. He hadn't spoken to her since his wedding when she'd walked off with his shirt. Wearing a wine-coloured cape and big earrings, she looked, with her dark hair and Roman nose, as if she was playing a gypsy. 'It *is* you!' she cried, shutting off the machine and setting down the half-filled water jug. 'I wasn't sure.'

She moved towards him, opening her arms, the cape parting to reveal the balloonish outline of breasts beneath her sweater. Overpowered by her potpourri of clashing scents, both hands round the basket handles, the basket between them, the moment awkward and surprising for him (but apparently good for her), he couldn't hug back. 'I heard,' she whispered while she still had hold of him. 'How is she? How are you?' Drawing back, she gave him one of those probing stares favoured by actresses no matter the situation. Years ago, when they were dating, she used to give him the same look over the top of a Chinese take-away menu.

'Do you have time for coffee? There's a place I always go to on the corner.' She released him only to slide an arm round his. 'I didn't recognize you at first. You've lost a ton of weight.'

'Twenty pounds. I had to buy new underwear.'

Topping up the water jug at the machine, she laughed. 'I just have a few more things to get. You don't usually shop here, do you?'

'I thought I'd give it a try.'

'Isn't it wonderful?'

She picked her basket off the floor and led the way up the next aisle, crammed on both sides with homoeopathic and herbal remedies. True to her vocation, she used broad telling gestures that could be easily read from the back row, moving her open hand along a shelf of teas until it seized a box. She deposited it in her basket. *PMS*, the label read, prompting Ross to recollect the predictable squalls of Hurricane Paula. The finger in her mouth, the furrowed brow, signified a decision's being taken. She picked out a second box, *Soul Restorative*, and set it in Ross's basket.

'Is tea all you're getting?'

'No,' said Ross. 'I'll meet you at the check-out.'

She was waiting there with her groceries already bagged. Watching his packages glide along the belt, she said, 'They've got ice cream.'

Ross looked at her blankly.

'Tofu ice cream.'

He turned and asked the cashier, because she was the only one remotely responsible. 'Is *nothing* sacred?'

The café was actually a bakery Ross was familiar with, with a few prettily clothed tables up front. As they entered, a man wearing an apron that proclaimed *Bakers Rise to All Occasions* was at the door that led from the front to the kitchen. He stopped to call out, 'It's Paula, so it must be Wednesday, or is it the other way round?'

'Ricky, this is my friend Ross. He's a caterer.'

'Fie,' said Ricky.

'He doesn't do desserts.'

'Oh, in that case.' Ricky came forward and flopped a hand over the cash register for Ross to squeeze.

'I'll have my latte.' Paula did that conjuring thing before the cake case. She wore her rings on her thumbs now, Ross noticed. 'And a biscotti.'

'What's that?' asked Ross, pointing to a cake inside the case.

'Pound cake with white chocolate ganache and berry confit.'

'That's what I thought.'

'You want?'

They took a table by the window. Outside, the rain streamed down. It had been raining for weeks. The sky stayed furred, a coated tongue. February swallowed up the sun and all they could do was wait for March to spit it out. Aware of Paula's concerned glances as she removed the cape and folded it over the chair back, Ross did not take his eyes from the window. He felt he could neither meet Paula's sympathy head-on, nor shield himself from it. She sat and, pushing up a sleeve, extended her hand across the table. 'Look.'

He thought she was showing him something in her hand, but it was empty. 'It's a Tibetan prayer. It's Sanskrit.' A tattoo bracelet, the blue forked teeth of the letters circling her wrist.

Ricky set down their orders. 'Enjoy!' Seeing her outstretched hand and misunderstanding, he pretended to be scandalized. As soon as he had scooted away, Paula plucked a sugar packet out of the bowl and slapped it twice against the table. 'You look just awful, Ross.'

He straightened. 'I thought you said I look good!'

'I said you looked thinner. You seem, I don't know, stiff.'

'I have whiplash.' He placed one hand to the side of his neck and, with the other, took up the fork and began toying with the cake.

'Have you tried reiki?'

He broke off a corner and lifted it to his mouth. It didn't taste the same. Berries were out of season and the icing stuck gluily against his palate.

'Is it hopeless? Is she really never going to walk again?'

'There was this guy I met while she was in ICU. He and his brother were with the Moscow Circus. His brother fell off the trapeze or something. He didn't even know who he was. He went over to rehab in a wheelchair around the same time as Iliana and walked out again.'

'Wow,' said Paula.

'So it's possible.'

'Absolutely. But what's she going to do in the meantime? She was a nurse, right? She can't do that any more.'

'They offered her a desk position, but she doesn't want it.'

'Oh, God, if it happened to me, Ross. I mean, it's hard enough to get roles as it is. Is she in therapy?'

'Is she ever. Rehab sets her up with a team. I think she's tired of talking about it to tell you the truth.'

'What about you, Ross?'

'What?'

'You're not yourself. Yoohoo? You're not even here.' She waved her hand in front of his face then leaned confidingly forward. 'I've joined this Buddhist meditation group, Ross. It's helped so much. You know me. You remember how I am. The Ritalin wasn't enough.'

He speared a half-deflated blueberry. He wasn't really listening. He was thinking of how clement Iliana was compared with the likes of Paula and how, all along, he had considered this a virtue. It was not so much that he longed for a storm now, but that he didn't know of any other means of clearing the air. He felt as if he and Iliana were both suspended in some grave, atmospheric portent.

'There's a retreat at the end of the month. I think you should come. You should both come.'

Ross set the fork on the edge of the plate. 'This was our wedding cake.'

Paula's eyes welled up on cue. 'Oh, Ross!'

3

For the big occasion of Iliana's first full departure from the horizontal, a team assembled around her. Over the course of several days the head of her bed had been raised by increments but now she was going to sit up. A nurse was there, a physio, an occupational therapist, though not Ross whom Iliana had finally convinced to go back to work. While she was still lying on her side, they bound her torso in an elastic bandage, warning as they tilted her that her blood pressure would drop. Indeed, as soon as she was upright she felt a violent rush of vertigo, as though she were suddenly perched high on a skyscraper's ledge during a windstorm, or on a crumbling shelf above a chasm. Reeling and nauseous, she clutched madly out, desperate to save herself. What lay below, she understood, was the bottomless drop into self-pity.

After that she spent almost half a year in rehab, every day of which was equivalent to someone else's month, relearning in an accelerated programme skills that had taken her all her pre-school years to master the first time round: sitting up, getting out of bed, washing, dressing, going to the bathroom. Every night she felt as if she'd blinked another day out of her eye. It wasn't until she was discharged at the beginning of February that the ground finally rose up to knock her flat.

It wasn't the chair. It was what she was going to do with herself. What could she do? She had loved her work, but now there were only grievances to nurse. Example: all her life she had been tall, but now everyone looked down on her. For the rest of her days she would be living with a child's unflattering view directly up everyone's nose. People treated her like a child too, making decisions on her behalf as to what she could or could not do, humiliating her with offers of help when she didn't need help, or withholding assistance as though deliberately forbidding her something. Or they would praise her in that singsong falsetto normally reserved for babies and dogs, just for completing some banal task.

Ross was not by intention guiltier of these offences than, say, their neighbours. He simply had more opportunity to offend. Before the accident, Iliana had worked shifts and Ross long, long hours. Neither had had normal weekends, or even weekends that very often coincided. Now, if not for Ross's many lunch engagements, they would be together all the time. Keeping up connections was part of Ross's business, and his personality, which was fine, but to Iliana's dismay he kept inviting her along. 'Come on,' he'd say, 'let's blow this joint,' as if it really had not occurred to him that she might have the place to herself once he left. (Ross, she was discovering, was one of those people for whom the time spent in the bathroom in the morning was his quotidian dose of solitude.) As if he really had not noticed what going out involved.

The week after she was discharged, two nursing friends invited her to lunch. With trepidation she agreed. It meant she had to change out of her pyjamas, which were what she wore round the apartment. Changing meant a transfer on to the bed and much struggle and awkwardness to dress her lower half, all for so disappointing a result; she'd put on weight from lack of exercise and very few of her clothes fit her now. But that was nothing compared with her fear of having an accident in public. She catheterized a second time – at least she did not need Ross's help for that any longer. At the last minute it occurred to her to call the restaurant to find out if it was wheelchair accessible. It was not. She'd had to phone round to make another reservation. Stephanie and Nina came to pick her up. The transfer into the car, the frustrating dismantling of the chair. The entire drive she kept thinking, *What if I pee in Nina's car?* It was one thing to pee in the chair, another to pee on the velour car seat of your friend who, taking pity on you, had invited you for lunch. The reassembling of the chair outside the restaurant. (Was it really ever going to be easy?) Then, in the restaurant, the obstacle course of negotiating her way to the table, the embarrassing removal of the chair she would not be using, the waiter asking Nina for Iliana's order as if Iliana weren't fit to order for herself. The conversation she'd had to endure. Nina and Steph talking platitudes, their subjects cheerful and trite, so-and-so at the hospital, what had happened on a television show Iliana had never seen. Anything serious or important might upset her. Eating, thinking *what if I pee now, in front of all these people eating their lunch?* Then the whole ordeal in reverse until, back at the apartment, she went straight to the bathroom and peed, then to bed, exhausted.

Not only did Ross try to get her out, he wanted her to do more round the apartment. Normally he was the one who brought up the mail. The key to the box was on his key chain and he collected it on his way in. This was how it had always been. 'You should get the mail,' he told her now, waving a handful of flyers at her.

'Why? You already brought it up.'

'Every day, I mean. You should get it every day.'

The last thing she wanted was to venture into the lobby where she was bound to run into the neighbours.

The kitchen counter along one wall had been lowered and the bottom cupboards removed. With the espresso machine accessible to her, Ross decided one arbitrary morning that he was going to teach her how to use it. That was how he put it, 'Since we got this counter lowered,' and it sounded as if he meant her to hop to and justify the expense.

'Push this handle to the left. This is where the coffee goes.' He knocked the receptacle twice against the edge of the sink, dislodging a cake of yesterday's grounds. 'Fill it with fresh Java. Tamp it down.'

She felt like a prospective employee being shown the ropes. Her gaze strayed and she began chewing absently on the inside of one cheek.

'You try now.'

Weary with uninterest, she asked him, 'Can't you just make it like you always do?'

It wasn't the chair. It was that she had come home three times before – Thanksgiving, Christmas, New Year – and each time had confidently assumed they would make love. But they hadn't. How to broach the subject of their abstinence? Her upbringing was a kind of gag; it was easier for her to have sex than talk about it. Ross had always been the one to initiate. Did he expect her to do *that* now too?

She was going to bed early now rather than enduring the nightly show-down, their version of *High Noon* where each of them would turn in the bed and, after taking ten sexual paces away from each other, *do nothing*. Their sex life before the accident had been so varied and fulfilling; she had come to him a virgin and he felt he should make up for what she had missed by showing her a good time in the style of ten different men. Iliana knew why his old girlfriends had come to the wedding. She had not been jealous. Why would she have been? She was the one Ross had made love to that morning, the one he was marrying.

He wasn't even wearing his wedding ring any more. The last time she'd seen it on his hand was Christmas. Just below her own ring a higher mound of flesh had formed where it was continually being pinched between the gold and the wheelchair's hand rim. She liked to scrape at this little pad, which was very hard and clearly swirled with her genetic print. Her blunted nails made a tag; she caught it between her teeth and ripped.

Ross came home, pausing briefly on the way to the kitchen, loaded with bags, the mail between his teeth. 'Sorry I took so long.'

Iliana tucked her hands into her lap.

A moment later he came back to the living room. Thinking he expected a reply, she told him, 'You weren't gone that long.'

'I ran into Paula Falcone.'

'Who?'

'She was at the wedding, remember?'

Iliana looked at her cuticles, swollen and freckled with dried blood. 'Which one was she?'

'Dark hair. Big nose.'

'There were so many.' (Phyllis Hamovitch had been the one to count them: twelve.)

As he headed back to the kitchen to unload the bags, the phone began to ring. 'Can you get that?' he called.

Ross was closer. The phone was on the low table in the hall, a mere step from the kitchen, while Iliana was all the way over on the other side of the living room. When she pointed this out, he said, 'Well, I'm doing something,' implying (she thought) that she wasn't. (She wasn't.) Grudgingly, she went over.

'Hello?'

A nervous female voice asked for Ross. Iliana dropped the receiver in her lap, wheeled into the kitchen and held it sulkily out to him.

'Thanks,' he said.

'Should I say hi to her?' Paula asked on the phone.

Annoyed to hear from her again so soon, Ross said, 'Why wouldn't you?'

'I only met her the once. I didn't think she'd remember me.'

There was a pause, which Ross did not attempt to fill. 'I won't keep you. I just wanted to give you the dates and times of the retreat. I've got Melanie's number, too.'

'Who?'

'My reiki practitioner.'

The kettle began its impatient aria. Ross pretended to be writing down what Paula told him.

'Think about it.'

He brought the phone closer to the whistle. 'I better go.'

After he had made the tea, he went and tapped twice on the half-closed bedroom door. Nudging it open, he saw Iliana over by the bed, her back partially turned to him. 'That was Paula on the phone.'

Iliana said nothing.

'She's a Buddhist now.'

'What was she before?'

'Italian.'

Her watch beeped. It was set to remind her to move in the chair so that she wouldn't get pressure sores, but Ross always heard it as an electronic rebuke, a reminder of his eternal culpability. 'What are you doing?' he asked.

'I'm not doing *anything*.'

She had been pulling something out of her eyebrows and eating it.

'I made tea.' He carried the mug over, and when he got closer to her he saw that she had been eating her eyebrows. There was a little bald patch in the middle of her right one, an actual divide. He knew an actor who had been scarred like this during a sword fight scene. It seemed a very bad sign to Ross that Iliana would do this to herself.

He set the tea on the bedside table. 'Paula recommended this.' Iliana looked offended; only then did it occur to him that Paula

117

had meant the soul restorative for him. 'Oh,' he bumbled. 'You've got a letter.' He drew the envelope from his back pocket.

Iliana took it, staring at its typed face. 'How did she find out?' she asked, not even opening it. 'Ross? How did she find out?'

The edge in her voice triggered his sweat glands. 'Who are you talking about?'

'My mother. Did you tell her?'

'No.'

'Then how does she know?'

'The hospital called her. She came to see you when you were in ICU.'

'I didn't want visitors. I didn't want anyone to see me like that, especially not her.'

She didn't know how uncharitable she sounded. She had her reasons, of course, not the least of which was that the last time she'd seen her mother, her mother hadn't seen her. That day on the farm Iliana's mother had refused even to raise her eyes and acknowledge Iliana's presence across the table. But at their next meeting these roles had been reversed. Ross, stationed on the other side of the bed, had watched (jealously, in fact) her mother gently wipe Iliana's face around the tube and bandage and blot her hair until the dried blood had been expunged. She had bent and kissed her daughter's forehead. The natural ease of maternal love, its practicality, had made Ross feel all the more deficient.

'I don't want anyone praying for me.'

'What do you want then? Tell me what to do and I'll do it.'

She tossed the envelope. 'I want to be alone.'

One hand to the side of his neck, Ross stooped to pick it off the floor.

Surprising to Iliana was how quickly the anger came back. She had not felt it since the day she and Ross had visited the farm.

She remembered walking in the house and seeing that nothing had changed in the two years she'd been away. Her mother, glancing up from where she was making a pre-emptive start on the dishes, had lowered her eyes and straightened her mouth as if she was tidying up her face; she had been wearing the identical nullified expression all Iliana's life. When Iliana went over to the sink to get a drink of water, her arm grazed her mother's as they stood there side by side. She felt her mother start, as if Iliana's body had shocked her when they touched. Only then did it occur to Iliana that her parents might be as nervous about seeing her as she was about seeing them. After all, none of their dire predictions had come true: she had not fallen upon rocks, but had landed firmly on her feet. It was not electricity in her body, but freedom. Suddenly, she felt emboldened. She felt that, after that day, she would never go back there again. Returning to the table where Ross sat helpless despite all his charms before the likes of her dad, she not only dared to speak to her father, but to speak her mind.

Only when the men had gone out to the barn did Iliana try to talk to her mother. She said, 'I moved, you know. If you're still sending those cards, I'm not getting them any more.' She was at the table, addressing her mother's back, bent as she watched the pie through the oven window, as if it would grow little legs and escape without her vigilance. 'I'm doing great, Mom.'

Her mother swung round. 'You are not!'

Iliana did an unforgivable thing then. She laughed. 'But I am. He's a wonderful man.'

The sound her mother had made was very like a gasp. Hands held mid-air, in fists, she ran from the kitchen, leaving Iliana sitting there stunned, then saddened. She had, she realized, just negated her mother's whole life.

As soon as Ross handed her the card, she knew even without opening it which passage it contained – the one about the cripple

119

lying outside the temple begging the two disciples for alms. It meant the worst possible thing: that they believed they were right. In her father's church she was being held up as an example of how harshly a sinner is reproved. Every Sunday her father was claiming that, if she would only return and repent, he could do the same for her.

In the name of Jesus Christ of Nazareth rise up and walk.

Her time in the hospital Iliana remembered mostly in sporadic dream-like fragments because of the morphine, but the exact moment when she knew she would never walk again she recalled with precise clarity. There was a man on the ward, a high roller, who one day came shooting past her door, first from one direction, then the other, moving the chair with powerful, swinging movements of his arms. When the nurses came to turn her, she no longer had a view of the corridor; it was at least two hours before she saw him again.

Back on her right side, she woke to him standing in the doorway. She was not mistaken. The big forehead and intense, close-set eyes were distinctively his. He rapped lightly on the doorframe and took a perfect step inside, without unsteadiness or hesitation, unsupported by crutches, not even making use of the wall. At first she thought she was dreaming it, but no. Striding unsmilingly towards her was a man who a mere two hours before had been wheelchair-bound.

The messages she'd been receiving about her own prognosis were contradictory. Ross had kept her pumped even as the doctors had cautioned her against unrealistic hope. In her other life she would have seen this man very differently, even as an angel. Now her heart sank because she knew there would be an explanation that, by virtue of its rationality, would preclude all miracles.

The man put his hand out. 'I am Vladimir. Your husband is my friend.'

The man she had seen earlier was his twin.

What upset her most about the card, more than the fact that, having opted out of faith, she had forfeited all right to miracles herself, was the feelings it brought back. Growing up, they had had to pray for everything: food, forgiveness, enough hot water in the tank. On bath night they prayed that the hot water wouldn't run out. Absolutely nothing could be taken for granted. They were utterly dependent on the whims of God. Now she saw her present life in comparison, lived at the mercy of ramps, cut-away kerbs, elevators, herself just as dependent, not on God, but on municipal by-laws and the probability that what she needed would be in a bottom cupboard. These weeks since her homecoming had felt just as isolating and abstemious as all the days of her childhood, excluding the summers she went to camp. They had been *no fun*. The difference was, as a child she had understood as a child. Now she knew how miserable she was.

4

Iliana's first glimpse of Bonnie was of a very thin woman dressed in black, arrowroot smears on her top, her hair short and dark, her jaw largish and tense. Ross, by contrast, was heavy, sandy-haired, and so relaxed as to seem almost boneless. It was hard to believe they were siblings, let alone twins. Later, as she got to know Bonnie, Iliana thought she knew what had happened. At conception the personality traits, instead of being dispersed at random, were drawn to either a positive or a negative ovum before developing into Ross and Bonnie, as though their mother had come near a very powerful magnet. In any event, Iliana tried to like Bonnie. Since she had given up on her own two sisters (who cared more about reconverting her than about her), Bonnie was going to be the only sister she had.

A few months before the wedding, Iliana asked for help. It made all the difference having Bonnie there to choose the dress, not just for the second opinion, but for how the sales clerk came back to life. His name was Serge, Iliana had learned the first time she went in, when he'd chatted amicably to her about the wedding and even got her to confess how she hated standing up in front of people because it felt like church. Slightly less friendly the second time, he was a different person by the third, sighing when he saw her and marching back to retrieve the two dresses that were still waiting on the hold rack, then thrusting the hangers at her.

'What exactly is your time-line? I mean, it is *this* millennium you're getting married in?'

'August the second.'

'Darling, you're *joking*, right?' He pointed to Bonnie and to himself, effectively forming a partnership with her. 'You and I are not letting this woman leave' – a different gesture for Iliana, a disdainful back-handed wave in her direction – 'until she buys a dress.'

'I'm with you,' Bonnie had said, shaking her head pityingly at Iliana. 'I'm with you entirely.'

Changing, Iliana heard Serge revert to the chatterer he'd been when first they met, and Bonnie (Iliana could not believe it), Bonnie was laughing. She'd heard her laugh, of course, but only sardonically, accompanied by the single sharp upward puff of disgust that set her bangs fluttering. Now she was cackling gaily with Serge and Iliana felt some reluctance to come out of the dressing room and interrupt them. She was almost in awe of how naturally they had fallen into the game. Iliana had never flirted in her life, unless you could call sitting on someone flirting, as she had done out of desperation that first time with Ross. Flirting was airy, mostly whimsy and suggestion, which was also how she would describe the white dress with its low-cut silk bodice and the sheer overlapping layers of the skirt and sleeves.

'Beautiful!' said Bonnie when Iliana finally stepped out. She turned to Serge. '*You* chose it.'

'I did.'

'I love it. Turn round,' she ordered Iliana before dispatching her back to the dressing room, Cinderella to the hearth, to put the blue one on.

The blue dress was sleeveless with a neckline appliquéd in cream and silver threads. The bodice, waist and hips fit closely while the skirt flared at the back, a mere suggestion of a train. The colour, a very pale aquamarine, looked almost sun-faded.

'Beautiful, too,' Bonnie told Serge, 'but my first instinct, without even thinking, is the blue. White is too . . .'

'Virginal.'

'Are you kidding? She's marrying my brother. Nobody's going to think that.'

Serge covered his ears. 'Don't tell me. I don't want to know.'

'Clichéd, I was going to say. Besides, she'll be able to wear the blue again.'

'People always say that, but where is she ever going to wear her wedding dress again? To a ball?' He went over to the glass-topped desk to get the box of pins. 'Maybe I should organize a ball so all my customers can have a second night in their wedding dresses. I'd make a killing on all you women willing to pay big bucks to feel like you're economizing.' He lifted Iliana's arm to pin the bodice. 'You will buy a padded bra? Darling?'

'What?' asked Iliana.

'I'm leaving you a teeny extra bit of room here so you can look your best on the big day.'

'Tell her she has to wear make-up, too.'

'You have to wear make-up,' said Serge, pins in his teeth.

'And what about her hair?'

He scooped Iliana's hair off her shoulders and held it to her crown. 'Ooops!' he sang and let it drop. 'We'll just pretend we didn't see *those ears*!'

As they were leaving the store, Serge gave Bonnie his business card and bid them goodbye with a fluttering hand. 'See you soon!' he called. To Iliana there seemed to be an emphasis on the 'soon' and that it was addressed to Bonnie.

'Looks like you might have a date for the wedding after all,' she commented when they were out of earshot.

'What?' said Bonnie. 'With Serge?' She laughed all the way to the car.

Next they went to the bakery so Bonnie could give her approval on the cake. 'The frosting is white chocolate ganache,' Ricky told them, cutting a slice for them to share. In the photograph in the bakery's album, the cake was shown in layers, square or round, ivy and fresh berries (currants, black and blueberries, Cape gooseberries) cascading down each tier.

'Oh, my God,' said Bonnie, 'I think I'm going to orgasm.'

'You can't do that here!' shrieked Ricky.

They were longest with Brian at the florist because Iliana would not be dissuaded from roses. 'Chocolate cosmos,' Brian insisted, showing them the photograph in Martha Stewart's *Weddings*. 'They're all the rage. Is the dress white?'

'Pale blue,' said Bonnie. 'They'll be perfect.'

Iliana said, 'I don't want brown flowers.'

Brian got up from the wrought-iron café set they were sitting at for the consultation. From the floor-to-ceiling glass cooler he took a brown daisy-like flower. 'Smell.'

Iliana sniffed it.

He held it out to Bonnie who inhaled, stirring up currents in the air with her hand. 'God, that's heavenly. It smells exactly like chocolate. Where do they come from?'

'The Andes.'

They turned to Iliana. 'It's brown,' she said.

In the end, she had to resort to the trump card, 'It's my wedding and I don't want brown flowers,' even though she knew it was not really true. It was Ross's wedding. The remainder of the consultation was so spiritless, filled with silences and ponderous sighs of disapproval, that Iliana understood it to be a shunning.

Driving back, Bonnie finally broke the silence. 'You realize, don't you, that the infrastructure of your heterosexual wedding depends entirely on homosexuals? I wonder if your baker has ever slept with your florist?'

It was an upsetting revelation for Iliana, not because she cared about the inclinations of her baker and her florist, but because she looked so naïve in Bonnie's eyes again. Her immediate instinct was to deny it. 'But Brian has a wife. He told me.'

'Of course he has a wife, but she's not a woman, dummy!'

This was how Bonnie treated Iliana, as if she were some rube from the sticks who knew nothing about men, which would have been even more offensive had it been untrue. In the hospital and in rehab, Iliana had not wanted to see Bonnie at all. She did not think she would be able to listen to Bonnie's problems with the patience that her sister-in-law had come to expect, or suffer her zoological categorization of the staff and other patients. Surprisingly though, the times she had seen her, at Thanksgiving and Christmas, Iliana had discovered that she actually appreciated something about Bonnie. She was the only person who treated her exactly the same way now as before the accident.

When Bonnie phoned and said she wanted to come over, her call coincided with a slight brightening of Iliana's mood. She'd woken that way and at first could not put her finger on the reason for it. Then it struck her. Ever since she'd come home an unrelenting gamelan of rain had played out on the roof of their balcony, a sound so cheerful it could only be a taunt. Now

125

she heard silence, or, rather, the non-sound of not raining. 'Sure,' she said.

The moment she opened the door, Bryce slipped past and began running through the rooms calling out for Ross. Bonnie, stepping in after him, exclaimed, 'God! What happened to you?' Confused, Iliana looked down at her legs, thinner now that her muscles had atrophied, feet perched primly on the footplate, knees touching. But Bonnie knew this.

'Your lips,' she said, already sifting through her bag. 'Yuck!'

Iliana licked them and tasted blood. They stung. She had been picking at them all morning, peeling off translucent strips of skin.

'Try this,' said Bonnie, producing a tube of lip balm, 'but use your finger. I don't want to catch it.' She snatched up Iliana's extended hand. 'Look at your nails! Oh, my God!'

'Ross?' asked Bryce, back from having sought him in every room.

'Ross is out,' said Iliana.

'Where?' asked Bonnie.

'Lunch.'

'Who with?'

'I didn't ask.'

'Let's go for lunch too, then. Why should he have all the fun?'

The neighbour they met in the lobby was the only one who could legitimately speak to Iliana in that maddeningly raised voice. (I'm not *deaf*, she wanted to tell them all.) Jim Marchand stood twiddling the dial on his hearing aid. Leaving the elevator, they heard the buzz but assumed it was the door.

'Iliana!' Jim roared when he saw her. 'They let you out again!'

'Weeks ago.'

'Bzzzz, bzzzz,' said Bryce.

'Damn it,' said Jim and he went back to thumbing the wheel behind his ear.

Out of the building, Bonnie gave an exaggerated shudder. 'I'm going to kill myself when I'm fifty. Remind me, will you?'

Iliana put on her gloves. 'How's the boyfriend?' She assumed that was what Bonnie had come over to talk about. On the phone she had implied urgency.

'Oh,' said Bonnie in a flutey voice, '*comme ci, comme ça.*' She gestured for Iliana to go first, because she was the handicapped one, but a second later was trotting after her just like in the old days.

'Troller!' cried Bryce as Iliana passed him.

'It's *not* a stroller,' Bonnie scolded.

At the corner, while Iliana waited for them to catch up, she checked her lap to see if the bulk of the two menstrual towels were noticeable. (She was not going to stoop to incontinence pads, no way.)

'I don't know what's the matter with him,' said Bonnie. 'He hardly knows any words.'

'I thought you were teaching him.'

'Teaching him?' They crossed the street. 'Can't he just pick it up on his own? He knows the names of different kinds of sushi, of course, and things with wheels. Animal sounds. Listen to this. What does a cat say?'

'Meow,' said Bryce.

'What does a dog say?'

'Meow.'

Iliana laughed. 'I thought you were talking about your Japanese friend!'

Bonnie rolled her eyes. 'He doesn't say much either.'

The café Iliana chose served deli-style. It was a place she'd been a few times, but didn't love; if she had an accident and was too ashamed to come back, she wouldn't suffer twice. Entering, they headed for the long glass display case.

'He can say "Ross",' Bonnie went on, 'but can he say "Bonnie"?

127

Can he even say "Mommy"?' She shook Bryce's mittened hand.
'Say "Mommy".'

'Troller.' He patted Iliana's wheel.

Turning to the selection behind the glass, Bonnie kept on in
the same complaining tone as she questioned the server on the
ingredients and freshness of everything. At the table, she unfolded
her burrito and poked critically through it before setting a piece
of chicken on the plate in front of Bryce. He spat it out with
exaggerated sound effects; Bonnie sucked on it before offering
it to him again. Through the rest of lunch she painstakingly
washed every morsel with her own saliva before presenting it
to him. Iliana, watching, could not help but be reminded of the
fretful regurgitations of a mother bird.

'I think he's seeing someone else.'

Iliana looked up with a start. 'Who?'

'Who have we been talking about? We've been seeing each
other for months, but he still won't introduce me to his friends.
He refused to come for Christmas.'

'I was surprised he wasn't there,' Iliana admitted.

'The fact that he's Japanese just confuses things. I say to myself:
Maybe this is how they do it in Japan. Maybe in Japan this is
normal behaviour.'

'But why do you think he's seeing someone else?'

'Phone calls.'

'Oh,' said Iliana.

'In Japanese, of course, so I can't even eavesdrop.'

'You've had a lot of experience with men,' said Iliana.

'All bad.'

'Still, you know more about men than I do. Can a relationship
be a happy one without sex? Do you mind me asking you this?'

'We're having sex. That's about all we're doing.'

'What does it mean when a man loses his interest?'

Bonnie plied Bryce with another morsel. 'That's not the problem, believe me.'

Leaving the café, Bryce got behind Iliana to push. When Bonnie tried to pry him off, he shrilled stubbornly. 'Here, sweetie,' said Iliana. 'Sit on my lap. I'll take you for a ride.' Bryce clambered up. 'Maybe those phone calls are nothing,' she told Bonnie. 'I mean, women phone Ross all the time.'

'Still?' said Bonnie. 'If I were you I'd put a stop to that.'

Iliana said nothing. In her lap, Bryce raspberried car sounds.

'Should I confront him?'

'Ross?'

Bonnie erupted. '*No!*'

'Confront him how?'

'Ask him if he loves me.'

'What if he says no?'

Bonnie sighed. 'I could live with that. At least I'd know.'

'I couldn't,' said Iliana grimly.

They reached the apartment. Bonnie looked at her watch. 'We've got to go. I'm meeting someone.'

'Him?'

Bonnie, making a face, lifted Bryce off. 'How about you? How are you? I haven't even asked.'

'I'm fine.'

'No,' said Bonnie, suddenly pressing. 'I mean *really*.'

Naturally, it began to rain immediately after they left Iliana in front of the apartment. Bonnie opened the umbrella and held it over Bryce, who would not consent to being carried so they might both benefit from its shelter. By the time they reached the bus stop, she was soaked. Talking about her unloved life depressed her; being with the admirably coping Iliana filled her with self-disgust. If what had happened to Iliana had happened to Bonnie, Bonnie would have killed herself, which would surprise no one, suicide being, at the best of times, at the top of her to-do list. 'Bus, bus, bus!' chanted Bryce when it came into view. He mimicked perfectly the hiss of its brakes, then clambered up the steps and showed his eight teeth to the driver while Bonnie paid the fare. Standing on a courtesy seat, resisting Bonnie's efforts to pull him on to her lap, he pressed his cherub's face against the window.

'Do you love me?' she whispered needily.

'Bus,' said Bryce.

As planned, Ross was waiting at the apartment when they arrived. Opening the door for them, he was met with jubilant screams from Bryce and a glare from his dripping sister. 'Who did you have lunch with?' she asked, throwing down the umbrella and peeling off her jacket.

'My Colombian friend Jaime Rios. You remember him from the wedding?'

'No.'

'He remembers you.'

She headed for the bedroom to get out of her wet clothes.

Ross helped Bryce out of his gear then led him to the kitchen where he had prepared a snack. Bonnie reappeared dressed in a quilted bathrobe. Even through the padded fabric, the angles of her shoulders showed. 'Well?' said Ross impatiently.

'Well what?'

'How was she? Does she seem depressed to you?'

'I'm depressed,' said Bonnie.

'What did you do?'

'We went out for lunch. Why didn't you ask her to go with you?'

'I did.'

'Hmm,' said Bonnie. 'That's funny.'

He had cut up fruit and skewered the pieces on a straw, a vitamin

C kebab. Setting it on Bryce's tray, he said to Bonnie, who was leaning against the counter with her arms crossed because she was angry, or cold, or both, 'What's that supposed to mean?'

'She said women still call you all the time.'

'She's worried about that?'

'She just happened to mention it. To tell you the truth, she seemed fine to me.'

'She's eating herself, for Christ's sake!'

'Don't shout at me!'

'I'm not shouting! I'm worried!'

'If you're going to leave her, then do it. It's cruel what you're doing.'

'What am I doing? Is that what she thinks? Did she say that?'

Bonnie looked huffily at the ceiling. When Ross came over and grabbed her arm, she pushed him off disgustedly.

'What did she say?'

'Nothing.'

'Then what are you talking about? What are you trying to start here?'

'Nothing!'

'You didn't want us to get married. You said as much. All you ever do is criticize Iliana. If you're still hoping this doesn't work out, let me put you straight.' Bonnie opened her mouth to object, but he wouldn't allow her a word. 'I love Iliana. I got married to her because I intend to spend my life with her. But you wouldn't understand that, would you? How could you?'

'I have a boyfriend!' Bonnie retorted.

'A boyfriend? Oh, for Christ's sake!' He went and grabbed his coat from the closet and, opening the door, kicked his shoes out into the hall. 'Don't call us!' he shouted, jabbing a finger. 'Leave us alone!'

5

Never in his life had Ross stuck to something he didn't like. He dropped out of university after just one semester (the professors kept telling him what to do) and walked away from so many jobs he'd had to start his own company. But for Iliana, for Iliana anything. While still in rehab she had told him that her greatest fear was to be dependent on other people, so once she came home for good he stopped helping her. He helped her less than before the accident when he used to do almost all the housework. He liked housework and the perks that came with it: how, clearing the table, he got to eat whatever was left on Iliana's plate, a third helping. How, sliding a hand between the sheets as he made the bed, he could treat himself to her residual warmth. Accepting her latte at whatever time of day was morning to her, she'd bow over the bowl, sip noisily, then lift her face and smile. He considered it a sacrifice now to do without his bonus third helping. For weeks and weeks he had been deprived of her smile that in these grey days might have meant the sun to him. As for the thermal comforts emanating from her side of the bed, he was a stranger to them now. She had asked him to move out to the couch.

In his despair, he thought of the crew signs posted all over the city, fluorescent pink or yellow arrows pointing the film industry's myriad labourers from location to location. He needed directing himself. He didn't know what to do. Consulting his library, such as it was, confined to one small section in the wall unit, surrounded by his faux food museum, he found nothing that could guide him, just three copies of Ed Snow's self-published war memoir *Who Tolled the Bell?* (spines unbroken), *One Hundred Years of Hockey*, *The Screenwriter's Primer*, *Amazing Trivia From the World of Hockey*, *More Amazing Trivia From the World of Hockey*,

Still More Amazing Trivia From the World of Hockey, Let's Go Europe '86.

As a last resort, he phoned Bonnie and asked her to see Iliana. Their argument afterwards reminded him of another they'd had not long before the wedding.

'Have you told her about all those women?' Bonnie had asked that day.

'What women?'

'About that stand-in and all the other women you've slept with. You've got fidelity problems, brother.'

'I have not!' Ross had cried, incensed.

'Have you been tested?'

He bristled. 'You're the one who should be tested!'

'Oh, *touché*!' she sneered. '*Touché!*'

The accusation had inflamed him. Monogamy! At last something he could believe in! So enthusiastic a convert was he that he found himself in the absurd position of wishing he'd come to it a decade earlier, except that Iliana, his inspiration, would have been a minor. (He pictured her father coming at him with a shovel.)

Unjustly accused again now, a year later, he'd really lost it with his sister. She had touched the pulsing, exposed nerve that was his marriage.

They had to get away from Bonnie; Ross knew that now. He could not be present for Iliana and for Bonnie too, not any more. Bonnie was his sister, his beloved, exasperating twin. As her twin, he naturally felt responsible for her, even more so because of Bryce. He owed Bonnie his help, had promised it. And she expected it without showing the least interest in, or understanding of, his own difficulties at home.

At Bryce's birth, Ross had been supposed to cut the umbilical cord. They brought him into the delivery room to do it. Between the scissor blades, the cord had felt rubbery, like a bicycle inner

133

tube stretched taut. 'I'm going to faint,' he had croaked. The nurse walked him right back out again.

That's what he felt like now with Bonnie. That there was flesh and blood connecting them and he had to make that cut.

Friday night, all day Saturday, all day Sunday. That Ross agreed even to Friday signified, not so much an opening of his mind or a diminishment of his scepticism, as his desperation. He honked the horn outside the saggy-porched, subdivided house in Kits where Paula lived, where, hanging in an upstairs window, instead of a curtain, was a coloured poncho, where multiple mailboxes were crammed beside twin front doors. A moment later Paula appeared out of the right door toting a bulging canvas bag, which she stowed in the back seat before opening the passenger door.

'Did you remember a pillow and blanket?'

'We're sleeping over?'

'Wait. I'll get you one.'

Impatient to get the evening over with, Ross told her to forget it. Paula got in the car. Maybe because she was wearing a hair band that exposed more of her face than usual, she looked weirdly pale to Ross, almost erased. It took him a minute to realize she wasn't wearing any make-up.

'She didn't want to come?'

'Iliana?' He shook his head; a lance of pain.

'Now, Ross, it's silent,' she said as they drove off. 'I told you that, right?'

He shrugged; more pain. Silence was nothing to Ross now. With Bonnie no longer speaking to him (at his own request, admittedly), and most of the time not Iliana either, he felt as if he were walking around in a movie out of which the sound had dropped.

The retreat was happening in a large pagoda-shaped building at the university. Other people were arriving at the same time, many also carrying bulky bags like Paula. Ross was relieved to see they were not the bunch of stubble-headed, saffron-robed cultists he had expected. They looked more like teachers and engineers, odd only in how racially homogeneous they were. The real Buddhists, apparently, had no need for Buddhist lessons.

After giving his name to the woman at the registration desk, who crossed it off the list without saying anything, he followed Paula into an anteroom where coats and shoes were to be left. 'Paula!' He pointed to his socks, one blue, one brown. She raised a finger to her lips, acting out the shush.

Inside the hall, which was very large and empty of furniture except for some chairs in rows at the very back, rectangles of folded blanket had been laid out across the buffed hardwood. People knelt or sat cross-legged. At the front was a platform flanked by two large austere flower arrangements, with a garishly coloured representation of the Buddha on the wall behind. Paula led him over to a place near the wall. Out of her bag came two blankets, a small collapsible bench, a colourful pair of Afghani socks. After opening and smoothing flat one of the blankets and pulling on the socks, she unfolded the ends of the bench, stood on her knees and slipped it underneath her. Her second thinner blanket she had evidently brought to use as a wrap (Ross saw some of the others swaddled this way), but she offered it to him instead and pulled the zipper of her polar vest to her neck.

He took some moments fixing the blanket, then, getting down on all fours, tested the kneeling position briefly and wincingly before adopting the cross-legged one, first with the left leg on top then, when that knee screamed, the right. He felt like a cat indecisively circling the same spot over and over and, embarrassed, glanced around. No one was looking at him. People were still coming in (there were more than he had expected, more than a hundred) and the ones who had already settled sat with their eyes closed.

'When does it start?' he asked Paula, who also had her eyes closed and her palms resting ceilingward on the slope of her thighs.

'Ross,' she whispered, 'please.'

'I just want to know when it starts.'

'It's started.'

'What has?'

Most of the day he was on his feet. Maybe this was why he found it so hard to sit. Trying for a more erect position in the hope that this would alleviate some of the strain on his back, he drew up his spine and forced his shoulders down, but within minutes, like a sock that has lost its elastic, he slipped back down. Frustrated and making unquiet sounds to show it, he got back on all fours and pushed the blanket along to the wall so that he could prop himself against it. Legs extended, brown foot and blue foot in full view of the room, he sat and waited, lifting one buttock, then the other, to stave off the numbing. Eventually the big double doors closed and a man and a woman padded silently past Ross on their way to the front. The woman took the microphone off its stand beside the plat-form and welcomed everyone while the man seated himself under the Buddha's banner. Apparently he, a fortyish Caucasian man in khakis, was the teacher. The woman at the microphone introduced him as Michael Goldfarb and listed among his credentials the fact that he had been a monk in Thailand for seven years. (Goldfarb? thought Ross. Goldfarb? How could his mother let him?)

The microphone replaced on the stand before him, Michael Goldfarb made a few introductory remarks. Meanwhile an ache cosied up behind Ross's kidneys and his neck felt on the point of spasming. He poked Paula with his brown foot, which, now that he was behind her, was their closest point of contact. She stiffened, but didn't turn. He had to move anyway (he couldn't hold the pose another second), so he got awkwardly back on to his hands and knees and crawled over.

'I can't sit like this any longer, Paula. I'm in agony.'

'Then lie down,' she hissed.

'Can I?'

'Yes, lie down.'

Michael Goldfarb asked for a show of hands from the people there for the first time. He looked directly at Ross still flailing on the blanket as he did this, but Ross was not the only novice. Around the room seven or eight other hands went up. 'For the benefit of those of you here for the first time, let me begin at the beginning – with the breath.'

He spoke modestly, yet with authority and humour, every so often pausing to chuckle, though whether he was laughing at himself or them was not clear to Ross. 'This is all there is to it, simple as it seems. Follow your breath. As you inhale, focus on where the physical sensation is strongest. For some of you this will be the rise and fall of the chest, for others, the air entering and leaving the nostrils. Let's do it now together. Inhale. Feel the air entering your body. Without trying to control this natural process, let it be the focus of your attention. Feel the pause between the inhalation and the exhalation. Feel the air flowing back out again normally.'

Even Ross, who prided himself on being unteachable, tried to follow the instructions. Beached on his back, with hands folded behind his head, he took a breath in. Just a year and a half ago the flow of air had been largely channelled through his right nostril. He remembered the night before the operation, waking with a start because of a strange feeling in his belly, like something coiling up – fear of the knife, he'd thought, but no. They were *hunger pangs*. For half the world a constant companion, but Ross didn't even recognize them. The real fear came later, when the dressing was removed. He thought of Iliana in her white uniform smiling reassuringly down at him, the gory length of gauze like bloody sausage casing in the metal tray, he blinking back tears, not only from the pain; something life-changing had happened. He felt that he loved her, yet had been as incapable of rising to the occasion as he was of physically getting off the table. 'You seem the sporty type,' he had told her, resorting to the old formula. Learning that her game was tennis, he had cried out, 'Tennis! I love tennis!' He never watched the game or played it, but he had claimed to love it.

'As we sit here together,' said Michael Goldfarb, 'you may find that your attention has wandered away from your breath. You are not alone. This practice is simple, but it is not easy. Thoughts will come and go and, with these thoughts, feelings pleasant, neutral or unpleasant. You may grow bored or restless or drowsy. You may feel physical pain. This is normal. There is no one, *no one*, to whom this does not happen. The important thing is that when you recognize that your attention has strayed away from the breath, despite how long it takes you to come to this realization, begin again. Try not to berate yourself. Don't feel guilty or assume that you've somehow failed. This isn't a test and it certainly isn't a contest. So why not do it? *Just begin again.*'

But Ross could not manage to stay focused for a complete in- and exhalation. He picked up either one end or the other before falling into random and entirely disconnected thoughts, like the rapid flickering of channels when someone accidentally sits on the remote control. One second he was thinking about his nose and the next about Bryce, whom he hadn't seen for two weeks and desperately missed, walking backwards and chirping, 'Beep, beep, beep, beep . . .' Then he was back to thinking about Iliana. The thought of her filled every little interstice between his hopes and his fears. A habit she had brought home from rehab was going to bed early. At least, he had thought that was why she retired at nine, until it became obvious that she was avoiding him (no easy task in a one-bedroom apartment). She was enlarging her sanctuary with sleep. A few nights ago, he had crept in, trying not to wake her. 'Do you have something you want to say to me?' she had asked him in the dark.

Startled, he remembered all the times in the hospital she had asked him to explain what had happened. 'You weren't wearing your seatbelt. Babe, there was a tennis ball rolling around on the floor and I was afraid we'd—' His nose beginning to leak, he'd wipe it on his sleeve. 'I asked you to get it. I should have stopped the car. I slowed down, but I should have pulled over.' He would be shaking with the effort of holding back. 'I'm sorry. I'm so sorry.' And when he looked up she would be asleep again, or a nurse would come in, or an orderly.

Confessing – how like vomiting. Preliminary to both, a douse of cold anticipatory sweat. Both brought you to your knees. Then relief, emptiness – but not for Ross.

He had sat down on the edge of the bed, clutching his head. He wanted to hold her, but she seemed so angry and remote. Afraid of touching her, of hurting her, of doing the wrong thing, of shaming himself, he did nothing.

'Oh,' said Iliana (heartlessly, heartlessly). 'In that case, I'd like to sleep by myself.'

A sweet-toned bell rang three times.

Paula shook him. He scrambled to a sitting position, looking around. People were rising and packing away their things so, dazedly, Ross did the same. He creaked to a stand, handed back Paula's blanket, then limped out of the hall after her. They found their shoes and coats and, still not speaking, walked out into the night. Around the pagoda was a Japanese-style garden surrounded by enormous cedars. The only light came from inside the pagoda. People streamed silently out of the building, becoming shadows. It might have been a nightmare, but it wasn't. His life, that stifling loop of guilt and misunderstanding, that was the nightmare. This was more like a dream.

They said nothing until they reached the parking lot and got into the car. Ross turned on the heater. 'That went faster than I thought.'

Paula made an untranslatable sound.

'It goes until five tomorrow?'

'Yes.'

'Hmm.' Ross looked behind as he put the car in reverse. 'It's the sitting I can't take. I actually started having fantasies about this La-Z-Boy I once owned. Explain it to me. They want you to be uncomfortable? Is it, like, part of the suffering shtick? Goldfarb was okay. Goldfarb I liked. I was expecting, you know, a sermon, but it didn't happen.'

'Actually,' said Paula, 'it did.'

Ross had assumed that Paula being quiet was just another act, a play at serenity, that her lack of make-up was, in fact, a costume. Now, turning out of the parking lot, he glanced at her in the seat beside him and met her barefaced anger.

'You slept through the talk!'

'I did not!'

'You did! You slept through the talk and you snored!'

'You accuse me of snoring?'

'I do! And you deliberately talked even though I told you it was silent! You kept talking to me even after I asked you not to!'

'I just wanted to know what was going on!'

'I told you no speaking! I told you no moving!'

'No moving? No moving? This is the first I've heard of that!'

'You are so infuriating! You haven't changed at all!' Paula's hand came down hard on the dashboard and then, abruptly, she turned to face forward in the seat again. Hands in her lap, palms up, she inhaled conspicuously through her Roman nose. 'Oh, Ross. Ross, Ross, Ross.' She giggled.

'I don't know if I'm coming tomorrow,' Ross told her.

'Oh, don't come!'

When they reached her place, Paula got out of the car. He looked over his shoulder at her ducking in the back to get her bag. 'Should I call in the morning to let you know?'

'Don't come!' She blew him a kiss.

Something occurred to him then, so he did not turn back to watch her go up the steps; neither did he drive away. He stayed exactly as he was, looking back, as if Paula were still there. When he finally faced forward again, she was just closing the front door to the house, waving goodnight. He didn't wave back.

Anyone watching what he did next might have thought he'd seen something come round the side of Paula's house, then pass along the right side of the car before disappearing behind it. They might have assumed this slow turning of his head was Ross tracking whatever it was he saw. There was nothing, though. He wasn't looking at anything. He was just turning his head to experience his suddenly full range of movement and how free it made him feel.

At some point in the middle of the first Saturday morning sitting the image came to Ross of those self-immolating monks. *Well*, he thought, cringing on the folded-up comforter he had brought, *who wouldn't? Who the hell wouldn't?* He was almost at that point himself. He glanced at Paula beside him and, seeing that she was no longer beside him, scanned the hall and caught her in the very act of sneaking off to install herself on the other side of the room.

After the sitting Michael Goldfarb explained that he would be meeting the beginners while the more experienced among them did a walking meditation. Hearing 'walking meditation', Ross rose and followed the people who were putting on their shoes and coats.

There was a wide concrete ramp that led out of the pagoda and, on either side, a square pond. The effect was of a bridge over a moat; Ross walked down it and stood watching for Paula. So intense was her concentration that she didn't see Ross even when she was right beside him.

'Paula,' he whispered.

She didn't stop or acknowledge him in any way.

'What am I supposed to do?'

'Walk,' was all she said.

He stood there watching how they did it. Many of the people seemed to have selected for themselves a path either in the gravelled Japanese garden or through the trees. Ross observed that they walked this path to a personal end, not necessarily a physical one, then about-faced and walked back again. While a few maintained a natural pace, most were moving in slow motion. It made for a strange sight, all of them plodding steadily back and forth within some imaginary confine, gaze set in the middle distance, passing and even crossing each other, but somehow not colliding. *The Night of the Living Dead* came inevitably to mind.

It had rained all the previous night and, though it had stopped that morning, water dripped from the pagoda's eaves and the shaggy branches of the cedars. Ross heard distant traffic, the steady crunch of gravel and, somewhere nearby, a bird pipping. So accustomed to cooking smells, he was surprised by the intensity of the woodsy odours that surrounded him. Through his unzipped GoreTex he felt a strip of chill air down his front while at the same time sunlight warmed the side of his face. All this he noted – the sounds and smells and sensations rising then falling away – in the few moments he was working up to take a step.

Ross had been the one to teach Bryce how to walk. Bryce was about ten months old at the time, and had been getting absolutely no instruction from Bonnie, so Ross took it upon himself to provide the lessons. Back then Bryce could stand on his own but needed to cling two-handedly to the furniture with his back to the room, craning over his shoulder to see what everyone was doing, and crying out of feelings of exclusion. Only Ross seemed to think it was worth the trouble to demonstrate the steps.

'Like this,' he had told his nephew, raising his right heel off the floor. At the same time he shifted his weight to the sole of the left foot and canted his left hip. His elbows bent slightly as he pushed off with the ball of the right. Breaking with the floor, he took the first step (toes, shin and knee gliding forward), accompanied by a flowing gesture of the right arm. By the time the heel had landed (arch, ball and toes in smooth succession), the left foot was already airborne, his pelvis already shifting, his left arm in mid-swing alternating with the right. He was amazed. So many intricate, simultaneous movements, all of them predicated on a delicate vertical balance, the stepping precisely timed to the unstepping so that, given adequate speed, there was a moment within every step when a walking person could conceivably be suspended in mid-air. What a feat! How wondrous and complex! Yet in just three days Bryce had abandoned his sofa and coffee table crutches and was crossing the room, albeit tentatively, arms floating at his sides, as if he were walking on the moon.

That did not happen now. Now, forcing the scrutiny of consciousness upon the action actually paralysed Ross. This had happened to him before, while driving, back in the days of Miss Stockholm. He would be cruising mindlessly along when suddenly the next decision he had to make – accelerator, clutch, brake? – would flash like neon in his mind. As long as he thought about it, he couldn't act.

When the step happened, it was because he stopped thinking. His right foot launched forward by itself. Oddly, it frightened him as much as if he were stepping off a ledge or over a threshold into the unknown. The walking seemed to be happening without him, he merely observing it. They were two different things, the walking and the experience of it, the physical act and the knowing. In that second he got the point of the weekend, or one of them at least. He understood that there is a difference between what we're doing and what we think we're doing, and between real life and the life we think we're living. His foot came down. He felt the firmness of the ground beneath it.

6

The easiest thing in the world for her to do, the natural thing, was to pray. The comfort it would offer was so tempting. To hand it all over to Jesus saying, *Here, take my pain.* And in return all she had to do was acknowledge that He had died for her sins and that she was unworthy of this sacrifice. All she had to do was go lower still.

She was determined not to take the drug. She was going to face the future exactly as it was. The weekend Ross spent on his retreat was Iliana's night in the garden of Gethsemane. She sat alone in the apartment, struggling to be free, at least in thought.

She was disgusting. Bonnie had confirmed it, had taken one look at her and said, 'Yuk.' No wonder Ross wouldn't touch her. Her legs were thin and marbled blue with bruises from running into the furniture. Probably she smelled of pee. If she leaked, she would be the last to know; she wouldn't feel it.

Here, take my pee.

In the morning she lay alone in bed playing with the sleep from her eyes, rolling the sharp grains between her fingers, flicking. The same with snot. She tasted it: salty. Her ear bled, she dug a finger so deeply, but with no nails to speak of she extracted nothing.

144

Vaginal mucus stretched in a clear string from thumb to index finger. Tears: salty.

On Sunday, Ross came home early. She was not expecting him back until dinner time and had just placed a hair, frayed like a shorted electrical cord, between her front teeth to bite off the imperfection. Hearing the door, she quickly ran both hands through her hair to tidy it, took the hair elastic off her wrist and redid the ponytail. Hands clasped in her lap (to restrain them), she watched him come into the room.

He was carrying a paper bag under his arm, which he dropped on the couch before sitting down, first working his neck, then leaning back with his hands folded over his much reduced stomach. He had finally made his mind up, Iliana could see. She had expected as much after he had openly spent the weekend with Paula. For weeks she had been waiting on his decision, had listened to him weep over it. Now the apology was right there on his face, his expression a veritable sympathy card. He opened his mouth, but instead of a verse inside, the card was blank. Evidently he was still at a loss as to how to break it to her. 'What's in the bag?' she asked to start things off and, despite how she had been steeling herself, her voice cracked.

'Books.' He slid the contents out, laying them out side by side so she could read the covers. All of them were about Buddhism. 'A funny thing happened on the way over this morning. I drove by a couple of churches. The parking lots were all nearly empty, and at one this forlorn-looking minister was standing at the top of the steps waiting for someone to show up. I got the impression that he wouldn't have been averse to dragging people in off the street. Then, this afternoon, I left early to go to this bookstore someone recommended. I could barely get in the door. It was standing room only at the metaphysical bookstore. What do you think that says about modern spirituality?'

'It shows that Moses was right. It doesn't take much for people to exchange one god for another.'

'Buddhists don't believe in God. I actually didn't know that until this weekend.'

'Did Paula enjoy the weekend?'

'Not the first night. After that, I'm not sure. I got one or two things out of it. Are you interested?'

Shrugging, she used her finger to free some hair from the ponytail.

'Beware of any pursuit that requires you to take off your shoes and go around in socks.'

Smiling, she went on scrutinizing her split ends.

'My neck came unstuck.' He turned his head so that his chin lined up with his right shoulder. 'The main thing I learned, though, is about suffering.'

All these weeks, suspended in his indecision, Iliana had been waiting for him to speak frankly, yet now she turned away from him. Outside the balcony window, clouds were regrouping for another rain. The same thing was happening under her eyelids.

'Things change, yet we cling to how we were. This is why we suffer.'

'What exactly are you saying?'

'We've changed.'

Iliana took umbrage. 'They told you that?' When he had first told her about the retreat, she had not believed he was really going. She had thought it was an excuse to see Paula. But it seemed that it had happened and, because she did not understand what he had been doing, she imagined it as a prayer meeting, with Ross standing before a group of strangers revealing personal, humiliating things about her.

'No. I read it in one of these books. This one.' He pointed to it. 'While I was sitting in the car.'

'How long were you sitting in the car?'

'I don't know. An hour? I cut out early. I was just about out of my mind. Anyway, the point is, everything's changed, babe.'

'I haven't. I'm the same person sitting down.'

'No. I've changed, too. That's the problem. I knew it when you came home at Thanksgiving, but I couldn't let go of how we were before. I just couldn't. I'm sorry. I'm sorry it's taken me so long. I'm sorry for my selfishness. I'm sorry I've hurt you.'

She was stunned by how calmly he spoke. It gave credence to his argument: he wasn't the same. The Ross she knew would have felt guilty (he loved his guilt). What she had expected was a self-flagellating finale, fists vigorously thumped against his soft breast, hair torn, avowals of a love he regretted he could no longer follow through on. The Ross she had married was capable of this kind of hypocrisy, but not callousness, no. She gnawed the skin on her thumb.

'I hate it when you do that,' said Ross. 'Please stop.'

She threw her hands in the air. 'What are we going to do with this place? I don't want to stay here.'

'We'll sell.'

'Just like that? Gosh. Last year you didn't even want to renovate. Now you're in a big hurry to get out. Where does Paula live?'

'Where does Paula live? She lives in Kits.' His face fell. 'Don't tell me you want to move to Kits. I don't consider moving to Kits starting over. I consider that moving down.'

'I'm not moving to Kits if you're living there with Paula!'

'What are we talking about?'

'I'm talking about Paula.'

'What about her?'

'You're in love with her.'

'I am not!'

'Then why won't you wear your ring!'

'What ring?'

'Your wedding ring!'

Ross stared at her for a moment, a piece of his hair standing up on one side of his head like a terrier's cocked ear. He seemed bewildered. Slapping his thighs, he got abruptly off the couch and walked out of the room. She heard the dresser drawer open in the bedroom. He came back wearing the ring on his thumb. Kneeling at her feet, he waggled it in her face. She took the circle of gold and closed her fist round it.

'Here.' He offered his hand again, the left one this time. Slipping the ring on his finger for the second time, she saw for herself how it no longer fit.

'*I do*,' said Ross. 'Did I get it right this time?'

He tipped his hand. The ring slid right off and fell brightly in her lap. 'I will,' he promised.

Surrounded and unrecognized in the score of newly arrived, Iliana stepped down into the field and looked around for Ross. Months ago she had asked him to stop apologizing for his compounding guest list, having long ago lost track of his total. Now, scanning the throng, she suspected that he had, too. Drawing near the fire where the crowd was already dispersing, she did not see him because he had just been whisked away by a woman in white to the back of the bartender's tent. Those who did not know the woman assumed she was the bride, a dark-haired beauty with a Roman nose and a regretful smile.

'Have you seen Ross?' Iliana asked a couple talking together.

The woman smiled. 'Never looking so happy.'

'I've never seen him looking unhappy,' said the man.

In the bar tent Ross, unbuttoning, asked Paula, 'What time is it?'

'One twenty.' She slid the shirt off his back. 'I see you still have breasts.'

He crossed his arms. 'Have you seen Iliana?'

'What does she look like?'

'She's beautiful.'

'Oh, Ross,' said Paula, stifling a giggle, 'hearing you say that makes me want to cry.'

'That's not crying.'

'I just remembered that time— Do you?' She draped the shirt over an open hand so that the wine stain was lying in her palm. In the fingers of her other hand was a piece of ice. 'We were undressing. You had your shirt off and suddenly the button on your waistband popped and flew across the room and almost put my eye out.' She scrubbed at the stain. 'I'm a Buddhist now, Ross. It's too late for us, I know, but I wanted you to know that.'

Staring, Ross wondered what the hell she meant.

The main effect of the ice cube was to saturate the shirt; Paula went off to dry it by the fire. As soon as she had gone, Ross got the good idea to have a glass of wine himself. Peering around the wall of stacked cases, he signalled to the bartender to hand him a corkscrew. He opened a Zin, filled and raised a glass. 'Iliana, you are my pearl,' he practised, immediately discouraged by the sound of it aloud. He was not a poetic man.

The Hamlet of Havarti poked his head in. 'Here you are. A little birdie tells me you need me to tie your tie.' He looked a second, frowning time at his son. 'Did you rent that thing without a shirt?'

'Is she here?'

'Who?'

Ross reached into the case for another wine glass and filled it for his father. They clinked a silent toast, nodding to each other, then Teddy said, 'I guess this would be the time for me to explain to you the facts of life.' He sat down on a case beside Ross, crossing his long legs, searching for the words. 'Son? The penis goes in the vagina.'

'Now you tell me.'

They both laughed.

'Seriously, though, is there any advice I can give you?'

Ross scratched his chest. 'Would you say that Iliana is a pearl?'

'A what?'

'I have a speech to make.'

'Oh. She's wearing a blue dress. Does that help?' He tapped his watch. 'Where's your shirt?'

'By the fire, I hope.'

'I'll go get it.'

Left alone again with his unformulated thoughts, it occurred to Ross that Iliana was not a pearl at all, but the whole oyster. At the thought of her oysterly parts, he smacked his lips, already purple from the wine, and touched himself through his tuxedo trousers, wishing she were with him now.

At last Iliana ran into someone she knew, or rather Phyllis Hamovitch recognized Iliana and sang her name out, baring the brilliant white teeth of a dentist's wife, which her lipstick had already smeared from effusive smiling. 'What a perfect day to get married. You look radiant. And such beautiful bridesmaids. When I married Ham in 1947, I had four, which was considered a lot in those days. But twelve, Iliana! Twelve! I counted.'

Iliana knew immediately who she meant, the apparitions all in white, skinny spectres of Ross's former loves, come back to haunt him, probably at his own invitation. Nearby, Ed Snow was talking to one, and when Iliana passed them he stopped her, saying, 'This is Vicky who used to moon around before your time,' but did not introduce her to Vicky as the one true bride. Iliana was not going to find Ross, she realized then; she was just one of many who wanted to be beside him now, so she turned and followed the music coming from across the field.

Waiting under the tree were a tall man with the worried air of a disgraced pastor and a long-haired cellist playing with closed eyes. 'Stella?' the pastor asked.

'Oh,' said Iliana. 'She's probably one of the ones in white.'

Seeing the bride walking straight towards her destiny, Phyllis Hamovitch, nostalgic, romantic, went too, tapping Ed Snow on the shoulder on the way. When Ham returned with their drinks, he saw his wife heading for the tree, which made four people with a clear destination. Soon others began to drift. Even the ones who had gathered early around the bar and shown no inclination at all to leave it, like the mother of the groom, reluctantly broke away after topping up their glasses. 'Is that her?' Iliana overheard as the first guests drew near. 'Could it be?'

Many of them had never actually met Iliana; more than a few of the female guests would probably admit they were disappointed by this proof that she was real. Or was she? One of the Vickies leaned into another and whispered more than audibly, 'What do you bet her bra is padded?'

Nothing had been rehearsed, especially not Iliana leaving her bouquet in the car. She knew about the made-for-TV Western. With the throng circling her, more than two hundred appraising stares, she felt as if she were making her last stand empty-handed. All at once the circle parted to form a makeshift aisle. At the end of it was Bonnie crouching to Bryce's level, nudging him forward with the flowers.

Now all that delayed them was Ross, sighted at last by those on the periphery of the crowd, at the fire with Jaime Rios, jabbing a long poker into the flames. When they shouted to him, he held up one hand to plead for patience, prodding on. At last, satisfied that the meat was cooking as it should, he threw the poker down. No one expected him to run, least of all Iliana, but they clapped in unison and chanted to encourage him along. Arriving breathless and sweating, he stopped when he saw her, as though astonished by the strange coincidence of meeting her here, of all places. Everyone laughed and the marriage commissioner, evidently fearing that one or both of the couple might disappear again, began the ceremony even before Ross had properly reached his bride: a long, grandly orated preamble on the institution of marriage. Next he asked if any of those gathered knew of an impediment to the union. Whoops of laughter. 'Do you Ross Alexander,' he continued, 'undertake to afford to this woman the love of your person, the comfort of your companionship, and the patience of your understanding; and to share with her equally of the necessities of life as they may be earned or enjoyed by yourself; to respect the dignity of her person, her inalienable personal rights, and to recognize the right of counsel and consultation upon all matters relating to the present or the future of the household established by this marriage?' He waited for a reply, and when none was immediately forthcoming from the groom, cued him in a stern whisper. 'Say "I do".'

Ross did. The crowd roared.

Iliana assented to the identical terms and conditions. The rings were exchanged, broad gold bands, Iliana's able to pass cleanly through Ross's. When he kissed his new wife (his better half, his life's sole reason), he did it full and long on the mouth and stuck his tongue in; he couldn't help himself. Not the lewd hoots and whistles or even Iliana's embarrassed squirming could make him stop, only the cello starting up again. He pulled away to beg the man to refrain from playing in a minor key at his wedding.

Now Ross would not let Iliana go. As if he believed too literally the words in the ceremony about the sole condition that might permit them to part, he took the hand that now wore his ring and would not give it back. Leading her into the heart of the crowd, he brought her face to face with every person who stayed gathered, lunging at them, lips Merlot-purple, lips stained Zinfandel, engulfing them in a joyful ursine hug. When they came to Iliana's friends, Stephanie, Nina and Claire, he introduced her to them, too. They moved on to the tables, to the people who were already seated, then to the guests who, tired of waiting their turn to congratulate the couple, had returned to the tents for drinks and appetizers. There they found Ross's mother with four martinis behind her; Ross knew this because of her habit of spearing the olive from each glass on to one stick in order to keep track herself.

'Is this my little boy who was afraid of the toaster?' She embraced them both, whispering to Iliana, 'Hurry up and give me a legitimate *grandchild so I can hold my head high again.'*

END

1

Clambering to a stand on the seat, Bryce leaned over and tapped the shoulder of the farmer riding ahead of them. 'Hey, Bud,' the man said, turning.

'Do you know Ross?'

'I might know him to see him. What's he look like?'

'He's, he's . . . a man!'

'I think I have seen a man around. Yeah.'

Bonnie had no idea if this exemplar of patience, to whom Bryce had chatted throughout the last hour of the trip (happily revealing in an embarrassment of detail their personal situation), actually was a farmer. He wore a John Deere cap and that was evidence enough for Bonnie. All of the other passengers, similarly capped if they were men, the women frumpy and gone to fat, seemed to her as bucolic, though she had only begun to see them that way after the bus, which they had boarded in the civilized core of the city, had transported them via the ferry from Horseshoe Bay to Vancouver Island, then into this void of woods and fields. Bonnie had no appreciation of the pastoral. The countryside was dirty. Dirt was the point of it. Last year, when Ross told her that they were moving over here, Bonnie had almost killed herself.

Finally, up ahead on the highway, sign of an actual settlement – Canadian Tire, Wendy's, Pay-Less Gas – that so North American, so comforting buffer of familiar franchises against the rural. 'When are we there?' Bryce asked the man for the dozenth time.

'Now.'

The bus turned and the depot came into view. Bryce, still wedged between the headrests, looked back at Bonnie, his mouth open, soundless with excitement. Facing forward again, he asked, 'Do you know my auntie?'

'Is she a woman by any chance?'

'She has a wheelchair!' Bryce squealed in anticipation of it.

Bonnie tugged at the hem of his shirt, which was on him backwards. 'Sit down.'

At the depot, a handful of people moved towards the bus as it pulled into the bay. Bryce, face pressed to the smeary window, declared that he did not see Ross among them. 'You haven't seen him for so long,' Bonnie told him, 'you don't remember what he looks like.'

But Bryce was right. Once the toing and froing had ceased, only the two of them were left standing on the sidewalk, Bryce fiddling with the scratchy tag at his throat, looking worriedly around. 'Here,' said Bonnie, trying again with the tissue. 'There's a bogey in your nose.'

He pushed her hand away. 'No. Leave it in.'

Was he picking up on her anxiety or she his? Standing there waiting (she hated waiting), Bonnie thought of her conversations with Ross over the last year and a half, the tone she used. She pictured the Strait of Juan De Fuca reaching boiling point as her words crossed the water. Ross had come back to Vancouver only twice and both times she'd sent Bryce up to Randall and Barry's. Could it be revenge, his bringing them all the way over only to strand them?

A man in sunglasses and an air-streamed helmet came riding up on a mountain bike, stopping right in front of them, foot on the kerb, toned, sun-browned leg extended. Bryce suddenly bolted for him, arms wide, and Bonnie, caught off guard, wasn't quick enough to hold him back. The bicycle clattered to the sidewalk as the stranger dismounted and scooped Bryce up.

'Helicopter!'

'Oh, my God, Ross!'

He whirled Bryce, then, mock staggering, deposited him back on his feet, herding him against Bonnie so he could hug them both at once. 'I can't believe it,' he said, squeezing. 'I can't believe you've finally come.'

Bonnie started to cry. She had her old reasons (his betrayal of her, her exhaustion), and now this: he had changed so much. As he held her, she patted disbelieving hands all over his damp back. Her fat friendly brother, the one she had been missing, where was he? Thirty or forty pounds were unaccounted for; the rest he'd shifted around and packed tighter. She could have been in the arms of an impostor for all she knew, someone who'd stolen Ross's face (a slimmer facsimile), copied his voice, and even made sure the signature stains matched up in a continuous dribble from T-shirt to shorts, but had failed utterly in reproducing his proper bulk.

At last the Ross-alike let her go. He held her out at arm's length, fixing on her a look of such undying fraternal love that she felt herself released from at least a portion of her bitterness. 'Well,' she said, using the tissue herself. 'Here we are.'

Ross stood the bicycle up again and, while Bonnie steadied it, lifted Bryce on to the seat. '*Bonjour, bonjour!* How old are you now?'

He held one finger up. 'Three.'

'You're more than three,' Bonnie said. 'You're three and a half.'

'You didn't have a birthday without me, did you?'

'He had *two* without you,' Bonnie reminded him.

'Your shirt's on backwards. God, Bon. He's grown so much. He's like a little man now. Where are your bags?'

She picked them off the sidewalk, her small suitcase and Bryce's backpack.

'That's it?' he said.

'Where's the car?'

'No car.' He took the helmet off and settled the bowl of it on Bryce's head, clicking closed the strap. 'Do you know what kind of bicycle this is? It's called a Giant. Fee fi fo fum.'

'Fee fi fo fum.'

'I don't believe it! Where did you learn to speak Giant?' To Bonnie: 'How was the trip?'

'Awful.'

Grinning, he slung one arm round her neck. 'It's so great to see you, Bon. Come on. I can't wait to show you round.'

They started walking, Ross's arms encircling Bryce as he pushed the bike. A logging truck rumbled past on the highway. They dashed across and, safe on the other side, Bonnie glanced down the long commercial strip again. They could have been anywhere in North America, anywhere.

'Driving in, we weren't impressed either,' Ross said, answering her thought. 'We were going to whiz on through. Then I happened to glance over and see that we were passing this— When I say it's the biggest hockey stick, I mean it's *the* biggest hockey stick. It's the world's biggest hockey stick. I looked at Iliana and she looked at me and we decided to turn in and get a closer look. Once we were off the highway – you'll see for yourself in a minute – we discovered this perfect little town.'

'Where's the hockey stick?' Bryce asked, looking around.

'Iliana will take you by it later.'

'How is Iliana?' Bonnie asked.

'She's amazing.'

They came to a railway track banked on both sides by blackberry brambles, the clusters of fruit hard and green. Stopping on the sleepers, he pointed to where a red brick clock tower with a high grey roof rose up several blocks away. 'That's City Hall.' His voice sounded cartoonish with civic pride.

On the other side of the tracks was a residential neighbourhood. Bonnie knew Ross expected her to find it quaint. Waving his arm, he took in the whole tree-lined street. 'We love Duncan, Bon.' But to Bonnie, a high-rise dweller from a peninsula of high-rises, these stucco and wooden bungalows, marigold-bordered, their roofs thatched with moss, looked like the houses of impoverished dwarves.

'It's got everything. Character. Culture.'

'And the hockey stick?' asked Bonnie. 'Which is that?'

'It's got a *theatre*. It's got cut-away kerbs and a post office with a ramp. There's a natural food store.'

'A natural food store?' She stopped, blinking at him.

'It's not only the place, Bon, it's the lifestyle. When Iliana was nursing, we never even saw each other. Now we're running the café together. And Bon?' He squeezed her forearm for emphasis, unnecessarily.

'What?' she asked.

The way he said it reminded her unpleasantly of other confessions made to her by men who had also gone half their lives without realizing something essential about themselves. 'I am *such* a café guy.'

At the next corner, they turned on to a commercial street brightened with bannered light standards and coloured awnings. Apart from the clock tower, no structure Bonnie could see was taller than two storeys. In the middle of the block a sign stood on the sidewalk: *Interesting Sandwiches*.

'This is it. Go on in. We'll stash the bike.'

She had already started through the gate when, hearing Ross say her name, she turned. No question he looked great – healthy, tanned, smiling even – yet all at once her twin-sense switched on. Like a smoke detector with a ten-year-old battery, it was activated so rarely she hadn't even known it still worked. 'What?'

'Nothing. I just want to say thanks for coming. We really need your help.' He disappeared into the alley, pushing Bryce.

Still, Bonnie couldn't shake the feeling off.

Inside the courtyard, at patio tables arranged around planters, two women sat drinking coffee together while a man played chess against himself. French doors led into the café, its interior so filled with plants it could have been a continuation of the outdoor space. It took a moment for the homonym in the café's name to register, the metal letters fixed into the stucco façade spelling out *Real Food*. Bonnie spotted Iliana inside, her back to the door. Strangely, whenever she thought of her sister-in-law, she thought of her standing, not so much because her early impressions of Iliana had been so indelible, as because Iliana had never acted the way Bonnie had expected a person in her situation to act (which was, of course, the way Bonnie would have). Seeing her now and seeing the chair, too, was almost shocking.

Ross reappeared holding Bryce's hand. 'Everybody?' he announced. 'I want you to meet my sister Bonnie. My nephew Bryce.' The man, who had a Mosaic beard and just enough long grey hairs to collect into an elastic, raised an open palm, while the women turned curiously towards her and regaled her with friendly 'Hi's. 'Go on in,' said Ross.

The three customers all got up at the same time and followed them into the café. Iliana, Bonnie saw now, was talking to an older, heavy-breasted woman with bad highlights. Seeing them, the woman leaned over to say something to Iliana, who then turned round in the chair. A Happy Birthday chorus started up. Sitting in Iliana's lap, a cake the shape of a helicopter with three lit candles in it.

Bryce trotted right over to Iliana. 'Is this your wheelchair?'

Iliana laughed. 'It is.'

'Nice.'

'Thanks. This is your birthday cake.'

Barely regarding it, he confided, 'I've got a lazy eye.' The song nearing its finale – *Happy birthday dear Bryce! Happy birthday to you!* – he looked back at Bonnie. 'Why is it my birthday?'

'I think we're celebrating your last one. Aren't you going to blow the candles out?'

Breath and saliva, in equal proportions, extinguished the three flames. Ross squatted beside Bryce, a hand on his shoulder, and pointed to the blackboard above the short-order window on which the fare was written in coloured chalk. 'I want you to pick a sandwich, any sandwich. I'll read what we have. We've got a Gary Fichter. An Iliana Alexander. A Deb Howland. A Bonnie Alexander. A Bryce Alexander. Should I keep reading or do you know what you want?'

Bryce nodded.

'What?'

He stuck his tongue out and moved it around.

'You want me to read the list again? A Gary Fichter—'

'Yeah!'

'You want a Gary Fichter? I haven't finished reading out the list again.'

'Gary Fichber.'

'I'll just tell you what's in the Bryce Alexander.' It was written

160

up on the board. '"Cream cheese and worms on sourdough".' You still want a Gary Fichter?'

Bryce said he did.

The big woman with the highlights returned from the kitchen carrying in each hand a platter stacked high with sandwiches, crusts excised. 'He wants a Gary Fichter, Deb.' Nodding, she set the platters down on the decorated table with the presents. 'This is Deb, by the way,' Ross said, 'our short-order queen. Where's Stevie Blake?'

'On the roof.'

The cake lifted out of her lap, Iliana turned to Bonnie and, smiling, opened her arms. 'It's great to see you, Bon. It feels like years.'

As she bent into the hug, Bonnie found herself looking over Iliana's shoulder at the menu board. *Soups: The Atomizer, Zucchini Chill-Out, Black Bean and Avocado.*

Soups?

Suddenly she was blinking back tears, for here was indisputable evidence of an internal transformation to match the physical; all her life she had known her brother as a person who had to sink his teeth into everything. Then her gaze strayed and came to rest on her own name.

Bonnie Alexander: no bread, no filling.

People started dropping by. They kept coming, everyone greeted personally by Ross, exhorted by him to join in the celebration with a complimentary mug of freshly brewed organic coffee, a piece of helicopter cake and a Bryce sandwich. The Bryce sandwich, a new item on the menu everyone was eager to try, was largely responsible for the party atmosphere as person after person took a bite, then lowered the crustless triangle only to find a worm, sticky with cream cheese, dangling down. They screamed, then screamed with laughter. The worms were made of fruit juice and came in red, purple, orange and yellow.

Old wooden tables and mismatched chairs were arranged on a floor of refinished planks. Big bright acrylic paintings of fruit and vegetables filled most of the terracotta-coloured wall space. There was a shiny Faema espresso machine, an antique cash register, plants in profusion. But for the people, it could have been, if not quite a Denman Street café, certainly a Main Street one. There was something the matter with the people and it didn't take more than a superficial glance around for Bonnie to put her finger on it. She meant the women, of course – the men she didn't bother looking at. It was their clothes. They all seemed to be outfitted in dated, faded thrift store wear, in crinkled rayon floral print dresses, drawstring batik pants, hemp vests, Birkenstock sandals with crumbling soles. It was their hair, too. Bonnie had actual nightmares about being out in public and catching sight of herself in a mirror and seeing her hair like that. Or it was their bodies. Visible under Deb Howland's T-shirt, not only the substantial infrastructure of her brassiere, but also the flesh caught between it and the waistband of her jeans. The room was filled with the kind of soft, lumpy bodies that Bonnie squeamishly imagined, after clothes were removed at the end of the day, bore the impression of seams and straps for hours. Yet such friendly unselfconsciousness! They kept coming up to say how much they liked her brother and how striking was her resemblance to him. One woman inexplicably referred to Ross as 'spiritual', which started Bonnie thinking of herself as a kind of priestess. As each woman approached, she felt herself being called upon to absolve her of her various sins against style. She wondered if they'd always been this way, or if town life had lowered their standards, or if they just didn't know any better. She wondered *how* to forgive them.

Finally, Ross, who had been weaving through the company with

Bryce on his back, extending the coffee pot for refills, took her away. 'Come. I want to show you the apartment.'

They left with Bryce through the courtyard where the party had spilled over. Near the back of the building, accessed from a lane at the side, was a set of steep wooden stairs that led to the roof. 'That's Stevie,' Ross told her.

He was bent over, hammering, shirt off, his back to them (on either side of his obvious spine the more obvious corrugations of his ribs). As they stepped on to the roof Ross called to him, 'This is my sister Bonnie and my nephew Bryce.'

Stevie paused to look over his shoulder. Bonnie saw a boy's smooth face and an untamed, almost feral squint, suggesting to her abandonment in a cave at birth and a lupine upbringing.

'Why aren't you down there having fun?'

Stevie resumed his work without replying to Ross. Motioning for Bonnie to follow, Ross explained, 'He doesn't say much.'

'Does he know how to talk?'

'He's building planters. We're going to have a herb garden up here.'

The partial second storey had been added on at the back and lived in by the previous owners. Ross unlocked the door and ushered Bonnie and Bryce inside, Bryce immediately sinking down in the entryway to strum the metal grate of the heating vent. He sprang up and ran to the one below the kitchen window. *Strum!*

Ross opened the window wider to clear the air of the fresh paint smell. 'What do you think, Bon?'

She followed him into the living room where he cracked another window for a cross-breeze. 'The view isn't quite as majestic as you're accustomed to,' he understated. The vista was of the parking lot behind the post office. 'And there's just the one bedroom, but that's all you have now.'

'But there's no furniture. What are we going to sleep on?'

163

'Oh, you're staying with us at the house for now.'

He was proposing that they come to live, Bonnie realized, and immediately she felt her fury rise. Ross, sensing it too, tried to pre-empt her objections. 'I can't stand the thought of all this water between us. It was bad enough before, with the bridge, remember?'

In their twenties, they had shared an apartment in the West End for a few years. He was alluding to when he'd got his own place in Kerrisdale and Bonnie had for several months refused to cross the Burrard Street Bridge to visit. 'I want to help with Bryce. I said I would.'

She gushed sarcasm. 'It's a little late for you to be saying that, isn't it? I mean, where were you the last year and a half? Thought you'd just skip the Terrible Twos? Well, I wake up screaming. I am scarred.'

'We needed time. I explained that to you. What's keeping you in Vancouver?'

'I have a life,' she lied.

'There's a job for you, too. I've been holding off hiring someone else.'

She actually took a step back, pretending to be affronted, when what she really felt was cornered. Though she knew this was not an ultimatum (there were no strings attached to Ross, despite his cheques), eventually she would have to work at something. Bryce was due to go to preschool, then kindergarten, elementary school, high school, and, unless he was serious about a career in valet parking, maybe even university – what then? And what choice did she really have? Life without Ross was hell. Her hand went to her chin, automatically feeling for hairs. Just then she remembered Wolf-boy outside, and the roof's perilous edge. 'Where's Bryce?'

Together, they started for the door.

Strum!

It came from the bedroom. He was sitting with legs in a V, the vent between them, waiting to put music to their entrance.

Ross laughed. 'What do you say, Bon?' He reached for her but she sidestepped him.

'Come on,' she told Bryce.

When Bryce was tired his eyes went slightly out of synch. While this did not affect his vision, neither did it contribute anything positive to his appearance, particularly when he could not be persuaded to wear his clothes the right way round. Rejoining the party, Bonnie went immediately to find Iliana. 'Look at my idiot child. Can you take us home?'

They went round the back where Iliana parked. Iliana transferred herself into the driver's seat and, after a brief struggle, popped a wheel off the chair and leaned it against the car. She popped the other wheel and leaned it against the open door. Bryce squealed in admiration.

'Can I help?' asked Bonnie as Iliana hefted the body of the chair in one hand.

'It's all right.'

The chair was not going to fit through the door, not with Iliana in the seat. Bonnie could see this. 'Here,' she insisted.

'It's okay. I've got a system.'

It was like watching the camel squeeze through the needle's eye, Bonnie thought. Somehow Iliana got the chair in the car and over her shoulder into the back seat, followed by the wheels, then Bryce, clambering eagerly over her to get in the back, too. Though Bryce did not really remember Iliana, he had been talking about the wheelchair ever since Bonnie had mentioned it to prepare him for the visit, foolishly hoping to forestall embarrassment. The chair had not disappointed him. He sat with one arm slung around it now, as if it were a friend of his.

'So how have you been keeping, Bonnie?' Iliana asked once they were on their way.

'Where are the brakes?' Bonnie asked.

Iliana slowed the car to demonstrate, but Bonnie put both hands on the dashboard just in case.

'What did you think of the café?'

'It looks great.'

'We did the house at the same time. It was crazy. Ross finally has enough to keep him busy. You don't mind helping out while you're here?'

Her thin shoulders heaved. 'No.'

'I'm making the bread, did he tell you?'

'How did he lose all that weight?'

'Well, we're vegetarian now for one.'

'*What?*'

'Didn't you see the menu? We're organic, too.'

'I knew it!' She threw her hands up. 'I knew something was wrong!'

Bryce interrupted. 'Why does a wheelchair have wheels?'

'Because that's what it is, honey,' said Iliana, 'a *wheel* chair.'

Unwittingly, Iliana had opened the question floodgate. From long experience Bonnie knew 'It just does' was the only defence against absurdity; she leaned back, glad not to be the one caught in Bryce's trap, worried about Ross again instead of angry at him.

'Why is it?'

'You mean why do I need it?' Iliana asked.

'Yes.'

'Because I can't walk.'

'Why can't you?'

Why, Bonnie wondered, was Ross not eating meat? What did it mean? He used to live on flesh. At his wedding he had served six whole lambs!

'Do you want to see the hockey stick?' asked Iliana, ingeniously freeing herself.

'Yeah!'

Ahead on the right was a yellow brick high school and, across the street, the community centre. Iliana turned into the parking lot and drove round the building, which Bonnie saw as they circled it was part of a larger complex including the arena that faced the highway. Iliana stopped the car and turned to Bonnie. 'I should warn you—' She had been about to tell her about Ross's Buddhism, but Bryce interrupted, shrilling, 'Lookit!' causing Iliana, too, to look up at the hockey stick. It was a familiar sight (they had lived in Duncan almost eighteen months), but all at once she saw it as her sister-in-law and nephew did, as though for the first time. A gigantic phallus rising, it was the very symbol of potent manhood. Why had she never seen it this way before? Subconsciously she must have, for the very moment she laid eyes on it she decided this was where she wanted to live.

Sighing, she told Bonnie, 'You actually get a better view from farther off.'

The same could be said of the Pyramids, the Statue of Liberty, the *Arc de Triomphe*. There was a town on the prairies Bonnie had heard about that laid claim to the world's largest pierogy and that, too, was probably better viewed from way, way back. The hockey stick, supported by four steel pillars, ran the entire length of the building at the height of its roof, part of the blade lifted into a sky from which the blue was already fading. Now, past seven, the sun had dropped behind the building, but at a certain point in the day the puck, raised up on a pillar of its own, probably eclipsed it. Bonnie tried to imagine herself here, living in the shadow of such kitsch.

No fucking way, she thought.

2

All is suffering. The first time Ross saw this, the First Noble Truth, in print (confirming both his experience and all he believed he deserved), he had felt perversely comforted. More than anything it had set him on his path and since then he had constructed, paperback by paperback on his bedside table, a leaning tower of spiritual guidebooks. These he did not consult as often as he knew he should. Avoidance (one of his personal weaknesses) was an unhelpful state of mind, but so too was that great Catholic motivator, guilt. It was a wonder he was not completely incapacitated by this clash of spiritual influences.

Every morning he made the effort. In the bed, white curtains incandescent from the sunlight behind them, he sat in quiet observation of his breath, experiencing for himself the ebb and flow that was life: the breath, sensations, feelings, thoughts, all coming and going. When, inevitably, he lost track of his breath and his attention snagged on, say, guilt, he would begin to suffer. Even when it snagged on a pleasant thought or memory he would suffer because then he would cling to it. In either case he would suffer because his mind was not free.

'Did you talk to Bonnie?' he'd asked Iliana the night before.

'Sort of.'

'Is she seeing anyone?'

'She didn't say.'

'She seems thinner. How does she seem to you?'

'Humbled,' Iliana had said.

He didn't know how Bonnie had coped without him. The times he had gone back to Vancouver she'd punished him by not letting him see Bryce. On the phone she'd sounded distant and cold, trying to make him feel that, after putting so many miles and so much water between them, it was not going to be easy to be close. Yet she suffered as much as he did over the separation. All of them had suffered.

'How long are they staying for?' Iliana had asked.

'I don't know.'

Thinking. He made the mental note: *thinking.* Then he started over. He simply began again.

It was called sitting practice, and when he had finished he went downstairs to wake up Bryce.

Bonnie was curled on her side with her knees drawn up, wrists crossed over her chest, hands fisted, exactly how she had slept in the womb with Ross, her back to Bryce who, in the spread-eagle pose of a mid-air parachutist, took up most of the bed. Crouching, Ross tapped the boy's cheek, then watched as he batted his lashes, disbelieving the end of his dream. Abruptly he pushed himself up and, looking drunkenly at Ross, smiled.

Ross tried to dress the boy quietly so as not to wake Bonnie, but when he went to pull the shirt over his head Bryce cried out, 'No!' and took charge himself. In the bathroom, boosting him at the basin, Ross saw dark hair pivoting on the back of his head in the same direction as the water spooling in the drain. (In the southern hemisphere, he wondered, did boys' rooster tails whorl the other way?)

'Where's Auntie Iliana?'

'She's already at the café.'

'Does she sleep in the chair?'

'No. She sleeps with me. Let's brush your hair.'

Bryce fended off the brush, like a boxer ducking feints. 'No! I do it with my hand!'

Only in freezing winter rain was Ross visited with nostalgia for his former sidekick, Miss Stockholm (RIP). The Giant had won his affection in a way the Camry never had. A pillow on the crossbar, he held Bryce tight against his body as he steered with his free hand. 'I'll take you past the train station,' he said, setting off through the empty streets.

It seemed like years ago that Ross and Iliana, searching for a place to start over, had left the highway to get a closer view of the hockey stick and inadvertently discovered Duncan. Sizing up the old clapboard train station, City Hall, and all the other buildings that gave the town its historic feel, Ross's first thought had been that the place would make a great film location. He was trying not to think like this now. Without realizing it, he had for years been appraising the world as if he were a director or a production designer instead of just a lowly set caterer. Now that he'd torn the celluloid from his eyes and silenced the soundtrack in his head, he was endeavouring to live in the world exactly as it was.

In the alley beside the café, he lifted Bryce down and deposited the bike in its usual place under the stairs, leaning against the bags of topsoil that had been delivered a few days before. Taking the boy's hand, he led him round the front and through the courtyard, conscious of how he had to cant just slightly to the left so that Bryce's hand could fit comfortably into his, how he needed to adjust his pace, to slow right down, so the boy could keep up. He liked having to make these accommodations because they forced him to be mindful.

Entering through the French doors, they were welcomed by the smell of bread. Iliana was in the kitchen rolling out the dough for her Cinnamon Mountains. 'Where's Bonnie?'

'Sleeping. I left her a note.' Ross went over to the corkboard and took down the button someone had given him from the Dalai Lama's World Tour. Out front there was a pad next to the phone, writing utensils, scissors. He traced a circle around the button then popped the plastic cover off. Coming back to the kitchen where Bryce was helping Iliana position the spirals of dough on the baking sheet, Ross pinned the refitted button to Bryce's front, which was, of course, his back. *I dress myself*, it read.

Bryce was put to work passing oranges out of the crate for Ross to juice. At ten to eight he was lifted up to flick the switch on the coffee maker, then, at eight exactly by the knife and fork hands of the vegetable clock, enlisted to help Ross carry the sandwich board out on to the sidewalk.

As people came in, Ross called out a salutation, addressing by name even those who had eaten there only once or twice before. This was a point of pride for him, as well as how he could approach a table where two or three regulars had just seated themselves and rattle off their orders for them to confirm, including what kind of toast they wanted and whether they took it dry or buttered. When he came back, he would be wearing plates along his arm, the handles of the coffee mugs gathered in one fist. He could pick up a conversation left off a day or two before. 'Great party yesterday,' everyone was telling Ross this morning.

Bryce sat on a stool at the counter, yogurt goatee dripping off his face, busily pouring raw sugar out of the little paper packets. When Ross, foaming milk at the Faema, asked him, 'How's it going?' Bryce paused in his mountain making to hold out his partially eaten toast.

'What's this?'

'Toast,' Ross said.

'A dog.' He took two bites then held the toast out again.

'Less dog?'

'A shoe.'

Ross laughed. 'I get it.' It was a kind of pre-school Rorschach, a breakfast psychiatric assessment.

Deb set two more orders out on the ledge of the short-order window. 'Don't forget Stevie Blake.'

They had been hearing the song of his saw from the roof since eight, but Ross had tables to clear and set, a till to man, babies to hold (Diane came in with her little Connor who miraculously shut up the moment Ross relieved her of him), people to greet and seat and see to the door, a nephew to keep an eye on. Gary, their organic produce man, arrived and Ross helped him lug the boxes to the cooler. He wished Bonnie would show up now and see just how badly she was needed.

When he took Stevie's breakfast up later, the first thing he noticed stepping on to the roof was gravity taking a pass on Stevie's pants. Shirtless and beltless in the full morning sun, Stevie fiddled with something in his hands, his frame pubescently lean, navel protruding like there was a finger behind it pushing out; all the waistband had to cling on to was hope. What Stevie was doing, Ross was sorry to see as he got closer, was rolling a cigarette. Lifting the paper rectangle to his lips, tonguing its edge, he watched Ross coming across the roof with his breakfast (no reason had ever been offered as to why Stevie could not go down and get it for himself), Ross, his *employer*, yet he acknowledged him with no more than a constriction of his glance.

Ross was careful not to sound accusing. 'I should have mentioned it before. You can't smoke up here. The patio's right below.'

At first Stevie showed no sign of having heard, though Ross was standing right in front of him now with the mug of coffee and plate of pancakes. He took his time: twisting one end of the cigarette, taking it in his mouth whole, drawing it back moistened through his lips, casually slipping it behind his ear. Ross really did not know what to make of this behaviour. Supposedly Stevie was well past twenty, but he appeared to have shaken off neither the physique nor the attitude (not to mention the *hair*) of adolescence.

He had come to Ross thanks to Deb, who had recommended him as a good carpenter and someone who would certainly need the money. Deb knew almost everyone in town; she'd lived here her whole life – more than forty years, but less than fifty, Ross guessed from her rather care-worn appearance and the age of her son, Brent, twenty-eight. She was friendly with Nana Blake, Stevie's grandmother.

When Stevie showed up to talk to Ross about building the planters, he had not seemed very eager. He had not seemed eager because he had not made eye contact. When Ross mentioned this unsettling detail to Deb, she shrugged and said, 'That's just Stevie.'

'What's the matter with him?' Ross asked her yesterday, after Stevie had started on the roof, but as Ross's native informant, his 'in' in Duncan, Deb was not as forthcoming as Ross would have liked. An anti-stereotype of the small-town gossip, she revealed little; she didn't even show her teeth when she smiled.

At last Stevie took the coffee mug from Ross, sipping noisily before setting it on the stack of lumber behind him. Real Food pancakes were served sprinkled with granola. Stevie lifted one from the plate Ross still held and shook the granola off before rolling it, too, and biting it in half.

'Hey,' Ross said. 'Iliana made that.'

Stevie looked up. Ross could almost see through the hair how his eyes unnarrowed. Then he did something really peculiar. He took the plate and, setting it beside the mug, proceeded to brush into his hand the granola that had collected around the pancakes. Ross expected some further act of derision, like Stevie flinging the granola off the roof. Instead he bowed and pressed his tongue to his palm, eyes closed, savouring what he had blatantly rejected a moment before.

Ross went back down the stairs, shaking his head. Ross the caterer would have sacked Stevie, but that was another life.

In the alley, he could hear Deb's son, Brent, talking to Bryce in the courtyard. 'What's your name then?'

'Birthday Cake.'

Coming through the gate, Ross saw Brent sitting with his ankles crossed on the chair across from him, shades on (the stupidest shades Ross had ever seen), arranging all his effects on the patio table: Discman, notebook, dog-eared copy of *Screenplays That Sell.* 'So, Birthday Cake, where do you come from?'

Bryce, on his toes, arms thrown over the back of the chair Brent's feet were on, chin balanced there, replied, 'Vancouver. I've got a lazy eye.'

'Have you? Well, why don't you tell it to go out and get a job?'

Bryce laughed with exaggerated gusto until Ross came up behind him and scratched the top of his head. 'You missed a great party yesterday.'

'Alas,' drawled Brent, 'I had a migraine.'

Ross went inside, taking Bryce with him, away from Brent's parasitical influence. This was a deeply impressionable period in his nephew's life. Too much exposure now to people like Brent Howland and Bryce might end up living with Bonnie for the rest of his life, hanging out in cafés, subsisting on — what? Grants.

Bonnie was in the kitchen, clearly having benefited from the extra sleep. She actually laughed when Ross rushed her and put her in their childhood chokehold. Elbowing him off, she said, 'Show me how to use the espresso maker.'

'She's already taken her first order,' said Iliana.

'That cute guy out front wants a latte.'

*   *   *

174

Now that Ross didn't have to drive his kitchens all over the Lower Mainland there was time in the day, natural lulls between breakfast and mid-morning coffee, between lunch and four o'clock, when he could do what he wanted. He either talked to people or messed around in the kitchen, following up on inspiration. 'Oh, no,' Deb would say when Ross came in and donned his apron, since it meant for her the inevitable trip back up the stepladder to make changes in her neat script to Ross's very mutable menu.

He found Iliana out on the patio taking her break in the sun. 'It's great having the kid here, isn't it?'

'Mmm,' she said. 'Can you ask her how long they're staying?'

Instantly, sweat prickled him. 'I thought you liked Bonnie.'

She frowned up at him from under the shade of her hand. 'I love Bonnie. I just want to know how long they're staying.'

'I'll find out. I've got a neat idea for a sandwich. Get Bonnie to cover for me.'

He headed for the Kitchen Kupboard. He should have taken the bike because he had to go to Overwaitea, too; loath now to double back, he continued on foot, taking much longer than he had intended. The lunch rush had started by the time he got back so it wasn't until the afternoon that he had the chance to start on his prototype.

The Rorschach toast had been his brainchild. He spilled the cookie cutters out of the bag on to the counter. For bread he chose sourdough, whole grain, and cranberry–pumpkin seed for that Neapolitan effect. First he prepared the tri-coloured layers, filling them contrastingly with cream cheese, strawberry jam and peanut butter. Then he cut the shapes out – moon, sun, star.

Bonnie was waiting to go home with Iliana, who always left at three then went for her run. 'Oh!' she exclaimed when Ross walked out with his heavenly clubhouse impaled on a Popsicle stick. Bryce, balancing on the rim of one of Iliana's wheels, reached up to take it from Ross and, biting into the moon, beamed.

'Deb! Can you come out here and write this up?'

The café closed at four, but it was several hours before Ross left. He boiled the potatoes for the next day's hash browns, skinned them and used the water for his stock. He liked to make the soups and heartier salads the day before to allow the flavours to co-mingle, his menu improvised from whatever Gary brought that morning. There were yellow tomatoes and yellow peppers so he decided on Golden Gazpacho. He made a second cold soup from baby beets, buttermilk and fresh ginger (Ginger Borscht he called it) and, since there was always call for a hot soup even in July, he also made one of lentils and peppers. For salads he concocted his popular curried potato, a faux tuna and a sesame noodle. When everything was ready, the dishwasher running, floors mopped, plants watered, all the chairs set back on their four feet, the French doors locked, he left through the courtyard, closing the gate behind him.

Going round to get his bike, Ross saw the dishes stacked on the bottom stair meaning Stevie had gone for the day. He slipped quickly up to the roof for a look. The second planter was finished. At this rate Stevie would be gone by the end of the week. Smiling at this prospect, he went over to look in the window of the empty apartment, feeling suddenly confident that Bonnie would decide to stay, that Iliana could be convinced that this would be a good thing.

He knew what was bothering Iliana. Ross was the one who had blamed their troubles on Bonnie in the first place. 'It's like I've got two wives and, in trying to please them both, I please neither. I don't know how the Mormons do it, frankly.' But it had turned out that his attachment to his first wife was stronger than he thought. He'd never really been apart from Bonnie for more than a few weeks and had not realized it would be like having a limb cut off. At the same time, he and Iliana had not exactly got their sex life back on track.

When he went down again, he saw that his bike was not under the stairs where he normally left it. Only the bags of topsoil were there. For a moment Ross just stood there at the foot of the stairs, staring as if he were seeing things, when in fact he was seeing nothing.

It took twenty minutes for him to walk home. Approaching the house, he saw Iliana and Bonnie in the yard and Bryce on the chair Iliana used on the road. Standing on the seat, Bryce spotted him first and waved. Only Iliana knew to be surprised he was on foot.

'I told you to lock it,' she said when Ross explained. 'Why won't you lock it?'

'Because I trust people.' This prompted a long, jaded laugh from his sister.

'What about insurance? Will the café insurance cover the bike?'

'Not if it wasn't locked,' Bonnie said.

Smiling, he summed up his take on what had happened. 'All is suffering, ladies.'

Bonnie threw her hands up. 'Tell us,' she said scornfully, 'something we don't know already.'

3

The day Ross's bike was stolen, Iliana came back from her run to find Bonnie sunning herself in a lawn chair in the yard. Instead of continuing the conversation they had had driving home, during which she had freely offered her opinion of the people she had met that, her first, day in the café, Bonnie asked if Iliana liked living on the island.

'I do.'

If Iliana had admitted this about living in hell, Bonnie would probably not have sounded as doubtful. 'Really?'

'You forget I'm not from the city.'

'So you're happier here?'

'I didn't say that,' Iliana told her.

She hadn't realized how dissatisfied she was until yesterday, when she took Bonnie and Bryce to see the hockey stick. Even if Bonnie had asked her outright (she didn't; she changed the subject), Iliana would not have done more than grudgingly admit to it. She would never have revealed the cause. A sister didn't want to know that about a brother. It would have been disrespectful to Ross. She even wondered if she had a right to dissatisfaction when things were so much better than before. With her bladder trained now, that infantilizing fear of wetting her pants in public was mostly a nightmare. She had a sense of purpose in a job she loved. Yet something *had* been taken from her and, when that happens, the first thing a person learns to do is live with less. She had learned to live sitting down, two feet below everyone else, limited by the places accessible to her, to live with inconvenience, and despite other people's attitudes towards her. She had learned, she realized yesterday, to accept affection as a substitute for passion.

'Why did you leave?'

'I wanted to go where nobody knew me. If we'd stayed people would always have been comparing my life now to my life before.'

'You've got an all right life,' Bonnie retorted.

Bonnie would never let anyone best her in misery, Iliana remembered, swelling with fondness, she reached out to touch her sister-in-law's hand. 'Thank you. Thank you for thinking that.'

'You weren't mad at me, too, were you?'

'No. Why?'

'Remember Thanksgiving when you came home from the hospital for the first time? I felt awful about that. Did I ask how you were doing? Did I show you any sympathy? No. I just went on and on about that . . . person. As if you were interested.'

'I was interested.'

'Oh, come on. I wouldn't blame you if you hated me at that moment.'

'But that's when I decided that I liked you.'

'You never said anything about the dress.'

'What dress?'

Lifting her sunglasses, she looked at Iliana. 'Your wedding dress. Don't you realize I stole your wedding dress? You had to stand up there in front of all those people in the blue one. I ruined your wedding.'

'But my wedding was the happiest day of my life!'

'The white dress was nicer,' Bonnie insisted.

'If I'd worn white how would anyone have known I was the bride?'

Bryce called then from the house where he'd woken from his nap. Bonnie leaped up to fetch him. 'I just wanted to be sure that you didn't leave because of me.'

Iliana started on her stretches, rolling her shoulders forward and back. A few minutes later Bonnie came back out with Bryce in tow, sippy cup clutched to his chest. Flopping down on to the lawn chair again, she told Iliana, 'Last year was just so horrible, I can hardly speak about it. I was on the verge of suicide every day.'

'Bonnie, you always say that.'

'It's true!'

'I wanna sit in the chair,' said Bryce.

Iliana went to the garage, switched chairs, and brought the one she used for running back out for Bryce. He climbed up

179

and settled in it, head thrown back, glugging drunkenly from the cup.

'I started this ritual thing,' Bonnie continued in a lowered voice. 'I'd set everything out like I really was going to do it.'

'Set what out?'

'Pills. It would have to be pills. You know how squeamish me and Ross are. We're Virgos. Blood would be out of the question. I'd set them out, really believing that I was going to take them. But I'd only take a sleeping pill and a Tylenol or two. When I woke in the morning and saw how close I'd come to dying – I never felt so glad to be alive.'

'Bonnie,' Iliana chided.

'It was the only thing that kept me going.'

'Ross!' Bryce clambered to a stand on the seat, flagging an arm at the sorry figure trudging in their direction. 'Ross!'

'How long are you staying for?' Iliana asked while she had the chance.

Ross put on a happy face for dinner, but Iliana would not meet his eye. Perhaps he thought she was angry about the bike. It was not until Bonnie and Bryce were tucked in and he finally joined her in bed that she told him what the matter was.

'I was going to tell you. She hasn't said yes.'

'You invited your sister to come and live with us without even consulting me?'

It was a whisper but it carried the payload of a scream.

'Not *with* us. In the apartment. I was showing it to her. We have this empty apartment and I shouldn't offer it to my own sister?'

'Ssh. She'll hear you. I thought we moved over here to get away from Bonnie.'

'We did, but look at her. What a wreck. It seemed the right thing to do.'

'Like how it seemed the right thing to invite Mike and Ham and Ed to the wedding we decided not to have?'

'Look how well that turned out.'

'I don't understand you, Ross. I really don't.'

'You want me to tell her not to?'

'Well, that would make me look pretty bad, wouldn't it?'

'What do you want me to do then?'

'How can you even ask me that?'

4

The door that led from the kitchen to the alley was open when Stevie Blake arrived. Ducking past it, he could hear voices and laughter inside. Ross's new bike was under the stairs, he saw as he climbed, leaning against the bags of dirt, with a blue and yellow trailer attached. He started with a smoke, afterwards stashing the butt in the apartment eave, then cutting the two-by-sixes.

Mid-morning Deb came up with coffee and a plate of French toast. 'Eat,' she told him, making herself comfortable on the edge of one of the planters. 'Sit down, why don't you? Use your knife and fork. Chew before you swallow.' Because Stevie didn't have a mother (he did, but she'd lived in Edmonton with that asshole for the last twelve years), Deb liked to step in when she could.

'I went in last week to play cards with Nana, did she tell you?'

'No,' said Stevie.

'She's quite the card sharp, eh?'

'That's why she moved there. More partners.'

'I said I'd go out and see how you're keeping the place up without her. Should I call first?'

Stevie ignored the hint.

'What are you going to do now?'

181

He licked the syrup off his wrist. 'When?'

Deb glanced around. 'You're finished, aren't you?'

Stevie shrugged.

'If you'd been a little more sociable, he'd probably have kept you on. He's got a hundred little projects on the go.'

'Who cares?'

'That's the spirit.' She placed her hands on her thighs and heaved herself up disgustedly. Before she went, she squeezed the back of his neck hard enough to make him hunch.

He puttered till two, cleaning up, loading the scrap lumber into the truck, even taking a nap. Then he went to the edge of the roof and sat with his feet dangling, getting a monkey's view of the patio. He knew she'd be in the kitchen because this was when she got the bread started for the next day. Ross, as he watered the plants, was chatting up a couple of women sharing a table. (How accurate would his aim be, Stevie wondered, if he spat from here?) The boy was there, too, parking toy cars in an intricate pattern. Someone wandered out and Stevie saw yellow daubs like bird shit in her hair. The second he realized it was Deb, he swung his legs back up and headed for the stairs.

The sister was still unaccounted for, but when Stevie looked in the kitchen, he saw Iliana alone, her back to him as she worked at the low counter. Her hair was in its usual ponytail and she wore a Real Food apron. (They sold these aprons, and T-shirts, too; all over town Stevie spotted assholes who'd paid $24.99 plus tax to be a human advertisement.) The muscles in her arms and back flexed as she bowed over the counter. It was probably pushing the chair that had made her so strong.

When her watch beeped, she stopped to lift herself. She seemed to sense then that she was not alone because she looked over her shoulder. At once her expression softened. 'You scared me,' she said. The smile she gave him then would have more than sufficed, but there was this, too: that he'd startled her by accident, but seeing it was just him, Stevie, had reassured her. Not even in his dreams would he have thought to count himself among the people she would be glad to see.

'Go on through,' she told him.

Stevie stayed where he was, pretending to look out into the alley but really watching her from the corner of his eye. There were four distinct parts to the action she was performing: a slow lean into the dough, the half-turn she gave it before straightening, the casting of a handful of flour, then the fold. He could separate these parts in his eye, but in actuality they blended one into the other.

She said, 'Ross is on the patio.'

'I'll wait.'

She stopped, her eyes on him, sussing for what the matter was. She didn't guess it, he could tell. 'Are you hungry?'

'No.'

'Want a drink?'

He shook his head.

'Have a seat then.'

Refusing the chair she pointed to, he leaned against the door-frame, watching her openly now. The ease with which she got around still amazed him. She seemed more graceful than a walking person. On a shelf under the higher counter there was a large blue and white striped bowl, which she lifted into her lap.

'How's it going up there?' she asked.

'I'm finished.'

'Stevie's finished,' she said and Stevie looked up and saw Ross smiling through the short-order window.

'Great,' he said. 'Let's take a look.'

Stevie went without waiting for Ross. A few minutes later Ross came up and proceeded to make a big deal out of Stevie's work, probably thinking Stevie was eating up his praise. Stevie was not.

183

Now he just wanted his money so he could fuck off. But there was something strange about the way Ross was talking to him, as if he were addressing someone standing behind Stevie, and when Ross asked what he was up to next Stevie concluded that Ross was, in fact, stalling. He shielded his eyes and tried to meet Ross's, which was when he realized that he could just go ahead and look at him because Ross wasn't looking back.

Kicking at the pea gravel, Ross asked, 'What about tomorrow? Any plans?'

'Why?'

'It's grunt work. Filling the planters. I don't want to offend you.'

'When are you going to pay me for the planters?' Stevie asked outright.

'Right now. I'll pay you from the register.'

He followed Ross back down the stairs. At the bottom, Ross pointed out the bags of topsoil stacked against the wall as if the place were being sandbagged against the threat of flood. Evidently he didn't think it necessary to seal the planters or provide any drainage. 'You can move the bike,' he said. 'I got a new one. Did you see it?'

'You showed me, like, yesterday.'

It made Stevie nervous to be offered the chance to return. Though he lived here and could have come to the café any time, he never would have. You couldn't have paid him to go in and order one of those asshole sandwiches. But with Ross's proposition a sickening feeling came over him that, until he actually did speak to her, Ross would just keep getting him to come back.

Afterwards, he drove to the Overwaitea to do Nana's shopping. Six weeks ago she'd moved to an old folks' home, the retirement wing of the complex where she was still responsible for her own cooking. For the convenience, she preferred frozen meals in microwavable packaging. He bought seven of them and biscuits, apples, instant coffee, tonic water. At the checkout, he selected the two tabloid papers that she liked out of the rack and asked for her brand in a carton and her lottery tickets, paying out of the wad of bills in his front pocket.

In the mall, he stopped at a food kiosk to buy a Coke. Directly across was a clothing store with a sale rack outside that a phalanx of teenage girls had surrounded. One looked right at Stevie, then whispered something to her friend. Stevie was not interested; he was way beyond such jailbait now. After a lot of phony giggling and unsubtle glances, they tired of him and moved off in a pack except for a girl who seemed genuinely interested in buying something. 'Sue!' they called to her.

Suey, Stevie thought. *Suey, suey.*

The first thing Nana did after he got her from the games room (breaking up a card game as it happened, to the obvious annoyance of the greybeards at the table with her) was ask for her lottery tickets. These she lined up on the table in her room and scratched one by one with a coin from the jar of change that she kept on the table. 'A double sawbuck!' she called to Stevie who was unloading the groceries. Chuckling, she went on scratching gleefully. There were six tickets but only the first was a winner. The others she pushed aside with a contemptuous snort. She struggled to a stand and came over to kiss Stevie, always keeping one hand on the furniture for support.

'How much was it?'

'Never mind.'

'How much?'

'I got paid.'

'Paid for what?' she asked hoarsely.

'I told you. I did some building for that guy.'

'What guy?'

'At the café where Deb works now.'

'Well, that's good news. Then you take this.' She slipped the lottery ticket into his shirt pocket. He tried to give it back. They struggled and Nana, with her superior will, triumphed.

Before supper they usually played a few hands of cards over drinks, then Stevie nuked the stuff and they ate it. Afterwards Stevie would watch TV while Nana read her papers and exclaimed over all the scandals. When he joined her at the table with a beer for himself and her G&T, she was fitting her cigarette into the holder.

'Have they figured out you're smoking in here yet?' The first thing Stevie had done when she moved in was disable the smoke detector.

'Probably, but what are they going to do about it? Evict me?'

He took out his rolling papers. 'Could they?'

'Let them try.'

'You can always come back home.'

She patted his hand, then it was all business, his card dealt, she waiting for him to look at it.

Eight of hearts. He lit his cigarette, then dug around in the change jar for a quarter.

'That much?' asked Nana, dealing herself.

'What are you playing for in the games room?'

'Canadian Tire money.' She said this with her teeth clamped round the cigarette holder, squinting through the smoke to scrutinize her card. By the tragedy mask of her face, Stevie guessed she was bluffing and, sure enough, she put down fifty cents. Stevie matched her out of the jar. She turned him over a seven.

'Where's Deb working again?'

'I told you. At that café. Same place I've been at.'

'Does she like it?'

'Wasn't she here? She told me she was here last week.'

'That's right. She said she liked it a lot. She said the coffee's good. Another?'

'It's not so great.'

'You're hard to please, I know. I don't have your standards. Oh, look!' She turned up her card. 'A jack.' She dealt herself a three, then a lucky seven.

'As if I have standards,' muttered Stevie, laying bare his eight.

'You do. What's the matter with the place?'

'I didn't say anything was the matter with it. You, like, asked about the coffee, didn't you?'

'I think it was very nice of that man to call you up out of the blue like that and offer you a job.'

He raked the cards in. 'Who told you that?'

'Deb.'

'You didn't even remember she was here. You didn't even remember I was working and you remember that?'

'How's he paying you?'

'Cash.'

'Government don't know then.' She winked.

'He's an asshole.'

'Why is that?'

The first time Stevie saw Iliana was the day he came to talk to Ross. They were sitting at one of the tables in the courtyard, Ross showing him the sketch he'd made on a scrap of paper. He was telling Stevie that he liked to use fresh herbs wherever possible. Everything they served in the café was fresh and organically grown. Had he ever eaten there? When Stevie shook his head, Ross said he hadn't thought so. He said he would have remembered Stevie. That got Stevie's back up. What the hell did he mean? Was he so weird-looking or something that Ross would never have forgotten him? It wouldn't have been the first time Stevie had blown off a job. (He was aware of a reputation sticking to him over this very

187

matter.) It was what he had been just about to do when he looked up and saw a woman in a wheelchair on the other side of the French doors. She had a big box in her lap and was trying to move the chair backwards and open the door at the same time. Stevie got up.

'Don't help her,' Ross told him. 'Sit down.'

Stevie was too stunned to do anything but that. Ross, meanwhile, jawed on about his herbs and the four rectangular cedar boxes even a monkey could hammer together, as if this woman weren't a stone's toss behind him, struggling for her dignity. Stevie sat there shifting in the seat, feeling as if he was the one stuck and outraged and furious, until he couldn't stand it any longer.

Seeing him on the other side of the door, Iliana backed up so he could swing it open. 'Thanks,' she sang as she wheeled through.

It was her smile that got him, flashbulb bright. He had not expected her to be happy.

He dealt Nana her card. 'He's a hypocrite. Hugging everybody, making like he's your buddy. What he's really making is a killing. Six bucks almost for breakfast and then you have to tip because he's, like, your best friend? Man, breakfast's three ninety-nine at the Sunshine.'

Nana put down a nickel. Stevie doubled her.

'And at the Sunshine you get sausages or bacon or ham.' He turned her over a six of diamonds. 'Another?'

She nodded. He gave her a two. She wanted another.

'Deb loves him, I bet. They all think he's a saint or something just because his wife's in a wheelchair.'

'What's the matter with his wife?'

'She's in a wheelchair.' Stevie began turning cards up for himself, one, two, three, until he purposely went over. 'Twenty-four.'

'What happened to her?'

'I don't know. She can't walk.'

'He married a crippled girl? I think that's very nice. '

'Don't say crippled.'

'Why not?'

'It's like saying nigger.'

'And she's a coloured girl, too? Well, I think that's very nice.'

The tiny room was so full of smoke now, it reminded him of Vegas where Nana had taken him three times. He crushed out his cigarette and leaned back in his chair while Nana commenced her pottering shuffle. Glancing down, he saw his whole leg vibrating with the foot he was unconsciously jiggling. He drew himself up straight, both feet flat on the floor, hands in his lap.

Are you hungry? Iliana had asked him. *Are you hungry?*

Wasn't it obvious?

Nana fanned the two halves of the deck with her swollen thumbs and laboriously nudged them into union. 'Stevie, honey,' she said, as if she could see right through the table. 'Don't touch yourself like that. It isn't nice.'

5

A truck stopped in the alley. She heard an extended riff of pings and rattles as soon as the engine cut out. A second later, a door slammed. It was six ten on a Saturday morning when no one of honourable intention would be out of bed. The alley door was ajar to let the heat out of the kitchen. Iliana started towards it, intending to close and bolt it, when footsteps sounded on the wooden steps. Backing away, she kept her eyes fixed on the opening. A face appeared. She saw a squint, a canopy of dark hair, but only for a second.

Puzzled, she went over to the door and looked out. By the truck now, leaning against it, hands thrust in pockets, shoulders of his denim jacket lifted, he appeared to be trying to fold himself laterally. Hair obscured his face. She was reminded of a very young child covering his eyes to make himself invisible.

'Stevie?'

When he looked up, she had to smile. It had nothing to do with his oddly expectant expression, but with where each of them happened to be situated at that moment, Iliana in the doorway three steps up, Stevie below by his truck. In the last two years she couldn't recall looking down on anyone but Bryce.

'What are you doing here? I thought you'd finished.'

'Hauling the dirt up for the planters.'

'Oh. Ross didn't tell me.'

Stevie toed the ground, saying nothing.

'I just took some bread out of the oven. Have a piece before you start.' As he lurched for the steps, Iliana almost laughed, thinking of Ross at the start of the week griping over Stevie's supposed recalcitrance.

At the counter, she tipped a loaf on its side and sawed the heel off. Steam escaped from the soft core. She cut a piece and held it out.

'It's, like, warm,' he said, bringing it to his face and inhaling. Tearing a piece of crust off with his teeth, he used his fingers to push it in his mouth. 'It doesn't even taste like bread.'

'What do you mean?'

'Like store bread.'

'No.' She watched as he devoured it. He did not seem so much uncouth (he kept his mouth closed and wiped his fingers on his jeans) as poorly trained. 'Another? Take it up with you.'

He stared at the bread she held out. 'I want to tell you something. Can I?'

'Of course.'

'Don't, like, take it the wrong way.'

'What?'

'I like you.'

She laughed. 'Thanks.'

'I mean, I'd like to fuck you. That's all. Thanks for the bread.'
He turned and pounded down the steps.

To say that she was stunned, that she was blushing – this would
be true. It was true that what he said upset her, but not because it
offended her. The last two years had been a period of adjustment,
of learning what she could and could not expect of herself and her
life. Now, in one crude sentence, this boy had uncomposed her.

He had done it with the F-word.

Without the rising shrill of the saw and the complement of the
hammer, she should not have even been aware of Stevie's presence,
but as she went about her work she was, acutely. She kept looking
over her shoulder. Creepy, in hindsight, the way he had been
watching her yesterday without her realizing it. She tried to think
when else she'd seen him during the week. Last Saturday, when
Ross was talking to him in the courtyard, he'd opened the door
for her. On Monday, Deb had introduced them, but he hadn't
met her eye. She hadn't given him a second thought, but now
she shuddered. Delinquency was written all over him. Couldn't
Ross see that?

She pummelled the dough, slammed the oven.

Deb asked from the grill, 'Is there a reason the door is closed?'

'Open it if you want.'

With her foot, Deb manoeuvred into place the stone that held
the door against the wall, and stepped out to cool off. 'That looks
like Stevie Blake's truck.'

'It is.'

'What's he doing here?'

'Ross is getting him to fill the planters.'

Deb turned and looked at her. 'That's big of him.'

'Why?'

'I didn't think Stevie made a good impression.'

Though she had not at any time then or now suspected Stevie, Iliana said, 'Ross's bike was stolen on Tuesday. It was an expensive bike and the insurance didn't cover it. He had to buy a new one. Did he tell you?'

'You think it was Stevie?' Deb asked.

Hearing the disappointment in her tone, Iliana was quick to reply. 'I didn't say that. I'm just wondering if he's ever been in trouble.'

'Oh, lots of it, but not that kind.'

Saturdays got so busy Iliana usually had to change her apron and go up front to help. She took the orders. Ross brought them, cleared the tables, worked the till. Bonnie had inconveniently chosen this day to beg off. Iliana liked the way the bustle brought her out of the kitchen for a change. Shuttling back and forth from table to table to short-order window, she was able to put what had happened into perspective. After today, Stevie would be gone and she wouldn't think of him again.

Next in line was a coven of female estate agents from the office across the street. Standing in the doorway, they looked around, ostensibly for a place to sit but really, Iliana suspected, for Ross. Irony of ironies: he actually *looked* sexy now that he'd lost all that weight. 'Here,' she called, waving them over to a table that was just being vacated.

'How are you, Iliana?' asked Beth Ann, who had sold them both the café and the house.

'Great. Ross will clear your table in a sec.'

Out on the patio, she took another order. 'What's ABC again?' the man asked.

'Orange, carrot, brewer's yeast.'

'And Ginger Snap?'

'Apple and ginger.'

Back inside, she saw Ross holding the estate agents in his thrall just by taking away the ketchup-smeared plates and smiling at them. 'Coffee,' she mouthed to him as she passed, holding up two fingers and thumbing in the direction of the patio.

In the kitchen, working the juicer, she looked at Deb's broad back with its various soft lumps. 'I didn't think it was Stevie,' she felt obliged to say again.

Deb raised a shoulder and let it fall. 'How's the line out there?'

'I'll check.'

'Where's Bonnie?'

'Where's Bonnie?' Iliana laughed. 'Deb, she's with your son.'

Deb, wiping the sweat off her brow, frowned.

The couple on the patio had their coffee by the time she returned with the man's juice. He sipped. 'Cool!'

She went to check the queue, telling the two women who were next up, 'It shouldn't be too long.' Something caught her eye as she turned and, without thinking, she looked up. Feet dangling over the roof's edge, wearing neither shoes nor shirt, he was literally half naked on his audacious perch. He did not avert his gaze when their eyes met. She considered trying to stare him down, but it was already obvious who had more nerve. Instead, to show him she had been unaffected by his flattery (if that was what he thought it was), she deliberately did not move out of the range of his vision, but went over to a planter and began deadheading the flowers.

Iliana's run was not a run, of course, but a 'run'. She changed her clothes, changed her chair, stretched, then worked her hands into cyclist's gloves. The first part was on residential streets, past older bungalows, then through the Seventies subdivision, to the road that ran a ring round the reserve, at points entering it. When she first adopted this route she was nervous about trespassing. The few houses she passed did not appear welcoming, or even fully constructed; siding stopped halfway up walls and plastic paned many of the windows. Signs of habitation were there (a chesterfield in a grassless yard, dismantled toys) but for a long time nobody seemed to be at home. It was at least a week before she began to see people. By then she realized that they, too, had probably grown less nervous of her. Soon they were hailing her, an interloper, from open doorways, or honking as they passed in cars. There was a man who was often at work on a truck in his yard and he would lift his head out of the engine, shake it, and call out that she was crazy. Hilly and winding, the road at points rough, this was her preferred route because it made a convenient loop the exact length of her stamina.

'Hi!' Bonnie called from the lawn when Iliana arrived back at the house. Bikini-clad today, she rose to her knees and waggled a tube of suntan lotion. 'Can you put some of this on my back?'

Iliana came over, arms and shoulders aching, hands burning through the gloves. She used her teeth to get them off and squirted a letter of lotion into her palm to smear across Bonnie's hot, freckled shoulders.

'You're panting,' Bonnie told her, disapproving.

'How was your day?'

'Brent's gay, isn't he?'

'You're asking *me*?'

Bonnie laughed.

Iliana said, 'If you're wondering if he's interested in you, all I can say is I haven't seen him talking much to anyone else.' She did not tell Bonnie about the many, many hours she'd had to observe Brent in non-action in order to come to this tedious conclusion. She passed the lotion back.

'Thanks.' Half smiling, Bonnie flopped down again. Her hand sneaked round her back, felt for and tugged open the tie. Both arms came up to frame her head, her cheek pressed to the towel. In full view of the street (two streets; it was a corner lot) wearing what was essentially a pair of panties, she relaxed indolently into the grass.

Iliana went into the house to run a bath, astounded by the way her sister-in-law spread her wares out on the lawn. Watching her in the café, she'd had the same reaction. Perfectly timing her appearance at Brent's table, Bonnie would stay to chat him up, intermittently deploying from her arsenal of touches the pokes and little slaps that signified her interest. Yesterday, sauntering past him, she'd flicked his earlobe with a spoon. Where had she learned to do that? At Catholic school? In her short skirts and high-heel sandals, with her painted lips, Bonnie had brought with her the idea of sex and confused everything.

The phone rang as Iliana was pulling off her sweat-dampened T-shirt. She answered to a man's voice. 'You're back.'

Instantly she pictured him on the roof watching and, flushing, covered up her front. 'Why are you calling?'

'To tell you how I'm feeling.'

She could not believe how suddenly cocky he sounded, how full of himself. If allowing him to look at her that morning had so emboldened him, she was sorry she had done it. (Why *had* she done it?) 'You already told me.'

There was a pause, then he asked down the now-refrigerated line, 'Is this Bonnie?'

'Oh. Just a second.'

She put the phone down, too flustered to take it with her, and went to call Bonnie, who flew into the house with a hand neatly cupping each breast, the bikini top swinging around her neck like a harness she'd broken free of. Iliana went immediately to the bathroom to turn off the water and cringe in private. 'I'm glad to hear it,' she heard Bonnie say. 'Yeah, yeah, I'll start reading it tonight.

195

'That was Brent,' she said when Iliana came back to finish undressing. 'He thought he was getting a cold, but now he doesn't think so.' Turning, she pranced back out into the sun.

Iliana transferred to the bed and began working her way out of her shorts and panties, but as soon as that was accomplished found that she did not feel like moving again. The island summer reminded her of summers in the Fraser Valley in that it actually got hot. From outside, the mesmerizing drone of a lawnmower. There was a fly, too, trapped between the window and the screen, hypnotizing her with its protest song. Hands resting on her abdomen she felt the stickiness of her skin on both her hands, though not the whole of her hands on her abdomen. After almost two years, she still had not accustomed herself completely to this.

When she was a girl her mother used to tell her that she must never, ever touch herself. Taking her words literally, Iliana had for years carried her hands out from her sides as if she were lugging around two invisible suitcases. In the bath, she used a washcloth so that her hand would not come into contact with her skin. Only later, when she'd got her period and her older sister was enlisted to explain sex to her, did she realize what the prohibition had actually meant. By then she'd been thirteen.

Reaching down, she felt the soft inside of her thighs. Her fingers pushed back the hair and baroque folds, but it was as if she were fondling some other woman. But if she touched her breasts, she felt more than the double pleasure of skin-on-skin. The nipples responded to the lightest sensation. She brushed them with her open palms; they turned to pebbles.

On the patio, the papery clusters of geranium, the sticky closed parasols of petunia, had released their sharp scent as she pinched off each spent bloom. She had smelled her fingers, conscious of him watching her lift her hand to her face. His gaze moving over her hair, straying at her ear, dipping inside it and, when she tilted her head back, following the contours of her throat. She had blushed as much with pleasure as with shame. There were people all around, yet he was doing this to her.

6

Almost two years had passed since the accident and, while Iliana claimed to have recovered from it, Ross hadn't. Not that he was living in hope of a cure for Iliana, or living in the past before the accident; to the contrary, he tried as much as possible to stay in the present moment, which is, after all, where life happens.

Ross loved Iliana, loved so much about her. She was the same warm person, the hearth of their home, and more: a person of resilience and fortitude. He thought her worthy of a statue. That he might lose her terrified him, and so he clung white-knuckled to his adoration. Yet there was aversion, too. In the emotional turmoil after the accident, he had not recognized this. His contradictory feelings had taken so long to come to the surface because he did not want to admit to them. He was not, for example (it pained him even to think it), particularly drawn to the sight of Iliana's legs. She had his mother's legs, it seemed to him now. If it had only been that – the terrible thinness, the matronly way they pressed together – he might have overcome the shock of the before-and-after contrast. But there was also the fact of the catheter (he didn't actually have to see it any more), and that every second evening (religiously) she came to him asking, 'Will you need the bathroom in the next little while?' It took him over a year to realize what she was really saying was, 'Please, don't interrupt.' Then she would be in there for over an hour, following her bowel programme. (Once he had opened the cupboard under the basin and seen *rubber gloves!*)

Guilt. Self-loathing. Shame. These were as unhelpful as his repugnance. They only made things worse. It was because of Ross that Iliana had the skinny pins of a sixty-one year old, because of Ross that she couldn't feel anything below the waist. What was he supposed to do? Get it off while she lay there watching? And if he admitted any of this to her – how hurtful! He couldn't bear to hurt her any more than he already had. Yet he *was* hurting her. Every night that he climbed into bed beside her and did not love her was a twist of the knife. It was worse than the accident, for both of them. The accident had been just that, an accident, but what excuse could he give her now?

In his twelve years in the film catering business, Ross had thrown himself annually into some sort of project to pass the time during the slack winter months: chicken fingers, his faux food museum, the nursing bra for men. Yet never had he embarked on anything so daunting as trying to change the way he thought. Identifying with his thoughts was to condemn himself. (What kind of man was he that he was so bothered by bodily functions? Was his love so flimsy, were his feelings so shallow? Was he really such a *prick*?) Yet denying them, refusing to think them, was as good as useless; an aversion suppressed redoubled. What he was trying to do now, instead, was sit back and allow these troubling thoughts in without judging, or identifying with, or reacting to them. These thoughts could be the very object of his meditation. Like everything else they were in a constant state of flux, arising and falling away continually. The sooner he disengaged and accepted them for what they were – impermanent – the sooner he would be free.

The afternoon Stevie Blake stole his bike, Ross had descended the stairs from the roof and stood gaping at the negative space that once surrounded and cushioned the physical reality of his bicycle, but had now moved in to replace it. He barely managed to suppress a howl of indignation. Was he not a man? he had wanted to cry. Did he not deserve a set of wheels? The ungrieved loss of Miss Stockholm flooded back. Where was she now? Compacted, melted down, reincarnated – but as *what*? 'That little fucker!' Ross had roared.

He had started for home on foot, head down, making fists, babbling to himself. Good people crossing his path had to leap out of the way. 'Hiya, Ross,' he sort of heard, but had not replied to. Reaching the corner he paused, still completely swept up in his mindless fury. Then that simple pre-school injunction, innately followed, forced consciousness upon him. Looking left: anger. Looking right: anger. When he put his foot out to cross, the coils suddenly fell loose and he stepped right out of them.

He started to laugh. He had, he realized, an aversion to Stevie Blake. Why wouldn't he? Stevie was insolent, and not only that, despite Ross's giving him the benefit of the doubt, he had turned out to be a thief as well. Ross considered himself easy-going and affable, someone who brought out the best in other people, but in Stevie's case he hadn't; he'd brought out the worst.

Yet these feelings Stevie provoked might prove useful to work with. Stevie could provide him the opportunity to practise tolerating aversion. Ross might practise on Stevie, so to speak. So he offered Stevie another day of work and towards the end of that day, Saturday, went mindfully up the stairs, placing a hand carefully on the railing, feeling the heat hiding in the rough grain of the wood. The movement created space under his arm, releasing the sweat that had been trapped there; it ran in a tickling rivulet down his side. (For over a year he'd been searching in vain for an effective natural deodorant, but none had proved a match for the old Ross spoor, that bite on the nose.) He bent his left knee, set his sandalled foot down on the first stair, shifted his weight, pushed off. Through the space between each riser, he saw his new bike (another Giant, but jujube green) and the blue and yellow trailer he'd bought for

Bryce at the same time. He could hear the voices of the people on the patio, smell the faintest trace of cigarette smoke, as well as food odours and his own persistent tang. Anchoring his attention like this on the climbing, he hardly noticed when he reached the top.

'Fuck,' Stevie muttered, hastily flicking the cigarette.

He had been sitting at the roof's edge without his shirt on. Ross watched him scramble to stand, then back away in what seemed like fear. Barefoot, he hobbled across the gravel and, when he could go no farther, pushed the hair out of his eyes. He smiled, but it seemed so out-of-character, so red-handed, that Ross wondered if Stevie knew that Ross knew about the bike. But if that were the case, why would he have agreed to come back and fill the planters? He was probably just sorry to be caught smoking a second time.

Pretending not to notice the cigarette (what did it matter?), Ross went over to the roof's edge and looked down. On the patio below, Iliana was deadheading flowers into her lap. He went and sat on the side of one of the planters, crossing his right leg over the left, interlacing his fingers and cupping his bare knee, concentrating on each small action as he performed it, noticing how detached it made him feel. Each of the planters was filled now with soil, the bags flattened, stacked and weighted with Stevie's shoes. He gestured to the opposite planter. 'Have a seat.'

Stevie ignored the invitation. *Rude*, thought Ross, *good*. Unfazed, he asked, 'Were you born here?'

Suspicion inflected Stevie's voice. 'Why do you want to know?'

Suspicious. Fine. 'I just wondered. My sister and nephew are visiting. It seems like a good place to raise a kid. Have you lived here all your life?'

He hunched one shoulder and rubbed his jaw against it. 'I lived in Edmonton one time for about six months.'

Sullen. Excellent. 'Which did you like better?'

Stevie shrugged.

Ross was not really trying to have a conversation with Stevie, merely drawing out the interaction and investigating his own responses, so he might stay open in Stevie's presence no matter how uncomfortable it made him. So far, so good, but he didn't want to push it. He stood. 'I guess I'm keeping you. You've probably got other things to do.'

Stevie eyed Ross through slits. Cautiously, almost crabwise, he edged towards where his shirt was balled up beside the plastic bags.

'Do you get a lot of carpentry work?'

'Why are you, like, asking me all these questions?'

Defensive. Good again. Ross was curious to know whether Stevie stole regularly, and, if so, was it out of necessity or spite? 'I'm just wondering. You know, in case something else comes up.'

Accompanying Stevie downstairs, Ross paid him out of the till and wished him luck, even offered to tape his card on to the back of the cash register for people to see. 'I don't have a card,' Stevie told him.

Contemptuous. Bonus. 'If I hear of any jobs, I'll let you know.'

Stevie stalked out. After he had gone, Ross hooked a finger on the neck of his T-shirt and bowed his head to sniff inside this tent-door opening. As far as he could tell, he smelled no worse for the encounter.

7

Bonnie had come with a week's worth of clothes, but soon the week was over and every sensible permutation of these garments had been exhausted. Apart from doing laundry, which did not address the real problem (appearing to others as a woman of scant wardrobe), one solution was to buy a few new things with all the tip money she had accumulated. They tipped surprisingly well here. 'Because they think you're a widow,' Brent had told her. 'You wear a lot of black. You have a kid. What else could it mean?'

She took Bryce to the refrigerated mall, dragged him up and down, shivering and appalled. There was a dollar emporium, a plus-size boutique, numerous cheap chain stores full of last year's offerings, stores that had 'shack' or 'hut' or 'barn' in their name, as if to rusticate the only remotely urban experience the town had to offer. There wasn't even a Bay. Already she was accustomed to the Real Food clientele, many of them health food aficionados, neo-hippies and refugees from city life who missed it more than they admitted. Here she found a wider, ruder demographic, and hordes of feral children.

Bryce begged to go into The Pet Barn to look at some kittens with runny eyes. The adolescent clerk, cheeks pebbly with acne, was mean enough to let him hold one. Afterwards, Bonnie had to sit down on a bench because she thought she was going to faint. During the long hot walk back to Ross and Iliana's, Bryce kept needling her. 'Why can't I have that kitten?'

'That kitten has a disease, that's why.'

'Why does it have a disease?'

'Because it's been in that mall too long.'

The real solution to her wardrobe problem, of course, was to go home and get her stuff. She had no choice. The year and a half of waiting in vain for Ross to come back had been the worst time of her life. Nevertheless, she found herself keeping up the charade of indecision, hoping that something might happen that would make the move seem less of a last resort.

Ross, instead of huckstering, had switched to subtler methods of persuasion. She was amused he didn't realize she was only stalling. He used the fact of himself, Ross, her beloved twin, without whom, truth be told, she felt like only half a person. His arm round her, he would pull her close until his armpit dampened her shoulder and she'd push him off with a disgusted squeal. In the café, he liked to come up when she was waiting on a table and, seizing her from behind to administer one of his paralysing sixty-second back rubs, say to his customers, 'This is my sister. Have you met my sister yet?' usually to the same table more than once, making a joke and a show of his affection at the same time. But Ross misjudged. A few days in his wearyingly charismatic company was enough to erase from her memory how much she'd missed him during the time they'd been apart.

What did please her was that he was tolerant of Brent in the café. It also surprised her for, no matter what Ross chose to call himself (cook, caterer, café owner), she knew him to be a businessman before all else. He talked a lot about food, about organics and the vegetarian lifestyle, but it was really the food industry he loved, otherwise he would open a soup kitchen, Bonnie thought. Brent did not tip. She supposed his mother had a running tab, because when she gave him his bill he told her Ma Pancake would take care of it. But even if Deb did pay for what he ordered, Brent was still bad for business, staying on through the lunch rush at the prime patio table he had staked out for himself, flagrantly ignoring the breadline forming on the sidewalk outside.

'Do you want me to tell Brent to go?' she asked Ross.

'Why? Is he bothering you?'

Not for a second did she think that this saintly display of patience, unprofitable to Ross and unjust to the people waiting, had anything to do with Ross's purported Buddhism. As usual, Ross had divined her unconscious motivation before she herself had. It would take more than brotherly love to justify her relocation, not just to the sticks, to the Stick.

Brent had been the first person Bonnie served at the café. 'So,

Bonnie Alexander,' he had said as she set his bowl of coffee on the patio table, 'what does a guy have to do around here to get a sandwich named after him?'

She took him in – blond, tanned, sunglasses with pink, reflective lenses the size of two dollar coins. 'Be related, I guess.'

'Gary Fichter's not related.'

'I don't know, then. You have to ask Ross for his criteria.'

'Deb Howland has a sandwich named after her. I'm related to Deb Howland.'

'You're a shoo-in, then.'

Full-throatedly, he laughed. 'Hey, a little birdie told me you live in Vancouver. Where?'

'The West End.'

'So did I.'

'You're kidding. Wild.'

A few days later, walking over to Brent's with Bryce, she realized she'd already passed by the house he lived in with Deb. It was in the older part Ross had led her through when she first got to town. The house was a dark green bungalow with painted figures cut out of plywood stuck around the sphagnum lawn. There was the standard back view of the bent over lady gardener (a self-portrait?) and a mother duck with four yellow ducklings in tow. Bryce declared his admiration for these decorations and for the 'Welcome' heart hanging on the door.

'Who have we here?' Brent asked, opening the door. 'Could it be Birthday Cake?'

'Sorry. I couldn't leave him at the café. It's their busiest day.'

'Did you try the orphanage?'

She goaded Bryce over the threshold, but Brent blocked his way. 'There's a park at the end of the street. Why don't you go play there?'

'He's only three and a half,' Bonnie said.

Bryce had already slipped past Brent and was trotting across the tiny, busy room. Well practised at scanning for potential hazards, Bonnie noted in one horror-filled glance the crystal menagerie displayed on a mirrored tray on the coffee table, laptop computer alongside it, the shelves crammed with probably irreplaceable and therefore irresistible china knickknacks. 'No!' she cried as Bryce lifted down a figurine to fondle with his dimpled, clumsy hands.

'He's only allowed to stay,' said Brent, 'if he promises to break something.' Pointing her to the kitchen, he headed for the couch himself. 'I can hardly stand. I feel decidedly in the grip of something. The coffee's in the freezer.'

The way Bonnie thought of Deb was forever changed now that she'd been inside her house. Instead of the he-woman Deb had seemed, she turned out to be the girly type. While Bonnie had been picturing her hunting moose and blackening her hands deep in car engines, she had really been doing crafts. Exhibit A: on the wall next to the fridge in the kitchen, a wreath made of shellacked bread dough stuck all over with dried wheat. Exhibit B: above the sink, a grandma and grandpa, desiccated apples for heads, in miniature rocking chairs on the windowsill.

'A summer cold's the worst,' she called to Brent in the other room.

'It might not be a cold. It might be the décor. Every time I come back here I am overcome with this generalized malaise. I should get a place of my own.'

Bonnie came back with the coffee. Brent's recumbent posture, his body stretched Ophelia-like on the pansied upholstery, forearm draped over his eyes, the other arm hanging limp over the side of the couch, knuckles grazing the blue broadloom, suggested a rapid demise. '*Are* you staying?' she asked.

'Until I finish the script. Who else am I going to live off in the meantime?'

'Then how can you afford a place?'

'I mean an office. A room, a ditch, anything. I've been doing most of my work in the café. This son of yours is shameless. Do you know what he's been doing? Tell her, Birthday Cake.'

'Kissing,' said Bryce.

Bonnie made room on the coffee table by removing the miraculously intact crystal menagerie to the top of the television.

'He's going round kissing all Ma's china dolls. Does he take after his mother or his father with these osculatory predilections?'

Bonnie brought a spoon down playfully on Brent's arm, then dropped it in his coffee before settling in the armchair across from him.

'You're not answering my question,' he teased and Bonnie could not tell if he was flirting in earnest or just for the fun of it.

'Tell me about the script,' she said.

He grew vehement. 'Oh, I want it to be scathing. I want there to be a lot of people sitting in that theatre four years from now—'

'Four years! Is that how long it takes?'

'Four years is nothing! Four years is because I have connections.'

'Ross worked in films.'

'I know, I know. He never fails to mention it. By connections I don't mean a caterer, believe me. I'm talking LA. Anyway, there are going to be a lot of people on opening night squirming as they recognize themselves.'

'What's it about?'

'That's what we're going to find out now that my trusty amanuensis has shown up.' Easing out of recline, he blew his nose.

'Honk,' said Bryce from across the room.

'Oh, ha ha.'

When he opened the computer, Bryce was suddenly right there, reaching out and turning it on before Bonnie could snatch his hand away. 'Don't you touch that!' she scolded.

'I hate that,' said Brent. 'I hate that a three year old can work a computer better than I can.'

Bonnie was not at all deluded about Brent Howland. She knew Brent wasn't perfect, that he only looked it. His faults – obsession, compulsion, narcissism (to start with) – she had recognized and sympathized with at once, just as a spontaneous bond may form between two strangers who by chance discover they have a disease in common. He was younger than she was, too, she could tell by the skin around his eyes, how it still lacked radial creases, decorations earned only by surviving into a fourth decade. More of a problem was that he clearly did not like children, but who was she to fault him for that when Bryce was the only child she'd ever been able to tolerate? In the mall it had been the marauding urchins more than the narcotized trailer-park types under-supervising them who had caused Bonnie such dismay.

She assumed (or let herself pretend) that Ross and Iliana (who was nice about Brent whenever Bonnie mentioned him) would smile upon a romance, should it come to pass. Iliana, scrub-faced and ponytailed, her beeping watch keeping her on her baker's ascetic schedule, so hard-working and decent and uninteresting, so admirable in her utter lack of self-pity, so *ordinary* now that Bonnie thought of it (which had to be the most extraordinary thing about her, considering) – she was the most sensible person Bonnie had ever met. If Bonnie had Iliana's blessing, she wasn't about to waste it.

Bonnie and Brent had figured out a way that Bonnie could help with the script at the same time as working in the café. Brent, as usual, occupied his table from late morning. Till early afternoon, he'd work on passages of dialogue that Bonnie would later input into the laptop and move from scene to scene, like the fairy-tale prince stuffing a shoe on to arbitrary feet, until an approximate fit was found. To Bonnie this seemed a convoluted way to work, but Brent called it 'process'. 'And it's supposed to be absurd, remember? It's black comedy.' He knew a writer, now an entertainment lawyer, who'd cut his script into scenes and thrown it in the air. The order in which he collected the pieces off the carpet was the final order; he'd got an option right away.

In synopsis the story concerned a handsome young writer (Brad Pitt would be the perfect thesp, Brent thought, or Leonardo DiCaprio) who returns from the city (New York or LA) to his hometown (picturesque Connecticut or New Hampshire) to work on a screenplay, but the peace he seeks is continually interrupted both by unwanted visits from undesirables from his past (including his mother), and by mysterious, vaguely threatening communications from various unseen characters he has evidently fled the city to escape. In tone, it was somewhat reminiscent of the early Cohn brothers, but made less sense. How they worked was Bonnie would hurry by with an order for another party on the patio and, as she passed, Brent would say something to her to which she had to reply with the first thing that came to mind. Anybody listening would not have known what the relationship between them was (as Bonnie herself didn't) or why they were playing this party game in which, apparently, nobody scored.

'Love interest,' he said one afternoon as she rushed past with a bouquet of juices, four glasses held in a cluster in her hands.

'Is extortionate these days.'

He wrote it down, grinning, but told her as she passed in the other direction, 'That's what we're missing here.'

Bonnie felt a smile crack open her face.

After Bryce's bath that night, both of them pyjamaed, Bryce buttoned up the back, he pointed to the heat register on the ceiling above the window and asked to be lifted up. *Strum!* He serenaded her like this every night.

'Enough,' said Bonnie. 'Auntie Iliana's sleeping right above us.' She tossed him on to the bed. '*People*, *Elle* or *Vogue*?'

'*People*!' Bryce shouted, scrambling to arrange the pillows.

'See the bad and beautiful woman loved by all the world?' Bonnie began, the magazine open across both their laps.

'Who is she?'

'The fairest of them all.'

'No!' he cried on cue. 'You!'

She gave herself a face-lift, the palms of her hands on her cheeks slowly drawing the flesh back to her ears. Bryce did the same, orientalizing his features, and they fell into each other, giggling. She turned the page. 'Here are the bad and beautiful woman's husbands. Here are her estranged children. Here's the hustler who took her for a ride.'

Later, after Bryce had fallen asleep, as she sat peering in the truth-telling circle of the compact mirror, tweezing, she heard Ross come in. He still put his heels down like a fat man. She could track his progress through the house by the overhead reverberations. When the thuds started down the stairs, she put the mirror away and took up the magazine again, erecting around herself a glossy, right-angled privacy.

'How was your day?' he asked from the doorway.

'Good, actually.'

'Can I talk to you?'

She cringed, dreading what he would say. His vegetarianism Bonnie actually approved of now that she'd got used to the idea. Gone the once constant threat of salmonella poisoning. As for his spiritual interests, she had overheard him in the café talking at people, though he hadn't dared approach her on the subject yet. Here he was now, coming towards her, wearing his earnest expression. Alarmed, too, by the way he made himself at home in her bed (he swung his legs up and leaned back against the headboard), she shrank further into her paper sanctuary.

'We're really glad you could be with us this week, Bon.'

Oh, relief! It was only that. Smiling, she slapped the *People* closed and tossed it on the floor. She adjusted the covers around Bryce and lay down herself, feigning a yawn.

'We're so happy here. We wanted you to see it.'

'Mmm,' said Bonnie, affecting grogginess. 'You've done really well.'

Ross touched Bryce's curls. 'I wish we could all be together again, but obviously that's not right for you. I just want to tell you you have my blessing. You want to go back to Vancouver. We understand.'

'Oh, but we're staying!' She sat up. 'I decided today.' Leaning over Bryce, she pecked Ross on the cheek. 'Actually, I should call Brent and tell him, too. What time is it? Never mind.' She threw the covers off. 'He'll be up.'

She nipped up the basement stairs in her nightie without a backward glance at her brother.

After four rings, she went to look at the clock. 'Hello,' said a stuporous man's voice, not Brent's.

'God, Deb, I'm sorry for calling so late. It's ten to twelve! I had no idea. Is Brent there? It's Bonnie. I thought Brent would be up.'

Deb put the phone down. A moment later Bonnie heard in the background an unfriendly exchange of words, half of them low-pitched, half of them high. The extension was picked up and the other phone hung up ungently.

'You weren't sleeping, were you?' Bonnie asked.

'I was nursing my wound.'

She laughed.

'Go ahead and chortle. I think I'm getting a sty.'

'God,' said Bonnie. 'How do you get one?'

'From looking at bad wallpaper.'

'I have good news then. You know the empty apartment above the café?'

She heard him gasp. 'There's an empty apartment above the café? Why don't I know about it? Oh, that Ma Pancake! She pulled a fast one on me.'

'We're moving in.'

Joy leaped in his voice. 'We are?'

'Not you, silly. Me and Bryce.'

8

A few days after he finished working for Ross, Stevie Blake found himself driving several kilometres out of town, over near the mountain where the hang-gliders launched. From the corner of his eye they looked like paper aeroplanes, all different colours, drifting down. Heading home, he passed the mall and could not resist turning a few circles in the empty parking lot. It was evening, almost dark. After a couple or three revolutions the truck began to bank and the wheels gripe, but that was not what made him stop. He finally noticed what was in the window of Field's. He'd lived in Duncan almost all his life, yet had never come across a sight like that.

The phone was ringing when he got home. He heard it from outside after he had pulled into the driveway, but didn't bother hurrying in because Nana would let it ring on and on. When he answered, though, it wasn't Nana; it was Ross Alexander asking if he was interested in another job. Stevie was still thinking about the tableau of naked mannequins, some standing with arms akimbo or raised, others kneeling or sitting with knees drawn up. The women's breasts were nippleless, pelvises blocky with deep creases to signify a hairless mound of Venus. The men just stood there, doing nothing.

The moment Iliana heard about the shelves, she knew what was going to happen, yet a few days later she was still pretending that she had control over the situation. Should she open the door to the alley or not? If she opened it, Stevie would think she was waiting for him. If she closed it, he'd think she was afraid. Either way would be a present to his ego. She decided to leave it open to show she was in charge.

Why had he picked her? Did he think she was easy prey? Angry, she tipped the bowl so the sticky mass of dough tumbled out on to the counter. She dusted it with flour. As she worked in rhythmic, unconscious motions – pushing, turning, folding, pushing, turning, folding – a moustache of perspiration formed above her lip. She glanced at the door. Closed, she decided, was a better message. She went over and slid the rock away.

The dough was taut and supple now, like beerily scented flesh. Back at the counter, she pushed into it with a little huff of exertion, then caressed it with more flour. Folded, pushed, turned. All at once her dream came back. It had shocked her to see herself starring in another person's fantasy again. Skin on skin, the sheen of sweat. She hadn't recognized the man she was with. In the morning, waking, she'd looked at Ross. For the last three nights she'd been lying next to him copulating like mad with strangers. His exhalation sounded like a sigh, as if he were merely impatient with her faithless antics.

Two nights earlier Ross had climbed into his side of the bed in the dark, trying to be quiet, trying not to wake her. 'Shit,' he muttered in advance of the cascade, the multiple slaps, paperback after paperback hitting hardwood.

'I was already awake,' she said.

He got up again to rebuild his bedside tower. 'I'm going to move these books out of here. I'm going to get some shelves built in the café.'

Iliana knew then. She knew what was going to happen.

'And I've got bad news,' he said, as if there were something worse than what he had just told her. 'Bonnie does want to move into the apartment.'

'So I heard.'

He slipped back into bed. 'When did she tell you?'

'I heard you talking to her just now.' Their bedroom was directly above the one in the basement. The heating vent funnelled up the sound.

'Is that what woke you?'

Iliana said, 'I heard you say that we're happy.'

Ross fussed a moment with the pillow. He lay back and breathed in and out. 'What do you want me to say to her? Should I tell her no? I will if you want.'

'Are you happy, Ross?'

'Babe.'

'How did this happen to us? We get into bed. We snuggle and talk. We're two consenting adults lying in bed together. We're married. All we have to do is do it. Why don't we?'

Ross said, 'I don't know. It's not that I don't want to. I do.' They both lay there. He reached for her.

'If you're not attracted to me any more—'

'No, no, no!' The hand flew up, without ever having touched her. 'I love you so much.'

'But I'm not talking about love.'

She drizzled oil in the bowl, smeared the sides, dropped in the dough. At the sink, she wet a fresh towel. She was beginning to doubt that he was coming after all (he hadn't yesterday, or the day before). To lure him, she went and opened the door halfway.

She wanted to see him alone first so she could show him that if he thought she had been complicit while he watched her from the roof, he was wrong. She was going to pretend that she hadn't even known he was there. If he came later, when Deb was here, he would have the upper hand. Unreprimanded, his presence would blackmail her with the embarrassment it would cause.

When the truck pulled up outside, she knew it was his. Unmistakable, the complaints of its engine. Her heart mimicked it, tachycardic. Reluctant to let him think she was waiting (she wasn't waiting), she covered the bowl and slid it in the warming oven. The timer sounded. She took the finished loaves out, upending the hot pans so they fell out on to their sides, exuding steam. The yeast for the next batch had proved. Stirring in a cup of flour, attention still focused on the door behind her though she'd heard nothing since the truck door's initial slam, she felt his gaze on her. Turning slowly, she saw he was indeed there, standing in the doorway, hair hanging thickly over his forehead in the manner of certain breeds of dog.

He'd smoked a cigarette outside first, collecting his nerve. Even from behind he could tell that she'd been waiting. She was hunched from the tension. Before she spoke, she moistened her top lip, showing just the tip of her tongue. For Stevie, inevitability coloured everything from that moment. He just relaxed into what happened next.

'Hi,' she began, not quite as coldly as she had intended. 'You're back.'

'Yeah.'

'I was hoping you'd come in early.' Seeing him start towards her, her voice dissolved.

'I need—' he started to tell her.

She cut him off with a 'What?' It sounded like a yelp.

'A pencil and paper.' He showed her the metal tape measure he was holding. 'I'm taking measurements. For the shelves. Did he tell you?'

'Yes. Of course.' Flustered then, feeling ridiculous, she stammered, 'By the till. There's a pad and a jar of pens.' She pointed to the swinging door that led to the front of the café. Her hand, she noticed as he took it, was white with flour and stuck all over with bits of dough and his, by comparison, brown.

After the kiss (long and smoky-flavoured), when they had finally separated, she saw flour on his shirtfront and dough in his hair. She wanted to think of this as evidence of a struggle when in fact she'd been the one to pull him down. As in her dreams, she had snatched him and begun, mantis-like, to devour him. She had never kissed a man who smoked before and could not help thinking that what she tasted on his mouth was sin.

He was a good kisser. He had to be. When he was twelve or thirteen, he used to make the okay sign with his thumb and forefinger and pretend it was a pair of lips. Only later did he realize that it was the sort of pathetic thing girls did, that boys humped the sofa back or jerked off with magazines. He wanted to touch her body, too, but wasn't stupid.

Iliana was the one to pull away. She seemed upset. 'Don't come back here,' she told him. 'Please don't come back.'

He hated that she felt she had to plead with him. 'Okay. But I should, like, take the measurements, so I have something to say to him.' He was deliberately not using Ross's name. Walking through to the front of the café, he felt so happy he didn't care if he never saw her again. (She smelled just as he'd thought she would, like bread.)

For Iliana the shock wore off once she was alone. It was an anaesthetic, blocking what she really felt. She waited for him to come back. After ten minutes, when he didn't, she panicked, thinking that he'd left through the front.

He was writing something on a scrap of paper. She tried to sound very, very angry. 'Are you going to do what I asked?'

First he wrote down the number so he wouldn't forget it, then folded the paper and put it in his shirt pocket. 'If you don't want me here, I won't come.'

'What are you going to tell him?'

'That I got another job.' He had taken down the pictures and moved a plant stand. Now he began to put everything back in its place, lifting a canvas gaudy with a still life of fruit.

'Did you?'

He had his back to her, raising and lowering the picture frame, trying to find the nail. 'No.'

'Then you'll be out the money.'

'It doesn't matter.'

Her tone changed. He could hear her relenting. She heard it herself and was appalled. 'When are you supposed to do this work?'

'Whenever.' Lifting the plant stand, he walked it back to the wall then turned and looked at her.

'You'll have to do it when the café's closed anyway, right? Why are you smiling?'

He straightened his face at once.

9

'I'm tickling you.'

Loading bread pans into the dishwasher, Iliana looked down and saw that Bryce had slipped a wriggling finger inside her shoe.

'Do you feel it?'

'Sort of,' she said. 'Now that I'm looking.'

'Why?'

'Why can't I feel things like other people? Sometimes I can. Sometimes I get an itch on the bottom of my foot that drives me crazy because what I can't feel is me scratching it.'

At the grill, Deb turned, 'When I was a kid we had a neighbour who'd lost an arm in the war. He said he could tell if it was going to rain because his ghost arm ached. Have you had breakfast yet, little boy?'

'Why did he have a ghost arm?'

'How about a pancake?' She slid one on to a plate for him and, taking his hand, led him into the café.

'Why did he have a ghost arm?' Bryce asked, going through the swinging door.

When Deb came back, she told Iliana, 'I have to say I'm glad he's staying.'

Iliana agreed. 'He's our mascot now.' A three-and-a-half-year-old interrogator with his shirt on backwards. What she especially appreciated was his frankness. When Bryce was around he asked the questions everyone wanted to but didn't. Like the day on the patio when he asked about the accident. As she told him, the conversations going on all around them dropped off one by one. They were all dying to know.

'Was Brent at all like Bryce?' she asked Deb.

Scowling, Deb picked an order slip off the window ledge. 'Yeah. Then he grew up, sort of.'

After she finished loading the dishwasher, Iliana went into the café. Bryce was on his perch at the counter, one arm absent from its sleeve, Ross at his side, tying a piece of string to a safety pin. Seeing Ross, Iliana's first impulse was to retreat to the kitchen, but Ross would know then that she was avoiding him. Instead she headed across the room, finding herself exactly where Stevie had measured the shelves that morning. He'd made some pencil marks on the wall. (What was she looking for? Some scrawled obscenity she could covet?) She glanced furtively back. Ross was fixing the pin to Bryce's empty sleeve. Tugging the string made the sleeve flap back and forth. 'There's your ghost arm,' he said.

Deb rang the bell. Ross went to fetch the order and, after he had delivered it to the customer, he began without reference to anything telling her about his disordered library at home, joking how a few nights ago he had accidentally knocked a stack of books off the bedside table, frightening Iliana half to death. Pointing to where Iliana was, where the shelves were going to be, he grinned, as if Iliana were in collusion with him.

Unfair, the way she had been treating him all morning, as if he were responsible for the kiss. But that was just what she was doing, blaming him for the taste of smoke in her mouth. Having already sent him out of the kitchen because she could load the dishwasher herself (thank you very much!), now she couldn't stand to hear him talking to this woman. She started for the door, scooting out of reach when Ross tried to touch her as she passed.

'I'm going to get the mail.'

It was the minister's daughter in Iliana who found it hard to respect the Buddhist in Ross. Her father was a man who sought scriptural justification for everything he did. So well thumbed were the velum pages of his Bible, the book had swollen to twice its original thickness. Some of these books of Ross's had never been opened. Many were flagged with bookmarks in the early pages. Yet he proselytized as shamelessly as any street corner evangelist.

Once she had asked, out of annoyance, if there was such a thing as a Second Noble Truth. He was constantly citing the first – sitting down to do the accounts, glancing at the morning's headlines, when he burned himself on the grill. It only followed that there would be a second, and sure enough, there was.

'It's the Truth of the Cause of Suffering.'

'What is?'

'The Second Noble Truth.'

'What is? What is the cause of suffering?'

'Desire.'

She had shuddered when he said it.

But her real objection to what he called 'his practice' was the one she applied to all religions: a former fundamentalist's distrust.

Up the post office ramp, bumping over the threshold. Picking up the mail was her job. As soon as Elsa saw her, she stepped briskly over to their box and had its contents ready to pass down to Iliana. Iliana always stopped to chat as she sorted through the pile. Elsa, in turn, always took her afternoon break at Real Food.

'I heard your sister-in-law went back to Vancouver.'

'Just to pack,' Iliana told her. Invoices. Flyers. 'She's moving over.' A postcard from a regular complaining about the breakfasts he was getting on his holiday.

'That explains why I saw Bryce at the café yesterday.'

Coming to the envelope and recognizing, not only the handwriting, but the return address, Iliana immediately lost her train of thought.

'I thought maybe she forgot him,' said Elsa.

Iliana looked up. 'Sorry? What?'

Two boys came to the door in the evening. They were older than Bryce, seven or eight, yet they said they wanted to play with him. The red-haired one lived down the street. The blond boy was his cousin, visiting for a few weeks.

'We want to push him in the wheelchair.'

Ross went out with them to get the chair from the garage, staying in the yard to supervise. Watching from the window, Iliana saw all three boys piled in the chair, Ross tearing round the lawn. Some time later he thudded into the house asking if they didn't have a ball. He disappeared into the basement. 'Found it!' The screen door slammed behind him.

The boys took turns trying from the chair to get the foam ball through the netless basketball hoop above the garage door, Ross intercepting the ball's trajectory and redirecting it to the backboard while cheering them on at courtside volume. From the kind of uncle he was, Iliana had always known he would make a good father. He might have been the mother of all fathers.

Even now, two years later, lost moments flashed into her consciousness, illuminating the present. Sitting at the window, she remembered waking in the hospital as they were rolling her, landing on her opposite side where her view was blocked by a rotund belly stretching taut a pale blue T-shirt. Dizzily, she'd stared at it. The nurse, bent in front of her readjusting the nasal tube, said, 'I think we were in nursing school together.'

Iliana remembered her, but in a svelter form, circulating with the blender, topping everyone's daiquiri. Straightening now so the belly stood boldly out in front of her, she moved partway down the bed, leaning over Iliana again, smoothing the covers. The belly nudged Iliana's drawn-up knees; she felt nothing. It was as if she had dissociated herself from part of her own body. She felt herself retracting but didn't know how much of this was the morphine.

'We were trying to get pregnant,' Iliana said. 'What if I'm pregnant?'

'I guess you'll be having a baby.'

'I can't have a baby.'

'Why not?'

'I can't move my legs. I can't even sit up.'

'You'll be sitting up before you know it. There's no reason at all you can't have a baby.'

Outside: screaming, Bryce in an epileptic-like thrash on the lawn, the two boys standing off to the side, staring. Iliana went out on to the porch. 'What's wrong?'

Ross knelt beside Bryce as he flailed, trying to get him to stop.

'What happened?' Iliana asked.

'He didn't want to take turns,' the red-headed boy said.

'Hey,' Iliana called. 'I think Ross made popsicles! Who wants one?'

The older boys came thundering up the ramp. Bryce, seeing them head into the house, immediately stopped crying and got up to follow.

'Fast thinking,' Ross said to Iliana as he passed.

Iliana got a tissue. Snot and tears were melting the popsicle Bryce sucked. He was at the kitchen table with the big boys, laughing as if nothing had happened. 'Just let me wipe your nose,' she said sternly over his objections. 'It will taste better. I assure you.'

'What was that all about?' Ross asked in bewilderment.

Iliana shrugged.

'I wonder about Bonnie. I really do. I mean, what's she doing that he flips out like that?'

'She's not doing anything. He's three and a half.'

Ross drew in his breath, shaking his head, unconvinced.

The game resumed without further incident, continuing until it began to grow dark and the summer round-up started, the boys' names called in a drawn-out shout from down the street.

After Bryce's bath, Ross asked Iliana from the bedroom door, 'Think there's room enough for three?'

'What? Are they sleeping over?'

Climbing in bed, Ross offered a hand up to Bryce.

Bonnie phoned. Bryce told her about his ghost arm, then Ross

221

took the phone and listened to her for a few minutes before passing her on to Iliana.

'So he was at the café same as always?' Bonnie asked. 'What was he doing? Any trouble?'

'No trouble, no.' It wasn't that Brent was trouble. It was that he never left and never paid his bill.

'I can't stop thinking about him. It's horrible. I'm going out of my mind here with all this packing, yet I keep falling into this sort of trance.'

'You're really that crazy about him?' asked Iliana.

'Of course I am. Where's he sleeping? Downstairs or with you?'

Iliana laughed. 'I thought you were talking about Brent!'

'Who? Brent? God, no!'

The rest of the week that Bonnie was gone, Ross was home every day by six. The three of them would have dinner and by seven Red (he had a real name, but that was what Ross called him) and his cousin White would show up at the door. Inspired by what had happened the other night, Ross was working on a popsicle series, fruit impaled on a stick then suspended in frozen juice. He was using the boys as his test group, all of them on the ramp in a huddle. Every night, Iliana came out to watch them playing. Neighbours out strolling would stop to talk. Red's mother came by to make sure the kids weren't making a nuisance of themselves. Later in the week, his dad dropped by and tried to interest Ross in coaching T-ball.

On Friday night when the phone rang, Ross said, 'That'll be Bon. Maybe I can convince her to stay away a little longer.'

That was when Iliana realized that it wasn't Bonnie Ross had missed and could not live without; it was Bryce. She understood, too, that the space in the bed that had opened since the accident (she had not thought of it, yet, as a void, but as an empty arm's length separating them) had already filled up. It had filled with Bryce, at that very moment nestling down between them.

At the post office she had not torn up the card right away. Neither had she read it beyond the address, not typed, oddly, but written in her mother's flowing script. She had simply weighed it in her hand, remembering what that other one had made her do.

10

The week he built the shelves, Stevie arrived at four thirty or five each afternoon. Sometimes the boy was there, sometimes not. Ross was always cooking in the kitchen and would come out to say hi, but that was all. He seemed as much in a hurry to get home as Stevie would have been himself had Iliana been waiting for him. The nosy questions and generally stupid comments about life that he had expected to have to endure did not happen. Instead, he got a key to come and go as he pleased. He could have built the shelves in two days, but he stretched it out to five.

As soon as Ross left, Stevie would put down his tools and go behind the counter where the stereo was to change the station, then pass through the swinging doors and take a look round the kitchen. The ovens were not the ordinary kind, but about half the height and twice the width, with stainless steel doors; there were three of them stacked one on top of the other at a height convenient for Iliana. He'd open each one and put his hand inside, but none was ever warm. Under the counter was where she kept her bowls, next to the empty place for the wheelchair to fit. She had three stacking sets in clear glass and a lot of different ceramic ones. The world's largest wooden spoon collection was housed there, too, and tea towels folded in a pile, and all the pans.

Across the kitchen was a walk-in cooler. He snooped around in there, too, the first night, curiosity piqued by the six big bowls covered with towels along a low shelf. Lifting a towel and seeing dough, he couldn't help himself: he touched the cool sticky surface. With his index finger he pushed. At first the dough only dimpled, so he kept pushing until, all at once, the surface broke and his finger penetrated. He drew it out, saw the ragged hole he'd made, the gluey dough on his finger, and wondered how the fuck he was going to fix it. Trying to smooth it out with a wooden spoon only made it worse. He could imagine her in the morning lifting the towel off, seeing the hole, knowing right away he'd done it and thinking he was pretty, like, fucked. Throwing up his hands, he went back into the café and started work in earnest. He was so upset he got ahead of himself.

Before he left, he went back to have one last look at the mess. The bowl he lifted the towel off first was the wrong one – a lot fuller than the other and unmarked. He checked under the towel to the right, then to the left, then under all of them. He'd been working about three hours, time enough to heal the scar.

Sometimes he didn't eat all day. It was sheer laziness. His stomach might start to grumble, but nine times out of ten he'd still feel lazier than hungry. If he was out, he'd stop and get a burger, but at home he could put eating off indefinitely. At the café, where he had to go in a few hours, the food Ross left for him did not exactly tempt him. He was not enamoured with vegetables and this was what finally got him off the couch.

In the kitchen he turned the stove on. Once the fat already in the pan had melted he poured it off into the peanut butter jar on the counter (topping up the jar, in fact). Outside a car horn honked. He turned off the stove and went to the living room to look out of the window. He was surprised, of course, but not entirely. She must have been there a while because she was already out of the car and in the chair beside it.

He came down the steps, right over to her. 'Hi,' she said. 'Deb told me where you lived.'

'Did you tell her you were coming over?'

'Of course not.'

Stevie ran his hand down his face. He had probably never felt as much regret in his whole life as he did right now for not having Deb over when she'd hinted at it. She would probably have cleaned up for him when she saw how bad things had got. Now he was screwed. 'Want to come in?' He didn't know which would be worse, her saying yes or her saying no.

'Um.' She looked at the stairs. Remembering, she backed the chair up, opened the car door and took a paper bag off the seat. 'I brought you this.'

Stevie looked inside and smiled, then handed it back so he could lift her. She was not expecting this. She let out a little cry that made him stop where he was, holding her. 'Never mind,' she said, tucking her face against his shoulder.

Inside, he set her down on the couch and went back out to get the chair. He didn't look at her, just set the chair down and left her there.

The danger she had put herself in! Her heart was punching to get out. *Go, go, go, go.* She didn't know anything about him. He could rape her. He could kill her. She looked in the kitchen where Stevie stood shirtless at the stove, his navel protruding like a child's, and somehow knew he would not hurt her.

'You want breakfast?' The package of bacon still in his hand, the strips he'd already put in for himself runching in the pan, their sweet smoky smell slow-releasing.

'It's after three,' she pointed out, adding in a wistful tone, 'I haven't had bacon for a long time.' He added three more strips and turned the heat up.

'Let me do that,' she told him when he took the bread she'd brought out of the bag. She did not approve of his knife. 'Don't you have a bread knife? How about a steak knife?'

The grease popped and crackled as the eggs hit the pan. He fetched some toilet paper to drain the bacon on, then cleared all the crap off the table. The dishcloth was in the sink six feet under all the dishes, so he got out one of Nana's tablecloths. (He hoped it was a tablecloth and not a sheet.) Iliana brought the toast over. The plates were clean, at least.

He had been a little sneaky about which chair he took away, giving himself the choice of seat. Across from her, he could look directly at her, but he didn't necessarily want that; he sat to her right, closer to her, and offered her the plate of bacon. She took a piece, hesitating over a second.

'Go on. There's lots.'

It was cooked just how Ross had used to make it, stiff as faux bacon. She confessed, 'It's the one thing I miss, being vegetarian.'

Stevie thought it was weird that she was a vegetarian. He thought that was weird, but he no longer thought the fact that she was in a wheelchair was weird. That in itself was weird. He punctured the yolks with the knife, smeared them over the toast. Into his palm he poured some salt from the box, offering it to her first. She seemed taken aback, then, smiling, took a pinch. He bit into the toast. She had cut the bread thick so it was crisp on the outside and still soft in the middle. He was on to the second piece in a minute.

'Do you want to know why I'm here?'

He shrugged.

'I'm married. I don't want you to think that doesn't mean anything to me or that I do this kind of thing all the time.'

'What kind of thing?'

'This.' She sounded disgusted.

'We're having breakfast.'

She reddened. She blushed easily, he realized. 'I can't have you coming into the café and making me feel uncomfortable because – I can't have that.'

'I said I wouldn't come when you're there.'

'Thank you. Thank you for that.'

She started on her last piece. He wondered if he should get up and cook some more, but didn't want to interrupt her. 'I don't want to make you uncomfortable. I won't come any more.'

She pointed to his bacon. 'Do you want that?'

He pushed the plate over to her.

'But you're there every day. Your tools are there.'

'I just have to paint. I'll be out of there, like, tomorrow.'

'When I turn the radio on, I get your station.'

'It's Island Rock.'

'I can't stand that kind of music.'

He wondered what kind of music she did like, would have given anything to have left it on that station instead. He had assumed it was tuned to Ross's station.

Sighing, she closed her eyes. 'You must think I'm awful.'

Stevie said, 'As if.'

Then she said something that made him feel like a complete asshole. 'You've got egg on your face.' She touched herself to show him where. Before he could wipe it off, she leaned over and put her own mouth on the place.

Sometimes it was hard for Stevie to look at people directly. It embarrassed him to be witness to the high opinion certain people had of themselves. Usually he looked away as he would if he walked in on someone in the bathroom. There were other people, though fewer of them, whose gaze he met instinctively even the first time. Iliana was one. He held her like that, not taking his eyes away from hers while he reached for her hand and put her finger in his mouth. It tasted salty from the bacon. He circled it with his tongue and, with it still deep in his mouth, began flicking the space between that finger and the next one. He'd never done anything like this before. It turned her on, he could tell (he was still holding on to her with his eyes), and so him, too, especially when he very slowly drew her finger out, lingering at the tip, sucking on it. Grabbing his hand, she showed him what she wanted him to do with it, using him to stroke her face, her neck. Her hair was what he wanted to touch. The band that held it slid off easily and it fell around her shoulders, concealing her face. When he put his hands under the curtain it made, the spaces between his fingers filled with hair. It was the colour of dried grass, but very soft, and for a while he kept catching it up like this and letting it slide through his hands as he listened to her moan.

She turned her head, exposing an ear. He leaned towards it. The kiss was no more than his breath, but it sent a shudder through her. Closing his eyes, he imagined filling her ear (it should have been wine or honey, but Stevie imagined beer), tipping the bottle then drinking the golden liquid. He lapped inside the whorl until her breath sounded as if she was on the point of climax and her fingers dug into his forearm. When she lifted her face to kiss him, he moved his hand out from between her legs. She didn't ask him to put it back.

11

Because he was busy looking after his nephew, Ross hardly saw Stevie the week he built the shelves. He had not really practised opening to his aversion as he had intended and, regretting an opportunity lost, decided to ask Stevie out for a drink on his last day. If he had actually liked Stevie, he might have done this spontaneously. As it was, he had to force himself.

Stevie was washing the brushes in the back room. It seemed that he didn't get many invitations because he looked almost shocked. Ross couldn't help warming to him then and, laughing, he put his arm round Stevie's sinewy shoulder, symbolically taking him under his wing. 'Come on,' he joked. 'Who knows when our paths will cross again?'

Stevie twisted away. He was not the touchy-feely type.

They drove off in Stevie's truck after Stevie had emptied his shorts pockets on to the dashboard. Cigarette papers, tobacco, Swiss Army knife, change, a wadded five, pencil stub, nails. Among these items was a single key unadorned by a ring, which he picked out and used to start the truck.

Further complicating the invitation was the matter of where to go. Real Food was the only worthwhile café in town, in Ross's opinion. He didn't know the bars. He let Stevie choose and Stevie chose the Legion.

Smoke, thick and stale, met them at the door. There were dartboards and a pool table as well as a stage with a console and a mike stand. A few old-timers slumped unheroically under the memorial plaques. Smoke accompanied them over to the bar where Stevie ordered a pint of draught and Ross a club soda. Smoke escorted them to one of the dozen circular tables in the room. By the time they'd taken their seats, Ross could taste the smoke.

Stevie rolled himself a cigarette. He fit in here, Ross could see, or he would perfectly in about forty years. He was already abiding by the smoking policy. The policy was, Ross deduced, to smoke as much as possible.

'You don't drink?'

'No,' said Ross. 'It's one of the Five Precepts. Do you know anything about Buddhism?'

From Stevie's nostrils – smoke, in a scornful ejection.

Ross told him the one about the hotdog vendor and the Buddhist. Stevie didn't seem to get the joke and Ross's attempt at explaining the punch line only made it worse, so he changed the subject. 'What's up with you next?'

Stevie opened the potato chips he'd got at the bar and set one on his tongue as if he were giving himself communion.

'Jobwise,' Ross said.

Pushing the bag into the middle of the table, Stevie shrugged.

'I like that.'

'What?'

'It's rare to meet a person who truly does not strive. This is something I struggle with myself. I used to work in the film industry. In film every extra fancies himself a lead. The second AD strives to be the first, the first to direct, the director to rule a small island nation. I never questioned this. I wanted to be the best film caterer in town. When we moved over here and opened Real Food, we hoped to get away from all that. But I have this enormous ego, see? Even when—'

'And what?' Stevie interrupted. His legs were crossed and the airborne foot, sockless under the shoe, jiggled with what seemed a furious impatience. 'Mine is *small*? How would you know?'

'Fair enough. My point is, all I'm saying – it's a general comment, not one directed at you – is the ego is behind most of what we do.'

'I thought the cock was.'

Ross laughed uncomfortably. He had been shooting off his mouth. If Iliana had been there she would have prevented this as she often did in the café, mouthing *earnest, Ross, earnest* from across the room. Though Ross had tried to persuade Iliana to take an interest in Buddhism too, thinking that it might help bring them closer after what had happened to them, Iliana, a refugee from fundamentalism, had steadfastly ignored his leadings. Some mornings Ross arrived at the café and with just one breath, one sweet lungful, knew in his heart that he would be better off following her example.

Making bread had been her idea. When she suggested it to him as a way that she might contribute to the café, Ross, knowing the disadvantage she was starting with, had not really believed she would succeed. Toast he thought her capable of, but never bread. In the beginning there had been failures, but she did not take them to heart. Jokingly, she proposed alternative uses for these charred or unrisen batches (door stoppers, bookends, bricks) then went right back to her cookbooks, annotating in the margin of the recipe the date and what she thought had gone wrong. Making bread was a fairly mechanical operation as far as Ross could tell. Though there was some variety in the ingredients, bread was basically flour, water, and yeast. The steps were tediously the same, too, yet Iliana did not grow bored with the repetition. Eschewing a machine, she kept at it manually, cheerfully, even *mindfully*. Watching her, he felt profoundly humbled.

And here sat Stevie, inscrutable and broody, either ignorant or contemptuous of the social convention that requires collocutors to take turns advancing new topics of conversation. With the lapse into silence, Ross began to doubt himself. What was he doing in this unbreathable fug with this bicycle thief, this person who so obviously disdained all he had to say? He shifted in his seat, fighting his growing inclination to leave. During meditation, he often likened his struggle to be receptive to negative thoughts and feelings to opening the door to his house and letting all the bogeys enter. It occurred to him now that sitting in the Legion with Stevie Blake was another useful analogy, that Stevie was the personification of an unpleasant thought, seated right across from him. If Ross left now, Stevie would remain hostile. On the other hand, if he stayed open and friendly, when next they saw each other Stevie might simply wave and walk on, right out of Ross's mind.

The bartender approached with a roll of tickets the size of a side-order plate. Stevie leaned back in the chair to gain access to his front pocket and gave the bartender a two-dollar coin. The bartender, heeding Stevie's nod, gave the ticket to Ross.

'What happened to her?'

Ross read the number on the ticket. 'Who?'

'Your wife?'

The last time Ross had been asked this was when Iliana was in the hospital. Vladimir, the Russian circus performer, had asked him. A few people he met in the waiting room, too. They had been commiserating. Now no one asked because it wasn't polite. That Stevie didn't know this was hardly a surprise. 'Car accident,' he told him.

'When?'

'Two years ago. She's okay now.'

'What do you mean?'

'She had a hard time at the beginning.'

'Does she feel stuff?'

'Pressure. Some phantom-like sensation. That's about it. She used to get these really painful spasms, but now she's got her medication sorted out. Why are you asking me all these questions?'

Stevie put out his cigarette, displacing some of the butts already in the ashtray. 'Don't feel sorry for her,' said Ross.

'Sorry for her? As if.'

The bartender was on the stage trying to raise the mike stand. He blew into it. 'Evening.' Feedback forced him back.

'It was a terrible thing. I guess that's what I learned from it.'

'What?' asked Stevie.

'That terrible things happen.' As soon as he said it, he lost his resolve completely. It sounded so harsh spoken out loud. Palms flat on the table, he prepared to rise. 'The smoke's really bothering my eyes. I'm going to get going.'

With his chin, Stevie gestured to the stage. 'Hold on a sec.'

'Evelyn?' said the bartender. 'Want to come up here and do the honours?'

At one of the tables a grey-haired woman in glasses and a sleeveless blouse rose and began weaving her way to the front, followed by a spiritless clapping. She climbed slowly up on stage and went over to the big glass jar identical to the one on the bar that contained pickled eggs. In the bottom the tickets looked like a handful of leaves. She reached an arm in, backscratcher thin.

'Four-oh-five-seven-two,' read the bartender off the ticket. 'Four-oh-five-seven-two's our lucky number.'

'Hey,' said Ross.

Stevie signalled to the bartender.

'And we have a winner right here. A winner over here.'

'What did I win?' Ross asked.

'They give it to you at the door. Come on. I'll drive you back.'

Ross got up and followed Stevie. 'I'm tickled. I never win anything.' At the door he said, 'Hey, it's your prize. You bought the ticket.'

'You got the drinks.'

'Are you sure? Hey.' He reached out to give Stevie a friendly cuff on the shoulder, but Stevie pushed open the door and stepped out just as the bartender approached with a large plastic-wrapped caterer's tray. With a brief congratulatory nod, the man deposited it in Ross's arms. Appalled, Ross turned to Stevie. 'I can't take this.'

Goose-pimpled drumsticks, a huge steak with a bone letter imbedded in it, bacon racing-striped with fat, and more, but he looked away. 'I don't eat meat.'

Ross followed Stevie down the concrete steps. 'You know that.' They reached the truck. 'You take it.'

'I don't cook.'

'Don't you know anyone who does?'

'No.'

Ross slid the tray over on the seat before climbing in himself. There wasn't room for the meat and the two of them; Ross had to hold it in his lap. As soon as he closed the door, he groaned out loud. 'Oh man.' He sniffed at his shirt. 'Open your window, will you?' He peeled his shirt right off and hung it out of the window like a flag.

He did not want Iliana to know he'd been in a bar. He didn't think she would care, but she would wonder what was going on. Stevie unrolled his window, smiling with half his mouth, and Ross could guess what he was thinking. It was what Ross was afraid Iliana thought about him, how he thought about himself, almost in tears five minutes before, then gloating like a schoolboy over his prize.

'Thanks,' he said, chastened, when Stevie dropped him in the alley. T-shirt around his neck, just as he reached in the cab for the tray he realized he had an out. 'Hold on a sec.' To be sure that Stevie did not drive away, he left the meat in the truck while he unlocked the back door and went inside.

He came out with a Real Food shirt for Stevie, too, and passed it through to him. 'A souvenir.'

The tray he took back inside and buried at the bottom of the freezer.

12

Iliana sat in Stevie's driveway appalled, not so much by his handiwork as by his confidence. The last time she came she had declared in no uncertain terms that what had happened was a singular event. Despite her assertion (which she herself had earnestly believed), he had taken it for granted that she would be back, and not just once, or he wouldn't have gone to all this trouble. Hammered together out of two-by-fours and plywood sheeting, the ramp smacked of the expectation of something regular.

Her first thought was to back out of everything – the driveway and the sex. She couldn't, though. It would have been easier for her to stop breathing than to arrest the momentum of her lust. She looked at the house, which reminded her of the house she had grown up in, right down to the plastic on the windows. Inside, of course, it could not have been more different. If cleanliness was next to godliness, Stevie Blake was the devil's personal friend.

As she sat there giving way to her body, allowing it to convince her mind, she remembered how he had leaned over and lifted her in his arms. Ashamed, she'd pressed her face against his chest. Though she hadn't said anything about how she felt, afterwards, when she'd asked to go, he'd said, 'How do you want to do it?' There were only the four steps. He'd bumped the chair down and left her at the bottom.

She went up the ramp and rang the doorbell. It occurred to her then that she had come empty-handed with no excuse for what she wanted. He opened the door in a pair of khaki cut-offs. She was eye-level to his navel. Without showing any surprise, he stepped back to let her through.

'Company coming?' she asked, protecting herself with sarcasm.

He had cleaned up. Two days ago the décor had consisted mainly of beer cans and dirty dishes. Now irregular tracks marked the carpet where the vacuum cleaner had been pushed haphazardly around.

'Anybody could drop by,' Stevie said, his open hand pressed to his bare chest, disingenuously, she thought.

She went ahead into the kitchen. 'How long did this take you?'

'Not as long as it took to mess up.'

Since they weren't pretending any more, she didn't see why they should confine themselves to the kitchen. Starting down the hall ahead of him, she stopped in the doorway to the bathroom. Something she hadn't noticed the other day: it wasn't a bachelor's place at all. The bathmat was the colour and texture of cotton candy. The toilet seat cover matched. There was a scale (did men weigh themselves?) and a couple of petit point pictures of pansies in oval frames.

'Do you live alone?'

'Why do you want to know?'

Further down the hall and to the right was a bedroom. She looked in at the bedspread and matching pillowcases, the cat-shaped lamp on the bedside table. 'This doesn't seem like a room you'd sleep in.'

'Keep going.'

The vacuum cleaner had come before her here, too, she saw when she got to the last door on the left. There was a neatly made bed with a green spread, a metal trunk, a small bookshelf. She went over and, for a joke, drew the covers back as if to check that the sheets were clean. Moving the spread released a slide of magazines from under the bed, a slope of half-revealed breasts and buttocks. Desire, like nausea, washed over her.

'This is a fire hazard,' she said.

He kept his eyes averted as she transferred to the bed. It was there, looking over at him hanging sheepishly in the doorway, that she finally noticed the cockiness was missing. 'I don't care what magazines you read.' If it had been Ross's stash she'd chanced upon, she would have felt differently.

'It's not that.'

'What then?'

He came and lay down carefully beside her, without touching her. He was so skinny she felt sorry for him and pushed the hair out of his eyes, holding it off his forehead. Pimples hid throughout his hairline. His eyebrows were thick and black. Resting on the curve of his cheekbones, the kind of lashes that were wasted on a boy.

'So that's what you look like.'

He sat up and, assuming a cross-legged position, reached under her head and drew the band from her hair, holding it in his teeth as he gathered up his mop. With perfect seriousness, he opened her blouse and for a long moment gazed down. Hers were not the breasts of the women living under his bed. Studying his face for signs of disappointment, she saw him round his lips. Instinctively, her shoulder blades moved together and her back arched her nearer to him. He was writing on her bare skin with his breath. Each time she opened her eyes, she saw him leaning over her with the crazy brown fountain bubbling on his head.

As the last time, he would not let her touch him. She reached for him and felt that he was hard, but he took her wrist and removed her hand. 'There are things I probably can't do,' she said, 'but other things I can.' Ross used to tell her that she was living proof that Christian girls gave the best head. With his mouth, Stevie stopped her talk.

What really bothered her about the ramp, she realized coming out of the house afterwards, was that it was in full view of the street. Stevie had neighbours. What did these people think he was up to? Beside the car, preparing to transfer, she glanced around to make sure she had not been seen. Three houses away a woman was sitting on her front step smoking. Iliana could make out the woman's face from this distance, but not so clearly that she would recognize her if they ran into each other on the street. The woman wouldn't have to see Iliana's face to know her again; she would know her by the chair.

Trying to hurry only made her clumsy. She could not get the wheel to pop off. Frustrated, she looked over a second time. There was a child riding a tricycle on the sidewalk in front of the house. The woman wasn't even looking in Iliana's direction.

She drove to Overwaitea to buy something in order to come home with the bag. Ross and Bryce would probably not be back yet from setting up Bonnie's furniture which had preceded her, but she didn't want to take the chance. In the parking lot, she took a comb out and flipped down the sun visor, somehow surprised that she did not look any different in the mirror. After the accident, she had thought the same thing. Yet it had been easier for her to accept herself then than it had been for other people. Seeing herself as an adulteress was going to be more difficult.

On her way into the store, she kept her head down, as if this could possibly prevent her from being noticed. She was not so paranoid that she still thought someone might have seen her leaving Stevie's house. What she was afraid of was that they would read it on her face. She thought of him straddling her, bowing over her, working just above her heart. She must have seemed drunk, weaving all the way to the back where the pharmacy was.

What to buy? Her mind went blank except for Stevie squeezing her nipples as he took her whole ear into his mouth. Behind her was a wall of lipsticks. Taking the tubes one by one out of their slots, she looked at the colours but had no idea at all how to choose. She read the names on the stickers: Rouge Kiss, Cherry Tease, Wet'n'Red. (Who made these up and how did they know about her?) The mirror was well above her head. She thought of Bonnie, who could apply the goriest of shades by feel and somehow not end up looking as if she'd been punched in the mouth. Pink would probably have suited Iliana better, but she picked the most culpable shade.

Technically, of course, she was not an adulteress. She had not had intercourse with Stevie Blake. Momentarily exonerated by this specious rationalization, she might even have sustained it, had she been raised in a different house. Instead, as she handed over the tube of lipstick to the pharmacist, she blushed the same colour as its contents. She had committed adultery in her heart the day she sat out on the patio and allowed Stevie to fuck her with his eyes.

Because of the café, it was perhaps inevitable that she would meet someone she knew. Almost every time she went out she crossed paths with a person who had eaten at Real Food. Privileged to park just outside the door, she had without thinking placed herself in the way of everyone arriving and leaving.

'Iliana.'

She looked up to see their real estate agent, Beth Ann, just then detaching a shopping cart from the line along the wall. 'What have you been up to?' she asked, coming over.

Iliana tensed with dread. 'What do you mean?'

'How're things?'

'Great! I was just—' she took her alibi out of her lap and waved it at Beth Ann, '—picking up some lipstick.'

'I hear your sister-in-law's moving into the apartment.'

'Yes.' Iliana coughed so she could cover her mouth and hide the fact that she wasn't wearing lipstick now, so Beth Ann would not remember that in all their meetings last year, and every time she saw her in the café, she never was. 'Tomorrow.'

'Nice to get some revenue out of it.'

'Mmm,' said Iliana.

'Well, see you around.'

There was a slight pause, awkward and (for Iliana) freighted with suspense. Beth Ann made the first move. Seeing her hand, Iliana thought of Bryce's cutting a swath through the air as he pretended to be an aeroplane. She saw Beth Ann's taking flight, sunlight glinting off her rings, and as her eyes followed its arching path up, up, she wondered what Beth Ann intended to do with it.

Down it came, on top of Iliana's head: pat, pat.

13

It had all the makings of a tragedy. It was very nearly Russian in the grandness of its themes: ill-starred love, displacement, omens of suicide. Still shaking, Bonnie boarded the Vancouver bus and staggered over to a seat, waving through the window to dismiss Iliana who had driven her to the depot. In the brown paper bag Iliana had pressed on her in the car, she found napkins to wipe her nose with. She couldn't remember feeling so empty and, thinking the feeling must be hunger, took out the sandwich, too, and nibbled off the crusts, leaving the middle for Bryce, out of habit.

As the bus pulled away a baby several rows back began to cry. When Bonnie turned in the seat to get a look at it, the feeling only intensified. Wondering then if she had forgotten something, she opened her suitcase on her lap. Though she was going home (what did it matter if she had left her toothbrush?), compulsion had taken hold and could not be reasoned away. She looked through her purse, too: bankcard, pills, tampons, keys. Again and again she inventoried her possessions, each time feeling more empty-handed.

She checked her watch to see how much of the trip was behind her. What if she phoned from the ferry terminal just to talk? She'd look foolish, she was certain. But now she realized what the matter was: she missed him. His voice, the funny things he said, how his tongue protruding signified cogitation. She thought of him that very morning perched on the toilet.

'Are you finished yet?'

'No. There's two more. A big one and a little one.' *A big one and a little one?* How had he come to possess so much self-knowledge when she had so little? He was a remarkable child, a perfect child. When she told him they were staying, from his adoring look she knew she was doing the right thing. She was doing it for him.

Ten days later, climbing back down from the bus after the return trip, Bonnie spotted Iliana's car. Bryce was not with her. She struggled over with her disappointment and her luggage, stopping every few steps to shade her eyes. In Vancouver, the sky had been as inconclusive as a photographic grey card. It suited her mood. Was it always going to be this tauntingly sunny here?

As soon as she opened the car door and saw Iliana behind the wheel looking like some species of angel, the question popped out of her. 'Are you pregnant?' Iliana denied it, but blushed so deeply that Bonnie was half inclined to think she was lying. She certainly had not had this glow about her when Bonnie left.

'It must be your hair then. Did you colour it?'

'Colour it?' Flustered, Iliana ran a hand over her head. 'Honestly, Bonnie.'

'You look nice. Where's Bryce? Why didn't you bring him?'

'He's got a couple of friends now. They're playing with Ross.'

'Friends?' Bonnie said, as if she'd never heard the word before. She flipped down the sun visor to inspect her reflection in the mirror. 'He wasn't too much trouble, was he?'

'No. It was nice having him around. Ross got right into it. We were a regular family for a week.'

'Then why don't you get pregnant?' Bonnie said. Embarrassed then, too, (she didn't even know if Iliana could have a baby), she didn't speak for the remainder of the drive. When they pulled up at the house, the aforementioned friends were there, two weedy-looking boys twice the size of Bryce, one red-headed, the other very blond.

'That's them,' said Iliana. 'Red and White.'

Bryce was at the top of the ramp in Iliana's spare wheelchair, the red boy, too, who just then gave the chair a shove. Down the ramp Bryce careered, screaming. Even before Iliana pulled up at the kerb, Bonnie had leaped out of the car. At the same moment the blond boy at the bottom stopped the chair before it shot out on to the road.

'What do you think you're doing! Do you want to get killed! Do you want to get hit by a car?'

Ross stepped out of the house, three popsicles in hand. 'Whoa. They're all right. I'm watching.'

'You were not watching! You were inside!'

The two boys stared as if she'd just broken off a leash. 'What?' she snapped.

'Let's all just chill out,' said Ross.

Bryce, crying, would not take his popsicle. When Bonnie tried to hug him, he pushed her away and reached for Ross. 'Fine,' she told him, stung. 'I'll go and pack your things. We're going over to the apartment.'

'Go later,' Ross begged. 'Go tomorrow. Stay with us tonight.'

'Why?' she heard herself screech. 'We're here for the rest of our lives!'

She stormed into the house and down to the basement bedroom where she threw herself across the bed. Outside, Bryce's cater-wauling went on for several minutes. Bonnie listened to it, cowed. They used to have these set-tos every day, tears and screaming on both their parts. It had been a test of wills, operatic in intensity, physically exhausting. One day it all just ended. Calm descended, a peaceful stasis achieved at last. Bryce was a completely different child once Bonnie had decided to obey him.

Upstairs the screen door opened and she heard the happy family come inside. 'You go talk to her,' Ross said.

'Oh, sure,' said Iliana.

The phone rang then and, answering it, Ross changed his tone. 'Brent! Hey! Yeah, she just got in. She'd love to talk to you.' He started down the stairs, one thud at a time. 'I'll just get her for you.'

Bonnie lifted her face out of the pillow to scowl at Ross. 'At least someone missed me.'

She did not go to the café the next day, but spent it trying to install order in her new life. Ross had kindly reassembled most of the furniture. Dismantling it in Vancouver, she'd been appalled at the ease with which everything had come apart. Squatting under the kitchen table, she'd twisted the four butterfly screws that held the legs on, then had to duck under her hands before the top crashed down. The wall unit reduced to a neat stack of boards. Apart from the mattress, the bed looked as if it could have fitted into a cello case. All the years she'd lived there she'd been living falsely, believing as she had in permanence.

She met Brent that evening at the cinema as planned. It was on the other side of the tracks just down from the train station, a nondescript cube of a building with the name of the blockbuster currently showing lettered on the marquee, a film that had played in Vancouver in the spring and was already lining the video store shelves there. Brent was standing well apart from the ticket line, as if to dissociate himself, hands in pockets, looking around, presumably for Bonnie; his pose and isolation, and the pink looking-glass lenses, made him seem both haughty and louche, like one of those beautiful swindlers who specialize in passing themselves off as aristocrats. He kissed the air beside her cheeks and, touching her watch, nodded.

'What? I'm on time.'

They got in line and, when it had advanced them to the cashier's window, Brent turned discreetly away while Bonnie paid. Inside, the cinema (red-carpeted and with the requisite profiteering snack bar) could have been in Vancouver, or anywhere.

'Want anything?'

Brent tucked his chin in to read the board over the top of his sunglasses. 'Oh, my. Civilization has arrived.' He meant there was an espresso machine. 'So much has changed since I used to come here as a pimpled lad.' He went ahead to find seats while Bonnie waited in line for his latte and six dollar ice cream bar.

Stopping just inside the double doors to look around for Brent, it occurred to her that she had not set foot in a cinema for almost four years. This was just one of the many deprivations motherhood had imposed on her (swearing was another, and sleeping in). A child is born. A video store membership is taken out. Endless is the chain.

She started down the aisle towards the hand that went up in the first row. 'There are seats further back.'

'But we'll be alone up here.'

Smiling, she dropped down beside him.

He opened the box, tipping the ice cream bar out. 'I notice you're off the board.'

'What?'

'At the café. Bonnie Alexander got the wipe.'

'Oh, I know. I don't think anybody ordered me.'

'I wonder who's going to take your place.'

The lights dimmed on Bonnie's shrug.

'I don't think your brother likes me.'

'He does,' Bonnie said.

'Well, Birthday Cake has *three* sandwiches named after him now.'

'You want me to talk to Ross?'

'Frankly, I thought you would have by now.'

The trailers, each of which seemed to Bonnie (now that she'd read *Screenplays That Sell*) to be the most crucial scenes, including the climax, held together by the cloying glue of heart-rending music, seemed interminable. When the feature presentation finally started, as if he had been waiting for just this moment, Brent reached for Bonnie. She was shocked, then (against her better judgement) delighted. The cool pads of his fingers grazing her forearm, caused the hairs on it to rear. Hesitantly (teasingly?), he drummed his way to her wrist. Was it the darkness that had emboldened him or was he actually shy? She glanced over and saw him in the strobing light from the screen, blond head bashfully lowered, the ice cream bar stuck in his face, soother-like. Gently he lifted her hand (she gave his soft fingers a conspiring squeeze), and as he toyed with her watch strap she shivered as if he were fumbling to undress her.

Dropped, her wrist struck the armrest. Pain sparked up her arm. Shaking her hand out, she cast him a wounded, unnoticed glance. He had her watch and was leaning over to read its face. He could not see the colour of hers.

Exactly ten minutes later, he leaned into her, whispering, 'Inciting incident, ten minute mark.' She smelled his mocha breath.

'Enter love interest, eighteen minutes.'

Hunkered in the insufficiently padded seat, holding her jacket closed with crossed arms, Bonnie sulked in discomfort. She was embarrassed, but also angry, and, because she could not rightly claim that Brent had led her on, she had to think hard for something to blame on him. Unable to concentrate on the film (it was terrible, insulting even), she shifted her numbing buttocks and gusted sighs. Finally it hit her what he'd done: Brent had robbed her of her innocence. Four years ago she would have liked this movie, three weeks ago even she would have accepted its fantastical premise and gasped at its predictable surprises. For ninety minutes she would have happily believed in the beautiful people in it. But now Brent had shown her that there was a formula; he had given it to her in a book. All at once she likened *Screenplays That Sell* to the kind of provocative and deleterious manual that incites controversy whenever one is discovered on library shelves, a *Suicide for Dummies*, or a *Pipe Bombs Step by Step*. Not only could she second-guess every supposed plot twist, she already knew by heart the ending. All endings were the same. Why had she never noticed this? Good was rewarded, evil punished, criminals incarcerated for life, lovers reunited, infidelity forgiven (seductresses blamed), marriages saved, families preserved, children spared, wounds healed, scars erased, lame set back on their feet, personality flaws overcome, addictions successfully treated, the dying allowed their dignity, the dead laid to rest, justice meted out, the innocent vindicated, order reinstated, communities strengthened. Unlike real life, in opposition to real life, in order to distract you from real life, to delude you about real life, everything worked out for the best.

At the forty-three-minute mark, Brent said, 'Watch carefully. This is why we're here.'

Covering her face, she watched through the interstices of spread fingers. Bonnie did not like to see other people having sex, even aestheticized sex like this. She did not like to think she was so driven by something that looked so ridiculous. The woman was lying naked on the bed, though her breasts stayed standing. The man slithered in beside her with the sheet taped to his bum (it never slipped down to show his crack, but travelled along with him as he humped his way up the woman's body). After a close-up of passionate necking (Bonnie was embarrassed by the way their noses got in the way), suddenly they were engaged in vigorous coitus in the seated position, the woman ululating in ecstasy, when in actual fact she was getting a rather rude shaking out.

'How are we going to top this?' Brent leaned over to snigger.

When the film ended and the rest of the audience was filing out, they stayed to watch the ceremonial scrolling of the credits, Bonnie because it used to be her habit to look for mention of Reel Food, Brent so he could pass knowing comments. 'Oh, look, they used a bird wrangler!' 'A friend of mine is a Walla Artist.' As they left, the lobby was filling for the nine o'clock show.

Stepping out of the cinema, Brent summed up the whole experience as Bonnie felt it. 'An uncategorical disappointment.'

'Mmm,' she said.

'That's what I love about you. We are so alike.'

Bonnie pretended to be rooting for something in her purse.

'Where to now? I hate to go home before dark. Ma will think I've been up to no good. How about the new pad?'

'I haven't unpacked yet.'

'I know, then. Let's go watch the sun set on the hockey stick.'

But the hurts had come too hard and fast, first his blithe mention of the erasing of her name (did nobody want her?), next the bruising of her ulna, then her realization that there was no refuge to be found anywhere, not even in entertainment. Finally this: her utter discombobulation leaving the cinema. She had expected it to be dark, but it was still light. She had expected to step out on to Granville Street, but Granville Street this wasn't.

What was she doing here?

Bonnie loved Vancouver. More exactly, she loved the West End (the West *Side* was where Ross had lived; the *East* Side? – frankly, she'd never been). She loved her building and her neighbours, every one of whom possessed superhuman powers of fun. Out of her window the ocean stretched to infinity, the islands humpbacked sea monsters. What was she going to do without the ocean? In the morning, after checking her horoscope, she always looked up the coliform count in English Bay to see how it correlated with what was in store for Virgo. She walked the seawall every afternoon. Inland, these little rituals would be

247

nullified. What then would bring meaning, or at least a semblance of it, to her day?

She saw herself, pink and sullen, twice reflected in his lenses. 'Can I have my watch back?'

14

'What are you looking for, Mommy?'

'For the box that has all the things from the bathroom.' Stifling a sob, she thrust her hand to the lower stratum of the box. This one had towels on top, but underneath, *shoes*! The whole packing ordeal, a blur to her now, could have been one of those psychological experiments wherein the execution of a seemingly mundane task reveals the mind's true nature. Hers displayed all the illogic, inconsistency and utter impracticality of a certifiable basket case.

'Why?'

'I'm looking for some medicine.'

'Why?'

She walked on her knees, a penitent, to the next box. Scraps of packing tape went with her, stuck to her. 'I have a headache.'

'Why?'

'Because nothing ever works out for me, sweetie, and it makes my head hurt.'

'Why does nothing ever work out for you?'

'Please, Brycie. Please. Go and park your cars.'

The top of the box was already speckled a bird's egg darker brown with her tears. Opening the two sides like doors revealed inner, unspattered ones. These she flipped apart and, at last, the omnium gatherum of her medicine cabinet appeared. Most of it was old make-up which she sifted through with both hands until a prescription bottle surfaced, what was left of the Zoloft she had stopped taking four years ago on the suspicion that it was making her nauseous (she'd been pregnant). Setting the bottle to one side, she plunged her hands in again and eventually the Zoplicone rose to the top, then Children's Tylenol, Sudafed, Robitussin, a bottle of One-A-Day Plus Iron, some Travel Tabs.

She got herself a glass of water and set it on the cardboard box they were using as a bedside table until the actual bedside table could be located in all the chaos. Letting go of her shirt hem, she watched everything spill on to the bed.

'What are you doing?' she called.

'Parking!'

She removed the lids from each of the bottles and set them out beside the water glass. The Sudafed was blister-packed. She slid the little silver tray out of the box.

In the living room, Bryce was arranging his cars in a spiral. She stood over him for a minute, fist pressed hard against her mouth. 'Bryce, I want you to go down to the café.'

He set the yellow bus down and adjusted its angle. 'Why?'

'Because I'm tired and I want to lie down. Take your cars and tell Ross you're there.'

'Why are you tired?'

'I just am.'

'Why are you crying?'

'Because I'm tired.'

'Can I have a Cimonum Mountain?'

'Go and see if there are any left.'

He sprang up, depriving her even of the chance to kiss him. She went after him, watched him going down the stairs, the curls on the back of his head and the words Real Food across his shirt front bobbing as he went. 'Go straight in!'

She hastened to the roof's edge to make sure he actually arrived.

It took him three times as long to round the corner as to descend the stairs. At last he appeared at the courtyard entrance, climbed up on the gate and pushed off, riding it backward as it swung him inside.

'Bryce! Open that or people will think the café's closed!'

He rode it out again, hopped off, and sauntered into the empty courtyard behind his stomach.

'Bryce!'

'What?'

'I love you, sweetie.'

Shielding his eyes, he looked up. 'Why?'

Ross was just leaving the kitchen when he ran into Bryce. He scratched the boy's head in passing. The next time he saw him, Bryce had scaled a stool at the counter and, having uncoiled a Cinnamon Mountain, was munching on it in a long, sticky strip.

'Where's your ma?'

He could not understand Bryce's dough-muffled reply.

'Upstairs?'

Bryce nodded.

'She unpacking?'

Bryce shook his head.

'What's she doing then?'

'Eyeing.'

'What?'

'Guying.'

'What?'

He swallowed. 'Crying.'

It was with some weariness that Ross climbed the stairs. Looking after his sister was not nearly as much fun as looking after his nephew. It was time-consuming and frustrating, repetitive, circular. He went over to admire his planters. He'd got Molly, the herb lady, to put in fairly mature plants because it was so late in the season, and all of them had survived the shock of transplant and flourished. Every few days Ross pinched the ends off as Molly had instructed him to do. Before his eyes, the basil sent out side shoots, the dill raised its ferny flag, blue borage flowers busted out all over. He squeezed the lavender and smelled his hands.

Bonnie was tired, so tired. She hadn't slept at all the previous night. Almost the moment she set down the water glass and lay back on the pillow, she fell asleep and began dreaming in weird, overlapping images. She was looking down on Bryce, not from the roof, but as if she were floating above him. He was crying inconsolably. *What now?* she was thinking in the dream. *What does he want from me now?* Somewhere in the background she heard Ross calling her name. He sounded annoyed and she was conscious of the injustice of this when he was the one who'd brought her here and ruined her life. Rolling on to her side, she drew her knees up and tucked her fists under her chin. Away she floated, bobbing off to Nod, bobbing on the ocean – oh, to see the Pacific one last time! – Ross's call coming closer until it sounded as if he was right next to her.

'For Christ's sake! Oh, Jesus, Bonnie! Bonnie!'

She didn't know what was happening. Lifted into the air from behind, then forced on to her knees, she began screaming before she had even completely woken up. He covered her mouth – who, she couldn't see. Someone had walked right in in the middle of the day! One arm tight round her waist, he forced her double with his weight. She tried to scream again, but something was rammed down her throat. The entire contents of her stomach came gushing out all over the bed – a lot of liquid, then the whitish pulp that had been Bryce's leftovers at breakfast, the pink pellet of the One-A-Day Plus Iron, two Children's Tylenols and a Zoplicone, as yet undissolved. Released, she fell face down in the wetness, bawling.

251

'Why did you do it? Why?'

Pushing herself up, she turned and saw that it was Ross. Ross crying, too. Stupidly, she thought that he'd saved her from her attacker instead of been him, and she wrapped her arms round his neck.

Ross pushed her off. 'What about Bryce?'

'Oh,' she croaked. 'But I didn't.'

'Then what's all this?' He swept his hand across the box, sending all the bottles flying, different coloured pills ricocheting off the cardboard surfaces all over the room.

'Don't do that! Why did you do that? Now I have to pick them all up!' Moving out of the wet spot, she hid her face in her hands.

Side by side on the bed, their shoulders touched. 'All I want,' Ross told her, 'is for you to be happy.'

'A fine way you have of showing it.'

'Look at me. I want you to hear what I have to say.'

'What?' she said, not looking.

'We haven't talked about this before, Bonnie. I think this is the time.'

'No!' She covered her ears, knowing what was coming. 'Blah, blah, blah, blah, blah . . .'

Ross pulled her hands away. 'Just listen to what I have to tell you!'

'I'm not interested!'

'You don't even know what I'm going to say!'

'I do! I'm not interested in becoming a Buddhist!'

'What do you even know about it?'

'I know enough!'

'What? Tell me one single thing you know.'

She threw it in his face, because she was right and he would not be able to deny it: 'I know that the Buddha is *fat*!'

* * *

15

'I called three times! Where were you?'

'What do you mean where was I!'

From Iliana's overly defensive tone, he guessed that he had been yelling (he wouldn't put it past himself after what he had just done to Bonnie), that Iliana was simply matching him decibel for decibel. 'There's an emergency here. Bonnie took a bunch of pills. I've been trying to get hold of you.'

'Get her to the hospital,' Iliana commanded, and Ross realized how long it had been since he'd heard that formidable nursy tone from her.

'She's okay. She didn't actually take them all. Maybe you should come and get Bryce, though.'

'Does she want me to?'

'I didn't ask her. I just think—'

'He's her child, Ross.'

He looked through the short-order window at Bryce at the end of the counter where Deb was showing him how to make a cat's cradle. 'I'm wondering if she's fit. I wish you could talk to her.'

'She thinks he'll be okay with Bonnie,' he told Deb after he got off the phone. 'Maybe you should go up and try to talk to her. She needs a woman's ear, I think.'

'Me?' Deb shook her head emphatically. 'I'm the second last person she wants to talk to. She didn't lend Brent any money, did she?'

Deb's comment rattled Ross because he hadn't realized Brent had anything to do with the crisis. He knew that Bonnie and Brent were friends and that she was doing some typing for him, but that was all. Now it made sense why Bonnie had changed her mind about moving. He took Bryce and a big bag of leftovers upstairs.

After he had put the food away in Bonnie's empty fridge, he found her in the living room, standing at the window with its view over the back of the post office, hugging her thin arms to herself.

'Are you going to be all right?'

'No.'

'Want me to stay?'

'No.'

He hesitated, wondering if he should mention Brent, say that Brent didn't deserve her, or something to that effect. He decided not to. 'You know where I am.'

'And you know where I am,' she told him coldly.

Her tone bounced right off him now that he knew it wasn't really him she was angry at. What did hurt was knowing that she was suffering.

It was one thing to accept that suffering was the inevitable condition of the world, another to see it at work on his own sister. 'All I can do,' he told Iliana in bed that night, 'is empathize with her. But why? Why does she keep doing it?'

'What?'

'Falling for those guys. You want to understand *samsara*? Just look at Bonnie's love life. Bryce's dad? I thank him for what he did, but smoke just poured off him. Positively flaming. Then there was Randy. He walked the walk for sure. Who was it last year? I can't even remember.'

'He was Japanese.'

'Japanese! Say no more!'

'You know why she keeps doing it, Ross. You pointed it out yourself.'

'Why?'

'Because it's you she loves.'

Ross said, 'Hmm.'

'So *is* Brent gay?'

'With shades like that? You have to ask?' He turned out the light.

'Anyway,' said Iliana, 'I don't think this has anything to do with Brent. She told me as much on the phone when she called from Vancouver. They're kindred spirits, that's all.'

'Well, Deb thinks she lent him money.'

'I also don't think she meant to kill herself. She has a pill ritual. Something she does when she's upset. It makes her feel better. She told me about it.'

Ross punched his pillow. 'She's nuts.' Exhausted, sick, he threw himself down. He'd stuck his finger down his sister's throat and made her vomit all over the bed. What a horrible thing to do!

'Good night,' Iliana hinted.

In the dark, lifting himself on his elbows, he leaned over to kiss her. Since his eyes had not yet adjusted to the dark, his aim was less than perfect. She took it on the side of the nose.

'I love you, Ross. You're a good person.'

'How can you say that? I stuck my finger down my sister's throat!'

Toss, turn, batter the pillow: over and over. Finally, just as he was edging closer to the void, a thought jerked him back. He sat up in the bed and cried out in the dark, 'Does my sister like it up the ass?'

'Oh, Ross,' said an exasperated Iliana. 'Go to sleep.'

The next morning he leaned the Giant against the wall under the stairs and walked back through the alley. It was too early to go up and check on Bonnie, but he would later, after she had had a good long sleep. She would, he hoped, wake to this new day (sunny yet again; the last rain they'd had was the beginning of June) and find herself in this great little town where the air was fresh and the flowers were in bloom and the people knew each other's names, with a job and a loving family around her, and maybe, just maybe, she would realize that it was possible to be happy.

He was hosing down the sidewalk when Brent Howland appeared at the corner and turned in the direction of the café, as if he intended to come for his free morning coffee, as usual. Flabbergasted to see him arriving at the gate, Ross lifted the hose as Brent was stepping over it, almost tripping him. He was able to rationalize this by telling himself that his other option was spraying him with water. By the time Ross had finished cleaning the sidewalk and had put away the hose, Brent was at his regular table, notebook open, Discman plugged into his head.

Ross marched over. 'What can I get for you?'

Brent pressed a button on the Discman. 'What?'

'Our usual waitress attempted suicide yesterday. I'll have to take your order.'

Hearing this, the man who had buggered his sister and cast her cruelly aside threw back his head and laughed. 'I'll have a latte.'

Here was the challenge, Ross thought, standing at the Faema. It was a simple matter to comport yourself with compassion and equanimity when everyone around you deserved it. But what now? What now? He flicked on the steamer and the Faema began its low-pitched growl. In his mind, he heard Deb say, *She didn't lend Brent any money, did she?* The Faema climaxing with a shriek, he slammed the steel carafe down hard. 'Shit!'

It was Brent Howland who had stolen his bike!

Out on the patio Brent sat, feet up on the opposite chair, head tilted back, catching the morning rays. What Ross would have loved to do was throw the coffee in his pretty face. Whether as an unconscious, watered-down fulfilment of this unwholesome desire, or simply because his hands were shaking with anger as he went to set the bowl on the table, a little coffee sloshed out and splashed Brent on the forearm. In an instant the chair was overturned and

Brent was on his feet holding his arm, backing away, screaming, 'You burned me!'

'What about my sister!'

All at once Brent froze, sunglasses sliding down his nose so that Ross saw his eyes for the first time. 'You weren't serious?'

'What did you do to her!'

'Nothing! I didn't do anything to her!'

Deb appeared in the French doors and, without even asking what was going on, came and caught Brent by the arm. 'I told you not to come here.'

16

Every other girl had disappointed him. Every time it turned out the same. He'd notice someone in the mall or working the concession in the arena, someone whose smile or hair he liked. After hanging around a bit to see what she was like, he'd finally get his nerve up. It went on from there, the same old story, until either he stopped calling or she got her brother to answer the phone and say she wasn't in.

There were a lot of reasons why things were different this time. He'd always hated the phone for the way it made you responsible for half the conversation. Iliana didn't want him to call. She didn't even expect him to talk. And while other girls grew sulky when he could not second-guess their feelings, it was pretty obvious what Iliana felt from the noises that she made. This was exactly what he needed, to know that she enjoyed the things he did without expecting them to lead to something supposedly more important. The others were always pulling back. They were embarrassed if they came in front of him, as if he had made them tell a secret about themselves while refusing to share one in return. As soon as it happened, he felt the pressure of reciprocation. He knew they would get together a couple more times and that would be it. Then either he'd blow it, or she'd think the situation was too weird. He would probably die a virgin was what he thought.

The stash under his bed notwithstanding, he'd never been as embarrassed as he was the next time he bought a magazine. He sat in the truck outside for a long time, just to make sure the place was empty. The guy behind the counter was instantly suspicious of the way Stevie walked in (head ducked to hide from the surveillance camera), how he sidled up to the magazine rack and grabbed the first thing he saw. 'This it?' the clerk asked, standing back, almost raising his hands in advance of the stick-up. 'Just a *Flare* for you today?'

Stevie told him, 'I'd like a bag.'

He'd bought it for the ads, for the full colour pictures of the women's faces, the profile shots that showed almost life-sized ears. He ran his fingers along their jawlines and over their lips, the way Iliana had shown him. He stroked their paper collarbones and necks. There were all these other parts to a body, other ways to feel. He hadn't known this before. It came as a relief.

And this, too: that he might press against her leg or hip as he caressed her and still stay completely in control. In the past, whenever he tried this, the girl had always misunderstood. She'd thought he was signalling his readiness when in fact he was trying to slow himself down. At this, the worst possible moment, she would touch him or pull him against her, and the whole thing would be over.

Iliana *couldn't* feel him.

That day she arrived at the usual time, three thirty, after she finished work. If she had mixed up the time, he'd still have known it was her because not even the Jehovah's Witnesses rang his doorbell any more. Inside, he took her face in his hands and kissed her mouth, which was how they broke the ice. She was always nervous at the beginning but already he knew the places to touch that helped her relax.

He let her go ahead to the bedroom, coming in after her so she could get herself on to the bed and undressed without the pressure of him watching. The first time he'd seen her lying down he'd been surprised to learn how tall she was. Today he was surprised because she'd taken all her clothes off, even her panties, so there was nothing to break up the long line of her body. Her pubic hair was darker than the hair on her head, straight and wispy like a baby's. He came and sat on the side of the bed, stroking it, kitten soft, while she watched.

'Oh,' she said, wincing when he stood and removed his pants. 'Don't.'

'All right.'

'I mean, you can take them off, but I don't want to— I thought I did, but now I don't.'

Lying down, he started on her neck. When he directed his breath into her ear, she responded with a gasp and dug her fingers into his arm, controlling the pleasure he gave her by how hard she squeezed him. He rolled on top of her and spent a long time on her face and mouth before working his way down to her breasts. Though he had always thought of himself as a tit man, he did not mind that hers were small. They were so excitable. He could take one in each hand and work the nipples with his thumbs.

While he was doing this, he sat astride her. If he had had any conscious intention, he would have tried to stick it somewhere less ambitious. Leaning to take a nipple in his mouth, he hovered over her, trying to decide – left or right? All at once he realized he *was* inside her. He stopped, hands at her shoulders propping himself up, feeling his pulsing self surrounded in her liquidy press.

She didn't know it either. 'What?' she asked, seeing the look on his face.

'I'm sorry.'

She stared up at him, confused. Then, shutting her eyes, she ran her hands down his back and gripped his ass.

He started to move, cautiously, a little forward, a little back. That was it. That was as long as he could last. A phrase popped into his mind the very moment he came: *make me one with everything*. It was the punchline of the joke Ross had told him at the Legion.

17

The Second Noble Truth is the Truth of the Cause of Suffering, desire. Not just sexual desire, Ross knew. Wanting things – love, success, material possessions – clinging to these things for fear that they will be taken away, that they won't last, then inevitably growing tired of them, wanting something different, wanting more. This ceaseless yearning distorts our vision so we do not see things as they really are, but rather through the lens of whether we want them or not, and how we might get them for ourselves. And because we hate those who thwart our desires, the cycle continues, desire inflicting yet more suffering.

Desire was clearly at work on Ross's sister, his perpetually dissatisfied, endlessly suffering twin. It was at work in Ross, too. He wanted Bonnie to be happy. She wanted love. If only she had love, they would both be happy. 'If only I had . . .' It was the open-ended mantra of desire, the circle most people trudged in all their lives.

Like a turnkey servicing the solitary block, Ross went up to the apartment three times a day bearing food, drink and sometimes reading material; he came back down with the old plates untouched. Bonnie was hunger-striking. She accepted the magazines, but the biography of the Buddha he found splayed open on the far side of the alley as if it had leaped from the second-storey window.

Bryce Ross kept all day, only bringing him back when it was time for bed. Bonnie did not object; neither did she thank Ross. She simply opened the door and, unsmiling, squatted to Bryce's level, kissed him, then, squaring his shoulders in the direction of the bathroom, nudged him onward. Essentially Bryce was in Ross's custody, but this did not make Ross as happy as he had once imagined it might. Instead, the entire situation served as a reminder of why one should be wary of happiness in the first place: it is so often contingent upon someone else's unhappiness.

Deb came to Ross and assured him that Brent would not be back. 'Enough is enough. I can't live with him. I sent him back to Vancouver.' Ross thought that Bonnie might finally emerge when she heard this. 'Brent's gone,' he told her. She tried to shut the door in his face. He stopped it with his hand. 'Why won't you answer the phone? Iliana wants to talk to you. She's been calling. She's worried. I'm worried.'

She pushed hard, shutting him out.

Truth be told, he was more upset about his own behaviour the afternoon Bonnie pretended suicide than Bonnie's, which he knew now had been a bluff. It distressed him that, after a year of consistent practice, when it came down to the crunch he had chucked it all. The whole reason for a daily practice was to develop wisdom and equanimity that could be drawn on in a crisis. When he thought of how he had practically assaulted Bonnie, how he had treated Brent (how he thought Brent deserved this treatment); when he thought of the false accusation he had harboured against Stevie Blake for so long, he grew positively hang-dogged with discouragement.

His friend Jaime Rios rang that week, as he did every now and then, and cheered Ross up. Ross both liked Jaime and felt indebted to him for taking over Reel Food (it had been a little easier for him to hand his beloved company over to a friend). It was Jaime who had given Ross the idea of what to serve at his wedding. At the time, though Bonnie and Iliana had been all het up about the dress, Ross had doubted that anyone would even remember what the bride wore. It was the meal that would make the day memorable. When, in the years to come, they heard the linked names 'Ross and Iliana', he wanted their mouths to water. Yet until Jaime came along Ross knew only what he wasn't going to offer: not the West Coast cliché of the whole stuffed salmon, not ribs or stuck pig. His minimum goal had been that none of the one hundred and eighteen guests who had returned their RSVPs, nor the thirty-two who had been remiss but would probably show up on the day, would eat something they had eaten at someone else's wedding. That they would all eat something they had never before tasted was his highest ambition. If he could accomplish this without having to resort to molding ground chicken into the shape of body parts, he would be doubly ecstatic on his wedding day.

'Jaime!' Ross said on the phone. 'How's it going?'

'Good, Rrross. Good. We're busy. Verrry busy. You don't miss it? You are sure you don't want to come back?'

'Not a chance.'

The morning of the wedding Ross had met Jaime at the Reel Food kitchen and together they had unloaded the salt from Ross's van. Back and forth from the parking lot they shouldered the heavy sacks. Afterwards Ross insisted on making them breakfast as a reward for having lugged in three hundred kilograms. (If he had not already conducted two preliminary test-trials, he would have sworn three hundred kilograms was too much salt.)

While Ross scrambled the eggs and Jaime cut pieces of canvas off the bolt, the two men talked about love. For this reason, too,

Ross was glad Jaime was back in Vancouver after a year away in his native Colombia. Two Canadian men might yammer all morning about sports, or maybe sex, but they would never mention love. Refused any other subject of conversation, they would prefer to sit in stubborn silence. Only a Latin could sigh *amor, amor* and grow weepy over his eggs.

'Rrross,' Jaime had said, '*amor* is like a pearl. It begins as a little irritation, then grows and grows to something precious.'

Because he was very short and plagued with over-productive sebaceous glands, Jaime looked at first glance adolescent, but the passion of his metaphor and his virile application of Ring of Fire sauce to his eggs greatly impressed Ross. 'Jaime! Promise you'll ask my sister to dance!'

After they had eaten, they laid out the first rectangle of canvas and poured in the centre of it, like the cone of white sand in the bottom of an hourglass, half a sack of salt. From the walk-in fridge, Ross brought out the first lamb studded all over with garlic. Pink and headless, it looked suspiciously like a flayed greyhound, and, when they poured yet more salt on and covered it, it looked like the carcass of a greyhound buried in a snowbank. They packed it in however much salt seemed like far too much, times ten, then very carefully, making sure that the salt stayed evenly around the whole body of the animal, folded the canvas round it and tied it up roast fashion. With all the salt, it was twice as heavy and required both of them to lift it.

'How's everybody?' Ross asked on the phone.

'Great. They all say hi. Mike says hi.'

'And? Any *amor*?'

'Oh, Rrross,' Jaime sighed. 'It is men like you who have all he luck.'

The next evening Ross rode over to Stevie Blake's. Deb told Ross where he lived – on the other side of the tracks, not far from the bus depot. He spotted Stevie's truck in the driveway of a blue and white bungalow fronted with dead grass, the last house on the block. A row of weed-filled tyres painted white formed a barrier against the road. Someone was home; Ross knew because the curtains were open showing the blue glow off the television, ripply through the plastic on the window. Only when he got right up to the house was he in a position to see the ramp.

On Ross's second ring Stevie opened the door wearing shorts held up with a bungee cord. Clearly he had not expected Ross (if he had, he might not have answered, which was why Ross had not called ahead). There were three distinct parts to his expression, or three distinct expressions played out in succession. Though it had taken two rings and an interval in between for Stevie to reach the door, he had swung it open without hesitation and looked out at Ross. In the second before it warped to something else entirely, Ross saw love. Unmistakably it was love. Normally Stevie looked so closed and suspicious, but now it was as if his face had been smashed with a hammer causing the hard protective layer to crumble away, exposing a soft and sentimental underneath. (Ross was reminded again of his wedding, cracking open the baked saline shell.) Then shock. Stevie stepped back as if he had just now felt the hammer. Then the same defensive squint that had attracted Ross's blame in the first place.

'I didn't think you were going to answer. What's the ramp for?'

Stevie looked at it for what seemed a long time. 'My grand-mother.'

'She home?'

'No.' Through the fabric of his shorts he fiddled with his balls 'She went over to the old folks' place a few months ago. I built i to dolly some furniture out.'

Ross pointed beyond Stevie, inside. 'Can I?'

The living room surprised Ross. He had expected from Stevie a standard of housekeeping to match his dress, which, ironically, was exactly what people always assumed of Ross, who was also scrupulous about his surroundings. He entered the room and saw that, not only was it spotless, but that Stevie was not alone; he had been watching TV with the vacuum cleaner. Stevie went over to where it was standing upright beside the couch and began winding the cord. 'You want a drink?'

'Sure,' said Ross. 'Water would be great.'

The décor did not reflect the tastes of someone Stevie's age (if Stevie had tastes). It was granny set-dec. There were a couple of women's magazines on the coffee table, left behind by the grandmother, no doubt. The one on top Ross remembered buying for Bonnie the other day, but when he moved it aside he saw that Stevie was using it to conceal a *Penthouse*. A frisson ran through him and he quickly replaced the *Flare*. Ross had himself indulged in pornography in his youth (what boy hadn't?) and on several occasions had been subjected to his father's half-hearted lectures on the dangers of excessive masturbation, though Ross had always got the impression that the chummy slap on the back Teddy concluded with summed up his real views.

Stevie came back with Ross's water. 'How've you been?' Ross asked, accepting the glass. 'Working?'

'Someone offered me something, but I didn't want those hours.' He dropped into the armchair.

'Night work?'

'It finished at, like, five.'

Ross didn't press for logic and none was volunteered. Instead, they sat unspeaking, Ross already wondering how he could ever have imagined even the remotest resemblance between Stevie Blake and Jaime Rios. At his wedding, Ross had tried to set

Jaime up with Bonnie, but Bonnie had resisted. Now that she'd fallen so low, Ross wondered if she would be as picky. But Jaime was in Vancouver, so he'd thought of Stevie, partially because he felt bad about blaming him for stealing his bike. Physically, there was a similarity: both Jaime and Stevie were dark-haired and dark-complected and both looked younger than their years, though Stevie was much taller. But if Ross had been sitting in Jaime's living room, there would be passionate outbursts and fervent interjections in Spanish, not this excruciating silence.

'Do you have a girlfriend?' Ross came right out and asked.

Stevie's foot stopped jigging. He let his head fall back. 'That would be so great.'

'It seemed like you were expecting someone else when you opened the door.'

He smiled.

'So you don't?'

'No.'

Though he had second thoughts now that he'd seen the magazine, Ross had not harboured any illusions about a relationship between Stevie and Bonnie anyway; he simply thought it would give Bonnie's morale a boost to be asked out on a date. But he didn't want to unleash a sex fiend on his sister either, at least not without a cautionary lecture, Teddy-style, first.

'I remember being single,' he told Stevie. 'It was exhausting. I was on the make all the time. I can't tell you how many women I slept with before I met Iliana.'

This was true. *A slut* was what Bonnie used to call him.

He set the glass on the coffee table and sat there with his elbows weighing on his knees. Opening the *Flare* to an ad for lipstick, he let the pages fan backwards while he chose his words. 'You're what? Early twenties? No offence, but you probably don't think about this stuff. I sure didn't.' He glanced at Stevie who was staring at him from under the dense overhang of hair. 'Now I try to be mindful. I try to focus on the action I'm in the middle of and only it. That way you're more or less forced to consider your intentions. Right intention, right action. So take sex. That's what we're discussing, isn't it?'

'Is it?'

'Well, it's what I'm talking about. Sort of. How did we get on to this anyway?' He chuckled nervously and, running a hand through his hair, got a noseful of himself. *Fuck*, he thought. 'Okay, so you go inside someone, right? I used to do that with women I didn't even feel close to.'

So unexpected was Stevie's outburst, it seemed to Ross that he was speaking for the first time in words instead of grunts. 'You can't fucking *believe* how it feels, not until it finally happens. It's like being a baby again or something. Or like you weren't even born. I'm not talking about, like, fucking your mother or anything like that! I mean that all the shit that's happened to you, it, like, disappears for those few seconds. If only it could go on for ever. I need a cigarette.'

He sprang up. Astonished, Ross watched him lurch out of the room.

Ross flipped the *Penthouse* open. A blonde on her knees and elbows looked back over her shoulder at him, the rosy folds of her vulva bracketed by lifted haunches. Transfixed, he gazed on at that place from where all men are born and to where they keep crawling back to experience their thousand exquisite little nullifications.

Stevie spoke from the door. 'I'm trying not to smoke in here any more.'

Ross slapped the magazine closed. Getting up, he followed Stevie out on to the front step.

The street ended in a barricade beyond which was an abandoned field. A shadow at this distance, the ridge curved in silhouette like a woman lying on her side. The sky blushed a labial pink. Stevie, rolling, asked, 'What's your wife doing tonight?'

Taken aback by the question, Ross floundered in his reply. 'She might be watching tennis.' Yet there had been a time when he knew her whereabouts at any given moment.

'She likes tennis?'

'She was the girls' champion of all Christendom. Before, I mean.'

'What else does she like to watch?'

'Um. You know those medical shows? She's addicted to them. She used to be a nurse. Look, did you ever meet my sister?'

Stevie aborted the inhalation. 'She used to be a nurse?'

It was a stupid idea, but Ross felt he should say what he had come to say. Then he was going to go home and make love to Iliana. 'I think you did. When I was showing her the apartment. You were working on the planters. She just moved in and doesn't know many people yet. Anyway, what I'm getting at is she's single, too. I'll leave it up to you what you want to do with this information.'

Stevie made a spitting sound, trying to get a stray thread of tobacco off his tongue.

'I've got to split.' Ross backed down the ramp. 'Come into the café sometime why don't you?'

He got on to his bike and rode off with a hand held high, without looking back, heading in the direction of Overwaitea, the only place he could think of that was open.

When he reached home, he strode excitedly up the ramp, eagerly, actually accompanied by an old friend of theirs who hadn't been around for a while. He thought about greeting her that way: *Look who's here!* 'Iliana!'

'Hi!' she called from another room.

He kicked his sandals off into the cupboard, out of her way. 'What are you doing?'

'I'm just in the bathroom!'

What day was it? Flowers crushed under his arm, he counted back two nights: Monday, Sunday. *Shit.*

Waiting in bed, trying not to look at the clock, trying not to think of the rubber gloves. He tried to keep himself pumped. He pumped himself, thinking of the *Penthouse* blonde, of Iliana in various positions, of Paula Falcone that time she— Susan Strangeway pretending to be that Hollywood— That girl in Grade Eleven who—

'Flowers?' said Iliana, twenty minutes later by the clock. She sounded more appalled than surprised.

'That bad? I was over at Stevie Blake's and by the time I left everything but Overwaitea was closed.'

Instead of asking what the occasion was, she wanted to know what he had been doing at Stevie Blake's. He told her his idea about Stevie and Bonnie. Clearly, she did not think much of it.

He turned out the light and leaned over to kiss her. *Rubber gloves, rubber gloves, rubber gloves.* He put his tongue in.

Rubber gloves.

'Good night, Ross.'

'Do you want to make love?' he asked, defeat already in his voice.

'No. Not tonight actually. I'm tired. Do you mind?'

Soft in his hand, his penis was already asleep. For a long time Ross lay there in the dark wondering which of them, he or Iliana, was paralysed.

18

That certain behaviours were inherently wrong and to be avoided, that there was such a thing as sin, had a practical as well as a moral application, Iliana realized now. Even people who were not religious understood this, even Ross, who preferred to call himself 'spiritual'; he adhered to a programme of moral imperatives called the Eight-Fold Path, which emphasized, instead of wrongs, the right way to live. But for someone who had rejected the commandments of her youth, who was not about to replace them with another alien set, Iliana had only her conscience as her guide, and the conscience, she knew by now, was as unreliable as a blind man at a crime scene, as self-serving as a monkey in a cafeteria. All there was to limit or control her was her fear of getting caught.

Then something happened that cut her loose completely. While it was true that at one time she was very quick to detect a patronizing attitude in other people, nowadays she could laugh it off even if it was indisputably there. She rarely considered any more how people reacted the first time they met her, whether they stared or avoided her eye. But outside Overwaitea, as her brief exchange with Beth Ann ended, as Beth Ann drew it to a close with that most asexual of gestures, a benevolent pat on the head, Iliana understood that there was in fact nothing to hold her back. She was exempt from societal scrutiny. It was almost as if the part of her that had no feeling was invisible, and, by extension, so was she (which explained why some people had to look at her so hard, and sometimes didn't seem to see her). Never would she be suspected of an affair because no one would suspect desire in her. The chair had neutered her. That this was not entirely true she only realized the next day, picking up Bonnie at the bus depot. Bonnie she would have to be careful around as, evidently, she possessed some kind of radar.

What had happened to Iliana's body after the accident was a normal neurological adjustment. Sensory perception below the waist had been cut off and, to compensate, had intensified in other places. It was as if all her pleasure receptors had migrated upward. The minute hairs in her ears, the skin of her lips, the dip in her collarbones, all became acutely responsive. She only had to draw a fingernail down her throat to cause herself to shiver. That young girl carrying her imaginary suitcases, hands out from her sides, had been more than strenuously pious; she had been prescient.

At first when she went to see Stevie it was enough that they kissed. Oh, the kiss, she had thought. Ever the appetizer, never the meal, but why? The flick, the suck, the lick: the kiss had all of this, and something, too, that she had never considered. When you inhale another person's exhalation, you take him in. His oxygen penetrates the lining of your lungs and you absorb him into your bloodstream. Was any deeper possible? But the nature of appetite is that more and more is required to satisfy it. As with food, she was suddenly voracious. Many people who cook or bake or serve for a living cease to be tempted; their palate wearies. Iliana's was the opposite case. She sneaked into the cooler and plucked savoury morsels out of the bowls. She licked her fingers. It was unhygienic. Ross would be angry if he knew, but she didn't think he would find out. She believed her immunity extended to this, too. Not surprisingly, the bread she baked these days was some of her best. Kneading, she pressed her whole body into the dough, eyes closed, moving in rhythm. She imagined that she was fucking it.

Stevie Blake had said that that was what he wanted to do to her and it did not take long after he had worked his way down to her most potent and surprising erogenous zone, the imaginary band that divided her unfeeling from her feeling self, before she wanted him to. She was confused as to why he didn't. If he thought he was being selfless, that she wouldn't feel it, she was sure that he was wrong.

When she was in hospital, a nurse had come at intervals to poke her with a safety pin. She would fold back the covers and lift Iliana's gown, then touch her with either the point or the bend, beginning at her midriff. 'Dull or sharp?' she'd asked. Iliana was not allowed to look or she would imagine the sensation. Once, glancing down, and seeing the sharp end pointed near her groin, she'd flinched.

'No peeking,' the nurse had said.

But Ross could make her feel it, too. He watched the procedure with bafflement and when the nurse asked, 'Dull or sharp?' Ross cringed.

'Sharp,' Iliana had said, cringing too. 'I feel it on Ross's face.'

'I'm sorry,' Stevie told her.

She opened her eyes. They didn't have many moments like this, when their eyes met and did not immediately veer off in opposite directions. If, while she was watching him, he glanced up to see what effect he was having on her, he'd look away. It was all very solemn, almost strict. No talking. No laughing. In her head she heard hymns. Apart from the fact that they happened to be in the same bed, they avoided each other. His expression was so serious and intense, Iliana assumed the pleasure he got out of pleasing her satisfied his ego, that he was doing it for himself. For who else? He didn't even know her. Now he looked down on her with the same mixture of pathos and embarrassment that a watched dog puts on when squatting to defecate.

'I'm sorry.'

He seemed to be begging. He was begging for it.

It was over before it started for her. Stevie collapsed with a cry and, lying on top of her, shuddered. Apparently he had the world's longest orgasms. It just went on and on until, finally, she realized that he was crying.

'What?' she asked. 'What's wrong?'

He lifted his face. Perhaps it was the tears running down his cheeks. He seemed drenched with them. He lifted his face and took a gulp of air as if he was just surfacing from water. It reminded her of someone in a baptismal font bursting through with hallelujahs.

When she left, she did that wordlessly, too. He would already have taken himself to another part of the house to allow her to dress and transfer. (He was discreet, which was her only indication, until today, that he was also sensitive.) In her mind, by dispensing with goodbye, she was demonstrating that she possessed enough self-control to come and go as she desired.

That same night Ross brought her flowers. She came into the bedroom and saw them on her bedside table, red carnations and baby's breath, a sprig of fern browning at the tips. 'Flowers?' she said, horrified.

He was sitting up in bed with his shirt off. 'That bad? I was over at Stevie Blake's and by the time I left, everything but Overwaitea was closed.'

Iliana had just transferred to the bed and, though it felt to her that her seismic reaction to this announcement must have been obvious through the mattress, he seemed not to notice. He did not even give her an opening in which she could blurt out a confession. 'Can you see Bonnie going out with Stevie Blake?'

She could not believe that he had not guessed who the ramp was for. 'You went to his house?'

'Yeah. He lives just behind the bus depot.'

Her heart was pounding. Surely he felt that, too.

'Stupid?' said Ross.

'What?'

'Getting the two of them together.'

'Who?'

'Stevie and Bonnie.'

She let out a sound, then stifled herself. Ross thought it was a laugh and said, 'You're right.'

Why did he pursue Stevie like this? It was almost as if he knew and wasn't saying anything. She hoped this wasn't so. She hoped that, despite everything she'd done, she still deserved his anger.

He turned out the light and leaned over her, a shadow, unexpectedly pressing his mouth over hers. His tongue, that slippery master of ceremonies, slid in. The kiss sustained itself, went on so long she had to pull away. 'Good night, Ross.'

'Do you want to make love?'

'No. Not tonight actually. I'm tired. Do you mind?'

For a long time he sat in the dark beside her, breathing in and out.

The next afternoon she went to see Stevie. Instead of immediately sinking to his knees, he went over to the couch. Wondering what the matter was, she joined him. He took her hand and, with his thumb, stroked the back of it. Iliana watched, realizing with some trepidation that he was going to speak. When all he did was turn her wedding ring round, she plucked her hand back. 'I'll see you in there.'

'Wait,' he blurted. 'Is it true you were a nurse?'

'Yes. Why?'

'I want to know more about you.'

'Know what?' she asked, appalled.

'Like, everything.'

She backed the chair up. 'I'll see you in there.'

Lying down beside her, he began to explore her, closing his eyes, seeing her with his hands. She kept her eyes open to watch how he slid down her waist, over her hip, along her thigh. She could still feel his hands even below her waist, but the difference was, on her legs, she could not feel the rasp of his callused palm.

Later, Stevie stopped to put on a condom. She was both relieved by the interruption and distraught. Of course a condom, but at the same time it made her cringe, not only to think of Stevie making this purchase, shifty in the pharmacy queue, but because precaution implied premeditation, and premeditation a graver degree of guilt.

On the edge of the bed, he pinched the tip with one hand while he rolled the condom down. (He was probably not all that enormous; it was just that he was mounted on so thin a frame.) Swinging his legs up, he climbed back on top of her. She watched his every movement, noting the almost trance-like intensity of his focus, how, as he slowly lowered himself into her, his face immediately took on a drugged expression. He shifted his weight on to one hand and used the other to separate her legs a little. The play-by-play on his face resumed. It, and her hands on his impossibly tiny buttocks, suggested to her what to feel, how slow or quick she should rise to match his arc (it was quick). He began to flex his jaw unconsciously. He breathed in short, equine spurts as he thrusted. All at once his mouth opened as if to scream, but there was no sound except the one she made.

Afterwards they lay together for a long time. She could feel him retracting. She had used to love lying with Ross after sex. He would sing the chorus of 'Seasons in the Sun' in an ascending falsetto as he shrank, until, finally, he would slip out of her, his liquid following in an unstopped gush. She felt that now, too, even though Stevie was wearing a condom.

'What?' he asked.

'Nothing.'

'What's so funny?'

'Nothing.' Carefully, she folded away the smile.

Sitting up, he moved off her and, at the edge of the bed, shed the snakeskin on the floor. He used the sheet to wipe himself. 'Did you feel it?'

'Yes.'

'How?'

'I felt it in my mind.'

He turned back to her and spread her wide, then moved down on her so his dark curls fell over her lap. She watched and, watching, remembered too how that felt. She began to feel aroused again. He moved down the inside of her thighs, slathered the hollows behind her knees; she was reminded then of Bryce and his experiments, how he liked to poke at her when she wasn't watching. She had long had a feeling about Stevie, that some part of him was three and a half years old.

Backing off the bed so he was kneeling on the floor, he took her toes one by one into his mouth. When he had finished, he crawled back beside her. 'You didn't like it.' He sounded sulky with disappointment.

'It's just that I'm thinking about the time.'

'When does he get home?'

'He might call and ask me to pick up Bryce.'

'You go and get him in the car?'

'Yes.'

'You're not afraid to drive?'

She looked at him, puzzled. 'No.'

'Do you miss it?'

'What?'

'Walking?'

'What I miss most is running.' She shifted a little in his direction, nudging.

'I'd kill myself,' he said.

She drew back the same distance. 'You have very little love of life.'

Evidently she'd spoken curtly. He got up at once and stepped into his shorts.

Dressing, she smelled bacon. By the time she got to the kitchen, the house was filled with its perfume. He was lifting a slice out of the pan with a fork and setting it on a nest of toilet paper on the counter. 'Are you hungry?'

'I've got to go.' She paused. 'How did you explain the ramp?'

'I could have told him anything. He's fucking clueless.'

She could not see his face for his hair; she didn't need to. She heard his tone and, though it shocked her, she realized that it shouldn't have. All along she had been careful not to mention Ross to Stevie, out of consideration for both of them. Ross, though, brought up Stevie all the time. He loved to be liked. Antipathy he could accept if it was mutual, or if Ross was the one disliking, as in the case of his old neighbour Ed Snow. But he really could not stand it when someone disliked him unilaterally. The doggy in him would be unleashed and, almost by reflex, he would rear up and, placing his big paws firmly on that person's shoulders, try to change his mind.

'Goodbye,' she said before she moved out of the doorway.

Stevie looked up in alarm.

She left thinking of their wedding, how the sky that morning had worried her. Ambiguously veiled in a colourless haze, it had implied either later evaporation or, sickeningly, rain. They had been about to have an entirely outdoor wedding in a geographic region classified as temperate rain forest, yet not for one moment had they given thought to the vicissitudes of the weather. Apart from dressing herself, Iliana had only been responsible for the flowers and the cake. Everything else had been up to Ross who had been so preoccupied with the meat that he referred to the wedding as 'the cook-out' or 'Project Lamb' and had even hired another caterer for the rest of the meal. Seeing consternation on the bridal face, he had followed her gaze to the window and guessed at once what was troubling her. 'Relax,' he told her. 'I have connections.'

He meant that with one phone call they would have tents and heaters, courtesy of this or that supplier. There was already a generator truck to run the lights and mike (the lights were film spots and floods) not to mention the portable toilets (all donated for the day), and a band formed ad hoc by various musician friends. The site itself was a former location Ross had catered, a farmer's field in the Agricultural Land Reserve where they'd shot the battle sequences for a made-for-TV Western. The resources available to them notwithstanding, Ross said he did not believe that it would rain. He said he didn't believe in rain any more, so fortunate did he feel to be getting married. Turning to her naked beside him, he had said with a wry grin, 'If you have any regrets, you'd better tell me now.'

'I wish I had different ears.'

'Your ears are wonderful. I have an appetizer in mind for them,' and he leaned in for a preliminary nibble.

Iliana did have one serious regret, though she did not voice it lest Ross misunderstand her: it was that in marrying him she was inadvertently obeying her parents. At the end of that day, 2 August 1997, she would have to admit that the only man she had ever had sex with was her husband. Not that she wanted anyone else (far from it); she simply objected on principle to the moral prescience of the man and woman who had disowned her.

Driving away from Stevie Blake's house, it struck her as high time to stop playing the rebellious daughter.

*   *   *

19

In the morning, pouring herself a glass of orange juice, Bonnie saw him from the window. He was sitting on the edge of the roof with his bare back to her, the line of it like some primitive percussion instrument. She didn't think anything of it. She assumed he was there to do something with the planters. Later his smoke, seeping through the screen and drifting all the way to the bathroom where she was peeling a pore strip off her nose, alerted her to his continued creepy presence. Only then did she entertain suspicion.

He had changed places and was sitting on the bench beneath her window. Rapping sharply on the glass, she asked through the screen, 'Does Ross know you're hanging out here?' Stevie half turned, but did not remotely meet her eye. He did not try hard enough and his hair was in his eyes. She noticed the way he held the cigarette, between his thumb and two fingers, like a joint. Presumably he did not possess motor skills fine enough to hold it properly. 'Does he?'

'He asked me to do something for him.'

'Then do it.'

A few minutes later there was a knock on the door. Wolf-boy again! she saw, peeping round the kitchen curtain. Abandoning all caution, she opened the door. 'What exactly do you want?'

'Come on,' he said, but it hardly seemed that he meant it. His top lip curled like the pages of a paperback read too long in the bath. 'I'm driving out to the bay.'

'The *Bay*?'

'You know, the ocean.'

'The Pacific Ocean?'

'Yeah.'

'Where is it?' she asked, stunned.

'About fifteen minutes away.'

'Fifteen *minutes*?' Inside her, Bonnie's grievance strained on its chain. In the last few days she had finally started feeling like she had it under control, had even considered venturing out to face her comedown. Now she was angry all over again. What could Ross possibly have meant by withholding the ocean from her, the one thing that might make her feel at home? Jaw clenched, she told Stevie, 'Wait a sec. I'll get ready.'

Jerking his head in the direction of the stairs, he waved her out.

Bonnie insisted, 'I've got to change.'

'Let's go.' He turned and started down.

She slipped on the sandals that were by the door. It took her a moment to lock up. When she reached the street, she saw Stevie getting into a big white pick-up with a distressed paint job parked halfway down the block. She ran to catch up, throwing all her weight back to get the passenger door open.

Stevie had emptied his pockets on to the dashboard and from the farrago of coins and crumpled things took a key. Bonnie flipped down the sun visor: no mirror. Unrolling the window, she leaned out to cringe at herself in the dirty one on the side. Without make-up, she felt vulnerable and exposed, a limpet with its shell ripped off.

At first Stevie could not get the engine to turn over. When it finally did, the truck lurched forward. In that logic particular to juvenile males, pulling out with a screech and accelerating all the way to the corner (where the law required him to stop) apparently made up for the vehicle's initial recalcitrance. Bonnie clung to the dashboard. 'I don't have my seatbelt on! Will you hold it?'

There weren't any seatbelts, she discovered as Stevie proceeded through the four-way stop. Tipping sideways as they turned, she hissed, 'Aren't you cool?' Maybe she should have been afraid of him, but she wasn't. She was more afraid of being seen with him.

Even after he slowed down, Bonnie still thought of it as a kind of joyless joyride, the window open, her hair lashing around her head as she bounced idiotically on the sticky seat. They crossed the highway and began a short jog through the suburbs (even worse than the countryside, in Bonnie's opinion, because of the people) until finally they connected with a curving road that on one side bordered a marsh. From behind the bramble boundary, blackbirds trilled sarcastically.

She took a tube of lipstick from her purse. 'What is it you're doing for Ross?'

'Driving out to the bay.'

She applied the lipstick by feel. Normally it would not be necessary for her to check her reflection, but the truck's suspension and the corrugated road jostled her out of the lines. As she made a correction with the tip of her pinky, she felt something spiky brush against her hand.

'How's your sister-in-law?'

'I haven't seen her lately.'

Stevie looked at her. 'Is she okay?'

She was trying to tweeze the hair with her fingernails. 'I guess.'

'Is she away?'

'No.'

'Then why haven't you seen her?'

Bonnie lifted one buttock to slip a hand under, then the other. 'I've been lying low.'

She didn't actually consider herself obsessive. The tendency was there, certainly, but wasn't it for any Virgo? Even Ross liked things a certain way and no one would ever accuse him of being OC.

And while she was fully aware of what she was doing when she was not behaving herself, she would never, except in this particular circumstance (call it a hair-trigger), concede that her behaviour was out of her control. An animal in a trap will chew its own leg off; Bonnie would pluck as relentlessly. In her lap, she clasped her hands, trying to hold herself back. She wrung them, then sat on them again; one or the other always sneaked back up to her face. Finally, out of desperation, she asked, 'Are we going by a drugstore by any chance?'

'A drugstore?'

They had passed a white clapboard church and houses that, though they did not look fit for habitation, evidently were. (None of them had any grass, but there was living room furniture outside.) She had no idea where they were. 'You have them here. I saw one once.'

Stevie gave her a sidelong look that wasn't very nice.

'How about a gas station?'

'There's a gas station.'

'I'd like to stop.'

A family picking blackberries into ice cream pails came into view beyond the next curve. There appeared to be three generations of them, a granny with salt and pepper braids and black spaces where teeth should have been, a middle-aged man in a baseball cap, a heavy-set woman of a similar age, and several children of graduating heights, the youngest, about three, looking out with a face stained purple. When Stevie pulled into the oncoming lane to give them berth, they waved.

Bonnie went on worrying the hair. 'How much farther?'

'Like I said, it's about fifteen minutes.'

'To the gas station?'

He pointed. They were approaching an intersection where the four red letters E-S-S-O stood on a square white building.

Stevie pulled in next to a finned Chevy on wooden blocks, its colour indeterminate under the dust. The station, with its single rudimentary pump, looked the same vintage as the unrepaired car. Bonnie hesitated before getting out, wishing she had been nicer to Stevie because now he just might take off.

The door to the office was propped open with a car battery. Inside, different lengths of exhaust pipe hung in a fringe around the window. Like the car outside, everything looked coated, but here, perhaps because air-borne grease had made the particles adhere more densely, it all appeared sepia-toned and stuck in time, even the Coca-Cola clock and the cash register like the one in Real Food. The only bright thing, not surprisingly, was the calendar, which showed the actual month and a high-gloss photograph of the ocean, as if to remind her of her destination. 'Hello?' she called out.

From the open door to the garage, she heard a scraping sound. 'Be right with you.'

A man in coveralls and a red polka-dot engineer's cap emerged, further dirtying his hands on a rag. He looked about sixty, with exploded capillaries ruddying in his nose and cheeks. 'What can I do for you?'

'Do you sell those little manicure sets? You know what I mean? They fold up and snap.'

He smiled lopsidedly.

'What I'm actually looking for is a pair of tweezers.'

'I got pliers.'

'Can I get the key to the bathroom?'

'It's open. Just around the back. I can't promise it's up to a lady's standards.'

Smiling, she backed out.

The truck was still there (thank God) with Stevie leaning over the steering wheel, knocking his head against it. She found the bathroom, the door ajar a few inches. The scurrying noises inside stopped when Bonnie flipped the switch and the light came on, the bulb hanging bare above her head. A revelation: some people are pigs. The toilet was the worst, the bowl stained inside the colour of coffee, the sink almost as bad, and above where the tap drip, drip, dripped the mirror no longer offered back a reflection. In her purse she found a scrap of paper (her bus ticket), wet it, and cleared a circle. There she stood, leaning over the sink but trying not to touch it, scraping at the whisker. It took about ten minutes for her to concede defeat. She stalked back to the truck with her hand over the mess.

'Take me back.'

He raised his head. 'What?'

'Take me back. Now. Let's go.' Touching her chin first to make sure the bleeding had stopped, she climbed in.

'Fuck,' Stevie muttered, starting the truck.

'Fuck you.'

He reversed, spraying gravel.

'Slow down.'

He did not. He gunned it back on to the road. The family of berry pickers was still there and they looked up with faces not as friendly as before.

'Will you slow down! Do you want to get us killed?'

'As if I care!'

'Well, *I* do!'

'Fuck!' Stevie shouted.

'What's the matter with you? Are you nuts?'

He kept on accelerating, tyres screeching along with Bonnie at every curve, the truck banking, Bonnie bracing herself against the impending crash. Maybe if she hit him on the head and grabbed the wheel, she thought, looking round for something to use. On the dashboard, among the contents of his pockets, was a Swiss

Army knife. 'Oh, stop!' she sang, snatching it up. 'Pull over! Pull over!'

They slid, fish-tailing as Stevie braked, until they had slowed enough for him to bring the truck on to the narrow shoulder of the road. Bonnie turned to Stevie. 'Don't follow me. Don't even think about it.'

Crashing through the ditch and up the other side through scrub, she reached the trees, out of Stevie's sight. With her thumbnail she pried at the little grey nub on the top of the knife; the tweezers slid out. Fingering her chin, she found the whisker, grasped it with the metal pincers, tugged. A little jolt of pleasure preceded her release. She squinted at the hair, assessing the tenacity of the root before blowing it off on to the forest floor where, from that exact spot, something prickly and invidious was sure to grow.

'Okay,' she said, climbing back up into the cab. 'Let's go.' She pulled the door closed and, looking down at her flayed shins, tsked good-humouredly.

'Where?'

'The ocean. That's where we're going, right?'

Stevie turned the truck in a U. Bonnie smiled and waved at the berry pickers. 'You would not believe that bathroom,' she told him as they passed the Esso.

Immediately the houses looked better. They were driving up a hill and the property values climbed along; she saw lawns, mail boxes, dahlia-crowded gardens. Suddenly the vista opened on to water. For Bonnie, it was as if she hadn't been breathing until that moment. She stuck her head out of the window and let the breeze – cool, fishy, faecal – flow around her. Greedily, she inhaled. They descended the steep grade to the bottom: a small gravel beach beside a government dock, a place to rent kayaks, a restaurant, a post office.

'Do you think it's clean enough to put your feet in?'

'It's not Vancouver,' Stevie replied contemptuously.

She hopped out of the truck and ran down to the beach without her shoes, her skip slowing to a hobble on the stones. As she waded in, water lapped frigidly against her ankles and stung her wounds.

After a minute Stevie came over and asked from the shore, 'Is Iliana still working every day in the café?'

'As far as I know.'

'Does she, like, finish at the same time as before?'

'Why wouldn't she?'

'I'm asking you.'

'I don't keep tabs on her.'

'I don't either. She can do what she likes. I just haven't seen her around in at least, like, *five days*. I used to all the time.'

Bonnie, as much annoyed by his presence as his questions, said, 'Why are you asking me? Ask her.' She didn't care if he abandoned her here. *Let him*, she thought, turning her back.

Boats of various sizes were moored at the wharf. Bryce loved boats second to cars. She would bring him here to look at them. (How? She'd have to get a car herself.) They could bring a pail and fill it with stones and throw them off the dock. Maybe they could rent a kayak. (She was making this part up.) Glancing back, she saw that Stevie had returned to the truck and was leaning up against it as he rolled a cigarette.

She was combing the beach for treasures when he finally honked. In the hem of her shirt she had collected several soft, intact exoskeletons of miniature crabs, green, brown and white beach glass rendered opaque by the waves, some interesting stones and shells. Like a courting crow, or a savage appeasing an angry god, she planned to offer these to her neglected son.

Stevie said nothing the entire drive back, for which Bonnie was thankful. She felt calmer now. The stress of the move was behind her, the shock of relocation almost. Or perhaps it was that she had finally accepted as inevitable that she and Bryce would end up here, at least for now. She did want all of them to be together, her and Bryce, Ross and Iliana. 'Thanks,' she told Stevie when he stopped in the alley behind the café, trying to sound grateful, because she was.

Then Stevie held her back by the arm, tight enough to hurt, 'Tell Iliana hi for me.'

Bonnie wrenched herself free of his grip. 'Tell her yourself.' She opened the door, but before she could climb down Stevie reached over and pinched the inside of her thigh, hard.

'*Ow!*'

'Tell her I did that,' Stevie said.

In the scramble out of the cab everything that she had collected spilled on to the ground. Deb must have heard both her squeal and the tyres' as the truck shot out of the alley. Out of the door she poked her head, still tortoiseshelled with highlights, but now with a wide unvariegated strip following the parting. Holding a hand to the stinging inside of her leg, Bonnie limped toward the stairs.

When Ross gave her a key for the apartment, he also gave her one for the café. That night, after Bryce had gone to bed, she went down. Empty and unlit, it seemed ghostly. Behind the counter was the stereo and, in a rack below it, Ross's CDs that she had glanced disdainfully through on her first day. She found what she was looking for, wrote a note and taped it to the stereo. *I borrowed a CD, Bon.* Sneaking back upstairs, she felt confident that Ross would see the note the next morning and read it as it was intended to be read, as the first gesture toward rapprochement.

In the apartment, she slid the CD into the player, turned out the light, went over to the window. The sound began so softly it was difficult to know when her expectation of what she was about

287

to hear left off and hearing itself began. It could have been, too, that all along the sound was there, steady in the background, but from this great a distance too faint to hear without a concentrated effort. With a gentle sigh, a wave rolled in. After a pause, it rolled back out. The lone cry of a gull reverberated to infinity. When she opened her eyes, it was to the darkened back of the post office and the boxy little red and white vans parked in a tidy row that, every morning, Bryce exclaimed over.

20

Just inside the café door, hanging on an antique clothes-drying rack, were the latest issues of *The Citizen* which Ross kept for people who wanted something to read over coffee if they were not interested in what was on the shelves. Removing the oldest issue to make room for the one he'd found rolled and secured with an elastic band in the courtyard, he'd skim the headlines of the new one to see in black and white what had already come to him by word of mouth. This was another thing he loved about the café: it made the news redundant. Ross was in the know, and not only because he overheard things. People told him things. He fancied not much happened in Duncan that had not been brought to his attention early on.

'Have you heard?' someone would ask, and if he hadn't, he would then. Shortly, someone else would come along and, posing the same question, corroborate the story. By the end of the week two dozen people might have asked him, but by then even *The Citizen* knew. This happened when the grow-op was busted up the valley, when there were lay-offs at the mill, when the new traffic light went up on the highway. It was how Ross found out about Iliana and Stevie.

Elsa Anders, who clerked in the post office and came for coffee most afternoons, mentioned that Stevie's friendship with Iliana had done him a world of good according to several people who knew Stevie and his grandmother. Like Ross, Elsa was in the know. The post office was another place where people stopped to gossip.

'He's on Bob's route and Bob says he can't believe how much better the place looks.'

'What place?' asked Ross.

'Stevie Blake's.'

Elsa's words struck him, but they did not penetrate. He went to put the coffee pot back on the warmer. Iliana had already left, so he couldn't ask her what Elsa had been talking about. Though he carried on as usual for what remained of the afternoon, his thought processes had muddied. The settled pond of his mind had been stirred up, and released from the murky layers at the bottom were confusion, grumpiness, and the first twinges of an inchoate panic.

A little before four he asked Deb if she would mind closing up. 'I'm just going to take Bryce home.'

He snapped closed the straps that kept Bryce from shifting around in the bike trailer. 'Ready to roll?' They set off, but instead of the usual route, Ross turned at the railway tracks, following the road that ran parallel to them, taking the right before the depot. From halfway down the street he saw Stevie's truck parked, not in the driveway, but in front of the house. He stopped at the bottom of the empty driveway and stood staring at the ramp.

At home he put the bike and trailer away in the garage, leaving Bryce in the yard while he went inside to get a popsicle. He heard the tub filling in the bathroom. He was sweating more than the ride had warranted, and as he opened the freezer to take out the popsicle tray his grip felt slippery on the handle.

'You're home early,' Iliana said from the doorway, causing him to turn.

She sounded as warm as ever, her voice cheerful with surprise, uninflected by culpability. Her colour was high, true, but that was because she had just got home from her run. Yet Ross was not able to look her in the eye. He went over to the sink. 'I guess you are, too.'

There was a pause that Ross, with his back to her, could not help but interpret as significant.

'What do you mean?' she asked.

Warm water ran over the tray. He loosened the popsicle. 'Someone told me you'd probably be at Stevie Blake's.' He turned off the tap, but water was still running like an extended echo in the other room, accentuating his sense of being connected to the moment. Suddenly he wanted to laugh because this was exactly the feeling he had been nurturing for so long without understanding how vulnerable and without refuge it might leave him. The last thing he wanted now was to be in this moment. He wanted the hell out of it and, turning, walked straight out of the house, letting the screen door slam behind him.

Sitting on the ramp while Bryce ate the popsicle, Ross answered all his questions. Bryce did not notice the monotone of Ross's replies, or how hard he was kneading the skin of his forehead as he repondered Elsa's words. Her tone had not implied scandal. Clearly, she had assumed Ross knew what she was talking about, so maybe Ross had jumped to an unfair conclusion (it wouldn't be the first time). He decided to wait for Iliana to come out and clear up his confusion and, when the tub shut off, he half turned towards the screen. She did not emerge. He was just about to get up and go back in when a realization forced him back into his cowed huddle: what he had been listening for so intently were her *steps*.

Bryce liked to line up his cars at the top of the ramp and, one after another, send them down. It was Ross's job to stop them with his foot at the bottom. This was what they were doing when Iliana finally came out. Bathed, wet hair combed and tucked behind her ears, she appeared fresh and composed. 'I'm sorry,' she said. 'It's over. I haven't been there for a while.'

The car leaped over Ross's foot. Another came flying down that he missed entirely.

'Do you want to know why?' she asked.

'Why?'

' It was because he looked at me.'

'*I* don't look at you?'

'Not like that.'

He walked back up the ramp, Iliana's eyes widening as he came. She seemed afraid of him coming towards her with his hands in fists. 'Excuse me.' Awkwardly, he slipped past her.

The bed crumpled and strewn with her sweaty clothes, he lay down, breathing hard. Lifting his head, he began smashing it against the pillow, shouting, 'Fuck! Fuck! Fuck!' He could not have ranked his feelings: whether he was more angry than hurt, or filled more with remorse than with humiliation. Grabbing Iliana's damp shorts, he threw them against the wall. He curled up to sob, but unlike his sister, whose capacity for weeping was record-setting, Ross could not keep it up. After a few minutes, he rolled on to his back and lay there with his eyes closed, listening to his own internal deceleration.

Iliana said to Bryce, 'I'm going to take you home now, sweetie.'

He looked up from where he crouched with his cars at the top of the ramp, one eye directed right at her, the other listing slightly. 'Does she want me back now?'

'Bonnie? Of course she does. You hop in the car. I'll be right there.'

291

Obediently, Bryce began collecting up his cars, holding them awkwardly against his chest with a starfish hand.

Inside the house, she took her keys from the hook by the phone. Ross was crying in the bedroom. She went back out. Bryce was still standing on the ramp. On the power line that ran from the end of the yard to the corner of the house an aerial chase was in progress, a grey squirrel bounding along the wire pursued by a chattering black one with a bald-looking tail. Black caught up and a vicious high-wire tussle ensued, punctuated by blood-chilling squeaks from both combatants. Suddenly Grey fell, bucking in mid-air, struggling to right himself. Landing on the grass with an audible thud, he uttered one last derisive trill before scampering off.

In the car Bryce asked how squirrels were able to run along a wire.

'Haven't you ever been to the circus?'

'Did it hurt when he fell?'

'It didn't seem to. He landed on his feet. May you always, too.'

She dropped him off in front of the café, waiting in the car for him to climb the stairs. He kept one hand on the wooden railing, bringing both feet together before taking the next step up. On the front of his backwards shirt was a dinosaur transfer; when it had disappeared from view, she drove back home.

She heard nothing behind the bedroom door now. When Ross did not answer her knock, she entered and found him supine on the bed, hands clasped over his chest, his face artificially composed. 'Are you sleeping?'

His answer was so long in coming she would have become alarmed if not for the rise and fall of his chest. 'I'm meditating.'

'Can we talk?'

There was another pause of equally maddening length. 'Go ahead.'

'I'm sorry.'

A wince marred his non-expression.

'I couldn't seem to help myself.'

'It's all right,' said Ross.

'It's not all right.'

'I'm prepared to forget about it. I owe you that much, I think.'

'You don't owe me anything. Do you think I was trying to punish you? I just want you to love me like before.'

Ross opened his eyes ceilingward. 'I love you more.'

'You know what I mean.' She hung her head. 'Why? Why won't you make love to me?'

'I want to. I tried to. You said you were tired.'

'When? When you brought me flowers? You couldn't have sounded less enthusiastic!'

'Okay, okay. It just doesn't seem fair.'

'What doesn't?'

'That I was the one who fucked up, but you are the one to suffer.'

'How am I suffering?'

He said her name reproachfully. 'Iliana.'

'How am I suffering?' she demanded, and when he did not reply she snapped, 'Will you sit up and talk to me?'

Dutifully, he lifted himself, moving slowly, as if he were very stiff or in pain. He crossed his legs, lotus-style.

Just then the squirrel fell again, its twisting freefall and nimble landing replaying in Iliana's mind. 'What happened to those Russians?' she asked. 'Did you ever hear from them again?'

He looked at her, confused by the change of subject. 'I guess they went back to Moscow.'

'He had a head injury, Ross.' She began to cry.

'What? What's wrong?'

'I just can't stand it.'

'What?'

'I can't stand that all this time you've been thinking I didn't try.'

'No, babe,' he said, crawling across the bed to her. 'You were incredible.' He took her hand. She pulled it back, infuriated by the brotherly gesture.

21

'Did you get my note?' Bonnie asked groggily. Ross sat up abruptly, looking around the darkened room as if he didn't know himself how he'd got there. Seeing Bonnie knock-kneed in her nightie with an empty water glass in her hand, he grunted and lay back down.

In the morning she thought she'd dreamed it. Their unexpected nocturnal meeting had become a springboard for actual dreams, further confusing the matter. Yawning, she stretched across the space Bryce had vacated (long enough ago for his astonishing residual heat to have already cooled off the sheets). A small voice warbled a Nick Cave song in the other room. She opened one eye to look at the clock. If it was almost nine, she wondered why Ross had not come to collect Bryce.

A little shiver ran through her, the frisson of déjà vu, for there he was, exactly as she thought she'd dreamed him: Ross lying on his side on the couch, his back to the room, a cushion where his head should have been. 'Ross!'

He rolled on to his back, blinking.

'What are you doing here?'

He rolled over again, reburrowing. Twenty minutes later, she and Bryce washed and dressed and ready to go down, he was still there, in exactly the same position.

They came in through the back in case of Brent, though it was still too early for him. Both Deb and Iliana were in the kitchen, neither of them speaking, and while that was not unusual, the harried state they were in was. A line of orders sat stalled along the window ledge. The sink swelled with unscraped plates. Iliana, turning out loaves, tossed the hot pans aside with an alarming clatter. 'Oh, good,' she said when she saw Bonnie. 'Can you take some of these orders out?'

Bonnie went over to the window, on the way glancing at Deb who seemed to look back at her with something more significant than her usual bovine disinterest.

The breakfast rush was on. Since she hadn't been the one to take the orders, Bonnie had to call out what was on each plate and look around the room for someone to claim it. (Every time she stepped out on to the patio she expected Brent to be there, flaunting her shame.) Everyone seemed unconcerned about the delay. No one complained. They asked where Ross was, and without exception seemed genuinely pleased to see her again. 'What've you been doing with yourself?' 'Haven't seen you around lately.' 'Settling in?' 'Welcome back.' More orders appeared on the window ledge, and when she had delivered them, she went behind the counter to get an order pad and pen. Her note, she saw, was still taped to the stereo.

Around ten, things slowed enough for Bonnie to go back to the kitchen. She found Iliana alone. 'What's going on?'

Deb came out of the cooler with a terse announcement. 'He made the salads, so that's one less thing. I don't know what we're going to do about soups.'

'Will somebody tell me what's going on? Is Ross sick? He's just lying there.'

'He's up there?' said Iliana. 'Oh, thank God.'

With no more information forthcoming, Bonnie joined Bryce on the patio to drink her coffee before the lunch rush started. Deb came out a few minutes later. 'I want to show you something.' Bonnie followed her back into the café and through the kitchen where Deb held a finger to her lips as they passed Iliana unloading the dishwasher. In the storeroom, she motioned for Bonnie to close the door. 'I don't want Iliana to know. She's upset enough as it is.'

'What's going on?'

'I have no idea, but it's bad. Look at this.'

Deb heaved open the freezer lid (Bonnie pictured her hoisting a car into the air with one thick arm) and, leaning into the icy cavity, tossed aside the frozen loaves of bread that were on the top. She asked Bonnie to hold the lid. With both hands, she lifted a large tray about the size of two cookie sheets. Frosted over as it was, Bonnie could not see what was in it until Deb rested it on the edge of the freezer and scraped away the white glaze.

'Oh, my God!'

Deb caught the lid before it fell and, reaching out, clamped her other hand over Bonnie's mouth. Cold and wet, it held her so tightly that Bonnie stiffened and didn't even try to free herself. 'You just pipe down. We don't need any of your hysterics here today.'

'What's he doing with meat?' Bonnie whispered after Deb removed her hand.

'I have no idea.'

'Is there any more?'

'No. I went through the whole freezer.'

'Has he been eating it all along?'

'I don't know that either.'

'You didn't say anything to Iliana?'

'No.'

'I'm going to talk to Ross.'

Bonnie slipped through the alley door without Iliana noticing

296

and hurried up the stairs to the apartment. Ross wasn't there. She went back down and looked under the stairs. The bike was gone.

Towards the end of the day an elderly woman bumped through the French doors behind a chrome walker that formed a three-sided corral around her. When she had negotiated her way to a table and settled herself, she began foraging through her handbag. Bonnie came to take her order. The woman pushed the pair of glasses that hung from a chain over plastic beads on to her face with the heels of her hands. Her lipstick had bled along the lines that radiated out from her lips, Bonnie saw when the woman looked up. The crimson millipede split to give her voice, a full octave lower than Bonnie expected. 'I hear the coffee's good.'

'Would you like a latte or a cappuccino, or just a coffee?'

'Coffee.'

'Decaf or regular?'

'Lordy. Just a coffee.'

Bonnie came back with the mug. The woman was screwing a cigarette into a holder. 'I'm sorry, you can't smoke in here,' Bonnie told her.

'What?'

'You can't smoke in here.'

The woman scanned the room, which was empty except for Bryce at the counter. 'Is Deb here?'

'She is. Do you want me to get her for you?'

At the short-order window she said to Deb, 'There's an old duck out here who seems to think you're going to give her a special dispensation to smoke.'

Deb lumbered over to the window. 'That's Nana Blake.' To Iliana she said, 'Stevie's grandmother. Come out and meet her. She's quite a character.'

Iliana looked up from kneading the bread, stricken. Bonnie came in for a tray and was about to follow Deb out when Iliana cried, 'Where are you going?'

'To get the ketchup bottles for refilling.'

'Do you have to do it now?'

Bonnie blinked. 'Why not?'

She went around collecting up the bottles. 'I don't know what's the matter with him,' the old woman was telling Deb. 'I've never seen him this upset since that time he went to stay with his mother in Edmonton.' Bonnie left the full tray of bottles on the counter and went over to refill the woman's cup, stepping round the barricade of the walker.

The woman interrupted herself. 'The coffee *is* good.'

Queasily, Bonnie smiled.

In the kitchen, she got out the bulk ketchup dispenser.

'What are they talking about?' Iliana asked.

'I don't know.'

As they were closing the café, Iliana suggested Bonnie and Bryce come along. She had a couple of stainless steel bowls in her lap and a place in mind.

They started down the street, Bryce capering along ahead like a boy born with a backwards torso. The shops petered into the credit union and the Island Savings Bank. At the train crossing, the sidewalk on either side made the picking accessible, the first blackberries pinging softly against the steel until a muffling layer of them had formed.

Bonnie had never been berry-picking and she felt almost fool-hardy inserting whole unscathed digits into the verdant tangle of razor wire. Each branch was as long as a whip and barbed with blood-coloured thorns.

'It's been a terrible day,' Iliana said. 'I haven't even had a chance yet to ask how you're doing.'

'*Comme ci, comme ça.*'

'Brent's gone.'

'I heard. Did you and Ross have a fight or something?'

'He walked out. You probably guessed I had an affair.'

The brambles seized Bonnie's hand. '*What?*'

'I thought you knew,' said Iliana.

'I thought this was about Ross eating meat!'

'What?'

'Deb found meat in the freezer!'

'When?'

'I can't believe this! Who with?'

Iliana hung her head, showing how the summer had bleached her to a glow. 'I was sure you'd guessed.'

'Who with?'

She looked up, mouth tight. 'I can't tell you that. Ross can tell you if he wants.'

'Tell me!'

'Does it matter?'

'Of course it matters!' Whenever Bonnie lost a lover, it always helped to know that it was to a man. (If it was a woman it would cast some of the responsibility, like a half-filled bucket of slops, over her, rather than her sex.) Bryce pulled on her arm as though she were a mechanical food dispenser. She plucked a berry, inspected it for insects, blew on it. When she popped it in his mouth, he wriggled with pleasure at the sweet-tart taste.

Iliana said, 'I thought you'd guessed or I never would have told you.'

Of the people who frequented the café, no one man came to mind. Instead a composite formed in Bonnie's mind, as if each feature were sketched on overlapping squares of acetate: an earnest cast to the eyes, a receding hairline and accompanying shaggy neck, all he stood for silk-screened across his chest. Certainly more than one man, more than three or four, fitted this description. Ross fitted this description! They constituted a type that, with the exception of her brother, Bonnie did not care for and could not easily tell apart. It had to be one of them, yet she could not offer Iliana a name to admit to. 'Tell me,' she said.

A man came across the tracks on foot – John Deere cap, plaid shirt hooked on his thumb and slung over his shoulder. He nodded to them, and when Iliana nodded back he stopped.

Bonnie ignored him. 'Tell me.'

The man flicked a berry in an impressive arc into his mouth. He winked at Bryce, whose stained lips, chin and hands made him look like the child of cannibals. 'Good, eh?' To Iliana he said, 'They're just the right sweetness.'

She concurred with a grateful smile.

'Any earlier, they're sour as the dickens. Say,' he added, encouraged by her friendliness, 'there's a crippled lady who works over in that café on Kenneth Street.'

'That would be me,' Iliana chirped.

'Well, good for you.' He popped another berry in and waved as he walked off.

'Tell me!'

'Stevie Blake.'

'*You slept with Wolf-boy?*'

Iliana looked back to see if John Deere was still within earshot. She gestured helplessly to Bryce, who should not have been hearing any of this either.

'Oh, my God,' said Bonnie.

'It's over.'

'Oh, my God.'

'I haven't seen him in almost two weeks.'

'You're not in love with him.'

'Of course not.'

'Why did you do it then?'

'Why do you think?'

More repelled now than slighted on Ross's behalf, Bonnie cupped the inside of her right thigh where Stevie's bruise stained her like dirty fingerprints that would not scrub off. 'But what about Ross? How could you?' Something ruinous occurred to her then. 'You're not splitting up, are you?' Her voice quavered insecurely. 'Oh, my God! If you split up I'll kill myself!'

'Stop it, Bonnie!'

'He loves you so much!'

'What do you mean by love?' Iliana countered. 'Idealizing someone? Putting her on a pedestal?'

'That's what I've been looking for all my life!'

'It is not. Anyway, you've already got something perfect.'

Bonnie looked blankly at Iliana who gestured then to where Bryce had wandered off. He stood on the tracks shielding his eyes with purple hands, hopeful that a train would come. Bonnie hurried over and pulled him off.

'I'm done,' Iliana announced, lifting the bowl and shaking it from side to side.

'It doesn't make sense,' said Bonnie. From conception she had known her brother and from conception Ross had always had an adoring female at his side. Realistically, she just could not see him, a man at whose wedding twelve additional brides had shown up, being cuckolded by the likes of Stevie Blake. 'Was he that good?'

'Who?'

Never again would Bonnie accept a naïve reply from Iliana. 'Wolf-boy,' she said sternly.

Iliana blushed. 'Actually, it was a little too much like church.'

'What are you going to do now?'

Iliana said, 'I think I'll make a pie.'

301

Lastly, Ross presented his new wife to Jaime Rios at the fire. 'Felicitations!'
Jaime cried. 'This is the beautiful day that will last the rest of your life!'

'Hold on to her, will you, Jaime, while I check the meat?'

'I am honoured to fulfil this task!'

'Done,' Ross called, 'done!' which was how he lost his bride again. Jaime
Rios let go of her to get the rakes. Those gathering curiously around the fire
quickly crowded Iliana out. She wandered off, glad of a moment to herself.

Two men handled the rakes, dragging the bundles off the coals, while two
more raised the board on which each blackened bundle was transported over to
the sawhorse tables. After much grunting and swearing not customarily heard
at a wedding, the six charred forms were set out for everyone to admire. If it
had been anyone else's wedding, they would have wished they'd had a sandwich
before leaving home. Ross had not managed to get his tie tied and now, as if to
further flout the tradition of the tuxedo, he stripped off his jacket and donned
asbestos-lined gloves. With a knife, he picked at the disintegrating strings. The
fabric, miraculously not burned away, had to be peeled off, revealing a shell of

heat-petrified salt. Roughly textured, pinkish from the wine, it appeared as a beautiful self-protecting secretion, or some kind of mineral-encrusted mould. To get inside required another set of instruments, a hammer and chisel no less. As if he'd done this a hundred times and not just twice, Ross tapped the chisel in several places, testing, before bringing the hammer decisively down. There could have been a hinge, so precisely did the shell crack. A second blow and it fell to pieces, releasing from the crowd an appreciative gasp and from the lamb steam, a gush of rosy juices, the heady perfume of garlic.

As Ross carved, people came holding out their plates as though begging to be fed. Jaime Rios and a few enthusiastic others opened the remaining lambs, but Ross insisted on carving and personally serving each of his guests. At the very end of the long, long line Iliana stepped forward with their two plates. Ross cried out again, in despair over the irresolvable conflict of responsibilities facing him as groom and host, and, naturally, in lust.

'Come on,' she told him. 'I'm starving.'

With no seating plan apart from a table reserved for the wedding party, it was perhaps inevitable that a good-natured mix-up would occur. Many of the guests could not find a chair beside the person they had come with, or a chair at all, and ended up next to a stranger or cross-legged in the grass. The bride and groom were the last to sit. To the chiming of close to two hundred and fifty knives tapping two hundred and fifty glasses, like the amplified ringing of the crickets they had displaced for the day, Ross and Iliana arrived at the table, Ross raising an arm to silence them long enough to say, 'Thank you for coming to my wedding.' Ross sat, bu before Iliana could take her place, one of the false brides beat her to it The guests would not desist. About to turn to his shy wife to see if sh would grace him with another kiss, Ross felt a hand slip down the back of his pants, way down, grasp his anal hairs and tug. He hollered mor in surprise than pain and, turning, saw that it was not Iliana in the chai beside him but the very woman his sister always referred to when citing who she believed to be evidence of his incurable promiscuity, Susan Strangewa in ivory lace, one-time stand-in for a famous Hollywood actress, sitting i *this time for his bride. He leaped up and, taking her arm, pulled her out of the chair. 'Sit down,' he commanded Iliana. 'For Christ's sake sit!'*

Teddy Alexander gave the toast to the bride and, in welcoming Iliana into the family, described her as a pearl, which prompted Ross to groan audibly and shake his fist at his dad, for, with no one from Iliana's side of the union to make a similar speech to Ross, it fell upon him, a man robbed of his only metaphor, to speak after dinner.

They ate. That the meat was a success Ross could taste for himself and see by the great quantity of bread being shuttled in baskets out of the caterer's tent for the guests who wanted to sop up the juices on their plates, by the people streaming back for seconds, and, at the end of the table, by the appalled expression on his sister's face.

Bonnie didn't want Bryce to eat any of the meat, but he gobbled up the shavings Ross had so treacherously laid upon his plate and gleefully hurled his vegetables into the grass. In this he was egged on by the shiny, soot-speckled teenager Ross had seated them next to. 'Eeet,' he kept encouraging Bryce. 'Eeet.' Red and runny, the meat was practically raw, lying in the hot pool of its own diluted blood.

As for the wine, just as in the Western, each dead soldier was promptly replaced. When the gorging was over and the sated guests lay down in the grass to digest, red-stained napkins strewn about, the field looked a scene of battle once again. Rising in triumph at this happy carnage, Ross turned to address Iliana. Everyone fell silent. 'My wife,' he began, 'mother of my children . . .'

'Is that a shotgun I hear?' someone called.

Clichés ricocheted in his head. He could not think of a single word or phrase that might adequately express what he was feeling. It was as if he were trying to describe exactly how something tasted. 'Intense blackberry and pepper characters with a liquorice nose supported by spice, oak and softly textured tannins' – these were mere words. They could not even approximate to the subtlety of experience. He could say he adored her, he desired her, he craved her, but these were just sounds, like his nephew's vocalizations.

Noticing the crinkled corners of his eyes, the side of his mouth twitching,

Iliana thought he was about to laugh, but to her astonishment and Ross's great mortification he let loose a sob. Iliana had never heard Ross cry. Like most other things, he did it loudly and with abundant feeling, sinking back down in his chair and leaning into the comfort of her arms. He was not the only one weeping either. All around them, soiled napkins were retrieved to blot eyes, and the Vickies, all sitting at one table, began to keen in unison.

Perhaps wishing to spare her son the embarrassment of public tears, Pal Alexander piped up then. 'Speaking of babies—'

'No!' Bonnie hissed.

Steadying herself with the chair back, Pal rose to her stockinged feet. The mint green pumps she had kicked off long ago. 'Ross was simply the sweetest child. Unlike his sister, all we ever got from him was smiles. When they say that a person's character is fully formed at birth, I believe it. He was the fattest, jolliest thing.'

'Ma?' Ross begged over the laughter. 'Ma, sit down.'

'Nothing troubled him. He hardly ever cried. Did he, Teddy?' Teetering, she turned to her husband, who nodded and returned her indulgent smile.

'She's pissed,' Bonnie explained to Jaime Rios.

'Except he did have these little moments in the bath. I suppose the warm water relaxed him. He'd do a jobbie and, seeing it floating there, scream.'

'Daddy!' Bonnie cried in desperation. 'Daddy, make her stop!'

'These weren't insignificant either. Not with his appetite. Even as an infant, it was hard for him to take responsibility for his own actions.'

Teddy rose and helped Pal back into her seat. 'Cut the cake!' Bonnie ordered Ross and Iliana over the cacophony of shrieks and cackles. 'Cut it before she gets up again!'

The cake stood on a table of its own, off to the side, six layers high, a terraced fall of multicoloured berries. Hands joined around the handle of the knife, Ross and Iliana looked at each other before they made the cut, their private gaze communicating exactly what Ross had been trying to find the words for earlier. He had been wrong about everyone remembering the meal, he realized then. What people would remember most about the day was the two of them standing here, devouring each other with their eyes.

As for his undelivered speech, Mike Lambeth bailed him out. 'It's great to meet up with Pal and Teddy again,' he began once everyone had been served cake. 'For those of you who don't know, they've high-tailed it out of the rain and now reside in Arizona. This leaves Ross fatherless most of the time and, since he lives below me, I find it necessary to step into Teddy's shoes when it's required.' Mike turned to Teddy. 'Was he always asking you for money?'

The musicians had gathered on the makeshift stage. They were more in number than they had said: the cellist, keyboardist and fiddler, two guitar players, a banjo and a bass player, and Ross's sous-chef, Dmitri, who played the harmonica.

'It's an annual thing for Ross to come to me with some sort of business proposal.' He told them how he'd almost invested in Ross's Ring of Fire Sauce, but that they could not agree on how to market it, as a condiment or an oral analgesic. He described the nursing bra for men, then had to wait for the laughter to subside again. 'Now, I'm not as stingy as I look. I'd happily get behind a worthwhile project. Ross's got that cracking little catering company and I'm always telling him, any time he wants to expand, just tell me. Instead he keeps coming to me with these hare-brained schemes that only the government would invest in.'

He paused, running a hand over his Man from Glad crown. On the stage, half of the musicians stepped down and headed for the bar.

'The golden rule of business is supply and demand. I venture to say that this is also the rule of happiness. When a balance is achieved between our desires and another's willingness to satisfy them, the result is a sympathetic, mutually rewarding relationship. This is exactly what I see here in this young couple, a thriving economy of love.'

Ross, who could not quite believe capitalism could be made to sound romantic, or even less that these sentiments could come from Mike, leaped up to shake his hand and tell him that he was touched. At that instant the banjo set off running. The musicians had decided to break into two bands. This one was Bluegrass. Beneath the premonition of a sunset, Ross dragged Iliana out into the middle of the field for the traditional first dance. With all the guests gathering around to watch, she felt once again surrounded, Ross tugging at her arm. She balked, so he started on his own with an unselfconsciousness Iliana didn't know if she admired or was embarrassed by. He danced as if he were putting out a brush fire, arms raised, feet stamping. Taking mercy on them, the band switched to a waltz. A waltz with Ross was his usual overwhelming embrace, plus a sway and shuffle.

After a couple of tunes, the second group of musicians took to the stage to play the Blues, starting with 'Married Man Blues'. Every one of Iliana and Ross's neighbours, even Jim Marchand who used a cane, got a chance to dance with at least one Vicky.

Bonnie rejoined the party after she had tucked Bryce in with his grandmother in the car. Technically she was free of her responsibilities, but when she spotted the oily-faced boy who had been seated next to them during the meal she felt robbed of her excuse. That he stood shoulder-high to her did not deter him from begging her in grandiloquent phrases to honour him with a dance.

'Sorry,' she told him curtly.

He trailed her, pleading. 'I am a friend of your brother. A dance with his beautiful sister would make me almost as happy as he is.'

'No.' She hurried on. Afraid he would give chase, she sat down at the table where all the other women dressed in white had gathered and was effectively camouflaged in their presence.

'I remember – God, it was hilarious!' one of them was saying. 'The button on his waistband popped and flew across the room—'

'Let's get up and sing a song.'

'It was the snoring I couldn't take. I just couldn't sleep.'

'But I hear he got his nose fixed.'

'Don't tell me that! Why not for me?'

'A couple of years and a couple of guys later. He's actually quite a catch.'

'He cooks! He cleans!'

'He was so much fun!'

'Come on. Let's sing a song for Ross.'

Someone tapped Bonnie on the shoulder. Starting, she turned, expecting her Latin lover, but instead seeing a man even older than her father, mottled hands folded over the handle of his cane. 'Care to dance?' Bursting into tears, she bolted from the table.

Someone turned a spotlight on the musicians just as the bands were swapping places again. This was the moment the Vickies chose to flutter en masse up to the microphone, like proverbial moths drawn to the light, and begin a drunkenly impassioned rendition of 'The Rose' in several keys at once. Iliana was just coming from the portable toilets when she heard them and, far from being jealous, thought smugly that no one would ever write a song called 'The Chocolate Cosmo'. Only because all the white dresses should have been up front did she notice the lone apparition wandering the field.

'Go and see how your sister is doing,' she told Ross.

By the time Ross reached her on the dark perimeter of the celebration, Bonnie was weeping the horrible racked sobs of all the too-thin women he had ever dated. His own eyes teared up hearing her, as if he also smarted from the mental pins she stuck in herself. 'Bonnie,' he implored. 'What are you doing out here?'

'I want to be alone.'

Alone, as far as Ross could tell, was how she spent all her days, captive in her West End tower until a man whose nature would allow it came along to love her.

'What happened?'

'Nothing. It depresses me, that's all.'

'What does?'

'This.' Her gesture took in the whole party. 'All these happy people in one place.'

He laughed and, opening his arms, drew her close, Lazarus-thin, swaddled in her gauze.

Under her cheek, her brother's chest had all the comforting properties of

309

a hot water bottle. Bonnie sniffed. 'Can I still phone you now that you're married?'

'What a question.'

'Will she mind?'

'She doesn't mind much, so far as I can tell.'

When Bonnie looked up, he saw behind her liquefying mascara a fear that was genuine. 'Come and dance.'

She cringed. 'A man is following me around.'

'Who?'

'He comes up to here.'

'That's Jaime Rios. Dance with him! Please, Bon. Do it for me.'

The floodlights came on, drenching the entire field. Ross imagined that, back on the highway, the people driving by would see the field illuminated as it had been during the shooting of the Western two years before and wonder what was going on. Real life, he thought. Real life was happening. Leading Bonnie to where the dancing had resumed, he went to find his wife, his better half, his life's sole reason.

Most of the guests would stay till dawn. They were drunk and still drinking and, in the morning, would be here yet, collapsed in the grass. The big artificial moon held in the sky on a metal stand provided groom and bride with light enough to slip away. 'Iliana,' Ross whispered, hands on her shoulders, feeling her anticipatory shiver. 'Let's go home and make that baby.'

BEGINNING

1

Without really knowing where he was going, Ross rode through the subdivision on the ridge. Light-headed from exertion and from not having eaten, he had to stop several times and lean over the handlebars until his vertigo subsided. When he got out of town and into farmland the road flattened and he found himself pedalling between the fields as if he were dreaming them. He dreamed the golf course, too, until the highway intersection when the rumble of a logging truck woke him. Lifting his head, he saw the mountain.

Shortly after crossing the highway, he came to the sign for the park at the top of the mountain and on impulse veered across the road, gearing down immediately because of the steeper incline. Trees thickened on either side. He geared down again just as a hatchback piled with teenagers overtook him, honking. The pedalling was not the difficult part now, but keeping his balance while climbing so slowly. He had to weave almost into the middle of the road. Thinking this was not such a good idea, he tried to gear back up. First he heard a click, then the violent ratcheting of the chain falling off.

He walked the Giant to the top. (The Giant might actually have walked him.) There were half a dozen vehicles in the parking lot,

311

a picnic area, a pair of his and hers toilets. Setting off through the trees, he soon reached the edge and, depositing the Giant against a log, climbed down on to a wide rock shelf where he sat cross-legged and removed his helmet. Duncan lay below him, a tidy grid snared by roads, the highway a diagonal slash. He saw the river's silvery convolutions and the ocean a surprising stone's throw away with Salt Spring Island floating in it. In his daily life he was aware of the river only when he drove across the bridge that spanned it. The ocean he'd forgotten entirely. They'd lived here almost two years but now he felt like a traveller looking down on a place he had yet to visit.

More from exhaustion than intention, he closed his eyes. The sound carried. Along with the breath he was still trying to catch, he heard a peculiar rippling noise he could not identify, as well as several distinct phrases lifting out of the conversations in the picnic area. *Where's the watermelon? Don't tell me we forgot the watermelon.* Someone else (one of the teenagers who had driven past him on the way up?) was talking about getting wasted one last time that summer. Laughter and, nearby, scurrying and chirring. He could smell himself, sour over the sweetness of the trees. And there was pain, of course. The rock he was leaning against dug its knuckles sharply into his back, his thigh muscles throbbed. His right ankle, bearing the weight of his crossed legs, pressed into the rock shelf. Pain because, after all, he was suffering. Ross could hardly pretend now not to know its cause.

His mentor Mike Lambeth came to mind because it was Mike Ross had gone to see in the penthouse the last time he'd had to let go of something he still wanted. He'd gone as usual with a proposition, one that Mike accepted: to buy Reel Food and hire Jaime Rios to run it. That evening Mike opened the door, a tea towel tucked into the neck of his shirt, surprise shining off his face brighter than his hair. 'Come in,' he had said, stepping aside to le this happen, 'come the hell in!' but, smelling the fug of commercial tomato sauce, Ross had hesitated.

'Have I come at a bad time?'

'Not at all! Ross time is never a bad time. Drink?'

At first glance all there was to indicate the source of the cooking odour was the open microwave door. The kitchen was spotless. Mike had a woman who came every week to clean, apparently the only woman in his present life. (His ex-wife, grown children and grandchildren lived back east.) Following him through to the living room, Ross happened to glance into the sink and was in turn stricken and embarrassed by what he saw: a steaming, half-eaten portion of cannelloni in a plastic tray with the fork still in it.

Then he was back to thinking about Stevie Blake. Unhelpful thoughts. The last time he'd seen Stevie, he'd felt as though he almost had his aversion licked. Now it had trebled, quadrupled. He felt the shocking urge to violence. All ninety pounds of Stevie (ten of them hair) Ross knocked over in his mind, kicked, spat on, punched. How many times in the last twenty-four hours had he pulped him like this? Yet Stevie kept on coming back.

He was distracted by the rippling sound he'd heard earlier, closer now. It reminded him of wind agitating a flag or a sail. Realizing what he had been caught up in he named the feelings – rage, hurt, betrayal. It was like calling off his dogs. They ran to him, tongues out, friendly.

Stevie was gone.

He'd lost track of his breath. He'd been lost in thought all this time. He was lost. He made the mental note – *thinking*.

He started over.

The pain in his ankle was gone, he realized as he tried to re-anchor his attention. Neither could he feel the rock behind him. He tried to focus on what he could feel but discovered that he felt nothing.

One concept that had always challenged him was *Anatta*, No Self – the idea that the personality was, like everything else, in a state of constant flux, feelings, perceptions, intentions changing moment by moment. For a person like Ross, who was known to others as well as to himself as a *character*, this was a frightening prospect. If there was no self, if he was simply a flowing mind-body process, then what had he been wrestling with all this time? Who was up here on the mountain if not Ross? Alarmed, he opened his eyes and looked down, confirming that his legs were indeed still crossed beneath him. His body had simply gone numb from sitting motionless for so long. Nevertheless, he trembled, for the question remained: *who was he?* Successful café owner and entrepreneur? Mike Lambeth was the most successful businessman he knew, yet there wasn't a person in Mike's life Ross could name apart from their mutual neighbours. Brother, uncle, husband? And without Iliana, what would he be? Divorced? Childless? Standing lonely at the kitchen sink to eat his dinner?

He heard the fretful snapping of cloth, then – *whoosh*! – slicing crosswise in front of him was a huge saffron-orange kite with yellow stripes, a man hanging horizontally off it. For a second this gigantic butterfly hovered there, air vibrating its nylon wings, face grinning audaciously under the sunglasses and helmet.

'How're ya doing!'

Astonished, Ross raised a hand, acknowledging the greeting.

He struggled a long time with the chain. Meanwhile, the sun began to set, making his eventual descent nerve-racking. Riding the bike headlong into the concentrating gloom, expecting at every bend to be blinded by headlights and struck or run off the road, he found that by the time he reached flat ground his hands and forearms were tremoring from the strain.

He did not plan on going to see Stevie Blake any more than

he had planned on retreating to the mountain. As he passed the hospital and headed down the hill into town, he simply recognized that he was exhausted. He considered going to the café, but didn't have the keys and would have to get them from Bonnie; he definitely did not want to see Bonnie. He might have checked into a motel except he didn't have his wallet. By then he had turned on to the avenue that ran parallel to the railway tracks, which was the way he had come twice before.

The street ended in a void demarcated by a linear constellation of lights from the subdivision along the ridge. From halfway down the block Ross could see Stevie's ghost truck in the driveway and that the front yard appeared to be strewn with something. The other houses were similar modest post-war bungalows, but only at Stevie Blake's had a hurricane struck, scattering boards and pieces of plywood willy-nilly over the grass.

He was not actually pedalling very fast when he fell. Maybe he hit something. Maybe he just collapsed. One moment he was up, the next down. One moment he was moving along practically in a state of torpor, the next he was writhing on the road.

When they had first moved to the island he had thought about finding himself a teacher or a *sangha*, a group to practise with, but Ross was a Do-It-Yourselfer, so he didn't. His pain now was outrageous. In a way, he couldn't have had a better teacher than this pain. That there had been a time when he did not feel it, that soon he wouldn't again, mattered not. Ross was finally and completely in the moment, suspended in it, attention bare, focus pure and unwavering. If only it didn't hurt so much!

The wreckage scattered across Stevie's lawn, Ross realized once he had pulled himself out from under the Giant and risen wobbling to his feet, was the demolished ramp. He limped towards the steps, steeling himself when he reached them, consciously regretting the

315

loss of the ramp. His right knee hurt too much to bend; he had to hold it stiff and step up with the left.

Stevie answered almost immediately, throwing open the door. When he saw Ross he cried out, 'Don't hit me!'

'Don't hit you?' said Ross, offended. 'I've never hit anyone in my life.' Evidently Stevie did not believe him, for he took a step back, still holding his arms protectively up, *asking* to be punched, Ross thought. He might even have obliged, as he had so many times in his mind, had he not felt about to pass out. 'I've got to sit down.'

Stumbling past the cowering Stevie to the couch, he eased himself down, mangled leg extended, and let his head loll back. After a minute or two, when the dizziness had passed, he opened his eyes. The hurricane had struck inside the house as well, depositing empty beer cans and pyres of butts on dirty plates all around the room.

Stevie had not moved away from the door. He was wearing the bungee cord again and jeans with one thigh torn in an L. 'What do you want?'

'To know what happened.'

'I love her.'

Ross flared. 'That's my wife you're talking about!'

'Don't call her that!' Stevie shouted. 'Don't you call her that!'

A tickle behind his knee aborted his scathing comeback. The outside of his right leg was skinned from shin to thigh leaving a long shiny wound beading at the edges. Drawn by gravity, the beads were trickling down his calf. 'I'm bleeding.'

Stevie had not let his guard down, but now he came away from the door and looked at Ross's leg. Turned queasily away from his own injury, Ross was not even aware that Stevie had left the room until he came back with a towel. 'Here. It's clean.'

'I can't look at it. I'll pass out. The bone's showing.'

Stevie came closer. 'It's a *scrape*. You better wash it.'

Ross didn't move.

'The washroom's there,' Stevie said.

Standing. How? He broke the action into units of lesser pain, sliding forward, pushing himself up. Somehow he got on to the good leg. He hopped woodenly, using the back of the couch for support. 'In here,' said Stevie, snarling it, yet showing him the way.

Inhaling sharply with every step, Ross followed. In the hall, he kept one hand on the wall. *Excalibur Hotel, Las Vegas*, read the tea towel over Stevie's naked shoulder.

Confronted by the bathroom mirror, by his own face warpainted with grease, Ross understood why Stevie had been afraid. He was still wearing the helmet. With blackened hands he unfastened the strap. Stevie, impatient, indicated that he should sit on the edge of the tub. Ross clutched the towel rack and, shaking his sandal off, stepped in with his good leg. Grimacing, he lifted in the right. Stevie turned on the showerhead attachment, adjusted the temperature, handed it to Ross.

'What happened? What's that black stuff? Grease?'

'I fell off my bike.'

Stevie made a derisive sound. 'Go. I don't have all day.'

Water hit the wound. Ross roared.

'Don't be such a fucking baby.' Stevie snatched the nozzle back. 'There's the soap.'

Ross lathered and gently daubed with the bubbles. Stevie passed him the nozzle. Pain again, that schoolmaster with a stick! That prick!

'Your arm's all fucked up, too.'

Ross saw that it was. He held it out and, with Stevie's help, gave it the same treatment as the leg. Very carefully, he blotted around his wounds with the tea towel, Stevie watching. When Ross

317

had finished, Stevie offered his arm. Without meeting Stevie's eye, Ross took it. As soon as both his feet were on the bathmat, Stevie stalked off.

At the basin, Ross washed the grease off his hands and face. He wet his hair flattened into a tight cap from the helmet, and, like his nephew, combed it with his hand.

The leg was stiffer on the way back to the living room. Stevie, in the armchair tearing off the end of the cigarette he had just rolled, did not look up as Ross groped his way along the couch. The sitting ordeal again. 'You're right,' Ross said when it was over. 'I probably shouldn't call her that.'

Stevie lit the cigarette. 'What are you doing here? What do you want?'

'I was up on the mountain. You know the one they hang glide off?' He leaned forward to inspect his leg but had to look away. His whole body sang with pain, one sustained note, ringing in every nerve. 'I was up there meditating when this weird thing happened. Suddenly I couldn't feel my body any more. It was like only my consciousness was up there on the mountain. Has that ever happened to you?'

Stevie had his elbows on his knees, head lowered, so Ross could only see the very top of his head, hair heavy, sheenless, matted-looking. 'It wasn't a good feeling,' Ross told him, his chest tightening. His nose began to run. He pressed it with the back of his hand. 'I wondered if that's what Iliana feels like all the time.'

At the mention of her name, Stevie looked up. 'I don't have to tell you anything.'

'I think I have a right to know how things stand.'

'Fuck you,' Stevie said.

'She was a nurse, right?'

'You told me that.'

318

'That's how we met. In the hospital. I was a mouth-breather. I guess she told you about the accident.'

Stevie stared at Ross through crescented eyes, smoke leaking from his nostrils. 'You did.'

'She didn't tell you anything?'

'I just said she didn't.'

'I was the one driving. I asked her to get something off the floor so she undid her seatbelt. I looked back for just a second – one second – and drove into a truck. She was in a coma for four days. They were the worst four days of my life.' He put his hand up to dam his nose. 'Well, last night was pretty bad, too.'

The tears started, as if he'd merely diverted the flow. 'Oh, fuck,' said Stevie, standing. 'I'm getting out of here.'

He stayed away a long time, long enough to finish the cigarette. He came back without it. By then, Ross had pulled himself together somewhat. Stevie set a can of beer on the coffee table in front of Ross and went back over to the armchair, dropping into it, legs crossed, pumping his ankle.

Reaching for the beer, Ross stopped with his arm out. The scrape was not bleeding now, but seeping something clear that made the wound look shellacked. He shuddered from the pain, which he had not noticed before because the pain in his leg was so much worse. It only hurt now because he was looking at it.

He told Stevie, 'There's not a day that goes by that I don't look at her and feel responsible.'

Stevie belched. 'That's stupid, man. It was an accident.'

'But you know what I never once did? I never once wished it had been me instead.'

Stevie said nothing.

'You know how she goes to the bathroom?'

He looked at Ross coldly.

'She puts a tube—'

'I don't care!'

'She has to put this tube up—'

'Who the fuck cares?'

'That really doesn't bother you?'

'You are such a fuck! I don't believe it! I thought that about you the first time I met you!'

Ross bristled. 'If you have such a low opinion of me why did you keep on taking my money and eating my food? Oh, never mind. I know why.'

'What's someone like her doing with you? That's what I want to know.'

'You stole my bike, too, didn't you?'

'*What?*'

He looked so outraged by the accusation that if Ross had not already exonerated Stevie when he put the blame on Brent Howland, he would have now. Nevertheless, he pressed sarcastically on. 'Someone stole it. You stole my wife. I should believe you had nothing to do with my bike?'

'*Don't you call her that!*'

'Why not? You think she's going to marry you?'

Stevie sprang up from the chair. 'I can't believe she even let me come near her! I never for a second thought she would! But she did and now I'm fucked! Now my life is over and I don't even know what I did! I just want to talk to her! I just want to tell her I never felt like this before!' With fists to both sides of his head, he cried, 'I just want to talk!'

'When's the last time you saw her?'

'Six days ago.'

'You haven't spoken to her since?'

'No.'

'Have you called her?'

'I never called her!'

'And you haven't been to the café?'

'No!'

With this confirmation from the other guilty party, Ross felt strangely heartened. 'Hey,' he said softly. 'Sit down.'

'I want to die!'

'How old are you?'

'What difference does it make?'

'Twenty?'

'I'm twenty-three!'

'Sit down,' Ross commanded and Stevie obeyed, dropping cross-legged on to the chair and folding forward in a sob. Within his reach, and Ross's too, the end of suffering. 'Let her go.'

'Get the fuck out of here!'

'You said you wanted to talk.'

He lifted his face, crimson, wet. 'Not to you!'

'I'm just the guy you want to talk to.'

'I hate you!'

'You think I don't hate you? You think I want to run into you tomorrow and next week and next year and every time be reminded that you fucked my wife?'

'I'm leaving town!'

'That won't make any difference. Every time I step on my own roof and see those planters, every time I take a book off my own shelf, I will be reminded. That's what I'm doing here. I hate you, too. I'm not leaving until I don't.'

2

Though Bonnie found something to dislike about all times of day, she was particularly not a morning person. Nevertheless, as they stepped out into the predictable sunshine she had to admit that there was respite in these early groggy hours before you really became conscious again of all your problems. The town quiet, nobody yet awake, she stopped on the stairs with a finger to her lips. 'Listen.'

Bryce pulled on his ear.

'Can you hear it?'

His face brightened. 'Yeah! I can!'

In the kitchen Deb, stolid in blue jeans, was chopping potatoes into large chunks on a board. (Bonnie could not help imagining her at home, in gingham, a cross-dresser.) 'Good,' she said, unsmiling at mother and child. 'I was just going to go up and get you.'

'Isn't Ross here?'

'Isn't he up there?'

For a moment they only looked at each other, Deb mirroring Bonnie's confusion. Bonnie said, 'Iliana didn't show up?' She realized then that she had woken without the usual sensory alarms – not the onions, not the bread's dream-sweetening transition. 'Should we phone them?'

'If they're at home,' said Deb, 'then everything's all right.'

'What if they're not?'

'Someone would call if that was the case. You'd better get started on the orange juice.'

Bonnie was aghast. 'You're not going to open!'

'I'm not going to let Ross down.'

'There's just the two of us!'

'There's the three of us.'

'What about the bread?'

'The freezer's full of it. We'll be all right. Good thing it's Saturday.'

'Good thing it's Saturday? Saturday's the busiest day! I can't do it! Yesterday was bad enough and we had Iliana!'

Deb brought the knife down on the board with enough force

to cause Bonnie to jump. 'Will you stop always thinking about yourself? You remind me of someone.'

'Who?'

'You know who. Bryce, show her where the oranges are. Bryce will explain how to work the juicer.'

Bonnie was not all that surprised that her child could work all the machines in the café. He could also choose his own videos and CDs despite not knowing how to read, and operate the stereo and VCR. He knew the tasks to be done before opening and in what order, and that, when they took the sandwich board out and set it on the sidewalk it would be time to let the hungry enter. Bonnie followed his command, taking additional orders from Deb. She was to run the frozen loaves under the tap before putting them in the oven; Deb assured her no one would know the difference from freshly baked.

'I'm not thinking of myself,' Bonnie said in her own sulky defence as she was cutting the fruit for salad (Bryce was not allowed to handle knives). 'I'm worried about Ross.'

People queued up for the opening, most of them ruffling Bryce's hair as they passed or demanding that he give them five. Bonnie watched, slapping the order pad against her open palm. Deb was right only in so far as Bonnie was not a people person. Who else would she think of? But maybe Ross was right, too. Maybe she could change. As the tables filled and expectant faces turned towards the menu board, Bonnie scanned the room and saw women who apparently didn't realize that just the teeniest bit of lipstick might brighten their whole look and men who seemed not to have heard of the ponytail's demise. These were people she could help. They knew nothing, but, like children, they did not know they knew nothing, so she had to be careful not to offend. Her advice would have to be subtler than a whisper, or better yet, disguised. Or maybe she should forget advice and try instead to provide a positive example. She could stay and live among them and just be herself. (Deb, though, Deb she was going to have to talk to. She was going to have to get that woman to do something about her hair.)

Stevie woke up. The night before he didn't think it possible, but here he was, blinking the sun out of his eyes. He lay there in case he was mistaken, just feeling what it was like. Sounds washed over him: a sprinkler raining intermittently against the wooden fence next door, bus engine idling, a dog. He was breathing. An empty hand clenched and unclenched in his gut.

It was the longest he'd gone without thinking of Iliana since the whole thing started.

Padding naked to the kitchen, he discovered it had reverted to its former state. There was no food. Not just nothing he cared to eat: no food. If it was Saturday (he thought it probably was), he hadn't showered in a week.

On the bathroom vanity: bloodstained tea towel, soap blackened with grease. The shampoo bottle stood on its head on the tub ledge. He had to wash his hair with Irish Spring. He had to cut open the bottom of the toothpaste tube and dig the Crest out.

All the junk in the yard. He couldn't even remember tearing apart the ramp, yet here was the evidence of it, here the crowbar.

He parked down Canada Way because of the farmers' market. Walking the three blocks to the Sunshine, he passed the barber's and, catching sight of his own reflection in the window, stopped. With his hair still wet, he looked like someone washed up on to land after weeks of clinging to wreckage. There was an old-timer in the chair, but no one waiting. On impulse Stevie went in and sat on the bench.

The curls straightened by the comb touched his shoulders. 'I get around to it, like, a couple of times a year,' he admitted to the barber.

'So I should go short then and make it last?'

'Whatever.'

The barber fastened the cape. 'Another nice day.' Having got the requisite conversation out of the way, he fell silent, which was fine by Stevie. He watched in the mirror the scissors snip off the hair she'd run her fingers through, his face emerging as if from a disguise.

'There,' the barber said, switching off the electric razor. 'Army'd take you now.'

'I don't wake up early enough.'

Stepping out of the shop, he felt cooler, especially around the ears. The sun was brighter, too, without the natural filter of his bangs; he started in the direction of the café with his head bowed. Halfway down the block, he saw the sandwich board. He'd walked right past the Sunshine. Then he thought, *why not?* Ross wasn't going to kick him out. After last night, he probably still wanted to be his fucking friend.

The gate was open, the patio tables full. At one of them the little boy sat gazing into a spoon. 'I'm upside down!' Stevie heard him exclaim as he passed. Inside, he paused to read the menu and, seeing what he wanted, took a table near the shelves. The skinny sister was clearing a nearby table that had just been vacated. 'I'll be there in a sec.'

It surprised Stevie that she spoke to him at all.

In the kitchen, Deb said, 'Well, you come over and do it for me then.'

'You don't mean you do it yourself!' said Bonnie, horrified. 'Isn't there any decent place in town?'

'Why should I pay all that when I can get them out of a box?'

'I'm going to take you into the city, girl.'

'It's just as good.'

'No. You and me are going to treat ourselves.'

Deb frowned, but Bonnie could tell it was a pleased frown.

She went back out to take Baldy's order. He was bent over one of Ross's books, a white sickle-shaped scar visible through the dark fuzz. Sighing at the seemingly insurmountable challenge ahead of her (the monk look was so, so out), she asked, 'Coffee?'

He looked up. The face was vaguely familiar, the forehead distractingly white. He inarticulated something she guessed to be a yes.

'Latte or a cappuccino?'

'Regular coffee.'

'Decaf?'

'Just coffee.'

First his tone belied his otherworldly appearance, then his curled lip. She recognized him by his order: he wanted an Iliana Alexander.

'Deb,' she hissed through the short-order window. 'That little creep's here!'

It took Deb a moment to recognize Stevie, too. She didn't know anything, Bonnie realized, because she didn't seem alarmed in the least. 'You do him,' Bonnie told her.

Stevie was trying to read the book, but he might as well have been holding it upside down for how much he was taking in. The sister had gone to get Ross, but he still couldn't help hoping it would be Iliana who came out of the kitchen. If it was her, he didn't know what he would say. He would probably start to bawl and she would think he was a complete fuck. Flipping through the book he found refuge in a blank page.

'That's some pig shave.'

He looked up at Deb pretending to buff her nails on the top of his head.

'What can I get you?' she asked.

'What's the matter with your waitress?' He jerked his chin in the direction of the kitchen.

'Your haircut scared her. How's Nana?'

'Good.'

'Did you have a look at the board?'

'I want Iliana.' Deb, filling his coffee cup, didn't notice how his voice skittered over an octave.

He wanted to bolt as soon as she had gone, but knew he'd start bawling then for sure. Staring at the page in front of him, eyes tearing up, was all he could do. There were black spots moving on the page. They were not on the page, of course, but swimming over his eyes. Dirt or dust that was probably there all the time. Now, staring so intently at white, his tears magnifying them, these motes showed up clearly, like fruit flies drowned in a glass of water, haloed in light. It made him think of something Ross had told him the night before, that we hardly ever see things the way they really are. Pressing the heel of a hand to each eye, he rubbed hard. When he took his hands away, there were coloured stars.

The skinny sister brought the plate over. She set it on the edge of the table and, grimacing, fled. It was open-faced, heaped with something gold and crumbly, a salad on the side. *Faux-tuna melt with a secret topping.* Stevie ignored the salad. He lifted one side of the sandwich, but it buckled under the weight of the hot load. Waiting for it to cool, he picked at the salty topping.

Deb came over with the coffee pot again, sitting down across from him after she had refilled his cup. He felt self-conscious eating in front of her and his foot jiggled under the table.

'Here,' she said, after he had finished. She took a napkin from the chrome dispenser and passed it to him. He wiped his mouth and fingers and left it balled on the plate.

'You sure wolfed that down. You must have been hungry.'

Stevie shrugged.

'Well? Did you like it?'

His hand went up and touched his bristled head while he thought about his answer. 'I could live without it.'

3

Despite the weight he'd lost, Ross still took up a lot of space. The house was twice as large as their old apartment yet he managed to fill with his enthusiasms, with his very Rossness, all the available space. Even without calling out to him Iliana knew when she got back from her run that he wasn't home; the house exuded emptiness. The fridge, too. Normally she brought home leftovers from the café, but she had neglected to today. All the fridge had to offer: an open box of baking soda, a bowl of blackberries.

She drove to Overwaitea. Basket in her lap, she headed down an aisle. Shortening was the first thing on her list if she was going to go through with the pie, then sugar for the berries. While she was gathering the pie ingredients, she scouted for something to make for dinner.

Accepting the bagger at the checkout's offer to take her groceries to the car, she made a quick side trip to the liquor store in the mall. 'What are you serving?' the clerk asked when she came seeking his professional advice.

'Ham.'

He led her down an aisle of green and golden bottles.

The ham proved foolproof. The thing was already cooked, it turned out. All she had to do was peel off its tight plastic jacket, plop it in a pan, and pour the bottle of Coke over it – her mother's recipe. She was pleased to have remembered when she chose the ham. The instructions on the label told her how long per gram to bake it and at what temperature. Scalloped potatoes were a cinch. As for the Brussels sprouts, she remembered her mother sitting at the kitchen table painstakingly carving a cross into the bottom of each, but surely this was zealotry. Iliana decided just to boil them.

It was the pie she found daunting. How had she imagined she could take on the technical challenge of a crust? There were only three ingredients. Anything that simple had to be difficult. Bread had already taught her this.

That she should find herself in this predicament was perhaps unusual for a woman of her upbringing. Her sisters had both learned to cook and, like their mother, probably brought to their own dinner tables every Saturday a freshly baked pie filled with whatever fruit was in season. (Sunday was the day of rest, the day of leftovers.) Five years younger than her next oldest sister, Iliana was the baby, the last child, the indulged one. Because her older sisters had always helped, she had been excused from kitchen duties. The most useful skill she'd left home with was to puncture the bag to let the air out before pounding it all over with a fist, then to slit the bag and shake the crumbled contents over the layers of butter-drunk potato.

With the potatoes and the ham in the oven and the Brussels sprouts ready on the stove, she took the shortening out of the refrigerator and reread the recipe on the box. All at once a familiar, unpleasant fluttering started in her stomach, the same queasy half-and-half of anticipation and dread that used to descend upon her during the prayer meetings. Everyone sitting in a circle, heads bowed in silence, waiting for the Spirit to move them, the feeling would come and she would know that she was going to have to speak. She disliked speaking in public and would always try to wait the feeling out, but it would only intensify until it resembled nausea. Finally, stomach lurching, she would rise reluctantly to her feet.

What she was going to have to do now, she realized, was call her mother. She was going to have to call and ask how she made her pastry. The clock conspired to make the phone call happen. At this time her father would be in the barn feeding the animals and her mother would be in the kitchen, as Iliana was now, preparing supper. Still she hesitated, wiping her hands against the apron bib, willing the urge to pass.

After two rings, her mother answered. To her surprise, Iliana felt an instinctive comfort in the sound of her mother's voice after so long. 'It's me,' the child announced. But in the ensuing silence, she realized that she had not really thought the call through. She had been too impulsive. She should have tried the recipe on the bottom of the box first.

'He's in the barn,' her mother said at last.

'I know. That's why I called now. I need to know how to make pastry.'

'Did you get my cards?'

'I didn't open them. I told you I wouldn't.' Already exasperated, she was on the point of hanging up when she heard a sibilant inhalation. 'Ma? Are you crying?'

Hastily, she sniffed. 'How are you?'

'Fine.'

'Really.'

'I'm fine.'

'Your father's just sold the farm.'

'He what?'

'We love you so much. We pray for you all the time. You broke your father's heart, you know.'

Her father had a heart? All along she had assumed it was just a four-chambered ego pumping away in his chest. Iliana said, 'It's always about him, isn't it?'

'No! We almost went to your wedding. I got him to put his suit on, but at the last minute he changed his mind. I can't tell you how much I regret not pushing him a little harder.'

Iliana wasn't sure she believed this. Her mother would never lie, but she was not above misremembering. 'Well, you missed a great party.'

'I'm so happy that you've called. Are you really all right? They told me—'

'What?'

'At the hospital. That you might not be able to walk. I came to see you. Didn't Ross tell you?'

'Yes.'

'The next time I called, they wouldn't give me any information. I couldn't go again. Your father would know something was the matter. I didn't tell him. It would have been the death of him. I didn't even tell Marina and Karen. I've borne it on my own all this time. Oh, I wish you'd opened those cards!'

Stunned, Iliana asked, 'Didn't you call Ross?'

'He was so angry at me, I didn't dare.'

She tried to think of something to say.

'Iliana? Are you there?'

'What are you going to do now that you've sold the farm?'

'He bought a mobile home. There's a trailer park close to your sisters. Marina had another baby.'

'How many's that? Three?'

'Four.' She lowered her voice. 'I'd like to come and see you. He doesn't have to know.'

Iliana smiled at the defiance. 'I'd like that, Ma, but this isn't a great time.'

'What's wrong?'

'Nothing's wrong. Another time would better, that's all. I'll let you know.'

'Will you?'

'I will. I promise. Back to the pastry, Ma. I've got to get this pie in the oven.'

'Lard.'

'What?'

'I always make my pastry with lard.'

'Oh, Ma. That's gross.'

The first thing Iliana learned to do after the accident was to sit up in the chair. Her centre, now that she was no longer a walking person, had shifted and she'd had to find her equilibrium all over again. From the way the telephone conversation threw her off balance, she had to wonder if she hadn't been propping herself up with resentment all along. A practical person, she was dismayed by waste. After the accident she had refused to indulge in false hopes precisely because it seemed a waste of time. Now she couldn't help cringing over all those hours bitterly misspent in anger. She had not imagined that she had been the unforgiving one. Horribly, she found herself nostalgic for that cold little house with its sign in the yard, soon to be bulldozed. (It was probably the sign that had kept them close for so many years; it scared everyone off so they only had each other.) The interminable prayers on hard chairs, those hair-raising chases with the belt – had it really been so bad? She even found herself retracting her scorn for her sisters and the lives they had picked out for themselves. What she really objected to was that they had married such dull men. She did not disdain their goals at all. In fact, she wanted the same things for herself, just more, of course.

The bowl in her lap, she wielded the paring knives as if they were the two blades of scissors come apart, sending chunks of shortening flying. Eventually she abandoned the knives in favour of her hands (her tools of preference) and when she thought she had the consistency right, she stirred in the ice water. The mess adhered into a sticky ball, which she kneaded quickly, then divided and rolled into a ragged circle.

They had never eaten in the dining room, not even at Christmas. Last Christmas they'd been renovating and had eaten in the café. She found a tablecloth, candles; she got out a china plate. In the liquor store she'd bought a corkscrew, a little silver man with a hollow head and a menacing phallus. She wrung his neck, but instead of raising his arms in surrender, he simply flailed them. In the end, she resorted to using the corkscrew as a hammer and forcing the cork into the bottle.

The wine, when she finally got it out of the bottle, glowed yellow in the candlelight. She took a sip. It tasted good, but the struggle with the cork and the cork flotsam in the wine had undermined her confidence. Pulling herself up, she took the knife and began to carve. Maybe she was more hungry than depressed and, momentarily cheered by this thought, she stabbed a few of the Brussels sprouts and slid them from the fork. A generous scoop of scalloped potatoes and then, in the pause formerly reserved for prayer, she regarded her dinner.

Plate full. Life empty.

Ross thought there had been a break-in. He saw the mess, but not at first that it was a culinary one. It registered – greyish entrail-like scraps of dough in the circle of flour on the counter, the midden in the sink, the aroma. Even as he limped forward, he recoiled in moral outrage at the thought of an intruder, a stranger, in his kitchen. He had just come up the ramp (the one and only time he had been gladdened by the sight of it), thankful that he had made it home at last and that the light was on, meaning Iliana was in. To be met with such a violation when he had entered with so full a heart only made the shock worse.

Iliana had finished dinner and was sitting with her chin propped in one hand thinking that the trouble with cooking was the disproportionate expenditure of time and effort. Hours it had taken her to prepare, but mere minutes to eat: the ends had failed to justify the means and all that lay before her now was a long lonely evening, the first in her uncertain future, and the penance of cleaning up.

She heard Ross come in. When at last he appeared in the doorway, she shivered unpleasantly with *déjà vu*. The kitchen light on behind him, his face in shadows, he reminded her uncannily of the abject and forlorn who used to stagger dazedly into her father's church hoping to be saved from themselves. 'I hoped it would be you,' she said. 'Is it?'

'What's going on? Having a party? Or maybe you have a date?'

'Don't be stupid. Sit down.'

'No. I wasn't invited.'

'Since when do I have to invite my husband to eat with me?'

He flushed with pleasure at the marital term. In the candlelight, that most flattering illumination, Iliana looked almost golden sitting with her hair tucked behind her ears. Wishing he had not come in slinging accusations, he about-faced to get a plate.

'Use the good dishes.'

He limped to the china cabinet.

'What happened?' she asked.

'I fell off my bike.'

'Oh, Ross. Do you want me to look at it?'

'It's all right.' The sound of her sympathy was the best possible balm.

He'd never seen the plate he took out of the cabinet. Probably it was a wedding present. After the accident, the presents had kept coming; for months he'd find them stacked in the lobby when he got home. Upstairs, he'd tear off the layers of wrapping and stash whatever was inside. One day a large cardboard box came. Inside, his own brandy-coloured Yonex that he'd bought because he liked the name 'Yonex' (in bed, he'd ask Iliana to whisper it). He lifted it out and, like the pros, straightened the weave of the glow-in-the-dark-strings, stuck all over with gold fuzz, like bits of animal fur on a club. Underneath was Iliana's racket, the miscellaneous contents of Miss Stockholm's glove compartment, and the ball that had changed their lives. After that Bonnie came over every few days to deal with the presents.

He laid his place in silence. 'Were you at Bonnie's all this time?' Iliana asked.

'No. I went up the mountain they hang-glide off. You bought white?'

'That's what was recommended to me.'

'How did the cork get in there?'

'Give it to me.' With the cork bobbing up and blocking the neck of the bottle, it took several tries to fill his glass.

Ross lowered himself on to the chair, making affecting sounds to win further sympathy. 'Did you cook all this?'

'And a pie. Are you hungry?'

'You cooked a *ham*?'

'It wasn't so much cooking as math. Do you want some? It's my mother's secret recipe.'

'Give me some of the potatoes.' He held his plate out. She was wearing a red, cap-sleeved T-shirt. The full round of her bicep showed as she lifted the serving spoon. Even her forearm had a shapely, sculpted look. 'More. I'll have some of the sprouts, too.' Halving one, he popped it in his mouth. 'You make these like your mother.'

'Really?' She was flattered.

'You boil them to hell.'

'Ha!' Iliana retorted. 'My mother wouldn't have anything to do with hell.'

Pushing the maximum load on to his fork, he conveyed it robotically to his mouth, which opened and took in the food even though he had not finished chewing the previous mouthful, all the while bending vigilantly over his plate, the left arm on the table curved around it, as if he expected someone to sneak up and take it. The unclean top of his head and stubbled jaw, even the weeping scrape on his arm – he seemed *exactly* like those salvation seekers. When he had almost finished, she dished the last potatoes out of the pan and served them to him. He cleared them and, straightening, used the back of his hand to wipe his mouth.

'That was excellent.'

'Thank you.'

He sipped the wine, reserving comment, and glanced around the table. Still eschewing the ham, he lifted the bowl that contained the sprouts and tipped it over his plate.

'Speaking of my mother,' said Iliana. 'I phoned her. She wants to come and visit.'

He looked up, startled. 'What did you tell her?'

'I said this wasn't a good time and that I'd call her later. They don't know.'

'Know what?'

'All this time I thought he was making an example of me. Preaching about me in church. He doesn't even know. I feel so—' Her shoulders sank and she looked away, blinking back tears.

'What you said to me yesterday, babe? About thinking you didn't try? It wasn't that. It was that I knew you didn't believe you could. I saw those Russians beat the odds by sheer force of will and thought you could, too. That's all. I believed in you.'

Iliana poured herself a little more wine and topped up Ross's

336

glass, too. 'I know. I hated waking in the hospital and seeing that look on your face.'

'What look?'

Dissolute though he had appeared (it was his ordeal, too) – unshaven, hair grease-darkened, eyes puffy (like now) – his first look of the day transformed him. He would gaze down at her, positively glowing with the expectation that when he asked, 'How are you feeling today?' she would kick off the covers and bound out of bed. 'The miracle look. Why don't you just have a piece?'

Ross withdrew his hand.

'It was already dead when I bought it.'

He waved the offer off.

'It's not that *I* don't believe in miracles, far from it. After I stopped believing in God, a.k.a. my father, they began to happen all the time. Remember our first date when you stopped at that fish store? I thought buying tuna in a fish store was showing off. I thought that bag you had slung over your shoulder was full of *cans*. Imagine my surprise.'

'Oh, babe,' said Ross, shaking his head. 'Is that true?'

'I was worried about your weight. More worried than about the penetration. I thought you might squash me.'

'Did I?'

'No. Another secular miracle happened. You lay right on top of me and felt so light.'

'I still feel responsible, babe. I am responsible. It was my fault.'

'I almost died, Ross. That I didn't is enough for me. I wish it was enough for you.'

How to accept things as they are? How? The food had reached his stomach and his energy was returning. He'd come to let her go, he remembered. He had to let go of his attachment to her, of his humiliation. He had to start again, *in this very moment.*

'Stevie Blake has an outie,' was how he began.

'For heaven's sake, Ross!'

'Was it good?'

'Please!'

'Tell me. I demand to know.'

'It was good but it wasn't fun.'

Ross nodded, trying to remain neutral, trying not to gloat. Their sex had been fun. They had been a couple of sex kittens, rolling over each other. 'Sex should be fun,' he said, as if reading from a manual. 'Hell, it should be funny.'

They both sat there solemnly remembering different funny things. For Ross it was the shaken-champagne eruption of the defective spermicidal foam canister, for Iliana the box spring jarring off the bed frame and collapsing, then Phyllis Hamovitch ringing from downstairs to ask about the crash. Ross picked some more rind off the ham and ate it.

'How did this happen, Ross? How did I become like a sister to you?'

'He was a virgin.'

'Stevie?' She looked at him, eyes widening. 'How do you know that?'

'He told me.'

'When?'

'Tonight. Not in so many words.'

'Did you go over there, Ross? Oh, my God, Ross.' She hid behind her hands. 'How is he?'

'He'll survive.'

'I didn't know. If I'd known—'

'I wish I was,' said Ross.

'What?'

'A virgin.'

'You?' Iliana laughed. Picking up the knife, she pulled the pan back over to her side of the table and, holding the ham steady with

338

her fork, sawed off a piece. He saw her arm extended to shake the impaled piece on to his plate.

She has beautiful arms, he thought.

'Are we going to bed or not?'

'You had an affair!' Ross reminded her.

'I'm not asking you to forgive me.'

'I don't!'

'Good. I hope you'll hold it against me. Maybe then you can start living with yourself.' She backed away from the table. 'I'm going to go freshen up.'

Ross flushed. This used to be her euphemism for installing her diaphragm, but now it meant something else.

It had been almost two years since he'd tasted meat. Back then he used to think that no meal was complete without a sizeable serving of flesh. Indeed, there was something satisfying, indeed natural, about having to use all of the specialized teeth, not just the mortar and pestle of his molars. That canine rip, it felt good. He was angry and, taking the ham in his teeth, he jerked back his head so that the piece of meat was rent.

Iliana called to him after he had served himself a second piece. He ate it slowly, savouring it, making her wait.

'Ross!'

He found her in the bedroom pulling her T-shirt over her head. Tucking one elbow into the elastic side of the bra, she whisked it right over her head in one Houdini-like movement. Ross glared at her cinnamon nipples. He was too soft a man. He needed to be harder, to stay angry.

'Are you coming or not?'

He raised an arm and sniffed. 'I'll be right back.'

He would have liked to take a shower, but did not want to wet his wounds, hardened now around the edges. He did not want to revisit that pain no matter what it had to teach him.

Iliana was lying naked on the bed by the time he got back. She looked right at him. 'The pie.'

'What?'

'I forgot the pie.'

'I don't want any pie.'

'It's still in the oven. Can you take it out?'

She heard him muttering imprecations all the way to the kitchen. The oven door slammed. A weight struck the counter. Ross said, 'Damn.' He reappeared, wearing a grave expression. 'Bad news, ma'am. It's about your pie.'

Iliana smiled.

'I was paying him! I was practically inventing jobs for him! How could you do that to me?'

'It didn't have anything to do with you.'

'How can you say that? We're married!'

'Maybe we shouldn't be.'

He stared at her from the doorway. 'Do you mean that?'

'Maybe.'

Let go.

'Why don't you lie down?' Iliana suggested.

Tentatively, he entered, hobbling over to the bureau. Shorts and briefs snagging on his erection, he slid them over the wound on his thigh, drawing air noisily through clenched teeth. Even bending was torture. He used the bureau for support. The surface wounds were only part of it. There were bruises, too, latent now, but sure to bloom by morning. Tomorrow he was going to be black and blue.

He straightened and looked at her spread out on the bed like a buffet. She laughed.

'What?'

'I know what your problem is. You're afraid you won't know what to do.'

This was true. This was so true. How many women had he given pleasure to? Scores, but his vast experience counted for nothing now. It was humiliating. He was like a thirteen year old again. He stumped over, slowly lowering himself on to the edge of the bed, his back to where she lay full of normal hopes and well-deserved expectations. Glancing over his shoulder, he saw her smile, meant to reassure him, though it did not. He was terrified that he would let her down while at the same time he was filled with a contradictory desire for her. So it was true! Pleasure and pain were the same. Reminded then of his practice, he got the idea to proceed mindfully, one increment at a time. He would begin again. Swinging his good leg up on the bed, using his hands to lift the bum one, he breathed into the pain, focusing on it. Anchored like this in his senses rather than his fears, he was able to lean back enough to fall on to the good elbow. 'You didn't put your diaphragm in, did you?'

'My diaphragm? I don't even know where it is.'

'Good.'

Staring at the ceiling, he wondered how to start.

Thinking. He made the note.

'We could just kiss,' Iliana suggested.

He reached for her hand, raising it, and with one finger began a languorous journey from the beautiful knob of her wrist, over her pulse point, down into the soft pocket behind her elbow, over the taut bicep, pulling it to his mouth. He bit.

'Ow!'

The kiss: open-mouthed, salty-tongued.

Ross pulled away. 'How about you do all the work?'

'With pleasure.'

'Wait,' he cautioned. 'Wait.' He closed his eyes and lay very still beside her, feeling the heat coming off her. He took a breath. As soon as she touched him, no matter where, he was going to blow.

'Tell me,' she said, 'how this feels.'